The ███████████████████████████████████████
thre███
tious███████████████████████████████████████
to ab██████████████████████████████████████
the empress, who is as yet unaware of his own identity.
Suddenly the empire faces further jeopardy – a violent
uprising of the inhuman Agaskan. Only the true heir can
save the kingdom, and survive the Rite of Endyear.

Richard Burns was born in Sheffield in 1958, and still
lives there, having taught in the city for four years before
becoming a full-time writer. *Khalindaine* is his first
novel: his mainstream work – *A Dance for the Moon* and
The Panda Hunt are published by Jonathan Cape. He has
also had poetry published in *The Gregory Anthology: The
Best of British Poets 1984–85*.

KHALINDAINE

RICHARD BURNS

UNWIN PAPERBACKS
London   Sydney

First published in Great Britain by Allen & Unwin 1986
First published in paperback by Unwin® Paperbacks, an imprint of Unwin
Hyman Limited in 1988

UNWIN HYMAN LIMITED
15/17 Broadwick Street, London W1V 1FP

Allen & Unwin Australia Pty Ltd
8 Napier Street, North Sydney, NSW 2060, Australia

Unwin Paperbacks with the Port Nicholson Press
60 Cambridge Terrace, Wellington, New Zealand

British Library Cataloguing in Publication Data

Burns, Richard, *1958*–
    Khalindaine.
I. Title
823'.914[F]   PR6052.U66/
ISBN 0-04-823313-7

Printed and bound in Great Britain by Cox and Wyman Ltd, Reading

Contents

1	The Rite of Endyear	*page*	1
2	Northreach		26
3	The Gilla Pass		53
4	Streetpoet		68
5	A Journey by Twilight		89
6	The Gros of Weir		112
7	Khalinrift		132
8	The Fevered Sun		162
9	Maldroigt		186
10	The Plains of Myr		204
11	The Death of a Pretender		229
12	Akhran the Golden		250

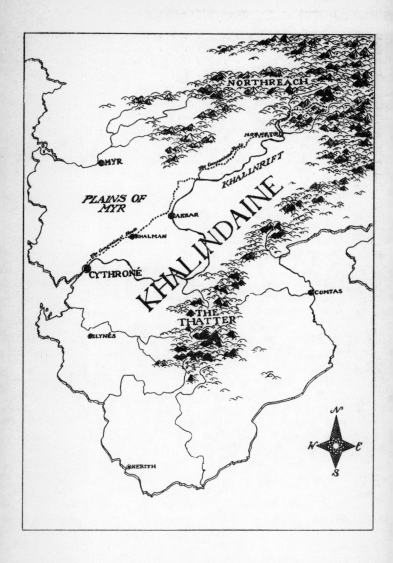

Chapter 1

The Rite of Endyear

The empress stood alone on the highest tower of the keep, raised the knife above her head, and plunged it into her breast. The crowd gasped in fear and wonder, and the empress fell to her knees.

At once the air was filled with a thousand doves. They were released from the boats and the banks, and confirmed that the ritual was complete. As they rose above the river, so too did the cheers of the crowd; the birds and the voices competed beneath the meridian sun. Then the doves flocked over the keep, and drawn by some nameless instinct, flew west away from the city. They passed high over the river and the estuary: the river-mouth beneath them was like an arrowhead piercing the land, and the gaping wound it made bled dull waters stained with brown silt. As the doves flew, fires were lit, pigs and sheep were roasted, and the celebrations began. High above them, on the keep, the empress Elsban slowly bled.

She had once been lovely, but her face had grown flaccid over the years, and acquired a soft maternal dignity. Our Lady of Khalindaine, the people called her, and Mother of the Empire.

Now something that was not age was tearing at her features. Her face was lashed and mauled by strange expressions that formed and welled beneath the skin: the eyes shone with black menace; the mouth was torn and stretched; the cheeks sank back to firm-boned shadows. As her human strength ebbed through her self-inflicted wound, the strength of her blood-ancestor Akhran flowed into the gaps in her consciousness. Akhran, founder of the empire of Khalindaine; Akhran, the barbarian; Akhran, the Golden. It was his immortal strength that knitted together the wound in her chest and made her whole again, just as it was his strength which had shaped the empire. Each year since the building of the Keep Akhranta, Akhran and his successors had climbed the highest tower and performed the Rite of Endyear, and each year he had used his strength to keep the monarch whole. She could feel him inside her as she lay on the bloody flagstones. His avatar surged through her body and mind. For a long time she lay still, and then, as the summer sun slipped from its midsummer solstice and fell slowly west into the sea, she crawled to the trap-door and lifted it.

She needed the strength of Akhran now, to carry her down those winding stairs. The trap-door fell shut behind her, and the wood above her head was warped and seamed with light. But though she let the avatar fill her body, she fought him with her mind. Sometimes she was not sure whose thoughts it was that filled her: the avatar or some screaming madness of her own. Together in a single body, empress and avatar descended through the arch at the foot of the stair, and out on to the gallery of the Great Hall. They crossed the gallery slowly, avoiding those places where the wooden structure threatened to give way, and reached the flight of wide oak stairs which led to the gallery from the floor of the Great Hall below. For a moment the avatar of Akhran called a halt: with his eyes her body surveyed the scene. It had been here, at the top of these stairs, that he had accepted the vacant throne of Nerith and thus become ruler of all Khalindaine; here where he had learnt of the birth of his firstborn, Deteth; here, a few steps lower, where he had smashed his axe into the balustrade and sworn to protect his empire for ever. The gash in the faded and dusty wood was still there, and beetles nested in it. The eyes of the avatar looked beyond the gash suddenly, seeking some spot on the floor of the Hall, finding the place, focusing furiously, and peopling the room with courtiers in archaic costume. The courtiers seemed to crowd around the corpse of a man in a crown: for the hundredth time Akhran witnessed his own death, poisoned by the hand of his queen and her lover, and in the middle of the keep built for his own defence. Rage filled the avatar: the figures of the courtiers flared up in Akhran's fury like flames in a wind; the cracks between the flagstones ran liquid with red anger; the high and vaulted ceiling clenched like a granite fist. And then all was over, all was gone, and the only movement in the world came from the dust twisting in shafts of sunlight and the bloodstained figure of Elsban, dragging herself tiredly down the stairs. She clenched her cloak at the neck as though she were cold, and hurried through the Hall.

The pikemen of Akhran, whose job it was to guard the keep, were all veterans of the Imperial Guard. Their backs were to the keep during the ceremony; they could tell only by the noise of the crowd and the faces of those courtiers who waited on the terrace before the main gate with them how the festival progressed. The sun had been rising across the sky when the empress had entered the keep; it had been at its height when the convulsive gasp and averted eyes had signalled her self-mutilation; now it was a golden orb in the western sky. Soon it would redden, roost and disappear. The pikemen of Akhranta, in their heavy blackiron helmets with their long black graceful plumes, grew tired as the long day lengthened, and it was with a relief none of them would admit that they heard the portcullis wind open behind them and saw the smiles on the face of the waiting court.

Elsban walked between them. She was dressed differently now: the long dark robe, embroidered with scenes from the life of the mythical hero Tlot, had gone; now she wore a gown of vermilion shot with jewels, that frothed at her neck with a ruff of the finest lace. Her body was pampered and restored with potions, preparations and perfumes, and all physical trace of the ceremony was washed from her; within her, however, she knew she would never have the strength to perform another Rite of Endyear. The knowledge frightened her, and gave her comfort.

She descended the flight of stone steps that led from the great gate of the keep to the quay below, and returned to her barge. Behind her, on its promontory jutting into the wide River Khalin, the keep was cold, grey, and sinister. The pikemen watched as the barge cast off from the quay, and then returned to their quarters. There they took off their helms, loosened their belts, and lit up their pipes. 'It's been a long day,' they agreed.

The royal barge moved serenely up the river, the effortless motion of the hull contrasting strangely with the abrupt synchronised strokes of the oarsmen. The barge was of purple

and gold. Liveried men of the Company of Rivermasters rowed
it through the water. They were stationed at the front of the
barge; the aft was occupied by a splendid pavilion of hung silk,
supported on gilded pillars. Beneath this canopy, surrounded
by her glittering court, was the even more impressive figure of
Elsban in her robes of state. Her vermilion dress shimmered
where it caught the low sun, and coiled about her throne.

The throne, a gift from the king of Ehapot, was of ivory
studded with dark precious stones; on her head was the tall
gold mitre that was the Imperial Crown of Khalindaine.
Despite the weight of the crown, despite the agonies of her time
in the keep, she felt alert and watchful, and looked around her.
Behind, the Keep Akhranta was a grey shape at the end of its
causeway, ugly and dramatic as the sun lit it from behind, and
topped with many towers. About her was a flotilla of tiny boats,
pulling upstream with her barge, and one or two larger boats
that rivalled her own. She recognised the nearest: the banner of
the Gyr Melinloth, with its blazon of white leopards on its pale
blue ground, hung from the stern.

The boats reached the Bridge of Towers. The stretches of
parapet between the towers were lined with cheering citizens
and decked with streaming pennons. As a precaution against
over-enthusiasm or malice the crowds were kept off the central
section of the bridge, beneath which the royal barge would
pass, by men of the Cythron militia in their steel cuirasses and
blue-plumed helms. Like their comrades of the Akhran
pikemen, these troops were tired and hot: merciless sweat
trickled beneath the brims of their helms, glossing their faces
and making them irritable. As the royal barge passed beneath
the bridge the crowd surged forward, and the militia drove
them back. When the barge had gone, and the central section
was once again cleared, two figures lay in the sunlight. One
moaned, the other was quite still.

The empress was oblivious of the skirmish above her. For
her the moment of shadowed darkness as the barge passed
beneath the bridge was a moment of hasty peace. The barge
burrowed its way into the arching stonework and the world
darkened and the cries were muffled; then it was through and
out again and the waves were diamond-shaped shadows flecked
with diamonds of light. To the north of her she saw the familiar

buildings of the city of Cythroné: she looked without curiosity at the towers and pinnacles of the new meeting-house, at the decorated façade of the law courts, and at the distant dome of the Grand Basilica beyond. Her eyes stopped roving, however, when they fell on the low bleak waterfront of the House of the Condemned. She peered carefully at the open square which formed the prison's roof, and then called to a courtier near her: 'Halfyndruth?'

An elderly man dressed in extravagant greens stepped forward and bowed before his sovereign. 'Your Majesty's pleasure is my command,' he said elaborately.

'Halfyndruth. Have there been any executions today?'

He strained his watery blue eyes towards the House of the Condemned, and distinguished hanging shapes on gaunt scaffolds. 'It appears so, your Majesty.'

'I thought so. Can we please not have executions on holy days. Send a message to the law courts and have them stopped. Better still, give a pardon to anyone in the House of the Condemned.' She looked blankly at Halfyndruth standing before her. 'I feel tired,' she said. 'I died today.'

Halfyndruth continued to stand there, not wishing to break the empress's reverie, whilst her head was filled with images of death. No: no one else should die today. She looked up to see the courtier, and dismissed him with a sad smile and a grateful nod. He returned to his place, and dictated a message to his secretary, whilst his manservant passed paper, pen, ink and sealing wax as required. With a flourish Halfyndruth coiled his signature across the foot of the page while Cluny, the manservant, dripped wax, and then carefully the courtier pressed his ornate ring against the blue wax to impress his seal. He handed the letter to Cluny, who held it tightly. He had never held a commission from the empress before, and now his master was asking him to carry the message back to Cynthroné from the royal palace after they docked. He was proud and happy.

The barge continued upstream. South of the river were the docks and the commercial buildings. The docks lined the Khalin's southern bank: those upriver of the Bridge of Towers served the narrowboats that plied the long River Khalin; those beyond the bridge served the sea-going merchantmen. A barge, fantastically painted in the style of Myr, was being unloaded against a granite wharf: for a moment the stevedores, half-naked in the sun, were still as they watched their empress pass, and then they returned to their work.

Then Cythron Bridge approached, its shop-lined form stretching high above the river. Again the echoing darkness; again the harsh return to cheering blinding sunlight. Now on both sides of the river was housing: prosperous merchants' houses gave way to lower older buildings that crowded the banks; in their turn the wooden houses gave way to mere shanties. Trees appeared amongst the buildings: charmless trees that served as support for lean-to huts or lines to hang drying clothes. Grass appeared in the streets. To the south now the buildings fell away to nothing: low marshy fields stretched towards swelling hills; occasional villages fed smoke into the early evening. North it was different. Between the shanties were enclosed houses, the homes of minor nobles who had moved out from Cythroné to the suburbs, and then rolling parkland, landscaped and beautiful. The barge was reaching Verdre and the palace.

Elsban saw little of this. Her mind was occupied with memories. The names of heroes floated before her: Tlot, Akhran, Ravenspur. Ravenspur – she pictured again the handsome man who had loved her in her youth, the warrior hero long dead who had fathered her child, the lost child, the bastard. She saw him astride his black horse. She thought of forbidden love, of how, being cousins, they had been unable to wed, even though Ravenspur was a widower. Jumbled lines of verse ran through her head, lines about heroes and lovers. She applied them all to her dead lover: 'He kissed her faerie hand and pledged his heart'; 'Tlot against all danger was in arms'; 'Scything from the north did Akhran come'. She would have the court poet make her a new poem about Ravenspur, she decided.

Ravenspur, and Tlot, and Akhran. The legends of Akhran, she knew, could not express the terrible blind force that was within her. Ravenspur she had known, lain with: he was mortal and gone, yet he too had been of the House of Akhran and had some ruthless anguish in his soul. And Tlot? Tlot was the earliest of the heroes, the first man, the man who had driven the Agaskan into the mountains. What had he been like, she wondered. Like Ravenspur, who for all his ruthlessness was human, and vulnerable, and had smiled at a young princess? Or like Akhran, terrible, all-powerful, demented? The modern ballads would have him the former: she was not so sure. The old song of Tlot described him as being very much like Akhran.

She looked up as the barge rubbed itself affectionately up against the bank, and saw Ravenspur's younger legitimate son, the Gros of Weir, standing on the deck in front of her. He isn't like his father, she thought.

In the hall of the meeting-house in Cythroné hangs a painting by the great Cythron artist, Vlatri tan Bul. It is a superb picture, one of Vlatri's masterpieces, and it shows – in the fashionable modern style – the landing of the royal barge at Verdre. The palace itself occupies most of the background: the shapely white marble building is distanced from the viewer by long lawns that sweep to the river, and playing on the lawn is a gentle fountain. But it is not the background which the viewer notices, for Vlatri's genius lies in the presentation of character.

He has chosen the moment when the empress in her flowing vermilion gown steps down from the throne, her hand entrusted to a courtier, the train of her dress carried by a lady-in-waiting. Between the empress on her barge and the palace the court is assembling. Viewed from an arm's length away these figures are no more than elongated blobs on the canvas, flashes and dabs of meaningless colour; step back, look again, and suddenly there before you is Halfyndruth's ingratiating stoop or Melkatan's long grey beard. The silver breast-plates of the guards march arrogantly across the landing stage; two peacocks strut behind them, mimicking. Other brush strokes resolve themselves into Ladies of the Chamber, calculatingly silly, waiting for their husbands or their lovers to help them from the barge, or into tired oarsmen, resting on their oars or stretching aching muscles after their long journey to the Keep Akhranta and back, but waiting silently as their empress disembarks.

Vlatri's talent extends beyond the portrayal of a scene of pomp and glory, however: a detailed examination of the canvas reveals the artist's eye for human detail. Notice, for instance, the tear in the Gyr Rilek's cloak where it caught on his spurs, or the manservant arguing fluently with one of the royal grooms for a horse to take him back to Cythroné.

The servant was Cluny: 'The orders,' he said, 'are Our Lady's.'

'The seal on this letter ain't,' replied the groom, who was unable to read but knew the royal seal when he saw it.

'It is the seal of Halfyndruth,' explained Cluny. 'He wrote the letter. He's my master.'

'I see.' The groom handed the letter back to Cluny. 'The letter's from Halfyndruth. Right?'

'Yes,' said Cluny, puzzled.

'Halfyndruth's your master. Right?'

'Yes,' Cluny repeated.

'Right.' The word was a statement rather than a question this time. 'Right. The letter's from Halfyndruth who is your master. It's not from Our Lady. So what I say is, if Halfyndruth wants you to have a horse he can find you one, but he won't find one here. Right?'

'You won't let me have a horse?'

'Right.'

I'll hit him if he says that once more, thought Cluny. He looked around for Halfyndruth, but his master, like the rest of the court, was lining up behind their empress ready to escort her to the palace. To disturb him now was impossible.

'Are you standing here all evening or are you going?' asked the groom.

Cluny turned his attention back to the groom. Like most grooms the man before him was small and light, in order that he did not tire the horses in his charge too much. 'Oh, I'm going,' said Cluny, with a note of deliberate innocence in his voice.

'Right,' said the groom, and Cluny hit him.

Cluny hit him hard, on the nose, with all the strength he could muster, and then, as the man fell, he pulled the reins from his grasp. The horse was shaken by the sudden pressure of the falling groom on its halter: it reared away from Cluny and it was all he could do to control it. The horse started to back away from the unfamiliar figure who now held its reins. It jerked its head and nearly dislodged Cluny's grip. Then it turned about and started to trot, away from the river, the palace, and the crowd. Cluny found himself dragged along behind it; he ran a pace or two to keep up.

There had been no plan in Cluny's mind when he had hit the groom, and no real thought save the thought that this silly little man was in the way. But now he had the horse's bridle in his hand. He hopped alongside the animal whilst groping for a stirrup with his other foot, found the stirrup, and lifted himself into the saddle, clinging to the reins and the pommel for support. His hat fell off as he climbed, and after raising an experimental hand to try to catch it, losing his balance, and grabbing wildly at the pommel again to retain his precarious seat Cluny let the thing go. It fell to the grass behind him, and lay on the lawn like some grotesque giant fungus.

The courtiers milling around their empress didn't seem to have noticed Cluny's dramatic exit, while the groom was still sitting on the ground trying to push his painful nose back into some semblance of its former shape. Cluny rode rapidly away from the courtiers, circuiting a large ornamental well that focused the lawn in front of him and heading west towards the setting sun, a line of trees, and Cythroné.

He slowed the horse to the quietest walk as they entered the trees, and ducked his head to brush aside the greedy branches. He rode through a small wood, wishing he knew the topography of Verdre better than he did, and came to a straight avenue. To the right of where he paused, reins slack, was the palace, its white walls rosy in the evening sun; left along the avenue was a wrought iron gate, and beyond the gate the fish-scale sparkle of the River Khalin. This was not the avenue Cluny had hoped to find: reluctantly he urged his horse forward, across the open space and into the trees beyond.

Another short journey of scratches and tugs through the woods of Verdre, and Cluny emerged on to a second avenue. Again, the view to his right was of the palace, for all the avenues radiated from that building, but this time to his left he saw the familiar posts and pillars of the Great Gate which led from Verdre to the Cythron road. This was the Western Avenue, one of the four principal avenues which approached the palace from each of the four compass points. Ahead,

accentuated by the dark lines of converging trees, the Great
Gate was silhouette and shadow between Cluny and the sun.

He rode towards the Great Gate slowly, his horse steadied to
a trot. He unfastened the lace at his collar, and cursed for the
flat felt hat he had shed in his flight. It had been one of his
favourites, small brimmed in the fashionable style, with a dark
green plume and a silver chain trimming it, and although of felt
rather than velvet it made him, he liked to think, look quite the
gentleman.

He reached the Great Gate. A massive arch of decorated
granite spanned the road; flanking the arch, with pointed
towers and heavy buttresses partitioning its length, was the
wall that guarded Verdre. The Great Gate itself was open: the
blackiron scrolls highlighted in gold that formed the gates
themselves were drawn back against the massive walls of the
guardroom. Groups of soldiers milled about. Cluny heard
voices calling from inside the guardroom: 'Wylek! Your ale's
been poured'; 'Stand up straight when I'm talking to you';
'Daft swine thinks he knows about bear baiting, but I soon told
him.' None of it had anything to do with him: he rode through
the gates unmolested and unquestioned; none of the soldiers
paid even a second glance to him, for what was another
leather-jerkined servant riding a horse from the royal stables?
It was a busy day, after all: the troops had seen scores like
Cluny, going about their masters' business. None the less,
Cluny breathed a sigh that was relief and gratitude when he had
passed through the gates, for questions might have proved
awkward.

The road he was now on was the Namamorn, the 'Road to
Morn', which led into Cythroné through the Anxious Gate,
one of the five original gates leading into the old walled town.
The Anxious Gate was the most eastern of these entrances, and
thus it earnt its name, for it was from the east that danger came
to Cythroné, and many were the hours of anxious waiting spent
by citizens on those towers. Now, of course, the gates would
serve little purpose as observation posts, being surrounded by
the spreading, growing city.

Expansion characterised the history of Cythroné. Once no
more than a fishing port on the north banks of the Khalin, luck
and local pride had made it the capital of the flourishing Old

Kingdom of Lorin. Later, in the Old Kingdom wars, Cythroné had expanded still further, as the population of the surrounding countryside was driven into the city for shelter. It was at that period that the city walls were built. Originally there had been a wide margin of grassland between the city and the surrounding walls, which could be used for grazing in times of war, but steadily the houses filled the open spaces and, doing what no army had ever succeeded in doing, they overran the sturdy walls. In the reign of Kythen I, the building of the first Cythron Bridge opened up the land to the south for development, and within two generations the docklands of Grenol and Carn, the commercial district of the Carpaccio, and the extensive slums of Molve, Nandra and the Quarter had spread uncontrollably over the southern marshes. In the same reign the court removed from the old citadel by the river, where now the meeting-house stands, to the healthier isolation of Verdre, trailing lines of shanty housing in its wake. It was through this shanty housing that Cluny now travelled.

Huts of wood and straw, leaning against one another or the occasional brick building as if for support, hemmed him in. The further from the city centre, the fouler the housing, thought Cluny, and then he smiled as he thought of the superb palaces of the nobility encircling the city and even the slums. None the less, despite these palaces, Cluny's observation was generally true, and as he grew nearer to the city the wooden shanties gave way to mean buildings of brick or stone, cold housing or dingy shops. Narrow alleys led from the Namamorn to noisome dark yards where children cried. The district was largely deserted now as the celebrations by the river continued, and it enveloped Cluny in a sinister silence in which the screams of children and the weak coughs that echoed from the shadows seemed appropriate and ominous. Cluny hurried his horse on.

The sun had almost set now: it was a vermilion dome beyond the darker domes of the city. Cluny passed groups of people returning from the fêtes by the river to their homes. This was but the vanguard of the exodus: when night set in the city's streets would be abandoned to the drunken mobs that always seemed to form after a celebration. Cluny threaded his horse carefully through the spasmodic crowds. The poorest were the first Cluny encountered: that they should leave the celebrations first was no surprise to him, for they had the furthest to travel and the least to spend. Despite the poverty of their pinched faces and ragged clothes, everyone seemed to have dressed for the occasion, yet the superficial extravagance of ribbons in their hats served only to accentuate the indignities of being so desperately poor. Many of them were not speaking Cythron, the official language of the empire, but rather their own languages, such as Taliolan from the beautiful hill country north of the Plains of Myr, or Earthscar patois. Cluny, well fed and prosperous despite his status as a servant, found himself wondering what sort of life these people could have led before: could it really have been worse than the dreadful poverty of life beyond the Cythron walls?

Cluny himself was an immigrant, a Plainsman of Myr who had been attracted to the city by the prospect of wealth and the romance of adventure, but only a slight rustic burr to his vowels now betrayed his origins. In all other respects he was the perfect Cythron servant, despite his impetuous nature, and Halfyndruth paid him and treated him well. Cluny drove his horse through the crowds that were thickening and damming the road. Common people, servants of masters who were not working that day, artisans and apprentices, ordinary people in jerkins and smocks, with dirty-bottomed skirts and grimy hose after their long day in the city, followed the poor out along the Namamorn. These were Cluny's people, the people he shared drinks and jokes and conditions with, but today Cluny rode a horse against the crowd, had been aboard the royal barge, and carried a message from the empress: he looked on the currents of shoulders pressing against his horse's flanks with something akin to contempt. Poor things, he felt: how they must envy me. But the crowd did not envy Cluny: they saw a hatless dusty servant doing his master's errands while they relaxed in holiday, and felt pity if they felt anything at all.

Cluny rode mechanically, hardly daring to think of the consequences of his action. He suspected that there would be trouble: he had taken a horse without permission after all. On the other hand, he felt, brightening, the mission had been undertaken on the empress's behalf, and Cluny – young, loyal, romantic – had enjoyed surmounting the trivial obstacles of his journey for her.

The road now led up to the dark mouth of the Anxious Gate. Torches held by iron brackets illuminated the streets ahead with patchy treacherous light. Although the gate was now surrounded by buildings it was still guarded by men of the city militia, and the great portcullis beneath which Cluny was riding was still heavy with the threat of its weight. Adding to the confused illumination from the walls, many of the crowd pushing and shoving their way along the road also carried torches now, and these threw wild disfigured shadows in the thickening dusk. The press of bodies about his horse was greater now, and the crowds were no longer all travelling in one direction, as they had been before the gate, but were pushing and shoving in all ways, creating swirls and vortexes, movement and blockages, all along the street ahead. From his position on the horse's back Cluny could see a flood of faces stretching before him down the road to his destination. He kicked his heels into the horse's flank and pressed on.

People were not the only cause of obstruction. Carts made their heavy way through the crowd, or pulled up outside drinking houses and reduced the street's width to a single file; pigs and goats wandered infuriatingly between human legs, tripping and fouling those they approached; barrels of rain-water, which had once collected water from the guttering by houses and shops, were pushed into the centre of the road by the constant pressure.

The congestion was at its worst in Fragma Square which marked the intersection between the Namamorn and the Mercantile Way. The Mercantile Way, which ran south across the Bridge of Towers, was a solid mass of humanity, and where the square opened out there was a virtual halt as they fought their way around the noble equestrian statue of Ravenspur. Cluny saw upraised faces, red with shock and lack of air; he saw heads bent down, tousled heads that shoved and laughed. He found himself in the middle of a gaggle of apprentices who wore silk cockades of red and black in their hats and who chanted egalitarian songs.

> In the past no first nor last,
> No king to rule nor serf to sweat:
> Better then when men were men,

But we'll have such days again;
We'll all be equal yet.

For tomorrow no more sorrow.
No king to rule nor serf to sweat:
    Streets will flood with noble blood,
    All blood's equal mixed with mud;
We'll all be equal yet.

'A chevalier!' cried one of the mob, grabbing Cluny's bridle. 'Hey,' he called to his companions. 'Look what's landed in the middle of us then.'

Cluny tried to push his mount through the press of bodies. That he was not a nobleman would do him no good: the lackey of a lord is, to a republican, worse than the lord himself, for the lackey has had his chance to be of the people, and has wasted it. Besides, Cluny also knew that a servant is more likely to be hit than the master. It is safer to hit a lackey than a lord, and in the law courts means the difference between a forty talents' fine and a hanging.

The crowd parted slowly and reluctantly before the muscular flanks of the horse. The apprentice who had first been aware of Cluny still hung on to the bridle. Cluny drew his sword. The apprentice received a sharp flat-bladed blow across the neck and loosed his grip. Another apprentice took hold of the bridle, but the pressure of the crowd and the strength of the horse forced him to let go. As the horse pushed forward Cluny was aware of the man at the horse's shoulder, then clutching at his own boots, and finally clinging to the saddle-cloth. Using his sword like a saw Cluny detached that corner of the saddle-cloth. The expensive silk gave easily once the first tear had been made.

With an oath the apprentice with the sore neck fought his way back to Cluny through the pressed bodies. It was like wrestling in syrup: each movement was exaggerated by the need to force aside the unwilling spectators. The apprentice climbed wildly on to the shoulders of two of his companions and made a grab for Cluny, throwing himself on to the back of the horse. Cluny turned in the saddle: for a moment the two figures were locked in unstable conflict above the indifferent element that was the crowd, and then Cluny, with the advantage of stirrups outweighing the disadvantage of having his assailant behind him, dislodged his opponent. In a sudden fury Cluny dug his spurs into the horse's flank, smearing blood, and the horse drove forward powerfully, wading carelessly through the resistant medium of the bodies whilst Cluny waved his sword.

The apprentice who had jumped at Cluny slipped quite slowly through the surrounding bodies, and eventually sank to the cobbled floor of the square. His friends tried to stop the crowd trampling on him. It was an impossible task. Whilst the fallen man curled up, foetal between the crushing legs, his friends were swept away by the tides and eddies of the crowd. In clumsy sightless agony he died beneath the legs.

Unaware, Cluny rode on. He was still quick with anger, but fortunately the crowd was thinner now and his violence subsided with passing time and easier progress. Subsided, but did not go altogether: smarting within him like an ulcer was the feeling that the apprentices had spoilt his mission. It had begun as a fine adventure undertaken on behalf of a queen; the brute reality of the apprentices' hands clutching for him had soiled the adventure and made it squalid.

Feeling dirty, with his own sweat staining his shirt and the sweat of innumerable others staining his hose, he rode on into Cythroné and towards the House of the Condemned.

In the great white hall of the palace of Verdre the courtiers performed their minuet. Beneath the glittering chandeliers and the arching gold-traced vaults they stepped the complicated steps. On a stand at one end of the hall, before velvet curtained windows, a group of musicians in the black and gold livery of the royal household entwined their strands of tune. A piping flute challenged a rasping viol; a complex rhythm disciplined the horns. On the carpeted periphery of the room stood old, abandoned or tired guests, watching the dancers on the polished wood floor. There the courtiers bowed and turned, concentric rings of men and women circling in elegant embrace.

The men of the court wore costumes of peacock hues, wore them indeed with peacock vanity. Ruffs of stark white silk and lace, folded into formal confusions that foamed about the neck;

doublets of rich satin, pricked and pierced to show tufts of ivory lining through elaborately embroidered holes; tight waists corseted into place and secured by brilliant sashes and narrow sword belts trimmed with precious stones; narrow useless parade rapiers contrasting with wide slashed pantaloons that extended to the knee, ending in ruffs of lace and cut open to expose yet more fluffed ivory silk; gorgeous hose of every shade; bejewelled slippers with raised heels and pointed toes. Over this fantasy of colour and design the court cloaks, long and light and uniform, indicated rank and station. The Gallants, young nobles of the various orders of chivalry, wore scarlet shot with gold; the Vaines, next in degree, wore green and gold; a Gros wore a cloak of royal blue and gold; a Gyr a much embroidered cloth-of-gold.

For the women of the court, in contrast, there was no such variety. Each lady, from the empress on her golden throne to the poorest Vaine's daughter looking for a wealthy match, wore dove-grey silk decked with diamonds and pearls, silver bracelets and chains, and a dark grey velvet eye-mask studded with jewels. Only the differing cuts of the dresses indicated personality; only the profusion of diamonds and pearls could indicate station. This anonymous fashion was an innovation of Elsban herself, and as she watched the prancing, dancing court she amused herself with the speculation that she might exchange places with any woman in the room, and no one would be any the wiser. That portly matron dancing with the dashing Gros of Nanx, for instance, or the blushing virgin over there who had attracted the lascivious attentions of the elderly Gyr Melinloth, High Admiral of the Warfleet. Not, thought Elsban dryly, that I'd want to swap places with anyone confronted by Melinloth on the rampage, but the idea of anonymity I still enjoy.

The dancers circled still, slow and precise, and then, with a cadence of harp and flute, a sustained note of the horns, and a rapid arpeggio on the strings, the music ended. At the last note the dancers stopped, turned to face their monarch on her golden throne, flourished a bow; then they turned to face their partners again, bowed once more, and broke the pattern of the dance floor by suddenly stepping from the rigid formality of the dance into irregular knots and clumps of conversation.

Immediately in front of Elsban as the dance ended stood the Gyr Orland, a distant cousin and yet her heir, for the seed and line of Akhran the Golden was fading and now only Elsban herself, the florid-faced nobleman before her, and this nobleman's brother, carried the blood of Akhran in their veins. Legitimately at least: for there was one other who could claim descent from Akhran, and as she thought of the bastard child she had borne and abandoned her heart seemed to balloon inside her like some useless emotion, instead of being, as modern doctors seemed to insist, no more than an organ for the pumping of blood. Elsban felt her heart swell as she thought of her lost child, and knew that the doctors were wrong: the heart is full of emotion, and the emotion was bursting to get out. She half rose from her throne, clutched her hand beneath her left breast, and stepped unsteadily down from the dais on which the throne was placed. The dancing had begun again as she stood. She did not see the whirling spectrum before her, nor hear the music play; she saw only her bastard child's father, and heard the sound of her blood rush in her ears.

Curval, leader of the court musicians, saw the empress stand, sway, and step down from her dais. For eight years he had composed and conducted at the court, but this was the first time he had known the sovereign interrupt the dance. Uncertainly he ceased to beat time with his heavy carved mace: the music ended as raggedly and untidily as the dance. Dancers found themselves posed in unexpected intimacies or barely balanced gestures as the animating music deserted them, and in embarassed silence they relaxed and stepped apart. This unexpected silence waited like a bride.

Elsban was as surprised as the courtiers by the silence, but long years of being the centre of attention had given her a poise and confidence. From her first startled glance around as the music came to a halt she slipped into her familiar regal grace. 'I thank you for your attention,' she said, with a note of detached irony in her voice. 'I have been thinking: it is time we made a Royal Progress of our domains; it is time we visited North-reach.' The pain in her chest gripped again, and she indicated to one of her ladies-in-waiting that she should like assistance. Supported under her elbow, guided by the lady-in-waiting, Elsban threaded her way through the silenced dancers and left

the room, nodding to Curval as she went. Curval in his turn
nodded at the band, some of them nodded back, and the music
began again. The music began; the dancing did not. Barely
twenty couples of the hundreds who had recently minueted in
the hall resumed their dance; the rest were too eager to discuss
the implications of the empress's announcement.

'Did you ever?' asked the Gros of Nanx's partner, deeply
offended by the informality with which the empress had
announced her decision. 'What a time to say she's going on a
progress.'

'A progress,' mused another lady in another part of the hall,
and then she turned to her husband and spoke decisively. 'You
must be sure to go with her. This is just the opportunity we
were looking for, and with your knowledge of butter prices you
should be invaluable.'

'Do you think she's just decided, or what, m'dear,' asked the
Gyr Melinloth, leaning rather too close to the ear of the
charming girl he had danced with, and dropping a glance down
her cleavage as he spoke. 'I'd have thought Elsban was a bit too
old for progresses.' There was a fascinating little mole in the
shape of a star on the girl's left breast. She smiled at him
demurely, and said nothing.

The Gyr Orland walked over to Melkhatan, the empress's
oldest and most trusted adviser, and demanded information.
'Well? What's this all about?'

'I assure you, your Gyrarch, I knew nothing of this
decision.'

The Gyr turned disgustedly away from Melkhatan, and the
latter felt a swirl of cloth-of-gold as the Gyr's cloak brushed his
legs. 'If you won't tell me, I'll find someone who will,' said the
Gyr. Melkhatan watched the receding back pushing ungra-
ciously through the few remaining dancers, and then turned to
repeat his denial to another insistent courtier. The Gyr
searched for his brother.

Cluny looked at the Gaolmaster's secretary, a round soft man
called Belphats who suffered from a perpetual cold. Belphats
looked at the letter, turning it distastefully in his fleshy fingers
and then holding it up to the candle's light. The letter, in its
turn, looked filthy.

'Well, the seal is genuine, I suppose,' said Belphats, in the tone of one who is looking for something positive to say. 'Well, Cluny. As I know you I'll believe you. I'll believe that this foul scrap of parchment really does contain orders from Our Lady of Khalindaine, and that it really was entrusted to your care by a senior judge. But Cluny, next time Halfyndruth gives you a letter to deliver, look after it will you?'

The Gros of Weir was elegantly dressed in crimson and black. He wore a short cut-off cuirass of blackiron armour that protected his abdomen and, following the line of his ribs, came to a point at the point of his breast bone; above this a swell of crimson doublet billowed out, emphasising the shape of the Weir-Lord's torso. Draped across his shoulders was the royal blue cloak that indicated his rank. He stood with one hand on the hilt of his ceremonial rapier, the other holding back the folds of his cloak, in that effortlessly asymmetrical pose currently fashionable in court. Like Melkhatan, he was trying to explain his ignorance about the empress's decision; unlike Melkhatan, the Weir-Lord was grateful to see the Gyr Orland approaching.

'Ahah,' said the Weir-Lord. 'My brother. He surely will be able to tell you all you wish to know.'

The Gyr sneered. 'I know nothing,' he said. 'Ask Melkhatan if you want to know anything, and I wish you more luck than I had with that closed-mouthed mincing sheep.'

'A very good idea,' said the Gros of Weir smoothly. 'Why don't you have a word with Melkhatan?'

The hint that the brothers wished to be alone was enough for most of the Gallants, several of whom owed their positions to the patronage of the House of Orland. Those who remained were dismissed with the curt 'Family matters' from the Weir-Lord's lips. 'Well?' he continued to the Gyr. 'What is it?'

They left the centre of the floor and made for a quiet corner. 'You know full well what it is, or you wouldn't have made such a fuss about speaking in front of those Gallants. You know as well as I do that there's only one reason why Elsban would go to Northreach, and that's the bastard.'

'I don't think you should mention the – the child – except in the strictest privacy.'

'But you agree? She's going to look for the – child.'

'I admit that it is possible,' conceded the Weir-Lord.

'It's common knowledge that she's dying.'

'It's treachery to say so.'

'She'll want to see the child before she does. It's obvious she's not well: look at how she behaved tonight. What can we do, that's what I want to know.'

'Let me think.' Although the younger by several years, the Gros of Weir had a better mind than his brother and knew it. 'I'll tell you what: don't worry about it at present. Not even if she were half-barmy, and we've seen no sign of that, would the empress look out the bastard – the child – at this time of year. By the time she got to Northreach it would be winter, and what earthly use would being there in winter be to her? If she's looking for someone it'll have to be summer when she goes, because she'll be wanting to get about, and that would mean departing in the spring. So you've three-quarters of a year to wait before you need worry, and she might not survive that long. And even if she does, it gives us time to make plans. We know that the child is some seven years younger than me; we know he was fostered off to some Northreach fur-trader. All we have to do is to kill off every fur-trader's pup aged between sixteen and seventeen summers and our problem is solved.' The brothers' eyes met, and they smiled at one another. Then the Weir-Lord continued. 'Although you do realise that it's our own flesh and blood we're plotting against: it could set an awkward precedent, could that.'

The Gaolmaster nodded, refolded the letter, and absent-mindedly poked a corner of it into his fingernails to release the dirt. 'It's got here a bit late, hasn't it?' he said. 'There's only one chap left in the place, and we were going to save him till tomorrow now. I don't like night executions: even in summer it gets too cold on the square.'

'You'll release this man?' asked Cluny, who didn't want to discover that his journey had been a complete waste of time.

'I suppose so, although it hardly seems worth it now. Do you know, we've had seventeen executions today, and with a premium of twelve talents apiece, that's two hundred, two hundred, two hundred and something, two hundred and something . . .'

'Too much,' murmured Belphats.

'Two hundred and four,' said the Gaolmaster triumphantly. 'Two hundred and four talents we've paid out in premium today, and we could have saved it all if you'd just got here at a sensible time. No, you can have this one that we've got left over, but the saving hardly makes it worth it.'

'I should think he'd think it worth it,' said Cluny.

'What does he know about it?' demanded the Gaolmaster. 'He's not the one who has to balance the books at the end of every session. Go and let me get on with this, Belphats; I've far too much work to do to worry about the prisoners.'

Belphats and Cluny left the Gaolmaster's office and returned to the ante-room which contained Belphats' desk. 'Well?' asked Belphats. 'Are you coming with me or do I have to go down on my own?'

'I'll come,' said Cluny. 'I might as well know who it is I'm saving. It's been hard enough work, by Menketh.'

'It wouldn't be worth doing if it didn't take an effort,' said Belphats sanctimoniously. Cluny found the remark rather obscure and conversation ceased.

They descended through steadily starker galleries, down flights of echoing stairs and corridors of unrelieved stone, and reached a small guard room lit by a smoky open fire and ventilated only by a narrow hole in the ceiling, so the fire illuminated and the smoke obscured the scene. A solitary guard was preparing a pot of cacauatl seed over the fire.

'You've got a prisoner down here?' asked Belphats, puckering his mouth against the grimy guard room.

The guard gestured over his shoulder using his head. 'Just follow the singing,' he said, thus identifying for Cluny the source of the noise which had been bothering them since they'd entered the guard room.

'He's coming with us,' said Cluny.

'About time too. What is it – garrotting or the drop?'

'Neither. We're setting him free,' said Cluny.

'You're letting him live!' The guard was incredulous. 'A voice like that and you're letting him live!'

'Does he sing a lot, then?' asked Cluny, who wished to learn something about the person whose life he was saving.

'Sing a lot!' The incredulity in the guard's voice was

squeezed to an even tighter pitch, making him almost falsetto. 'Daft swine never stops. Still, if you're not killing him at least you'll take him away, and that's what matters to me.' The goat's milk for the cacauatl seed suddenly boiled up the side of the pan and sizzled in the flames below. Blaspheming, the guard dropped the cup and made to mop up the mess. 'You two go and see to the swine. Keys are on the hook.' He made the same gesture with his head to indicate their approximate where-abouts. 'I'll follow you when I've cleaned up.'

Belphats lifted a heavy bunch of keys from the hook by the door the guard had signalled, and then they opened the door. The noise was much louder at once, and recognisably singing.

'Shut the door after you,' demanded the guard, and they complied. The sound led them through further dingy corri-dors, identical to those they had passed along before, and then to a wide vaulted room, with a ceiling that stretched into arched darkness and walls lined with tiers of wooden galleries.

Belphats listened attentively, trying to trace the singer, and then led Cluny up an echoing wooden staircase to the left. Black straw littered the floor and spread in unenthusiastic strands up the stairs. Beneath the light of flickering brands malevolent rodent eyes flashed at Cluny as he passed. They climbed to the gallery.

The slats that formed the gallery floor were smooth with wear but warped and parted, admitting light from the brands on the tier below. Cluny and Belphats made their way, the former cautiously and the latter impatiently, across the hollow wood, and their footsteps sounded around them in accom-paniment to the singer. Cluny could make out words now:

> It's a funny day to die,
> > Tra-la,
> A funny way to die,
> > Tra-la,
> But man was made to die
> And so I'll stay to die,
> It's a funny way to die
> > Tra-lala-la.

At the end of each line a mandola was strummed. The voice was not tuneless, nor unpleasant, but was singing with such a casual drawl, and echoing with such a bizarre effect, as to make silencing it seem imperative to Cluny. It was with gratitude, therefore, that he realised they had reached the singer's door. Belphats handed him the torch to carry and fiddled with the keys until one fitted.

'Not today thank you,' said the singer, as Belphats let himself in. The room was in utter darkness, and the light from the torch Cluny held was lapped up hungrily by the cold flagged floor, the rough domed ceiling, the narrow walls, and the figure cross-legged on the rushes before them. 'I'm trying to give up seafood,' the voice continued. 'It's an aphrodisiac. Or, if you must bring me oysters, bring me a woman as well. I'm very partial to a woman. And they're often partial to me.'

His mind has gone, thought Cluny. He was not surprised. The stagnant dark of the House of the Condemned was turning his own mind, he felt. Belphats, Cluny noticed, had drawn his dagger and was pointing it at the prisoner. 'Go and have a look at him,' said the secretary, in a voice which implied he wanted nothing to do with the whole situation.

With the torch stretched before him like a weapon, Cluny approached the cross-legged singer. What he saw surprised him. A young man of sixteen or seventeen looked back at him with level humorous eyes. 'Wouldn't want you to garrotte the wrong one,' said the young man in response to this inspection.

Cluny licked his lips before he spoke. 'We've come to let you out.'

'Oh.' The youth smiled pleasantly. He had a thin, elfin face. Dark brows framed firm dark eyes. Light from the torch highlighted white spots in those eyes, made a straight line down the right of his nose, lit his forehead and the bow of his lower lip. All the rest was darkness. 'Why?'

'Halfyndruth's orders,' said Belphats, stepping forward.

'From Our Lady of Khalindaine herself,' added Cluny, impressively.

The young man was not impressed. He stood up, looked around the cell, and strummed a minor chord on his mandola, followed by a major chord one tone below, and then, alternating these chords and using them to punctuate his song, he began to sing.

> Locked away in this prison fastness,
> Fast pining away, away from the pines
> And streams of my home, that Northreach vastness
> That meant far too much to my imprisoned mind;
> Locked away, awaiting no one,
> No one to save me, for who cares enough . . .

The tempo increased, and another major chord was added to
his accompaniment.

> Then I'm saved and I've got to thank someone;
> Thank half a man called Halfyndruth,
> For it's the truth that Halfyndruth
> Was the one who saved us.
>
> Yes, half in jest and half in truth
> Let's sing all praises to Halfyndruth,
> For he's the one who saved this poor youth,
> He's the one who saved us.

The young man put down his instrument suddenly, gathered
up a small number of ragged possessions, and collecting his
mandola again and strapping it across his back, made for the
door. 'Shall we go?' he asked.

They led the singer back to the guard room and asked the
guard to show him out. The guard mumbled something about
his drink going cold, and Cluny and Belphats returned to the
Gaolmaster's office, where they were asked several complicated
multiplication and long division questions which referred to
rations and arms.

At length Cluny decided it was time to return to Verdre. The
dance at the palace would be almost over now, and his master
would be wanting his assistance to undress; they had answered
all the mathematics questions to the best of their ability,
although not to the Gaolmaster's satisfaction, and Belphats was
yawning and not bothering to hide it.

'All right,' said the Gaolmaster. 'All right, leave me. Leave
me with all this. People never understand what goes into
running a place like this, they really don't.'

They did leave him. Belphats was trying to decide what sort
of nightcap he would have before going to bed; Cluny was

wondering how to explain the torn saddle-cloth on his borrowed mount. They walked down to the stables.

Cluny need not have worried. The torn saddle-cloth was no longer likely to be any sort of problem to him at all. The horse had gone.

'That's odd,' said Belphats, which wasn't what Cluny would have said exactly. 'This courtyard is locked and guarded.' He called out loudly, and the word echoed around before a small hurried figure appeared: 'Watchman!'

'Yes sir,' said the ancient watchman breathlessly.

Belphats adopted his most self-righteous tone. 'Watchman, have you been in dereliction of your duty?'

'Eh?'

'Have you been bunking off?'

'No sir.'

'Then where's this man's horse? He left it here earlier this night. It is here no longer. Hence, someone has taken it. Hence, you were bunking off.'

'I don't know nothing about no horse. Only person been in this courtyard since I came on duty was a royal messenger, and he left on his own horse ... '

'A royal messenger,' interrupted Cluny. 'I'm the royal messenger. You old fool, you let someone take my horse.'

'Well, well, well.' The old man was chuckling; Cluny wanted to throttle him. 'Is that a fact? Well, would you credit it. Bold as brass he was, I wasn't a bit suspicious, despite him being so mucky and all, and that despite one thing that really should have put me on my guard.' The old man was forced to stop as his laughter bubbled into his voice.

'Well man, what was that?' demanded Cluny desperately.

'Well, they don't often carry musical instruments, royal messengers, do they?'

Chapter 2

Northreach

It had been a long night, and Hedch had travelled a long way. As he looked out at the welcome sight of the valley before him he reined in his horse and eased his aching muscles. He pulled off his gauntlets and rubbed his rough hands together, blowing on them to help the circulation, and then he removed his helm and ran a finger round the stiff leather lining of his gorget, probing the tense tendons of his neck and shoulder. He was hungry, tired, and very cold, and for the thousand-and-fifteenth time since he had accepted the Gyr Orland's commission he wished he had stayed in Cythroné. He tried bending and straightening his neck to see if that made it feel better; all that happened was that the leather lining chafed him. I'm getting too old for this sort of game, he decided.

He looked at the peaceful town beneath him. The morning sun shone through the valley ahead of him. It was not high enough in the clear cold sky to illuminate the town yet, but it caught the suspended plumes of smoke that rose breathless above the houses and made them clean and proud. I could retire to a town like this, thought Hedch. He watched as a small group of town guards shoved the great wooden gates apart, and saw a small line of herdsmen, mounted on asses, leave the town for their steep mountain pastures. He looked at the web of intricate streets and the angled slabs of the roofs. It looked a nice town, he felt, as he urged his horse on with a swift kick of his heels.

He had been waiting for the gates to open. He knew that no Northreach town would open its gates before first light, and knew too that too early an arrival would bring questions he could well do without. All he really wanted was a bed. Now that the gates were open there was at least the chance that he could slip into the town unnoticed.

It was a forlorn hope. The town of Fenras, nestling in the Heront valley where the Heront river met the Glanth before the two rolled as one into the mighty Khalin river, had heard no news from over the mountains since the fall, a quarter-year ago. A group of children, washing briskly in the icy waters of the Heront, saw the messenger first, and ran back into town to report his arrival. Their flesh was still red and white from the chill river.

'A stranger?' The adults tried to hide their curiosity. 'Are you sure?'

'Yes,' said the children, impatiently.

Children and adults walked out to the gates to see the stranger ride in. He was unimpressive: an armoured figure on a tired horse, with a wooden lance that had no pennon and fur-edged boots with much-patched soles. The children, whose faces were level with his boots, ran out and grasped the stranger's legs. He smiled at them: it was an old, tired smile and as cold as the day.

With the children frothing at his boots he rode in through the gates, while the adults with greater reserve watched him from the margins of the streets. One of the guards, a young chap with a rheumy nose and a discouraged looking blond moustache, stepped out into the street to challenge the stranger.

'Halt!'

Hedch halted. The guard looked at him, at the worn armour and the haggard horse, and turned red with an embarrassment that was mostly inexperience. 'Yes?' asked Hedch politely.

'Proceed,' ordered the young guard. The people watching tittered, and one or two called out to increase the guard's embarrassment. Hedch smiled at the guard, the same slow cold smile which he had used on the children. It was a smile without feelings, a formal exercise of the face muscles rather than an expression to reveal an emotion.

'Can you show me the way to the inn?' asked Hedch. 'I'm rather tired.'

Whilst the guard tried to decide what he should do a heavy man with a jerkin of black fur that parted at the waist to reveal a bulging belly in a dark brown shirt stepped forward and spoke. 'Oi,' said the belly. 'You want the inn?'

'Yes please.'

'I'll take you. You not been to Fenras before?'

'No.'

'Come over the Gilla Pass, did you?' asked the man.

'Yes.' Mental images: white snow turned grey by heavy night; deep silent abysses that plunged to black; long-legged bodies that scuttled across his path and watched him from above.

'You'll be the first through this season.'

'Really?' Flurries of snow that blinded him; treacherous ice on the path; the darkness and always the eyes.

'Yes. Me, I'm a stranger here myself.' The belly thrust its way along a narrow winding street, leading Hedch and his horse. Behind came a crowd of children still bubbling though robbed of their captive; behind the children were the honest citizens of Fenras, hoping to catch some news of the outside world. 'You probably guessed by my accent. I'm a Cythron man. Arrived here just before the snows to do a bit of fur-trading and got stranded. Be a lesson to me, that will. Still, you can do worse than this place. Here we are; here's the inn.' The procession drew up outside a wood-framed building, distinguished from its neighbours only by the painted wooden sign that hung from a black iron pole and the fat man in an apron who wrung his hands in the doorway. 'Stranger for you,' called Hedch's guide.

'Bring him in,' called the innkeeper.

Hedch dismounted stiffly and stood at his horse's neck until, at a signal from the innkeeper, one of the children ran up and led the horse away. Hedch patted the animal affectionately on the nose as it was taken from him, and then allowed himself to be led away too, as the innkeeper and the belly, escorted by the crowd, led him into the inn. He was seated at a table in the tap room and a tankard of ale placed in front of him. The citizens of Fenras pressed into the dark narrow room around him and watched approvingly as he took an experimental sip of the ale. The faces arranged in a semi-circle before him. 'Well?' asked a voice. 'What news?'

Hedch smiled grimly once more. It had been like this in each of the towns he had visited: hello stranger, what news? The smile turned inward. 'The empress is ill, they say.'

A mutter of indignation and sympathy ran the half-circle. 'Nothing serious we hope?' asked a different voice.

'They say that it is in her heart,' continued Hedch. 'She has announced a royal progress to Northreach for this season, but I'd left Cythroné before any more had been decided.'

Another chorus of mutterings greeted this information. 'Imagine,' he heard a heavy female voice say. 'Imagine the empress coming to Northreach. I remember last time she came: slip of a lass she was then, and so was I.'

'Aye, we all remember that,' said another. 'All of us as are old enough at any rate. And the least said about that visit the better. We don't want none of your gossip spoiling Our Lady's progress, do we.'

Hedch looked up from his ale to see two toothless old women discussing the empress as they might talk of a sister-in-law. The landlord was looking at them also. 'Ladies,' said the landlord. 'If you've nowt better to do than talk about things best forgotten you'll kindly do it elsewhere.'

The one who had spoken first looked sharply at the landlord and at Hedch, a curious stare facilitated by the fact that she had a curious squint. 'You know as well as me all them stories about the bastard,' she said. 'And chucking me out of your filthy tavern ain't going to stop me nor anyone else talking about it.'

'Out,' said the landlord, moving round the table to assist the old woman in her exit. She stood before he got to her.

'I'm going,' she said. 'Fine thing when you can't even talk about your own empress.' She spat expertly on to the wooden table top; the landlord apologetically rubbed the spot with his apron.

'Get out, you old drab,' he said, and she was gone, leaving only a darker stain on the table to mark where she had been.

Hedch looked up. Like everyone else in Khalindaine he had heard the rumours about the empress's bastard child, but he had never heard them spoken with such force before. The old dear who had spat on to the table obviously believed the rumour; and the landlord too judging by the strength of his reaction.

The pot-bellied Cythron was talking now. 'What brings you to these parts anyhow?'

'Business,' said Hedch. 'I've a commission from the Gyr Orland.' Hedch thought for a moment and then decided not to announce the nature of his commission until later in the day, when he had the ear of some people of authority instead of this ragamuffin crowd. He stood up with a clanking of armour on wood and put down the tankard. 'Thank you for the ale, whoever provided it. Put it down on my bill. And now, if you don't mind, I'd like to go to sleep.' Vaguely dissatisfied, but with the twin news of the empress's progress and the illness to discuss, and the old woman's indiscretion to condemn, the crowd broke up. Wearily Hedch climbed the stairs. His bed was in the room upstairs, a long narrow room that ran the length of the inn below. Part of this room was curtained off: behind there slept the landlord and his wife, with their children. The rest of the room was occupied by two large beds, four-posters obviously bought second hand from some nobleman who had no further use for them. There was no mattress on either of them, just grubby straw indistinguishable from that which covered the floor. Hedch did not mind. He removed his armour carefully, unbuckling the leather thongs with fingers dulled by wear and cold, and piled it by the side of one of the beds. Then, dressed only in his hose and a stained grey shirt, he stretched out on the bed, and slept.

Va'alastar the Shaman stepped out from his house. Rain had made the street muddy and awkward: the shaman found his long crimson cloak trailing in a puddle and irritably pulled up the offending material, tucking it under his arm. He closed the door behind him. Above the stone lintel hung a blue and gold banner, symbol of the shaman's trade, and made dark and heavy by the previous night's rain-water. The banner was intricately patterned with fine scarlet lettering that ran through and about the design in vast loops and knots of language. Beneath its arcane splendours Va'alastar turned a large key, whispered a secretive incantation, and watched the keyhole vanish into the wood. Doing his best to avoid the worst of the standing water in the street, the shaman turned to walk towards the town centre, where the hoarstone stood on its granite plinth.

The morning had worn on, and commerce had increased visibly. Men and women plied skins of milk in the streets around him, or offered faggots and bright spring flowers. Va'alastar turned from one street into another: now he was in the Street of Merchants. Here canvas canopies above the stalls made a roof across the street, and within the cream and luscious light that illuminated this world through the canvas the merchants carried out their trade. Spices and leathers were offered at knock-down prices; poultry vied with yards of cloth; bone buttons and needles competed with salted fish. It was an opaque and busy world, coloured by the curious luminosity of canvas and flavoured by the rich animal smells of commerce and spice. Black-dressed matrons haggled with skinny traders; gaudy young men quarrelled with fur-clad merchants; heavy stomachs rested on unstable stalls. Va'alastar the Shaman, in his yellow robes and with his crimson cloak carried fastidiously under his arm, walked through the crowds without seeing.

Suddenly: a small dark head had caught him in the midrift; the air was jerked from him in a jet; he was doubled up and sitting down; he was damp.

He reoriented himself gradually. The first thing he realised was that he was sitting in a puddle. This was only too apparent. The second thing was that he had no breath to ask why. The third thing was that he was not alone in his puddle: a small girl with a grubby face stared up at him contritely from the region of his loins. 'Oh, Va'alastar, your shamanship,' she said. 'I'm sorry.' Va'alastar thought a number of thoughts unsuitable for a man of his position either in society or the shared puddle about making her sorrier, but fortunately he had not the breath to say them. She continued. 'I was looking for you and I couldn't stop.'

With as much dignity as he could assume under the circumstances, Va'alastar lifted himself out of the puddle. The child rolled off him as he rose and leapt clear, still talking breathlessly.

'You see, Va'alastar. It's happened. The rathga's opened. A stranger's come to town and the rathga's opened. Isn't it good.'

Va'alastar, his robes now thoroughly soaked in a circular patch where he had sat in the puddle, was less enthusiastic. Nonetheless, he had to concede that the arrival of a stranger, if what the girl said was true, on the same day as the rathga's flowering, was a good omen for the coming season. He straightened out his robes and continued on his way to the hoarstone, with the little girl trotting helpfully behind him like a ragged page.

They entered the square at the centre of the town. The shaman looked around him in some surprise: usually there was a sprinkling of people in the square, but today there was quite a congregation. He recognised one or two faces as they stepped aside to let him approach the hoarstone. 'Good morning, Mabeta,' he said to a soberly dressed woman as he passed her. 'What brings you here?'

'The news.'

'That the rathga has opened?' Va'alastar was amused. The opening of the flower had some ritual importance, but hardly warranted a crowd.

'No. Haven't you heard? They say the empress is dying.'

Va'alastar paused. Perhaps that explained the curious crazed vibrations he had received from the hoarstone recently. Certainly it had not behaved in its usual predictable way in recent days. He was going to question Mabeta further about the empress when he realised that she could know nothing. 'It'll be your daughter's initiation this year, will it?' he said instead, while all the while thinking that the girl must be correct when she had said a stranger had ridden into the town.

'That's right,' replied the woman. Va'alastar continued towards the hoarstone.

It stood on a plinth in the centre of the square. The stone had been there first: they had built the town around it. For hoarstones were rare and valuable, monoliths which connected the surface world of Man to the deeper, wiser areas below. It was common knowledge that the earth is no more than the great curved skull of the father-god, Hrakar, and that the hoarstones connect mankind with the great universal mind of Hrakar, alert with his potent thoughts and vibrant with his eternal knowledge. The shaman reached the hoarstone, bowed briefly, and in the same movement bent right down to inspect the small purple flowers that grew at the foot of the plinth. The girl was right; the rathga had opened. He pulled one of the flowers up by the roots with a quick tug of the wrist and examined it: seven petals of purple, each the shape of a tear and the colour of a bruise, radiating from a tiny velvet circle of dull black seeds. Still facing the monolith the shaman took a step backwards and touched his forehead with the middle finger of his left hand in what was the Northreach gesture of prayer. 'Menketh! Deliverer! We honour you!'

The milling crowd, which had been talking cheerfully about health and illegitimacy amongst monarchs, fell silent at the sound of the shaman's prayers. 'Menketh! Revenger! He who hath freed us from icy winter's bondage, and who hath sent this rathga flower in token of our liberation, be praised!' Va'alastar raised his right arm high, the fingers spread. 'Menketh! Master! Lord of summer, we praise you and love you!' The shaman held his exaggerated pose for a moment and then relaxed. 'The Menkethfeast is begun. Ring out the bells.'

At this instruction activity entered the crowd, spilling occasional figures from the edge who were dispatched on varied duties. Some went to spread the word, others to ring the great town bells. Outside each of the public buildings hung such a bell, and all but the great bronze bell high in the watchtower were rung to announce the Menkethfeast. From the basilica, the armoury, the archives and the meeting-house came the tumbled appeal of the bells: long changes and lolling tongues, winking and blinking in the morning sunlight, ringing into the day. Other people went to their houses and fetched out the food and drink they had set aside for this day. A fire was set up in the square before the basilica, and a live pig fetched from the edge of the town. Its squeals were poignant and human; its flesh was tender and tasty. Yet another group fetched long tables from the basilica and arranged them in the square, with equally long benches bordering them like the frills of a petticoat beneath a long dress. To add to this image and to give it credence, they covered the tables in gaudy cloths, bright patterned materials of yellow and silver and blue and dark brown that poured over the benches in eddying waves; dressed in their variegated patterns, the tables crowded the square.

Flags and banners were unfurled across the main streets. The yellow stallion that reared on a cloth of black was taken down from the watchtower, and, instead of this symbol of the temporal rule of the house of Akhran, the blue and gold flag of the followers of Menketh was raised. Blue and gold: a blue sky and a golden sun, that flooded the blue with waving narrowing willing warm rays; illuminated letters that circled the golden orb, and proclaimed the love of Menketh; a golden border rich with embroidered designs. Va'alastar watched the flag as they pulled it jerkily up the pole on the watchtower, and felt a sense of longing for the olden times, when the love of Menketh was a man's only motive, and when life was simple, noble and brief. He carefully picked the heads from several of the rathga plants, and separated the purple petals into a small soft leather pouch.

Disturbed from his sleep, Hedch listened to the bells and the crowd. He had never seen an initiation ceremony: in his distant homeland of Lorin such things had long since been abandoned. He looked forward to it. Not only was he in many ways a traditionalist, who approved of the old ways; also he had heard that the initiates must wrestle naked, male or female, and this too interested him.

The bells disturbed Lara too. In her mother's house, not far from the high towers of the eastern gate, she struggled towards wakefulness. The bells rang urgently, carelessly, in the morning air.

She sat up in bed, bleary-eyed and uncertain, with the blankets wrapped around her like a tent, and then the blankets were thrust off and she was standing as realisation struck her. 'Mother!' she called. 'It's happened, hasn't it? It's time for the initiation.'

Mabeta had just arrived from the square to hear her daughter's question. She hurried up the wooden stairs, sending creaks and echoes through the wooden frame of the house as she climbed. 'Yes daughter, it's happened,' she said, opening the heavy curtain that separated Lara's chamber from the corridor. 'Va'alastar's in the square getting ready; it's time you were doing the same.'

Lara grasped her mother's hand joyfully, and felt how cold it was. 'You've been out,' she said. Mabeta's hand was wrinkled and aged in the chill that came from the bones; her daughter squeezed it to give it heat and energy. 'You shouldn't have let me sleep so late.'

'A fat lot you'd have thanked me if I'd woken you earlier,' replied her mother with some justice. 'I went down to the square to look for something fresh for the morn meal and actually heard Va'alastar make the dedication. I was in the square before even him, believe it or not.'

'Hurry, mother, we mustn't be late,' interrupted Lara,

pulling a pair of baggy working trousers on over her night-creased grey shirt.

'We won't be. I told you: I was with the first to hear. You'll be in good time.' Mabeta bent over a carved wooden chest that butted her daughter's bed. 'You'll wear your new jerkin?'

'Yes mother.' The girl pulled a dark brown fur jerkin over her shirt and fastened it with the thongs that hung in front. It was cold in the room despite the sun that reached in through the window in patchy brilliance.

'Shall I plait your hair for you?' asked Mabeta.

'Please.' The girl took a mother-of-pearl comb from the chest and ran it through her long fair hair. She held her hair in a long bunch that rose like a horse's tail from the centre of her head and then spilt on her shoulder and then, kneeling down, let her mother shape it into a heavy plait. While her mother made patterns in her hair, the girl was busy also: she took the cork stopper from a phial of rathga juice that she kept in the carved chest and, tipping the bottle quickly on to her forefinger and back, made a practised mark on the centre of her forehead, twisting her finger as she touched it against her temple so that the mark that was left was a neat purple circle.

'Have you seen Ormaas yet, this morning,' asked Lara.

'Not yet. He'll be getting ready himself. He'll be ready before you, I'm sure.'

'I'm sure,' said Lara, with a bored certainty in her voice. 'He'll have had all his nice new clothes ready and waiting by his bed for the sound of those bells, you can bet.'

'Someone in that family has to have sense,' said Mabeta.

'Oh, he's got plenty of sense,' continued Lara, agreeing with her mother yet using a tone that implied that sense was not enough. 'He's just so . . . ' The peal of bells without was joined by the high harsh hollowness of Mabeta's doorbell. 'That'll be Ormaas now.'

'Talk of Araketh and summon him here,' said Mabeta, using the familiar saying of Northreach. 'You finish off getting ready; I'll let him in.'

Ormaas stood outside in the cold shadow of his aunt Mabeta's house, wondering whether to ring again. Mabeta opened the door. 'Come in quick,' she said. 'Don't let the cold in. Come on through to the kitchen where it's warm.'

The two of them walked through the hallway, down a few rough steps, and beneath a low arch which led to the kitchen. A scruffy maid curtsied and left abruptly as they entered, vanishing behind a vast black iron pot that hung from a wooden brace. Ormaas smiled at her after she had gone. He took a chair from the corner, where several were piled up seat-to-seat with their legs in the air like despair, and politely placed it by the fire for his aunt to sit on. She, however, only waved for him to sit down before running away in the wake of the servant girl. He sat, feeling the heat of the fire through his breeches. Mabeta returned and demanded he stood again, to be inspected.

'Oh, jump in the Heront if I lie, you do look smart.' Ormaas was dressed in shades of green, apart from his white novice cloak. On his chest was a small gold brooch cunningly fashioned in the shape of a leaping hare. 'Is that your father's brooch?' asked Mabeta. 'I remember his father giving him that on initiation day.'

Lara called down. Ormaas heard her pleasant insistent voice reaching down from the staircase. 'I expect she'll be needing some help with her cloak,' said Mabeta.

Ormaas went to sit again, decided not to, and stood, slightly nervously, waiting for his cousin to enter. She did, and smiled at him hostilely. 'Hello, Ormaas,' she said.

'Hello, Lara.' He stumbled over what he had intended to say. 'Thought we might go down to the initiation, if that's all right.'

'I was intending to go down there, yes.' She sweetened her smile to condescension. He wilted. '*I* intend to get initiated today.'

'Don't embarrass your cousin,' said Mabeta. 'I'm sure it's very nice he wants to go down to the initiation with you.'

'He just daren't go on his own,' said Lara, unjustly. 'Besides, he isn't my cousin. He's adopted.'

'Lara!' exclaimed her mother.

'It doesn't matter,' said Ormaas hastily. Whether it didn't matter that he was adopted or that Lara had mentioned this was not explained.

'See,' said Lara, triumphantly to her mother. 'Come on

then,' she said to Ormaas. She turned back to Mabeta. 'You're coming?'

'Of course.'

'Where's your father, Ormaas?' asked Lara.

'I don't know. Perhaps he'll be in the square already.'

'More likely he'll be in the tavern off Hujyar Street. Do you remember last year's Rodenfestival? We had to carry him upstairs. And that servant, Bilda-what's-the-name, dropped his arm into the chamberpot. Good job it was empty, but uncle Murak didn't know that, and when he was asked why he wouldn't use it to eat with the following morning he was horribly sick.' Lara grinned with relish; her mother and cousin both blushed.

The shaman stood by the hoarstone and raised both his hands and his voice for silence. The crowd shuffled slowly to quiet; the last voice ended mid-sentence as it realised that it was alone. Pitching into the silence as an experienced speaker must, Va'alastar spoke to the people. He told them the familiar tales of the gods: he spoke of Hrakar, father of the gods, whose skull is the earth; of Araketh, the god of the winter, the binding god who holds men in eternal bondage; of Menketh, the lord of Mankind and god of liberty and the spring. He told them the legend of how Araketh had first tried to win control of his father's skull, which contained all knowledge, and of how Menketh had thwarted him by distracting his brother with the fiery juices of a small purple flower; he went on to describe the way that the flower, the rathga, now opened this day to symbolise the coming of spring and the victory of Menketh. He added a few words of caution: he told them that today's victory was but a temporary one; that Araketh was a potent and terrifying force; that there was no room for complacency in the hearts and minds of any of them. 'To this end, therefore, do we the people of Fenras then dedicate the bodies of these our children. Step forward the novices!'

A small group of youths in white cloaks stepped forward. There were eighteen of them in total, each of them under eighteen years of age. They formed a stiff, self-conscious ring around the shaman, pressing close against the base of the hoarstone.

'Step back, step back,' he instructed the crowd, and willing assistants helped clear an open space in front of the hoarstone and between the long tables. Satisfied that there was enough room for the wrestling, Va'alastar began the ritual questioning which begins the Initiation. 'Art thou ready to offer thyselves to the service of Menketh.'

'We are.' They spoke together, solemnly.

'First you must prove yourselves worthy. With pokers of glowing iron you will fight one another: you will endure any pain in the sure knowledge of Menketh's healing grace.'

They nodded as he looked at them. He stepped down from the dais and spoke to the blacksmith of Fenras, a large bald-headed man called Gyrtjud who wore a sinister outfit of black leather. The blacksmith smiled cheerfully, left the crowd, and walked to his nearby shop. Meanwhile, a young man, who had been initiated the previous year, stepped on to the dais into Va'alastar's place. He held a large leather bag, weighted with some heavy hidden contents, and offered it to the novices. Each in turn reached into the bag and drew out a large coloured pebble. There were a few words of consultation, and then the novices compared their stones. Lara examined hers against that of her neighbour: her stone was pink and shot with veins of cream; her neighbour's stone was yellow, and smooth and round as an egg. She turned again, the stone displayed in the upturned grip of her hand. Hands likewise framing stones were passed around; various hands and various stones. She saw soft blue colours, and black stones shot with white; grey stones that were dimpled and rough, and green stones as smooth and liquid as an eye. Then she saw a pink stone, the twin of her own. She looked up to see who owned it. It was Ormaas, and he refused to meet her eye.

The novices split up, to return to their families, friends and servants. Whilst tactics were discussed, and the implications of the draw, the novices took off their clothes in preparation for the fight.

'Looks like your Ormaas has drawn his pretty cousin,' said a tailor called Mysla to Murak.

Murak, Ormaas' father by adoption, took the skin of wine from the tailor. 'Lucky old him. Wouldn't mind getting to grips with her myself.' Murak lifted the skin to his mouth and squeezed a long jet of red wine into his throat.

They watched appreciatively through the crowd as Lara stripped naked and then stood still to be rubbed with oil by her mother. It was cold, and the girl pressed her arms over her breasts in a gesture that was part modesty and part the need to keep warm. Then the blacksmith returned, pushing his way through the crowd. He carried a heavy metal bucket, and staggered under its weight; in the bucket were ornate iron pokers. He placed them in their bucket in front of the hoarstone and then drew one out. It was red hot. He brandished it at the crowd, who withdrew; his big sweat-lined face was smiling as he cried, 'Get 'em while they're hot,' in parody of the chestnut vendors.

As the crowd moved back to form an arena in which the fighting could take place Va'alastar summoned the novices to him. Lara found herself between two other girls. Where their shoulders touched the oil was tacky between them. She looked down and saw goose-pimples in the curve of flesh between her breasts. 'Come on,' she found herself thinking. 'I'm freezing.'

She did not have long to wait. They were instructed to each take a poker from the bucket. The tips of the pokers had cooled to dusty grey in the cold air. Then each in turn was ordered to step forward. With one hand touching the hoarstone, the shaman touched the other to the first novice's forehead. The boy tensed at his touch, and orange bands of power licked the length of his poker. Another stepped forward, received the strength of the hoarstone, stepped away. Then it was Lara's turn. The nervous fear she experienced as the shaman's hand reached for her face disappeared at his touch: the hoarstone's ancient vibrations pulsed through her body, draining it of the old, familiar sensations of cold or tiredness or embarrassed nakedness and replacing them with fire that ran through her veins and along the handle of the poker until it cracked and crackled at the end.

Excited, tense, the novices lined up: two lines like a guard of honour before the hoarstone. Va'alastar stared between them, one hand still touching the hoarstone, and then nodded angrily for the fighting to begin. The novices looked up, got the measure of their opponents, and stepped forward.

Ormaas confronted his cousin. He had never seen her naked before. Whilst one part of his mind followed the lean contours of her body another assessed the grip she held on her poker and the way she was balanced, her weight on her front foot, ready to dart forward. Behind him Murak was laying his money on Lara, because he doubted that Ormaas would have the courage to hurt his cousin.

Lara shared this opinion. There was a tight smile in the corners of her mouth as she stepped forward. She felt again the surge of power course through her. 'Come and get me,' she murmured.

He did. The poker swung suddenly into her ribs, burning where it touched. Shock replaced confidence in her face. 'You hurt me!' she cried, indignantly.

'Va'alastar will repair the damage.'

Angry, she advanced a pace towards him, drawing back her poker to strike. She was artless, made over-confident by the power of the hoarstone within her, forgetting that Ormaas shared that same power. Her blow never landed. He struck the poker against her shoulder: she dropped her own, and before she had chance to move to pick it up he had struck her again, full on the side of her head above the ear. Lara's eyes lost expression and her legs lost strength. For a moment she still stood, as though too surprised to fall just yet, and then she tumbled to the floor.

Ormaas let the weight of his poker drag his arm down by his side. Around him the other fights were also ending: he had to step aside as his neighbour was driven down towards him, crashing to the ground at his feet, with a raw scarlet burn running from her neck to her navel and a broad darkening bruise on her wrist. And then all the fighting was done, and the crowd stepped forward to engulf them.

They revived Lara with a bucket of cold water, wrapped her in a blanket, and led her to the shaman. Ormaas offered to help support her: the look she gave him was more violent than their combat had been. Va'alastar washed her face and body with the diluted juice of the rathga petals, pressed his hands to her wounds, and restored her in all but pride.

Then the novices were led to the basilica, to perform their

nightlong vigil whilst the town celebrated. With them was the first of a succession of judges who would watch them to see that none dozed or spoke throughout the night. The doors closed behind them, shutting them in, and through the long cracks that outlined the doors they saw the day turn from steel to lead and evening fall. As the day darkened, activity in the square resumed.

A whole pig turned on a spit; a troupe of jugglers performed inadequately after too much wine; Hedch spoke to Murak.

'They say you're the fur-trader?' asked Hedch.

'One of them, one of them,' said Murak complacently, chewing meat off the bone and swilling it down with wine.

'But the biggest? You are the biggest?' insisted Hedch. He was bored by this fat drunkard, and his remarks were not without irony: it was difficult to imagine a bigger fur-trader as Murak reclined on his chair, stomach thrust between a beautiful fur jerkin.

'Oh, yes,' agreed Murak cheerfully. 'I'm the biggest.'

'I have a feeling you're a family man,' probed Hedch.

'No wife, never have had,' said Murak. Hedch smiled his relief: the man the Gyr Orland had told him to look for was a fur trader with an adopted son of some sixteen years; this drunken bachelor would hardly fit that description. 'Only me and my boy,' continued Murak, confoundingly.

'You and your boy?'

'Ormaas. Nice lad. You might have seen him laying into the pretty lass with the long hair during the Initiation.'

'I missed the Initiation,' said Hedch, slightly bitter. He had slept through it, despite the tumult of bells.

'Never mind. P'raps you'll meet him tomorrow.'

Hedch smiled and refilled Murak's goblet. 'If you've never married, who is this boy? A friend's son perhaps, or a servant?'

'He's no servant,' said Murak, with brief animation, and then he slumped again. 'He's adopted. Don't no one know where he's from. Found him on the doorstep; looked a nice lad; took him in. Not regretted it.'

Hedch fought mounting excitement: this must be the one. 'That's all you know?' he asked.

'That's all I know,' agreed the fur-trader.

Hedch began his rehearsed lines. After trailing around

Northreach all these long days, after the endless journey north from Cythroné, after the time wasted and the false starts, here was someone who matched his master's description. 'My master, the Gyr Orland, is looking for some furs. He wants a man he can trust to select and dispatch a sample to him. He promises twice the usual price so long as he can have the very best. Are you interested?'

Murak was, and much more sober. 'The Gyr Orland, you say? Him that will be next emperor?'

'That's right.'

'How do I know you're speaking the truth?'

Hedch produced a couple of letters, both sealed with Orland's signet. The latter missive interested Murak particularly, for it contained details of the prices the Gyr was offering. 'Forty-five talents for otter, 85 for badger, 140 for boar, 280 for bear.'

'Are you interested?' asked Hedch again.

'When do you want them?'

'As soon as possible. There's just one condition: you must send your boy down with them, as a mark of good faith, you understand.'

News of Murak's good fortune spread rapidly; Hedch slipped discreetly away. With any luck his search was over, although being a thorough man he would press on up to Brokmild the following day, to make sure there weren't two fur-traders with adopted sons in the region. He doubted there would be: this Ormaas, initiated today so obviously of the right age, fitted so very well. Hedch smiled as he climbed on to the hard bed and rustled himself comfortable amongst the straws: I've found the bastard, he thought. The Gyr hadn't mentioned the bastard, actually, but Hedch was no fool, he thought, as he dropped off to sleep. Outside, the celebrations continued.

Mabeta spoke to her brother as soon as she got the chance.

'I hear things are looking up,' she said, looking down.

'Yes,' he grinned from his chair. 'Never heard of so much money.' He looked carefully at his sister. 'You're not worried by anything are you?'

'It's too much money,' she said.

'Nonsense. There's no such thing as too much money.'

'How much is he offering? Over two hundred talents for a bear pelt. That's twice what you could get normally.'

'Forty-five apiece I got for the last lot in the Mornet market,' said Murak regretfully.

'Exactly. So how can anyone afford to pay this much?'

'Gyr Orland can,' said an unexpected voice. Brother and sister turned to face the speaker, and then turned away quickly, for the speaker was a crippled beggar. 'No, don't turn away. I know a bit about the Gyr Orland. Served under him one bit, which is why I've no legs left to speak of now.'

Murak risked a glance at the cripple. It was true he had no legs: they had been cut off above the knee and replaced by short wooden stumps. He pulled his body about on wooden crutches, and wore leather patches to protect the stumps. 'Say it then,' said Murak resignedly. 'I don't suppose we'll get any peace until you've done.'

There are cripples and beggars in every town in Khalindaine, sometimes itinerants, sometimes forming small communities within the community. In the Quarter of Cythroné, for instance, the Land of the Maimed has become a famous destination for those in search of the bizarre or the grotesque. Nowhere has more cripples than Northreach, however, because of the Northreach tradition that Menketh had once visited the mountains disguised as a cripple: the legend has now become law.

'Gyr Orland is the son of Ravenspur: I served under Ravenspur too, though the old man was past his best by then, I reckon. Ravenspur was just a nickname, you understand – he was really the Gyr Orland too. Don't think they've got a nickname for the present Gyr, though the troops used to call him all manner of names. He wasn't much of a soldier, you see,' said the cripple, looking at Mabeta.

'Is that all you've got to say?' asked Mabeta, but her brother was more charitable; also, he was intrigued by the man who was to make his fortune. 'Carry on.'

'Have you heard of the Débâcle of Othmasht? No? That was where I lost my legs. Eight years ago it was now, come this Endyear. He lost 3,000 troops that day, did your Gyr Orland, and gave up soldiering. But you should have seen the money he spent on that campaign. Three thousand talents on a suit of armour, 2,000 on a horse.' Mabeta was scandalised; Murak rubbing his hands together joyfully. 'They do say he once spent 8,000 talents on a banquet, and that in a single night's gaming lost two castles to the Gros of Nanx.'

'Ridiculous,' said Mabeta. The cripple's authoritative tones had attracted a small crowd, meanwhile, who were anxious to learn more about Murak's benefactor too.

'What battle did you say it was you . . . got hurt,' asked Mysla the tailor, not quite able to say 'lost your legs'.

'The Débâcle of Othmasht. That's where it happened. Remember it clear as tonight: clearer than some of you will remember tonight, from the looks of you. We was hunting out Agaskan in the foothills of the Thatter, way south of Khalindaine across the Rift; they'd been raiding some of the villages in the foothills, and had pressed almost to the east bank of the Khalin once or twice. The Gyr Orland had never led an army before, but being the son of old Ravenspur everyone had high hopes for him, and he had no trouble gathering an army.

'We set out from Hyjurak, which is a sort of garrison town west of the Thatter, and just marched east towards Agaskan territory. It was a foul journey: we set out just after the Endyear, and tried making our way into the mountains for about a turn of the moon without any success. We knew there was Agaskan all around us, because we kept finding men that they'd killed, but we didn't often see them. Sometimes a shadow on the hillside would get up and run; sometimes you could make out a distant figure on a distant crest; most times there was nothing, save cries in the night as they killed another bloke. We marched round in a great circle in that month, and were nearly back in Hyjurak with nothing gained and two hundred men dead, when the Gyr decided enough was enough and that we should go out and find them. He divided the army into three and sent us off again, straight into the mountains.

'I was in the second column, under the Vaine of Ythret. There aren't any scouts for that sort of countryside – you just carry on till you find something, without knowing what you're looking for. We carried on, and found an Agaskan road. We could tell what it was at once, because there were wheel marks all along it, and skulls, human skulls, grinning at us from posts all the distance of it. It was like a ridgeway, this road, climbing up from the foothills into the mountains proper, and as we'd been ordered to press on into the mountains we followed it.

'Mountains, I call them, but they're not like Northreach mountains. They don't go to points like our mountains, and there's no snow ever settles on them either as I know of. They're just lumps, all piled up and ugly and brown, like a muddy path that dries all scuffed up and bumpy. And they're hot: you've never known heat like it. I've crossed the Rift a couple of times but even there the wind still blows, whereas in the Thatter there's nothing except hot orange stones.

'We climbed and climbed. Soon we could see Hyjurak behind us, like a smudge on the landscape, and the foothills rolling away. And there were rivers, rivers that burst out from underground places and ran between the foothills like silver thread stitching together the ochre. There was the Khalin, too, far away on the horizon; black it looked, and curling like a serpent as it does when it nears the sea, and slow and old and tired. That was behind us; in front of us there was just mountains.

'The road started to drop. We left the ridge and the view. Suddenly we were alone in the world. Just us, and stones. And Agaskan. We couldn't see them but we knew they were there: you could feel them watching, and smell them moving, as if they were right on the edge of your senses and yet never quite ... tangible.' The cripple paused, wondering if this was the right word. Before he had the opportunity to decide, he was egged on to continue.

'Where were we? Going down? That's it: going down into this defile, this gap in the rocks. You couldn't call it a valley; a valley is somewhere homely, with trees and birds and running water. This wasn't like that: this was like Roagazg.' He used the archaic word for the kingdom of the Dead; a Cythron would simply have said 'hell'. The cripple continued. 'A shadow passed over the valley and we looked up. The sky was thick with arrows, slanting like rain from the lips of the pass. We dashed for cover, and found there wasn't any cover. Men were trampled in the panic, and the horses and the wagons went wild. I was pressed against the side of the defile, with my back against the rock, when a wagon went past. The driver had an arrow in his back, and next to him a young man in armour was hanging on for dear life. Then an arrow hit the horse in the neck. The horse fell. The wagon careered into the horse. The men were launched into the air as the wagon reared against the dying horse, and I saw the man in armour hurled into the path of a flight of arrows. And that was all I saw. A wheel burst off the wagon as it landed again, and when it bounced it bounced on me. Both my legs were crushed as thin as a leaf, and as the wheel rolled on its journey I watched as my legs bent as though I'd new knees and then I hit the floor.

'When I came to, I knew I was dead. There were flies everywhere, crawling in my mouth and ears and nose, and in the mouth and ears and nose of the man I was pressed against. I tried moving. I seemed to be pinned down, except for my legs, so I kicked with my legs, and I swear I felt them moving, but then I remembered, and I wriggled myself around beneath a pile of corpses until I could see myself, and there were no legs. I think I cried, but the tears would have been dry in that heat.

'I was in a heap of bodies. The Agaskan must have killed everybody who stood whilst I was lying down, and then heaped body on top of body. I suppose they saw my legs and figured no one could have survived that, and hadn't checked if I was alive.

'I didn't dare move, once I'd thought about it. I just stayed there, beneath a slowly stiffening weight, and let the flies crawl over my flesh. I could hear sounds of the green-skins going through our stuff, emptying purses and stripping off armour, and I was dreading they might search me. But maybe someone had already taken anything of mine worth taking – and there wasn't much anyway – because my shield was gone and my money-bag.

'Don't even try to imagine what I felt like,' cautioned the cripple. 'Sometimes in that long time I even felt like letting the Agaskan know I was there, calling out to them to end the agony. I felt like appealing to them, saying, "Help, you've got it wrong, I'm not dead." I felt like it, but I didn't do it, because I knew I would be dead if I did, and bad as my situation was I knew it was worse for the dead. I could see flies laying eggs in their eyes.

'At last it was quiet, and I opened my eyes up to find that it had gone dark. I waited even then for an age, and nothing stirred still. So slowly, quietly, I pulled myself out of the heap of bodies, edging forwards by pulling with my arms and dragging my useless legs behind me. And suddenly I was free. That first breath of foul Thatter air was superb to me then, like the honey of the Grove of the Red Rock; I pulled myself out and took stock.

'Fortunately for me the green-skins had left most of our food – they don't like it, I suppose; it's not the first time I've heard of that happening – so I was all right on that score. The biggest problem was that I was four days' march from home, and I'd no legs to march on. Four days' march is a long time crawling, I can tell you.

'I did it, as you can see. I crawled out of that stinking valley that night, eating all the food I'd been carrying in celebration as I reached the top. Day came and I stayed still, not wanting to be seen. I'd blundered into a shield in the night, that was just lying there in the Agaskan road, dropped by one of our men on his way in. I picked it up and sheltered under it. I've still got that shield now.

'I was five days on that causeway. Always I could see Hyjurak in front of me, and always the mountains behind me, and I lived in constant fear that an Agaska would travel along that road and see me. On the fifth day I had a bit of luck though: I was at the edge of the road trying to keep in the cover, when the edge of the thing gave way, and I dropped on to this scree slope. I tumbled down and down, cursing because some day I'd have to get back up, and went and got myself knocked out again. And this time when I came to I found myself in a bed, in the fort at Prahkit, with what was left of my legs sawn off and these pads in their place: some shepherd had found me, see, and taken me back there. They were decent folk in Prahkit. They gave me a bit of money, and had a chap make me some crutches, and then they paid for me to get back to Cythroné. Which I did. And from there I came back to Northreach, where I was born if you didn't guess. For a year or two I stayed clear of this place, Fenras, as my parents were still here and alive – they were poor and a cripple like me's no good around the place – but this year I've come home for good, back where I was born.'

Murak clapped, Mabeta smiled sadly. 'What's your name?' she asked. She didn't want to know: she wanted to show sympathy and she enjoyed feeling condescending.

'Khayrik,' replied the cripple. 'Khayrik of Fenras.'

'Thank you for telling us your story.'

'Thank you for listening,' said Khayrik, avoiding irony, settling for flattery. He watched as the brother and sister turned away, and then called out diffidently: 'Perhaps a talent for my tale?'

The fur-trader turned. A coin spun in the light from the open fires of the square, and landed noisily on the stones. The cripple picked it up. 'One lousy rubek,' he said, slipping it into the purse that hung around his neck. 'Huh.'

At dusk they had been novices; now they were initiates and, as they stepped out into the early morning, they were tired but pleased. They handed their white novice cloaks to Va'alastar, who would save them for next year, and received the congratulations of their families.

Murak's pleasure in his son's achievement gratified Ormaas. He wasn't used to such praise. It was only when he realised his father's elation was more due to some business deal than Ormaas's Initiation that he listened carefully to the words, rather than the tone, of his father's pleasure. '. . . Best bit of news I've had . . . Of course, it took careful negotiating . . . Something for me to leave you too.' Murak paused.

'I don't understand,' said Ormaas, filling the pause.

'No, you wouldn't. You were in the basilica. Good fight you had: pity it had to be your cousin. Still – nice looking girl she's grown into.' Murak gestured a pair of breasts in the air, expressively if inaccurately. 'We've been given an order, from the Gyr Orland no less, to take him some furs. You're to take them. To Cythroné. You'll go, won't you.'

'The Gyr Orland. What's he?'

'Only heir to the throne. And the prices!' Again Murak gestured in the air, using much the same movement only to indicate riches this time.

'I'm going?'

'I'd go myself if I wasn't so old. It's a fair old way to Cythroné, even these days. Anyway, you probably wouldn't want me along. I'd only get in the way. Especially if that pretty cousin of yours goes, eh?'

'Father,' said Ormaas, tiredly.

'What?' asked Murak. He recognised some sort of threat in Ormaas's tone, and misinterpreted it. 'You're not going, is that it?'

'I was just thinking . . . ' Of Lara, but he didn't say that.

'I suppose you're going to turn against me, is that it? I've seen plenty of young men do that when they've got Initiated. And I took you in off the streets too, found you abandoned in no more than a cheap linen wrap.'

'I'll go,' said Ormaas quietly. 'Now can I go to bed?'

'I knew you would,' said Murak. 'Now all we've got to do is persuade your cousin to go too, but I'm sure a good-looking young chap like you, specially with the prospects you've got now . . . ' Ormaas endured this until they got home. Then, pleading righteous exhaustion, he went to bed.

Lara took no persuading, although her mother did. They argued back and forth. In the end Lara turned her back on her mother and sulked, letting a delicate tear contrive to roll down her cheek.

Mabeta had seen it all before. 'Oi. Less of the histrionics. You're not in Cythroné yet.'

Lara's mind pounced on that word 'yet'. 'True,' she agreed. 'I'd better be getting some things ready.'

'What sort of things?'

'Clothes, provisions, things like that. I'm going to need all sorts of things in Cythroné. You wouldn't want me dressed like a servant there now, would you. There'll be all sorts of people in Cythroné. Perhaps the Gyr Orland will fall in love with me. I'd marry anyone to be empress.'

'I haven't said you can go yet,' said Mabeta.

But Lara knew her mother, and simply smiled.

The cripple swung his body between his crutches. He had no difficulty, despite everything, in keeping up with Murak, whose belly overhung his belt and whose hung-over head still throbbed. 'Stop following me,' said the fur-trader. 'I'll have you run out of town.'

'Make me run anywhere and I'll be grateful,' said the cripple, not pausing in his pursuit.

'Leave me alone.' Murak deliberately hurried, confused his

own breathing in doing so, and had to stop by a drinking fountain to get his breath back. Khayrik stopped too, resting contentedly on his crutches.

'Let me go with your son,' said the cripple. 'I'll be his guide.'

Murak laughed, which brought on a fit of coughing. When he had finished he took a drink from the fountain.

'What's wrong with that?' demanded the cripple.

'You'll slow him down.'

'Did I slow you down?'

'You made me stop.'

'You stopped because you're fat.'

'Nonsense. Just a bit of breathlessness.'

'Is your son prone to breathlessness?'

'Of course not.'

'There you are then. I'd not slow him down.'

'You wouldn't earn your wages.'

'I haven't asked for wages.'

'What do you want then?'

'To travel with a purpose.'

'You're daft.'

'Perhaps. You'll let me go then?'

'You'll do it for nothing? I'll have to ask Ormaas.'

'Of course.'

'He'll probably say yes.'

'You'll not regret this.'

'You really are daft: I'm regretting it already.'

Ormaas thought about the idea, and it seemed a good one. Neither he nor his cousin had ever left the Heront valley before, and crossing the Gilla Pass as they must do on their journey to Cythroné was itself a worrying thought: he could not even contemplate the journey beyond. The cripple had a pleasingly blunt common sense, had been everywhere, and knew everyone. He could do no harm; Ormaas thought he might do some good.

Hedch made inquiries. No one else in Fenras had adopted anyone, that was known of. He paid for another night in the tavern, and went back to sleep. Tomorrow he would leave for Brokmild.

Tomorrow they would leave for Toothaas. It would mean a night in the Gilla Pass, but that should be safe enough: although there still were a number of Agaskan in the Gilla it was unlikely that they would attack; the Gilla Agaskan were degenerates, sad reminders of the proud Agaskan kingdom which had once flourished in those mountains before the days of Akhran and the First Khalinrun.

They had decided to leave so soon because of the difficulty they might have getting a boat in Mornet. The journey to Cythroné was a long one, but not a complicated one: they would travel overland to Mornet, the major town of Northreach; from there they would take a boat to Akbar, on the far side of the Rift, and finally another boat would take them from Akbar to Cythroné. The journey would be done in two moons' turning. As none of them but Khayrik had ever been further than Mornet – Mabeta had once gone there for a religious painting she had commissioned, and Murak went there at the end of each winter season's hunting to take his pelts – Khayrik was the one who planned the journey. And he insisted they leave early before all the Khalin barges were taken. 'We don't want to go overland across the Rift if we can help it,' he said. 'I've done that trick before.'

Preparations were hurried, therefore, but thorough. Again Khayrik's experience proved valuable. 'Not your best horses,' he warned Murak. 'We'll have to sell them when we get to Mornet anyhow.' And so mules were settled on. In a similar way Khayrik designed himself a saddle, and had one of Murak's leather cutters make up a series of straps which would hold his deformed body in place, and also decided what they would need in the way of food and other provisions. 'Fire-spell,' he said, 'and salt-beef, and biscuits, but nothing more. We'll only be a night in the open before we get to Toothaas, and we don't want to be too laden.'

Whilst Khayrik was supervising these preparations, Ormaas and Lara were making their own. Ormaas, as befitted the son of a leading fur-trader with a fine house and its own court, already possessed most of the things he would need; nonetheless, he delighted in travelling around the craftsmen's shops with her, spending Murak's money. They found a small silver shield for her, in a disreputable stall in the Street of Merchants that was

run by a dirty overdressed Myrian with an ingratiating stoop
and a nimble tongue. The man told him a story about the
shield, which they did not accept, and then suggested a price,
which they did. He said the shield was bought by a sailor in
Ghanay – its workmanship was certainly exotic – but almost
lost in a shipwreck off the coast of Myr; the sailor and the shield
were lost at sea, but washed up on the Myrian shore where they
were found by a monk of the Order of the Bronze Way; the
monk was robbed and killed by a Kapatar who worked in a
travelling fair; the Kapatar gave it to his brother, who was
senior partner in a knife-throwing act. The knife-throwers used
it professionally for many years until an accident forced their
premature retirement; it was sold to a whore in Akbar, who
used it as a decoration in a house of ill-repute in that town of
ill-repute; she gave it to a swarthy merchant whose caravans
traversed Khalinrift, because he liked it and she liked him. He
lost the shield, and an eye, in a fight with Khalinrift bandits;
one of the bandits, bearing the shield, fled to Fenras for safety,
and was run over by a cart in the Street of Merchants.

Khayrik brought out his own shield from the small bundle of
possessions that was his home. It was a large round hide shield,
old-fashioned but purposeful, with only a few patches of paint
suggesting that once it had been of dark green and bore the
rearing stallion of Khalindaine across its field. It had served as
bed, shelter, begging bowl and boat in its time, and was the
only think Khayrik owned that he cared about. That the
colours were not even those of his regiment was irrelevant:
Khayrik, and this shield, were the only survivors of the
Débâcle of Othmasht; they owed a lot to one another, and yet
owed nothing.

That night Murak held a party to mark the departure of his
couriers. The couriers themselves didn't attend; as Khayrik
said, 'They're too tired and I've got more sense.' Murak let him
go, and drank the night away with his friends. Khayrik
returned to the dirty streets where the beggars found room to
sleep, and there was treated to a dance by his friends. A fat
dwarf danced with him as a Kapatar played reels: her skirts
swirled as he swung his legless body, and the dance lasted till
dawn.

Chapter 3

The Gilla Pass

Fenras is cupped like a jewel in the palm of the Heront valley. Two rivers meet there, and two landscapes. In the valley floor it is verdant and domestic: drystone walls pace out the fields, squat self-important barns stock feed for the winter, small bustling homesteads twist columns of smoke towards the sky. Yet beyond, where the mountains rear up like breaking waves and the only vegetation is desperate bushes clinging to the rocks or dark green pines standing sentinel, the scenery is very different. Here no one lives, save the occasional Agaskan renegade and the rarer mountain hare, and the flat safe world of the valley is smashed into crowded fragments that push up against one another in planes of snow and ice.

Hedch said his thanks to the tired guard in the mean fingerless gloves, and then heard the postern close behind him. Fenras had been a pleasant town, but Hedch was glad to be on his way again. He followed the river northwards between the rough flanks of the mountains. Rabbits scuttled off the track in front of him, their idiotic white tails flashing in the half-light before dawn; birds sang in ever-increasing numbers in the shadow-bound trees, anticipating the coming of the sun. It was cold, and Hedch felt the chill settle into his flesh, working its way towards his bones like a parasite. Still, he thought, it isn't far up the valley to Brokmild, and there's meant to be a good tavern halfway.

Whilst Hedch travelled north, along the valley, preparations continued for Ormaas's journey west, out of the valley and the familiar world he had known all his life. Hedch was the first person to stir in Fenras that morning; Khayrik and Ormaas vied for second place.

For Khayrik the primary concern was to continue to be important before Murak and Ormaas could change their minds about letting him travel with them. As soon as the first sun struck the western mountains he was up, rubbing hands together in the cool morning, and then lurching his way through the streets to the house of Murak. In the silent streets the rhythmic tapping of his crutches, and the low scraping of his padded stumps, echoed in a sad tattoo.

Arriving at the fur-trader's door, distinguished by the wide antlers displayed above, Khayrik was uncertain how to proceed. A servant who had opened the door to throw out the night-soil solved that: Khayrik simply walked straight in. He found himself in an open court. A group of mules were being laden with whicker panniers. Khayrik noted with approval that the lead mule bore a specially adapted saddle instead of the panniers.

Servants went about their business. Two were carrying rich and delighting furs out to the mules, where Murak supervised the packing and folding. Two more watered and fed the animals. One was sent to Va'alastar's house to buy a bottle of fire-spell.

The shaman was already at work. The servant stood in the street in front of the windowless ground floor and looked for a bell or a knocker. He found neither, so tapped on the door itself. It opened at once, mysteriously, but then the servant saw that Va'alastar was standing just by it and the mystery was explained. Fumbling, the servant handed over a coin wrapped in a note; Va'alastar read the note, took the coin, and disappeared into the recesses of his house.

The servant looked around. In the windowless gloom only low-burnt and grotesque candles, melted into fantastic figures, cast light, and what light they threw was muffled by a faint sulphurous fog that enveloped all. He stared to penetrate the fog, and saw that the walls were lined with books and shelves, and that the shelves contained the arcane instruments of the shaman's trade. Va'alastar's charts of the stars and the moon were piled up on a decorated desk with turned oak legs; on top of these, like a paperweight, was an old human skull, its cranium marked out like a map.

This was Va'alastar's representation of the skull of Hrakar. Khalindaine's vast peninsula thrust out into the centre of the cranium, extending down to the frontal bone; surrounding Khalindaine from every side but the north, where the peninsula was rooted, was a great sea that extended to the curved crack of the skull's squamous suture, just above where the ears would be; below the suture were other lands, marked with exotic names such as Wembey, Ehapot, Ghanay and Fildo. The servant wished he could read.

The shaman returned with a green phial in his hand, containing the fire-spell. Such spells were the staple of the shaman's trade in these irreligious times: like any other shaman of the day he simply could not exist on the old magic of hoarstone and Hrakar alone, but needed to supplement his income by selling cheap tricks like the fire-spell, an inflammable liquid that would take fire in any conditions. Perhaps it was the knowledge that he was compromising the traditions of his trade by selling such inferior spells that made Va'alastar look so fierce when he re-entered the room; whatever, the servant put down the skull rapidly and then made an equally quick retreat to the door, pausing only to take the proffered phial before letting himself out and dashing up the street and back towards Murak's.

As soon as was possible, and later than everyone except Mabeta would have liked, the mule-train was ready. Mabeta stood on a wooden-framed balcony that overhung the courtyard and wept at the loss of her daughter and nephew, whilst Murak stood by her encouraging everyone on. As the door to the court was opened to let the mules through, Mabeta rushed down the spiral staircase to kiss them a long, delaying, goodbye, and then followed them into the street.

Their route took them past the shaman's house. Va'alastar stood outside, with a puzzled look on his face, and watched the string of mules pass. Then he returned to the dark interior, and to his plotting and star-worrying. The hoarstone had been anxious recently, there was no doubt, and the shaman sought through his books for the cause.

Across the continent, where the Khalin runs into the sea, the Gros of Weir was lying in bed with his concubine. Rich tapestries of crimson and gold covered the bed and surrounded it, sealing it in between four carved posts against the world outside. Not that there was any special reason to shut out what was outside: a log fire burnt in a marble fire-place; wood-pannelled walls were enriched by the fire's orange glow; the moulded ceiling hung with luxuriating designs.

Two servants entered, wearing the pale blue livery of their master and carrying a tray of hot food between them. They set the tray down on a marble-topped table and drew their master's curtains for him. The Gros sat up in bed carefully; one of the servants rearranged the pillows behind his master's back to support him. Bowl after silver bowl of food was passed to the Gros, who tasted of each before passing them on, sometimes barely touched and sometimes all gone, to the girl in the bed beside him.

The companions followed the rapid trickle and spill of a stream that led down from the mountains, climbing with it towards its source. They kept going upwards, leaving the Heront valley behind them now, reducing its homely scale to the scale of toys as it dropped away behind them.

Half a day's travel took them to a vast bare corrie knocked out of the massif by some unknown geological action in the past. From the lip of the corrie they could just make out the wooden gates of Fenras set in the lighter stone walls. Khayrik called a halt.

'We'll eat here,' he said. 'Once past that fat boulder with the little boulder on top of it – the Good Friend they call it coming down, but no friend to anyone going our way – there'll be no sight of Fenras till we get back here. So you'd best take the view in now; give you something to remember when we're in distant parts.'

They ate quietly, overlooking the valley. Lara and Ormaas felt subdued; Khayrik was elated. At length Lara turned to their crippled guide. 'Have you been this way often?'

'Bless me, yes,' said Khayrik. It hadn't taken Lara and Ormaas long to learn that the cripple enjoyed talking: they waited patiently for him to continue, knowing that he would. 'I've a few tales of this place,' he said. 'Why, the first time I crossed the Gilla pass, which is the way we're going today, I was nought but a nipper.'

He wiped his mouth with the back of his hand and took a drink of water from his skin. Each of them carried a skin of water, a length of rope, and a short stabbing sword. 'Be prepared,' Khayrik had said. Now though he was carrying on with his story. 'I was only small, four winters to my name, no more, and me mam and me dad – he was a soldier too – were having this real battle. Biffing and a-banging they were, so one day he picks me up and carries me all the way to Toothaas up the pass. Took us two days and two nights but we didn't hardly seem to stop. Had a temper did my dad. In the end we gets into Toothaas, and me dad tries it on with this woman he knew lived there. She sees me though and she's not having any of it. "I can't just leave the lad," said me dad, so she says, "Take him back where he came from then," and me dad answers, "Right then I will," and before I'd had time to spit in the Leva there we were going back again.'

Despite the bright cold sunlight the way ahead of them was dark: they saw a deep cleft in the mountains that provided the stately route for an inadequate little stream, and alongside the stream an even narrower path of frozen mud. The sun rarely penetrated that cleft. They finished their meal, remounted, and pressed on. 'Don't look back,' said Khayrik as they passed the rock he'd called Good Friend. 'Let's just be making our way on.'

For a time the track followed the stream. The first corrie led to a second, smaller one, from which their stream rolled gently. There was no sign of how the pass would continue, and only a wall of rock ahead of them, with a towering peak just visible beyond. They could tell that the peak must be a long way off because it was purple and faint against the sharp edge of the rock wall ahead.

Faced with this Ormaas thought they must have gone wrong, but Khayrik did not even hesitate. Although the only marker for the trail was one of Hedch's hoofprints in the occasional patches of snow that still survived there, sullen against the thaw, he led them confidently.

At a large black rock they stopped, and Khayrik insisted that they check each of their mules for any sign of lameness. 'The path ahead's so narrow you can't get a mule to turn round at all, some places, and you certainly can't get them to go backwards. So once we start climbing proper we've to carry on to the other side.'

As soon as the climb had begun Lara and Ormaas saw what the cripple had meant. For beyond the black rock, as though deliberately hidden there, they could see the beginnings of a track which curved up and around the peak in front of them.

'Do we have to go all the way up there?' asked Ormaas.

Khayrik laughed. 'All the way up there – and then some further. Come on, don't say you've lost your taste for the journey already. You wait till we get to the top: what a view.'

And so they climbed. 'This way for the high life,' called Khayrik as they set off. The ledge was barely two strides wide. It took them out of the gully in a wide, vertiginous sweep, then widened into a corrie before doubling back on itself to make an assault on the summit. They travelled first south and then north, barely moving westward at all as they rose over the gully, and then their route took them around the summit of their first mountain, just as the last sun caught the west-facing slopes and angles behind them. From where they were they could make out the deep shadow of the Heront valley – it amused Ormaas to think that in the valley it would already be dark – looking surprisingly sinister and unfriendly behind them. 'Where are we?' asked Ormaas, trying to work out which of the mountainscape he had grown up with was involved in their route, but although Khayrik tried to point out landmarks that were visible both from the town they had left and their new position, such as the gap in the mountains where the Heront river flowed into the valley of that name, the disorientation was too severe. Ormaas admitted as much; Khayrik laughed loudly.

Whilst Ormaas and Khayrik were looking back, Lara had ridden ahead. Now, eyes squinted against the low sun, she looked across the vast sweeps and falls of landscape in front of them. The mountains seemed to stretch on forever: high cold peaks capped with snow that was the colour of amber in the evening sunlight, whilst between the peaks there was nothing but a silent drop into distant darkness. Lara looked carefully into the drop that edged the path, and counted slowly in her head to keep herself calm. She thought of the cripple, and his father, and smiled, and for the first time realised what a good thing it was that they had Khayrik with them. 'I can imagine what Ormaas and I would be like on our own,' she thought.

'Always fighting, never getting anything done. He'd get all lovey-dovey; I'd keep being nasty to him. No, I don't fancy that at all.'

She waited for the others to join her. As Khayrik had said, the mules would not turn around on that narrow path, nor would they go backwards. So she waited alone as they watched the view.

Suddenly, on the track ahead of her, was a curious deformed figure with long arms and legs. It scuttled along the path for a stride or two and then, to Lara's horror, went straight over the edge. She saw no body fall, and heard no screams, yet the impact of the creature's sudden disappearance stained her mind like a bright light.

Ormaas and Khayrik were not long in catching her up. They talked of the splendours of the scene, of the contrast between the view from the valley, where the mountains had been oppressive and formless, and from here, where the sun-struck peaks were as pure and as perfect as freedom. They asked Lara her opinion; she neither replied, nor moved on, and they had to wait behind her, unable to pass her on that narrow track, until she spoke.

'It threw itself off the cliff,' she said at last.

'What did?' asked Ormaas, but Khayrik had anticipated the answer. 'Was it a shambling ugly thing, like a man yet not like a man, and with a greeny-white skin?'

'I couldn't see the colour of its skin.'

'But the rest? Did it answer to the rest?'

'Yes.'

There was a pause. 'Agaskan,' said Khayrik, and the word was as harsh as the mountains now seemed. A complete silence fell between the companions and no one moved. Only the rough clinking of the harnesses interrupted their thoughts. At last Khayrik, almost impatiently, encouraged his mules forward with the reins, forcing motion in the cousins ahead of him on that path. 'Come on,' he said. 'We'd best be moving. It'd only be a degenerate or a renegade, nothing important. They don't attack unless you're on your own, and even then they're pretty cowardly. The greenskins here aren't like the warriors of the Thatter or thereabouts. They're just the weak leftovers. We'll be all right, you'll see.'

'Why did it do it, though?' asked Lara.

'Do what?'

'Throw itself off the edge.'

Khayrik smiled. 'It'll be all right,' he said, with a harshness in his voice. 'Have no fear on that score. Made for the mountains, those things. Can't hardly walk on the flat, some of them, so I've heard tell. No, it'll have jumped down safe enough, you mark my words. But we'd best be getting on: if it jumped down there then there's probably a cave; we don't want to find ourselves perched above even the most degenerate Agaska's cave come nightfall if we can help it.'

Thus, they continued on their way, traversing the high dusk. The cousins were silent, and hiding their fear by little, unconvincing, shows of nonchalance; Khayrik did their talking for them. He explained to them that they would not have to cross all the mountains they saw stretching before them to the horizon; in fact, as he told them, Toothaas lay between the two large mountains on their left. Lara was relieved: when she had seen the endless ranks of the mountains stretching away ahead of them she had been discouraged, and something to cheer her up was necessary. Yet, despite her relief, she could not shake off the feeling that they were being watched.

It was late afternoon in Cythroné and the Weir-Lord, gorgeously attired in dark blue and silver, recalled a poem he had been taught as a child. The poem described the scene before the Gros of Weir, and rather to the surprise of his equally well-dressed companions, the Weir-Lord recited it.

> Cythroné: the docks in spring.
>   Decks and wharves rich with treasures
> Of long journeys made to bring
>   Merchants' prizes, Northreach furs,
> Ilynes glass, Cayrab muslin,
>   Ghanay spices, Gold Shore sugars.
>
> The hopes of usury and pride
>   Voyage in wind-blown boats around
> A shrinking world; investments tied
>   Not to homely Lorin ground
> But to restless seas provide
>   The fortunes of this Lorin town.

Silk and satins, furled, disturbed
   By the life in lithe blown air
Are roughed and wave, then reassured
   By the bales, then flap and flair
With the next gust. They are birds
   Of bright colour, and more rare.

In the same way, furs are soothed
   Into action by the wind
On the bales; each skin moved
   Appears alive, no longer skin
But bear or boar. And thus the truth,
   Like Cythron wealth, waits on the wind.

He stood on the banks of the River Carpaccio, near to where it flows into the Khalin, and watched one of his ships being loaded. The ship was called the *Doret-vaine-Salgo*; its destination was the Gold Shore. It was a three-master, sixty strides long, bearing the yellow and black pennons of Khalindaine at its mast-tops, and with the complex arms of the Gold Shore Company displayed at its stern. He added to his previous recitation the motto of the Gold Shore Company: 'Brave traders braving exile bring the food of gold and goods which serve as Cythron blood.'

'You are cheerful, Weir-Lord,' remarked one of his companions, a subtle, red-faced merchant called Iuseth.

'I like the ships,' replied the Weir-Lord, simply.

His companion smiled. He had half the Gros of Weir's wealth, and was twice his age: he knew nothing about the Gros of Weir was ever simple. 'You like the money they earn you,' pursued Iuseth.

The Gros returned the smile. 'Perhaps,' he said.

The darkness thickened, making the always dangerous track doubly so, but still Khayrik showed no signs of stopping. Lara and Ormaas, dismounted now and leading their mules, went first, but Khayrik was undoubtedly in charge now. From time to time, as they passed places where it might be possible to camp, they cast questioning looks back at the cripple on the first of the string of mules: each time he shook his head.

Their path followed the side of the peak they had climbed for several thousand strides, and then, quite suddenly, there was a bridge in front of them connecting their mountain to the next. They looked down into the darkness below, but were unable to see the bases of the great stone pillars that supported the bridge.

'Who built this?' asked Lara.

'I don't know. They say it was built before the time of Akhran.'

'Is it safe?' This time the question was from Ormaas.

'I reckon so.'

Ormaas encouraged his mount forwards, but the mule had other ideas. 'That mule's got more sense than you,' said Khayrik. 'We'll spend the night on this side and cross in the morning, when we can see what we're doing.'

They looked about them. It didn't seem to be a very good place to stop: exposed, barren, and cold. But they accepted the cripple's explanation that there was no danger of avalanches here, unlike the earlier places, and arranged the mules in a tethered ring. They removed the panniers from the animals' backs, and arranged them in a rough shelter; Ormaas lifted the cripple from his mount, whilst Lara collected together some stones. The stones made a sort of cairn, over which she threw some fire-spell: at once a brilliant white light flared up, reflecting off the ochre stones she had gathered but doing nothing to penetrate the surrounding darkness. Then the light settled to a comfortable orange which lit through the stones and made them glow like coals. For a while the companions sat around the fire, eating a filling meal of salted beef boiled in rich spices, and then Khayrik instructed Ormaas and Lara to get some sleep, which they did gratefully, wrapping themselves against the cold spring night in thick furs borrowed from Murak's consignment.

Khayrik did not sleep. Long years of living in the vulnerable open had taught him to rest himself without sleep, and his clear honest conscience rarely needed the solace of dreams. Instead, he arranged himself on a low outcrop of rock, with his mutilated legs comfortably stretched in front of him, and drew his fur about his shoulders. He fancied a pipe, but decided against it. Instead he eased his aching arms, and waited for what the night might bring. The fire-spell cast its glow upon the plateau; beyond was a night as dark as super-stition.

In the Lady Treslan's chamber, the Gros of Weir was growing bored. The Lady Treslan reclined naked upon a couch of crimson velvet in front of a good fire while Vlatri tan Bul painted her portrait. The conversation with the few guests she had invited to keep her company whilst she posed for the painting was witty and daring, but the Weir-Lord was tiring now of the chatter. He walked to behind the painter and watched the skilful hands translate the Lady Treslan's volup-tuous form into patterns and planes of paint, and then strolled to behind the sitter.

'Don't stand in front of the fire, darling.'

He moved on, sighing ostentatiously, and drew back a velvet curtain to look at the clear night. The lights of Cythroné were like a constellation from the Lady Treslan's tower. He let the curtain slip from his fingers and returned to the predictable conversation.

Long, grimy fingers, with soft tough pads, clawed their way for a grip on the plateau's edge. Strong, sinuous arms lifted a pair of narrow eyes above the level of the plateau. Silently, the creature watched the sleeping group around the fire, then it lowered itself back into the crevice, swinging itself carefully down the wooden substructure built between the side of the mountain and the first pier of the bridge. When it had descended some thirty strides it stopped, reached out a long muscular leg, and finding a narrow ledge loped towards its home.

Khayrik shuffled rapidly along the ground around the fire-spell, crossing the circle of light, and awoke the cousins with a delicate touch he knew would not make them call out. 'Shh,' he whispered. 'We've got company.'

He told them urgently not to get up yet, but to lie where they were, prepared to move instantly. For little escaped the cripple's attention, and he had been suspicious of that wooden substructure from the moment he had first seen it. Two narrow eyes throwing back the light from the fire-spell had confirmed his suspicions.

The cripple's apparent lack of fear gave confidence to the other two. Lara reached out her arm and grasped her bow, slotting an arrow into the bowstring with a movement that was almost automatic, although she had never used the bow against anything bigger than deer before; Ormaas felt his knuckles whiten as they tensed against his sword.

They did not have long to wait. Again the grasping hands appeared on the plateau, and again the narrow eyes blinked in the light of the fire-spell. But now the rest of the body followed. The long muscular leg, culminating in a large foot with bulbous toes, reached for the surface of the plateau, found purchase, and pushed a short torso, naked except for a dirty white loin cloth and a large round shield which was strapped to its back, into the light. Khayrik, hidden behind the back of one of the resting mules and peering between the mule's legs, held his hand flat and low in a cautionary signal to his companions. He waited as the Agaska ducked down and pulled its shield from its back, to crouch in a warlike way behind it, with his long thick blade pointing threateningly towards the huddled shape of Ormaas. Lara's grip on her bow grew tighter. Despite the cold of the night she felt hot. She could see, over the shield, the strange distorted face of an Agaska, with its long upper lip leading to a pinched sucking mouth, its high sharp cheekbones and long jaw, its heavy eyebrows over thin eyes.

Still Khayrik's hand indicated caution. The cripple watched as a second pair of hands appeared, a second face was raised into sight, a second knee hoisted a second body upwards. They stood barely ten strides away, the new Agaska kneeling behind its leader, arm dangling over the edge. And then its body tensed and heaved a third in sight. Suddenly Khayrik cried out. 'Now!' he shouted, and Lara let off her arrow. It missed the Agaskan and vanished into the darkness beyond. Kneeling now, Lara threaded a second arrow which almost fired itself as the Agaskan charged, a dreadful shot that ran parallel to the ground. There was a hideous scream from the leading Agaska; the arrow had impaled its right ankle, and brought the creature to the ground. It lay there, quivering behind its shield in paroxysms of pain.

A fourth Agaska had by now heaved itself from the gorge beneath the bridge, and joined his comrades. They moved forward in a group, rapidly covering the ground on their long legs, and stepping over the fallen body of their leader. The mules, wide awake now, brayed fearfully into the night, and the noise echoed horribly between the mountains.

Ormaas was on his feet to receive them. He swung his sword wildly as the Agaskan broke through the ring of mules, and was shocked as his swing was halted by the soft resistance of Agaskan flesh. Rapidly, as though disgusted, he drew his blade back from the pot belly of the Agaska; the latter stood, as amazed as Ormaas, for the space of two heartbeats, and then slipped gently to its knees where it remained, as if in prayer, and quite dead. But Ormaas had no time to think of this, for another was on him now, harrying him with a short barbed spear and making him parry clumsily with the flat of his blade.

Khayrik too was using the flat of his blade, and like Ormaas this was not from choice. He struck his opponent in the ribcage but did little damage, whilst the Agaska's downstroke nearly caught the cripple on the shoulder. Lara ran forward to Khayrik's assistance, but as she did so another Agaska appeared over the edge of the drop. She turned rapidly to face the newcomer, slashing but missing with two hasty strokes.

Ormaas was doing little better. He too tried to slash at the Agaska that faced him, but the creature was too quick for him, weaving back on its long legs to keep just out of danger. Meanwhile, Khayrik's position was desperate. The Agaska he had fought towered above his crippled form, striking down at him again and again. Khayrik twisted to avoid the blows, parried with a frantic crutch waved in the air above his head, and tumbled right under the feet of the Agaska, which stepped back quickly without striking a blow, and nearly overbalanced itself over one of the ropes tethering the mules. The mule, terrified, pulled back its head as the Agaska tripped, ripping the peg from the ground as it did so, and in panic the animal swung its haunch between Khayrik and his adversary.

That the mule saved Khayrik's life is beyond doubt, for the Agaska had been poised above the fallen cripple ready to deliver the final blow; its actions went further than that. For, as the mule jerked the peg out of the ground the rope catapulted back, striking the Agaska facing Ormaas a cutting lash on the shoulder. The Agaska, thinking it was being set upon from the rear, lowered its guard for a moment as it half turned to look; again Ormaas felt the curious weight of a body on his sword as with a vicious upthrust he cleaved the Agaska's chest. The Agaska fell back, blood foaming at mouth and chest as its damaged lungs struggled for air, and nearly took Ormaas with it as it collapsed, ripping the sword from his hand as it went.

Quickly Ormaas picked up the discarded blade of the first of his victims, for he was unable to look at the creature with the rent chest, much less remove his sword from its ruined body. It still writhed mercilessly in the corner of his vision as he tested the Agaskan sword in his hand, feeling its unaccustomed weight and narrow handle, designed for hands which were not human hands. Wielding this unfamiliar weapon experimentally he dashed to help his cousin, whilst Khayrik, balance restored, swung an astonishing blow from behind his shoulder, over his head, and straight into the Agaskan face leering over him.

The Agaska parried rapidly, cut from forehead to lip but still agile; Khayrik though was sharp and angry now, and slashed at the long legs in front of him. The blade of the sword bit deep into the grey-green flesh, clashing nauseatingly with the bone and releasing a flood of dark blood that welled for a beat on the edge of the wound before pouring down what remained of the shattered leg. At the same time, Lara had caught her opponent on the arm, breaking the skin in a long shallow tear, whilst Ormaas came up behind it. It turned on this new attack and Lara struck at it again, on the other arm, as Ormaas swung at it. Agaskan blade clashed with Agaskan blade, and but for Lara, who caught the creature an ugly blow on the back, Ormaas would surely have been killed, for the impact knocked the sword from his hand. It arched over the fire-spell brilliantly before vanishing from the plateau in a noisy gathering clatter.

Khayrik stabbed the Agaska he had fought once more, in the stomach, as it stood in wordless agony on its shattered leg, and then turned to see the last of the Agaskan leap towards the plateau's edge with Ormaas following desperately. 'No!' cried Khayrik fearfully, for the creature would have every advantage on the rockface, but already Ormaas had checked his pursuit as the Agaska leapt towards the wooden scaffolding erected around the bridge supports. There was a sudden scream as the creature, its eyes not yet adjusted to the darkness below the bridge after the bright of the fire-spell, realised it could see nothing. The companions, rushing to the lip of the drop, heard the sound of the creature's impact against a stone pier, the scrabble of hopeless fingers on smooth masonry, and then a long hollow scream that took too much time to fade to nothing as the creature plummeted into the abyss. Sickened, Lara and Ormaas turned away from the drop, only to see Khayrik's sword raised above the neck of the wounded Agaska who had led the attack.

'No!' Now it was Ormaas's turn to object, but the sword was already swinging before sinking with a savage weight into the exposed throat of the Agaska. Khayrik stood in the orange light of the fire-spell, both hands gripping the hilt of his sword, whilst at its black blade blood oozed from the riven neck. He was smiling.

The Gros of Weir lay between the silk sheets of the Lady Treslan's bed, dreaming of tall ships and distant shores.

Chapter 4

Streetpoet

Ormaas and Lara rode some distance ahead of their crippled guide. The sun had crossed the sky now and begun its leisurely descent to the west; they hoped to make Toothaas by nightfall. There must have been four hundred strides between the cousins and Khayrik; indeed, to the solitary Agaska who watched their progress from his precarious ambush in the rocks, it looked as though there were two separate groups of travellers beneath him, and he cursed his luck that so tempting a target as the cripple and the mule train should follow so closely in the wake of the dangerous-looking young couple ahead. Another thousand strides, he thought, only another thousand strides would the horsemen have to be, and then I could have him, so I could. I could have the legless one. But there was no point in such wishing. The Agaska took a regretful last look at the cripple with his mules, spat in annoyance, and then slipped away through the troubled rocks to the dank security of his cavern home, where he gnawed an old bone and brooded silently.

Once the Agaskan of the Gilla had been a great race, unchallenged masters of the peaks: times had changed. First there had been the prophet Sumtran, who had led the war between mankind and the Agaskan, and then the fearsome Akhran the Golden – 'Soulcleaver', the Agaskan called him – who had taken the prophecies in Sumtran's Book of Voices and turned mankind's war into mankind's victory. The Gilla Agaskan were destroyed utterly, except for a few degenerates who still lived there. But at this thought the Agaska smiled his foul-fanged smile: for he had felt the call of the earth, whispering of Agaskan revenge, and he had smelt the sweet stench of the Ingsvaal, calling him on to victory. His laugh barked raspingly in the tight confines of the cavern: victory; victory; victory.

It was no accident that had separated Khayrik from his companions: they had chosen to ride on ahead, to shun his company. In his anger the previous night he had forgotten the innocence and inexperience of the cousins, and when he had slain that last, defenceless Agaska, he found their eyes when they looked at him full of disgust and abhorrence. A sad certainty filled him: the cousins would learn soon enough that compassion was a luxury on a journey such as theirs. Meanwhile, that they were not talking to him was inconvenient, but hardly a situation that would last all the way to Cythroné; he turned his attention to more urgent matters, as to why the Agaskan had made that uncharacteristically daring attack the night before. He hoped this didn't mean trouble, and prayed silently to Menketh.

The path wound through a high defile between two great rocks. Khayrik watched as Lara and Ormaas disappeared from his sight, and smiled too as the boy, involuntarily, half turned in his saddle to check on Khayrik's progress. Satisfied that the cripple still followed them, Ormaas goaded his mule on into the fissure.

It was dark and ominous in there, yet the darkness was relieved by the faint glow of daylight ahead, a glow which hardened as they approached into the firm shape of their exit from this narrow passage. Even though they knew it was coming, the daylight surprised them, and they found themselves in a new valley, lined with pine trees and fed by a foaming and playful brook. Yet it was neither the daylight nor the trees that most caught the attention of the cousins, but rather the densely packed buildings on the steep hillside ahead. 'Toothaas?' asked Lara.

'It must be, I suppose.'

'Thank Menketh for that.'

They rode down a narrow track, which curved down the bank of the river opposite the town, doubled back, and crossed the river by way of a small stone bridge immediately below where they had first entered the valley. From there they could see another building beyond the town, perched perilously on a volcanic plug by one of the large mountains Khayrik had pointed out the previous evening. Even at this distance the building had a dark and brooding appearance, and without needing to be told the cousins guessed it to be the Krantan-brunsvag, the Castle of the Damned, where the ancient hero Tlot had fought and beaten death, only to find life to be the greater torment.

The cousins rode up the hillside towards Toothaas. As they climbed they could see Khayrik and his mules crossing the bridge behind them, but they did not wait. They entered the town through the eastern gate, beneath a heavy black iron portcullis poised above the cobbles. Lara looked around. This was the first town she had seen apart from Fenras, and she found herself collecting and editing experience rapidly.

The first emotion was of the difference. Fenras stood in a valley whilst this stood on a hillside; Fenras smelt of paprika and Toothaas of garlic. But then the similarities started interfering: the same harsh grey stone, the same radial layout, the same architecture to many of the buildings.

They reached the town square. 'Khayrik will know where to find us. This is the inn father told us to stay at.' Murak, who knew the inns in the surrounding area well, had assured Ormaas that the Golden Eagle was the only one in Toothaas worth giving a second glance. They tethered their mules at the small metal rings set in the wall for that purpose, and approached. Outside the inn was a slight, half-bearded young man, playing the mandola and singing. He winked at Lara in a companionable way as she passed, and made her feel that the song he was singing, and had been singing long before she came into view, had been written specially for her.

> Lady, let me seek the white hart for you
> And hunt the boar and the benjamin bear;
> Oh, I will bring you any thing
> And brave all fears for you are fair.
>
> Lady, let me love you and you'll be clothed
> In jewelled words and thoughts of pearl;
> I'll imagine you are clad in
> Thoughts of mine – go naked girl!

Ormaas took two rooms, bought a cheaply printed broadsheet containing the local news from the landlord, who kept a stock of them, and went upstairs to read it. Lara wandered purposelessly out into the square, but when she got there the singer was gone.

The sight of a lone cripple with a string of laden mules excited little curiosity among the busy population of Toothaas, although one or two small boys found it amusing to jeer at him and ask him if he knew that his legs had gone missing. Khayrik found leading the string of mules through the crowded streets difficult, and it took him some time to reach the inn recommended by Murak. The strong smell of garlic, the staple flavouring in this part of Northreach, reminded the cripple that he was hungry, and it was with some relief that he recognised the mules of Lara and Ormaas tied outside the inn.

Dismounting alone was a problem: he had to unfasten the crutches first, and throw them to the ground, and then the various straps which secured him into place had to be undone; after that it was a matter of lowering himself to the ground in such a way that the damage he did would not be too painful. He almost achieved this, grimaced with pain from his shattered legs, and pulled himself into the inn.

The landlord greeted him with a mixture of respect and hostility. The respect was Ormaas's doing. The boy may not have approved of Khayrik's behaviour, but he did believe in being fair, so he had told the landlord to expect, feed and look after Khayrik. The hostility was endemic in his trade: of all the people in Northreach, publicans have least sympathy for beggars and cripples, as they deter potential customers.

Khayrik, however, had already decided not to sleep in the inn. A man who is damaged as Khayrik was damaged, a man who knows he can never be whole again, has to rebuild a new life to replace the old; Khayrik had succeeded in doing this, and he was not going to bring back a thousand painful memories for the pleasure of a night in a bed. He said he'd sleep in the stables, with the mules, and the landlord was glad.

Some time after dark, Ormaas, who had been worried about Khayrik, spoke to the landlord, who said that the cripple was sleeping in the stables. Vaguely disturbed, and wondering whether he should invite the cripple to share his room, Ormaas went out to look for Khayrik. He didn't find him, and assumed that Khayrik had gone out for the evening; in fact the cripple was sleeping almost under Ormaas's feet, but Ormaas would not have guessed that. The first art any beggar must learn is the art of sleeping without being disturbed.

As the following day dawned the man they called Streetpoet picked himself out of the straw, checked his sparse possessions, and wandered into the fresh new day from the heavy odours of the stable. From the sand-coloured leather pouch at his belt he took the money he had earnt for the previous night's perform-ance, and counted it as he walked across the stable yard. A heavy gold piece, a gold bittern worth five whole talents, glimmered in the cup of his palm. Streetpoet smiled to himself at the sight of the coin: here was just the sort of opportunity he needed after the bad luck of the previous few weeks.

He washed himself quickly in the horse-trough, wincing and blinking at the touch of the cold waters, and then let the water settle into a placid mirror again. He frowned slightly; his hair was a mess but he had enough money to get a new haircut without breaking into the bittern; more worrying was the condition of his clothes. These tatty old things might be picturesque in the ale houses, but a man with a gold bittern at his belt deserves something more. Streetpoet looked around the stable yard. Tethered beneath the arches of the stable buildings were a pair of horses kept warm by good quality blankets of a heavy black material.

'Just borrowing it,' he told the first horse as he slipped off its blanket.

He returned to his unsteady looking glass in the trough, trying to work out the best way to wear the cloak. I need a brooch, he decided, and again looked optimistically around the stable yard. The pump by the horse-trough attracted his ingenious eye: it had a black plaque attached to its wrought blackiron handle by a small bent pin which proved equally suitable for attaching the plaque to the blanket. Streetpoet spat on the plaque and rubbed it against the hem of the horse-blanket; it rewarded him by polishing up rather well. Then he fastened the blanket around himself at the neck, and practised a flourish or two.

It was better, but it was certainly still not right. Wrapped around him, the blanket gave exactly that appearance of respectability he was trying to convey, but the moment he moved his grimy faded jerkin gave a truer picture of his circumstances. He tried various ways of walking to avoid opening the blanket-cloak, and even succeeded with a tiny mincing step, but always he ran up against the same obstacle: as soon as he moved his arms the cloak fell open. Reluctantly, Streetpoet let the blanket fall to the ground at his feet, and then he took off his jerkin. There was another jerkin beneath, in the same undyed ochre and with the same stains and fraying seams. The roughened edges of the material caught the morning light and gave him an aura of dusty brightness, a halo of sunwashed threads. Streetpoet examined this jerkin carefully but decided it was no better than the other: with no more than half an idea in his head he took this one off too. The clothes at his feet curled up like sleeping pets.

The sight of his half-naked body looking up at him out of the horse-trough formed his half-idea into something practicable but audacious. Stealing himself against the cold, Streetpoet splashed and rubbed water from the horse-trough over his torso and felt it run in icy rivulets down his body. The water was sharp as a slap on his flanks, and the way it discoloured his flesh was like a blow too. He gasped, convulsively.

His toilet completed he jumped up and down for a few moments, slapping himself in an effort to restore the circulation, and watching with interest the mottled blues and reds which now appeared on his chest in response to the cold. He slipped on a jerkin, folded the other into the blanket, and hid the discarded items in the place where he had slept. Then he raced out of the stables, to return a few moments later with a small phial of blue powder.

For the last time he pulled off his jerkin. He dabbed a finger into the horse-trough and then into the powder, watching as the dry blue stuff on his fingers absorbed the dampness, became powdery balls to begin with, and then grew darker, shinier, more mobile. He rubbed it into his palm with the index finger of his right hand and then, when he was sure that the consistency was correct, he put the finger to his chest and made a widening zig-zag of blue from his breast-bone to his diaphragm. He knelt down over the horse-trough, applied a little more powder to his moistened finger, and carefully made a line inside each eye socket, just below the brow, from the outer edge of the nose to the outer edge of the eye, and then curving upwards smoothly and symmetrically to the hairline.

He stood up again, replaced the cloak which had once been a horse-blanket on his shoulders, and again practised his swirl and flourish. He smiled at his reflection as he looked down into the trough and then, in the guise of an Initiate of the Third Order of the Daln, he left the stables in search of a haircut and breakfast. As he walked he rubbed his finger tip against his palm, until the tell-tale smudge had grown faint.

Ormaas and Lara sat at a heavy wooden table, scored by a decade of eating knives until its surface was a network of cuts, and ate their breakfast. Each had an omelette of cow's milk and eggs, flavoured with black peppercorns and that firm, flavourless cooking cheese from the Plains of Myr that they coat in red wax to make it look tastier. Their blackbread was spread thickly with butter, and both butter and omelette reeked of the strong local garlic. Breakfast was a leisurely one: they only had the short safe journey to Levafoln to contend with that day.

Streetpoet stood outside the covered market of Toothaas. His five-day beard had been shaved, his shapeless, colourless hair trimmed. Except for a furtive smile and the way he looked at the gold coin he held in his hands, lifted it to his lips, and kissed it, he looked every bit the poor but respectable member of a religious order he was pretending to be. He flicked the coin into the air with a practised thumb and caught it dexterously in the same hand before slipping it into the leather pouch at his waist. Then, composing his face into one of pious solemnity he walked under the eaves.

The market traders set up their stalls in an octagon beneath the shelter of the market place, each of them facing out from the shelter's high strong central support. Already, despite the early hour, there were many customers about, and Streetpoet deliberately chose a long queue, hoping that others would soon draw up behind him.

They did. By the time he had reached the head of the queue he had some seven people behind him. 'Good morning, brother,' said the butcher to the preacher who stood in front of him.

'Good morning, and may the blessings of Our Lady be upon you,' replied the preacher. 'And a whole roast ham, if you have one.'

'Certainly.' The butcher laughed: 'Feeding the whole order, are we?'

'I have a long journey ahead of me.'

'Ah. Getting out while the going's good, is that it?' asked the butcher, cheerfully, without looking up from the joint he was preparing.

'Pardon?'

'I thought all you religious types were in a regular muddle over the hoarstones' messages these days.'

'There have been rumours,' said the preacher. It was true: apparently the hoarstones were becoming less and less predictable, and more and more violent. 'How much do I owe you?'

'One talent twelve rubeks please.' For a moment the butcher looked up, quite serious. 'And you'd better throw in a prayer as well, just in case.'

The preacher pulled a five talent gold piece from the pouch at his waist and held it out. The butcher leant over to take it. 'Just a moment,' said the preacher. 'I may have the change.' The butcher waited as the preacher delved into his money-bag, whilst the queue behind got longer in length and shorter in temper. 'One talent and one, one talent and two,' counted the preacher. 'Oh dear, dropped it again. I must start from scratch. That's a two rubek piece, and another makes four, and. . .'

To prevent further delay the butcher groped in his own large money-bag. 'Eighty-eight rubeks makes two, and here's three, four and five talents,' said the butcher, counting coins into the preacher's hands. 'And don't forget your meat,' he added as the other turned to go.

'Thank you very much.'

'Remember that prayer.'

'I will, my son. May the blessings of Our Lady fall on you. Goodbye.'

The butcher had already turned to his next customer; the preacher, with his joint of meat clenched securely beneath the crook of his arm, walked out of sight of the market trader and then tossed a coin high into the air. The gold bittern glinted and winked in the morning.

'Never fails,' said Streetpoet, cheerfully.

Khayrik's first sensation was one of pain as the suede boot caught him bone-jarringly in the ribs; his second sensation was downright agony as two knees dropped heavily on to his chest. He opened his eyes to look at his assailant: in the half-light the man looked ridiculously like an initiate of one of the Orders of the Daln. Then the pressure on his chest eased and the man stood up. The bright light flooding through the open doorway illuminated a long parallelogram of straw which stretched across the floor: in the brilliant chiaroscuro the man's features were reduced to eye sockets and cheekbones.

'Menketh alive,' exclaimed the cheekbones. 'I didn't see you.' Khayrik gulped for the air so rudely expelled by the offending knees and tried to reply, but then the figure peered over him menacingly. 'Khayrik?' The question seemed to come from the deepest part of the shadowed sockets.

Khayrik controlled his heaving chest just enough to speak. 'How do you know me?' he asked.

'It is Khayrik.'

'I know no preachers,' said Khayrik, as though this were his choice.

But the chiaroscuro features simply smiled. 'You don't recognise me, do you?'

Khayrik reached for his crutches. The cripple had little liking for men of religion, and even less for people who kicked him and then knelt on his chest.

'Look at me, you stupid sod,' said the preacher.

Khayrik looked.

'Well, who am I?'

'Bless Menketh. Streetpoet?'

'The same, and at your service, O Prince of Cripples,' said Streetpoet with a bow.

'You've not taken to preaching then?'

'Merely a deception I devised.' The young man bent down, lifted Khayrik's body awkwardly but affectionately to the doorway, and returned the items he had borrowed. The brooch was again a washpump plaque, the robe once more a horse-blanket. Then, in a frenzy of icy water, Streetpoet washed off the blue. He returned to the stables shivering.

'And what did that little performance earn for you?' asked Khayrik sardonically. 'A night on the cold stone floor of the basilica? A meal of gruel with the shaman?'

'Not quite, Khayrik-friend.' The younger man searched about the straw for his clothes and possessions, and dressed rapidly in the light of the sun shafting through the open doorway. As he dressed he picked up a parcel and tossed it to Khayrik.

Khayrik unwrapped the cheap grey material and produced a magnificent whole roast ham.

'A little better than you'd get from a shaman, don't you agree?'

'How much did this cost?'

Streetpoet grinned and made no reply.

'You didn't steal it, did you?'

'Not exactly.'

'What does that mean?'

'Let us say that there was a bit of a mix-up. I offered to pay, honestly I did. But the butcher must have made some sort of error in his calculation, because when I counted my change I found that not only had this superb joint of meat cost me nothing, but also that I was three talents better off than I had been before.'

Khayrik, annoyed with himself for being amused when he should feel severe, muttered something about the law catching up with Streetpoet someday. The latter was quite unabashed by this.

'They already have. They were going to execute me last Endyear.'

Khayrik looked disbelieving, which was all the encouragement Streetpoet needed to tell his tale. It was a tale that had already earnt him countless suppers in his half-year journeying north. Rapidly he outlined the affair of the loaf and three fish which had led to his imprisonment; with lingering pleasure he described the trial at which he had been condemned; grim precise details conveyed the atmosphere of the House of the Condemned.

'Well?' asked the cripple. 'Why aren't you dead yet?'

'Oh, I don't know. Perhaps they forgot about me.'

'Don't be ridiculous. Even if they had forgotten about you, you'd still be in there.'

'That's true. Are you going to Levafoln, today?'

'I am. Finish your story.'

'I have. Why not come with me then.'

'I can't. And you haven't.'

'Oh, all very well then. I was pardoned. Why not?'

'Why?'

'It was Endyear. You haven't answered.'

'I'm working.'

'Working.'

'For a fur-trader. We're going to Cythroné.'

'I'll come too.'

'Might not be wise.'

'Dressed as a preacher?'

'Still not wise. They don't like me.'

'Why not?'

'I saved their lives.'

The two vagrants collected their possessions. 'We must be good if we can sleep two strides from one another and never notice,' said Streetpoet.

'Or unobservant,' said Khayrik.

A cook, dressed untidily in a filthy apron over a filthy smock, walked into the courtyard with a bowl of vegetable scraps to feed the hens that clutched and cluttered about the yard. He saw Streetpoet and Khayrik through the open stable door.

'Oi. You lot. What you doing here?'

'I work for Murak of Fenras, fur-trader to the Gyr Orland,' said Khayrik

'Oh yeah. An' I'm the Gros of bleeding Weir.'

Khayrik was about to argue but Streetpoet stopped him. 'It's not worth it. Besides, I've got to get off. I want my supper in Levafoln tonight, and if I'm going to cook this,' he tapped the meat, 'I'm going to need a good pitch.' He turned to bow to the greasy chef. 'Greetings, my good man,' he called. 'And may all your headlice have harems.'

'Just bugger off.'

The track from Toothaas to Levafoln was a well-trodden one. It ran down the valley made by the swift River Leva and past the Krantanbrunsvag on its high plateau, twisting cheerfully in a youthful skittishness, until it arrived at the confluence between it and the already mighty River Khalin at Levafoln. For the companions it was a journey without incident, although looking back it was easy to identify the significance in a couple of overlooked events. The still short days of early spring were no problem on this short stretch of the journey, for from Toothaas to Levafoln could easily be travelled in daylight. Indeed, Ormaas had wanted to press on for Mornet immediately, instead of spending the night in Levafoln, and Lara had agreed, until Khayrik had pointed out how wild and inhospitable most of the landscape between Levafoln and Mornet was, how dangerous the track would be in bad light, and above all how little would be gained by arriving in Mornet exhausted one morning when you could arrive sedately that same evening. Khayrik's experience prevailed.

It was the only conversation that passed between them. If the journey was without incident it was also without interest, and Lara was bored as they rode alongside the tumbling river. Lara disliked Ormaas's silence almost as much as Khayrik's violence; indeed, as her memory of that night faded to the condition of a vivid dream, out of context in the world she had lived in all her life, she lost the urgency of her indignation. After all, she reasoned, without Khayrik we'd all be dead. She mentioned this to Ormaas, and he agreed, and his attitude remained just the same. 'You can be grateful to someone without liking them,' he said.

Travellers on such a route were frequent. Once the companions were overtaken by an armoured Gallant on a chestnut charger, whose steel armour was battered and tarnished, and whose green caparison and cloak were rent in many places. The Gallant hurried past them, hardly noticing them as he galloped by: his urgency gave them a curious feeling of smallness, of inadequacy, as though their destinies were unimportant when compared to the arcane mysteries which motivated armed knights or controlled the fates of nations. But then the companions passed a travelling player, travelling light, with his mandola strung to his back and a joint of meat beneath his arm.

The player stopped to let them aside, and winked at Lara as he did so. Lara stared on ahead of her as her mother would have wanted, and wondered if this was the same man who had been playing outside the inn in Toothaas. The dress and the mandola were familiar, but this minstrel looked cleaner and tidier than the last. Then they were past, and the troubadour had the track to himself. He sang a raucous song as he walked, and failed to notice the dark crouched shape on the hillside above him, or the signal the Agaska gave to his companions concealed just beyond the brow.

Shortly after passing Streetpoet the companions reached Leva-foln. Unusually, the town's famous carved ash gates were shut, and a small crowd of people waited outside like a queue. Ormaas dismounted and went up to the nearest part of the crowd.

'Could you tell me what's going on please?' he asked of those who waited.

'I don't know myself,' replied a large patient woman, obviously pregnant. 'But if they don't let us in pretty soon I reckon they'll have an extra one out here to contend with.' She sat on the back of a white donkey. She had a large comfortable face and a good-humoured smile. 'We live over there,' she confided, pointing out a small hamlet a few hundred strides away from the town walls. The hamlet stood in a pleasant grove of trees by the Leva, at the crossing. 'Some soldiers came a while ago and told us to get our things together as they were moving us into the town. That was some time back now, I can tell you. Anyhow, we all gets ready and then they dump us out here. I ask you. And me with this kicking and fighting like a good 'un.' She patted her distended stomach contentedly.

'Don't worry lass,' said another woman to the first. 'How many bairns you had by now?'

'This'll be my fifth,' said the woman on the white donkey. 'And all of 'em still alive bar one.'

'You've done better than me, at any road.' Whilst the conversation drifted Ormaas wandered about, trying to decide what to do. He went up to the gates and examined them. Two great carved figures stared back at him. On the right door was Menketh, on the left Araketh; one entered the town via

Menketh, and left through Araketh. Except for today, when everything seemed to have come to a grinding halt. He was returning to Lara, Khayrik and the string of mules when a voice reached out to him.

'Hey. You.' It was the woman who rode the white donkey. Ormaas mimed that he was puzzled that she wanted him; she mimed back that she was certain it was him she was wanting.

'Yes,' he said, coming over.

'My husband wants a favour. If you would.'

Ormaas noticed for the first time a small, insignificant man who held the donkey's halter. 'Could you do me a favour?' asked the man.

Ormaas indicated that he couldn't think of an excuse with a shrug. 'Can you hang on to this donkey then while he goes and has a pee?' asked the wife, and the man smiled shame-facedly.

'I suppose so,' said Ormaas carefully. 'Don't be gone long.'

'He'll not,' said the wife, from the donkey's back.

'I'll not,' echoed the dutiful husband. 'She's all right really,' he whispered to Ormaas. 'Just a bit sharp sometimes, You'll get used to her.' The man walked away, leaving Ormaas feeling uncomfortably as if he had somehow acquired the woman for good.

The gates opened with a hollow wooden clatter, and a group of the town's militia stepped out, surrounding the waiting people outside and herding them in. Lara and Ormaas found themselves led rapidly through the gate by a tall soldier in an old-fashioned full helm.

'I'm an old soldier, fellow,' said Khayrik. 'Come on. What's the trouble?'

'Agaskan.' The soldier took off his archaic and sinister helm to reveal the face of a youth no older than Lara or Ormaas. 'They've been reported to be moving about up river. Did you see that Gallant who came down the Gilla Pass today?'

'The green knight?' asked Lara.

'Aye, that'll be him. Travelled night and day from Brokmild, they say, to bring news of the Agaskan rising, and he's been alerting each town as he's passed.' Khayrik and Lara found themselves ushered into the town as they talked to the soldier, and then the soldier had gone and they were left.

The soldier stepped outside, placing his heavy helm over his face once more as he walked through the gates. A captain of the militia, in a scarlet jerkin and dark green hose, wearing a warm fur pelisse and waving a sharp fencing sword, called to him. 'Go round up those few over there, will you. Seem to be straggling a bit.'

The soldier walked over to where a well-dressed youth held the halter of a white donkey. On the donkey was a heavily pregnant woman. The soldier tried to guess the connection between these two, but could think of nothing.

'You'll have to come in to town with me now,' called the soldier.

'A moment please,' called back Ormaas. 'We're waiting for this lady's husband.'

'All right,' said the soldier, joining them. 'We'll give him a bit longer.'

Time passed impatiently. 'What's he doing?' muttered the soldier.

'Don't ask,' laughed the woman.'

'This is daft,' said the soldier. 'You're sure he didn't get into town without you seeing?'

The woman shrugged. 'He might've done, I suppose.'

'We'd best go look for him. Which way did he go?'

'Over there, I think,' said Ormaas, pointing to some nearby rocks.

'Oi!' shouted the soldier, stepping in the direction Ormaas had indicated. He turned to the woman. 'What's his name?'

'Petgarth.'

'Oi! Petgarth! Hurry up will you. We're sick of waiting.' There was no reply. 'Are you coming?' the soldier asked Ormaas.

'Might as well. You'll be all right?' he asked the woman as he relinquished the halter.

'Right as rain,' she replied.

Ormaas and the soldier walked into the tumble of rocks, looking for Petgarth and calling out his name. They didn't have to look far: he lay, stretched out on the ground and just out of sight of the city walls, with his stomach split open and both eyes removed. There was a gag of dirty material in his mouth, but the gag was unnecessary now as Petgarth was dead.

'Oh no,' whispered the young soldier. He kept repeating it, even when he was being sick. 'Oh no, oh no, oh no.'

The two faced each other. 'Agaskan?' asked Ormaas in a low and unfamiliar voice.

The word seemd to shock the other into rapid action. 'Menketh!' he said. 'We'd best be getting away from here. Let's get this poor sod into town.'

Ormaas took off his cloak and they covered the mutilated body. Sickeningly, a bulbous tube dangled from the man's slit stomach, trailing on the ground as they dragged the corpse. The young soldier pushed the entrails under the cloak with his foot. 'Sorry,' he said to the corpse.

Ormaas called out to the guards, who came running. The woman on the white donkey looked unconcernedly at the activities of the anxious men: at first she didn't understand what was wrapped in the cloak that they dragged from the rocks, and then she did, and then the labour pains began.

Ormaas found Lara and Khayrik in a small inn near the walls of Levafoln. He wanted to ask why they had chosen this inn, rather than the one Murak had recommended by the basilica, but the question now seemed unimportant. Exhaustion confused him and shock exhausted him.

Lara and the cripple were in conversation in the deserted tap room. Lara sat at a table; the cripple balanced on his crutches nearby. As Ormaas entered the couple fell silent. He walked straight past them into a private booth, curtained off from the tap room by a faded tapestry that imitated the hunting tapestries found in noble homes. The curtain wrapped itself behind the corner of a stool and Ormaas let it stay there; they could see that he was pale and drawn even in the limited light of the tap room.

'Landlord!' called Khayrik. The landlord appeared, wearing a stained cream apron which he used to wipe down the tables. 'A glass of strong wine.'

With little sense of urgency the landlord left them to return with a pewter goblet which he offered to Khayrik. But the cripple waved him towards Ormaas: the landlord put the cup on the table beside Ormaas and moved away.

'Go on,' said Lara. 'Drink it.'

For a moment Ormaas simply looked at the cup, and then he lowered his eyes down its crude unpolished stem, nodded, and lifted the drink to his lips. A tall and heavy looking blackiron candlestick with a stubby grey candle stood on the table; Khayrik lit the wick and the rough light filled the booth with highlight and shadow. As the peculiar heavy smell of candle-wax drifted in the air, Ormaas told them his story.

'Why did they do it though? Why kill him?'

'Who can say,' replied Khayrik, gently. 'He was in the wrong place. They always kill those they capture.'

'Always?' Ormaas shook his head. 'It isn't right, it isn't right,' he said sharply to Khayrik.

Lara thought Ormaas was questioning Khayrik's information, but he wasn't. He was questioning the world, and finding it lacking.

Khayrik spoke quietly, staring into the candle-flame. 'Who is to say what's right and what's wrong. I've killed folk in my time: people, Agaskan, it doesn't really matter which after a while. Does that mean the Agaskan are like people, or that people are like the Agaskan? I wonder. I've killed them, and I've hated them, but I don't hate them now. That's interesting too: I hate them for what they've done, to me and to hundreds of others, but I don't hate them.' Ormaas listened, confused. He understood something of what Khayrik said, and looked carefully at the cripple, waiting for the phrase or sentence that would make sense of the whole muddle. It never came, and as he waited his tired mind wandered. Poor Khayrik, he thought, and held out his hand. The cripple looked at the hand, forgot what he had been about to say, and then shook it warmly. They smiled at each other in a curious masculine fellowship that excluded Lara, and then Ormaas stood up. 'Let's get some more wine,' he said. The others nodded, and he went away, fetching a large jug and two more goblets. The inn was filling now and the landlord was busy; Ormaas was served by a mousy barmaid with grubby fingernails.

'Why did you chose this place?' he asked when he returned.

Lara shrugged, but Khayrik told him straight away. 'There's someone I know still out there. A young chap I used to look after sometimes.'

'The musician,' said Lara. 'The one with the mandola.'

Ormaas shrugged blankly. He hadn't noticed Streetpoet. 'Out there?' he asked. 'Is it someone you knew well?' The tense of that question was accidental, and ominous.

'You could say that. A lad about your age, had a rough time of it at home. He was adopted when he was young by this couple in the fur trade, but they didn't want a son, they wanted a slave. When he was about eight winters old he ran away, and I found him. Took him back to his parents twice, but he said he wanted to stay with me. I was younger then, and had legs, and went off to war. When I next saw him we were in Akbar, waiting for a boat to Cythroné, both of us. He'd given up being a slave again, and I'd been a beggar a long time. so we joined together a while. He always had a nice voice: we got him that mandola and he took to being a musician. Last I heard of him before this he was on his way to the Grove of the Red Rock, wherever that is, to learn to play properly. Poor lad: he was a devil, but a good one,' said Khayrik, contradictingly.

'I said you wouldn't mind us staying here,' put in Lara.

'No. Of course not.'

'He'll be all right, I expect,' said Lara. It was the sort of ridiculous thing she knew her mother would have said, but it seemed the right thing to say; the others seemed to agree, because they cheered up.

'Aye, perhaps you're right,' said Khayrik, whilst Ormaas nodded and let a smile play on his lips. Ormaas was on his third glass of tawny wine by now, however: he was just beginning to feel like smiling when he started to feel ill.

From beyond the booth they could here the garbled sounds of drinking and talking. 'It's getting noisy,' said Ormaas.

'Pardon,' said his cousin.

'I said – oh never mind. There are a lot of drunks out there.'

'There'll be one in here too if you carry on like that. That's fortified wine you're drinking, not water. If you're going the way of your father I'll not go any further with you,' she announced, playfully.

'Oh, shut up,' said Ormaas. Lara looked at him in surprise. He had never told her to shut up before. She was still looking at her cousin, and he was still looking at his goblet, when Khayrik lifted a hand for silence. There was a puzzled look on the cripple's generous, weather-beaten face. A song began in the tap room, and Khayrik seemed to be straining to catch it, although from what the cousins could hear it was not much of a song. A pleasant voice, piping through the pipe smoke, yet it held the cripple transfixed.

I'll sing you a song about my day;
My song's not all that ambitious.
You'll find my day is dreary and grey
And very repetitious.

At six o'clock I hear the cock crow
As it does every morning;
At six o'clock I feel my cock grow
– Don't you find that in the morning?

At seven o'clock it's time to get up,
I'm full of joy and vigour.
At seven o'clock I'm all set up
– Who was that I heard snigger?

At eight o'clock I fancy a meal,
Smoked herring or cured bacon;
At eight o'clock I steal my first meal
– Yours? You're surely mistaken.

From nine in the morning till nine at night
I can't think what to do
But from nine at night till they blow out the light
I try to entertain you.

And it's twelve o'clock and I have learnt
It's hard to entertain you;
Even so, I think I have earnt
Maybe a rubek or two.

Maybe a rubek or two, lads,
Maybe a rubek or two.
It's twelve o'clock and I think that I've earnt
Maybe a rubek or two.

Khayrik flung open the curtain which separated the booth from the outside world, and set off as fast as he could on his crutches. 'Streetpoet!' he cried.

'Khayrik!' Streetpoet stood in the middle of the now crowded room, a glass in one hand and the mousy barmaid in the other.

'I thought you were dead when I saw you hadn't come in through the gates. Did they open them again?'

'No. I had to get in through the water supply. Very cold and wet. That's why I'm performing unaccompanied tonight – unless you count this charming creature,' he added, making the barmaid giggle. 'The water has got into my mandola.'

'Come and join us.'

'Gladly. Is that pretty mistress of yours still with you. I wish she was a mistress of mine.'

'You're drunk.'

'You're being stern again,' scolded Streetpoet. 'It isn't every day I come back from the dead.

'No? It must just seem like it then.'

Streetpoet gave Lara and Ormaas his most practised mock bow, bending from the waist like a rag toy and waving his arms madly, one in front of him and the other behind his back, before arrving at a position where his chin rested on his knees. 'Hello,' he said to Lara, from that position.

'Hello,' she smiled.

'I liked your song,' said Ormaas, for something to say.

'Good,' said Streetpoet, still looking admiringly at Lara.

'But I thought it was perhaps rather rude.'

'Not a bit of it,' said Streetpoet. 'Now if you really want a rude song' – he returned his eyes to Lara again, and she blushed most gratifyingly; Ormaas felt like hitting him – 'you must wait until I know you better.'

'That will be a long time yet,' said Ormaas firmly.

'Oh, I make friends easily. Goodnight, handsome sir; goodnight, beautiful miss.' Streetpoet turned sharply, his torso apparently pulling his legs around, and his legs his feet, as though he had been turned from the shoulders by a giant hand. He walked away.

'He's drunk,' said Khayrik.

'So am I,' said Ormaas, standing up as if to fight the departed figure: they would be evenly matched, he thought, and then he staggered, forgot what he was standing for, and went to bed.

'Will he be all right?' asked Lara.

'He's your cousin,' replied the cripple. 'He hasn't drunk much; why's he like that?'

'He's not used to it. His father drinks like a fish. Ormaas stays clear.'

'I think he's right though, about going to bed,' said Khayrik.

Lara leant across the table and caught the other's wrist. 'Aren't you going to tell me some more about your friend? He's very interesting, but a bit frightening.'

'Some other time,' said Khayrik, 'Unless he tells you first.'

Khayrik returned to the stables; Lara climbed the stairs to the hot, crowded bedroom she was to share with ten other women. Before she got undressed for bed she looked into the men's room: Ormaas was the only one up there, as the other men were still in the tap room, drinking. She blew him a gentle kiss, and left without him knowing she had been there, so absorbed was he in his bitter jealous love.

His was not the only disturbed night. The guards on the town walls were alert to every sound, and the night seemed full of noises; Streetpoet was on his back in the street watching noisy stars revolve: Khayrik couldn't settle as he thought of the Agaskan and his poor destroyed legs. And in that town, that night, a child was born, and they called him Petgarth after his father.

Chapter 5

A Journey by Twilight

A low inhuman threnody, and the dull brushing beat of many feet, filled that long night. The Agaskan warriors were filing past Levafoln at the beginning of their long mad journey south to the Thatter, where the Wells of Glavkcha throbbed and pulsed to the sound of the Mind of Hrakar. These were not the bitter deposed decadents of the Gilla Pass, but sleek confident armies from Orgral, the highest part of the Northreach range. No man had ever gone to Orgral and returned alive. For two nights that followed the air hummed with their sounds and the hillsides were splashed with the light from their fires. After that, the Agaskan host appeared to have passed, and all was quiet outside the town gates. To those within Levafoln, there was threat even in the silence.

The days had not passed without incident for them, although the clammy impotence of waiting made them seem interminable. On the first day of the passing of the host, the Gallant in green had set off for Mornet on a fresh horse, and on the second day his corpse had been displayed, naked and impaled on a high post, in the open space in front of the town gates, where it had remained until the soldier in the old-fashioned helm had braved the silence to bring him down. On the third day a meeting was called, by Clarel-vaine-Leva, the local lord, to discuss the situation.

People crowded in the square. Khayrik chose to stay in the tavern: 'I'm not too happy in crowds,' was all he said, and the others understood. Lara and Ormaas found themselves unable to enter the square proper because of the crush of people, and had to be content with viewing proceedings from a side street.

The Vaine had instructed a platform to be built on the steps of the basilica, and there he and three other dignitaries waited as the citizens continued to assemble. At last he stood, holding his hands in front of his chest to order silence. The crowd shuffled their way to quiet as he began. 'People of Levafoln, comrades, friends. We live in troubled times – perhaps the most troubled since the Dark Years before Sumtran gave our people the Book of Voices, if Va'kin is right.' Va'kin, the shaman who shared the platform with three armoured men, nodded his grave agreement to the Vaine's suggestion. 'I have no experience in augury myself, yet I cannot but share Va'kin's foreboding, nor believe this strange movement of the Agaskan brings anything but peril. I will let Va'kin talk to us about this later; before that, however, two other people are going to speak. The first is Consatiné-vaine-Mornet, the son and heir to the Gros of Ra himself; the second requires no introduction from me as he's my old friend – our old friend, perhaps I should say – Harval, the Captain of the Watch.' Despite the tone of the Vaine of Leva's speech, no one clapped. The memory of the green knight's corpse was still fresh in their minds.

The Vaine of Mornet stood up as the Vaine of Leva sat down. The Gros of Ra's son was a good-looking young man with dark hair and a dark complexion. He wore a fashionable soft velvet hat, decorated with pearls, and an equally fashionable magenta tunic. As a concession to the weather he wore a long sleeveless fur which hung off his shoulders and was joined at his throat by a heavy gold chain; as a concession to the situation he wore a silver cuirass. His words were brief; his face, when he spoke, seemed to move too much, creating a sense of nervousness. 'Citizens of Levafoln. I and my body-guard will be returning to Mornet tomorrow, unless that course of action proves quite impossible. Should any wish to join me they are welcome: I promise neither safety nor comfort, but companionship on the journey and the knowledge that Menketh will watch over us. If you do wish to come with us, please meet me tomorrow at dawn at the gates: be warned, however, that I shall take no one who might hinder me. My purpose is simple – to get word of the Agaskan menace to Mornet and the Empire as soon as is possible. Thank you.' He sat down again, and Lara noted how much better looking he was when he wasn't talking. She pretended she was the Vaine of Mornet for a while, chewing on words as if they were toffee, until, after a short pause whilst they decided who should speak next, the Captain of the Watch stood. He was not a practised

speaker, and lacked both confidence and volume. 'Er . . .
friends . . . citizens. You know . . . I suppose . . . Look. It's
like this. We don't know what to do or how to do it but, I'm sure
I'm speaking for every one of us when I say that what must be
done will be done.' For the first time there was applause, which
made Harval smile. 'And speaking for myself, I'd rather be
fighting the Agaskan any day than standing here talking to
you.' People actually laughed, for the first time since that cold
day had broken over the body of the green knight.

Finally the shaman stood. Va'kin was a small portly man
with a long fair beard shot with silver. Like Va'alastar, he wore
a tall hat and a long robe of crimson, over which was added a
long brown cloak. He spoke intensely, yet fluently, pausing
only to mop his brow from time to time as the sweat ran into his
eyes.

'First, perhaps you are unfamiliar with the perverted religion
of the Agaskan. The Agaskan do not have hoarstones but wells
whereby they can contact the Mind of Hrakar: to these wells
they make cannibalistic sacrifices, hurling down their own
children in order to learn what the future will bring. In our
religion we have the Book of Voices which gives us the truth
and tells us how to worship our lord Menketh; for the
worshippers of Araketh there is no book, and no set method,
but rather there is the Ingsvaal, which no man can ever
understand or feel and yet which seems to run through the
whole race of the Agaskan and to motivate them as ants are
motivated, so that they work together without thought and
fear. When an Ingsvaal has begun they have a strength that
makes them unstoppable; they will work together without fear
of consequence, fanatically driven by Araketh. For remember,
as Araketh is the binding god of winter, who holds all things
together and tries to freeze the very waters of the Khalin, so
Menketh is the god of freedom and of the spring. We are
fighting for the spring and for mankind when we fight the
Agaskan: remember this and learn.

'The last time there was an Ingsvaal was in the Dark Years,
when Sumtran was inspired to write the Book of Voices and
when destruction was so near. An Ingsvaal is a time when
prophecy breaks down, when so great is the energy that thrills
the hoarstones I fear no man can control it. But this much we

know is true: the Mind of Hrakar is disturbed, and all the help
that Menketh can give us will be of no use unless the Mind be
appeased. How much of this is due to the irreligious ways so
prevalent elsewhere in the Empire at present I would not like to
say, when for the sake of fashion' – he spat the word – 'men
scorn the names of the gods, but I would say that the lack of
love and respect shown to the Old Religion by those who live in
the south could well have disturbed the balance between Good
and Evil which has always existed.' Ormaas saw the Vaine of
Leva lean over to Consatiné-vaine-Mornet and mouth a few
curt words. The Vaine of Mornet nodded in agreement. 'The
same strength which flowed through Akhran the golden and
forced forward the first Khalinrun is available for all; yet in this
godless age can we depend on this?' The two Vaines tensed as
Va'kin continued. 'Perhaps the avatar of Akhran shall desert
us; why should the power of the gods be used to save those who
believe not? I can do nothing, nothing save hope; and I can
hope for nothing more than a change in mortal heart which will
save us.'

There was much clearing of throats. The shaman's words
might have been true, but many in Northreach too had
wandered from the Old Religion, as well as those in the south;
it made them feel no better to learn that the responsibility for
their predicament might have been their own. The Vaines were
still murmuring to one another, and then the Vaine of Leva
rose to his feet. 'I'm sure we all take heed of the words of our
shaman,' he said. 'However, I can reassure him on one point at
least, because our guest here, Consatiné-vaine-Mornet, is
recently returned from Cythroné and has recent information
from the capital. Our Lady of Khalindaine, whose body
contains the avatar of Akhran the Golden, has not forgotten the
Old Religion, and neither has she forgotten Northreach: as
proof of this latter, she has already sent messages to the Gros of
Ra, whose son we have with us today, instructing the Gros to
prepare for a royal progress which will take place this year. The
strength of Akhran will still be with us, should the situation
turn to war.'

Relaxation was tangible: relaxation and relief. Clarel-vaine-
Leva added a few words of departure and the meeting broke
up. One or two muttered that the messenger, what-was-his-

name-Hedch, had spoken of a royal progress so it looked like there must be one; others said there was a fat chance of the empress coming to Northreach when the Agaskan were on the march.

Lara and Ormaas returned to Khayrik in the inn. Ormaas had tried to change inns, for this one, near the closed gates of the town, was dreadful and dirty, but it was too late: they were not the only travellers caught in the Agaskan rising, nor the only ones who needed a bed. They explained, meanwhile, to Khayrik what had been said, whilst sitting in the comfortless grime of their tavern, and Khayrik nodded his head. 'Nearly treason, what that shaman said,' he commented, and then: 'Well, are we going with this Consatiné-vaine-Mornet in the morning or not?'

The cousins looked surprised. 'We hadn't thought of it. He said he wouldn't take anyone that would slow him down.'

'A lot of mules won't slow him down on that journey. He's going to have to descend by the side of the Mornet falls: mules is better than horses for that. If he's been born here, and I guess he will have been, then he'll know that mules'll be no problem.'

'Should we?' Ormaas turned to Lara.

'I don't know. What's the advantage?'

'We'd get to Mornet quicker, get a boat sooner. There'll be more people than ever wanting to take boats away from Northreach if rumours of this Ingsvaal get around; if we don't get to Mornet soon it won't be worth our going at all.'

'Is it . . . safe?' Ormaas hesitated, too young yet to know that fear is sometimes legitimate.

'I can't say,' replied the cripple. 'But at least it's moving on.'

The night had been a quiet one; the hillside fires and shuffled noises no longer disturbed the darkness. As the sun rose a group was assembling behind the great carved gates; the gates opened with a long-drawn groan; a small procession trotted out on to the road to Mornet.

Khayrik had been right about the mules, although wrong about the Vaine. The Vaine had been against them, saying that they would slow them down; it was only when Malver, the huge sergeant who commanded the bodyguard, explained the advantages the mules would have over the rough ground that the companions were allowed to join the party.

Also with them were Streetpoet and a pedlar called Blavni. Streetpoet had determined to travel with Khayrik, whatever Ormaas might feel; Blavni had pressing debts in Levafoln and even the thought of the Agaskan seemed preferable to staying to face his creditors. Khayrik was pleased that Streetpoet was with them: the minstrel had a restless courage that encouraged those around him. At the same time, though, he hoped that Streetpoet would not try to get too familiar with the pretty Lara; he knew what Ormaas's reaction would be like.

He need not have worried on that score. Streetpoet's greeting to Lara was purely formal. Khayrik guessed that the minstrel had a lady-friend in Levafoln, which would also explain his absence these past few days, but in this supposition he was wrong; sober, the minstrel was quite perceptive, and recognised Ormaas's affection for his cousin for what it was. Normally Lara might have been worried by Streetpoet's coldness, for she enjoyed gallantry; today she was preoccupied.

The Vaine of Mornet led them. He wore an ebony helm with a pointed visor, and rode a dappled grey. His helm was plumed in red and white, his tabard striped diagonally in these two colours, his horse trimmed in them. With him was his standard bearer, who carried a large silk flag of scarlet, in the centre of which was a gold trimmed lozenge bearing the diagonal stripes, surrounded by a complicated twirling gold-thread design of stylised flora and bees. Like the other members of the bodyguard the standard bearer wore the same red and white tabard as his master, albeit in an inferior material, and a steel helmet with a large curving rim, pointed at front and back and with a contoured comb. There were eleven men in the bodyguard, including the standard bearer. Malver arranged them on either side of the mules, in escort; Lara, Ormaas amd Khayrik led the line of mules; Blavni and Streetpoet, the latter on a horse purchased with his gold bittern, a sorry-looking nag that was unlikely to carry him further than Mornet before dropping, made up the rear of the column.

Consatiné-vaine-Mornet, at the head of this meagre force, urged his horse through the ford across the Leva; Ormaas, following, looked at the comfortable, simple houses in the trees by the crossing, and thought of Petgarth who had lived there.

They travelled south now, following the Khalin. The river here was fast flowing and dangerous, unnavigable except for the wood-cutters, who annually rode their own timber, lashed into great rafts, down the rapids and swirling white waters. And even the wood-cutters balked at the Mornet Falls, which plunged vertically from the heights of Northreach to the Khalinrift below.

The noise of the river was constant and wearing. It cut them off, each of them, from their companions, and made the journey a private and lonely affair in which the rush of waters got confused with the sound of their own blood.

It was not long before they came to the crow-ridden carcase of the green knight's horse: they rode past without comment. Lara tried to catch her cousin's eye, but he was staring fixedly ahead. She did not want to guess what he was thinking, but she knew he was remembering that insignificant, harmless man, whose stomach the Agaskan had slit open. The crows wheeled around the carcase as they passed, and then settled again. They were strips of black against the sky, that seemed to grow and shrink with each wingbeat, making them flicker. Lara watched them, and felt frightened and exposed in a way she had never known before. As they reached a small tributary to the Khalin, a nameless stream that fed the great river, and rearranged themselves into single file to cross the narrow stone bridge, she was wondering whether she would rather have stayed at home, and then for the first time realised that she no longer could be certain that her home would still be there. The green knight had been coming from the Heront. He had crossed the Gilla Pass. What if the Agaskan had attacked Fenras, destroyed it? What if her mother was dead? For the first time she realised that this Agaskan rising was not simply a hazard of travelling but something new, unforeseen, dreadful.

The reorganisation, although well handled by Malver, took time. First the left-hand file of troops, then the mule train and the other civilians, then the right-hand file. A voice interrupted Lara's thoughts as they were crossing. 'Don't look into the water,' instructed Khayrik, and naturally she did. What she saw horrified her. For the river-bed was strewn with bloated bodies, olive green and white, with puffy faces and grinning jaws.

'What is it?' she asked, as they crossed the bridge and could ride two abreast again.

'Agaskan,' replied Khayrik, straining his voice over the sound of the Khalin. 'They always get rid of their bodies that way, as deep down as they can. Nearer to Hrakar I suppose. That shaman in Levafoln wasn't quite fair if he said the Agaskan are cannibals: they throw their own children down the wells, but it's a mark that they love them. Here, the Agaskan have put their dead in the river. That must mean they're travelling fast, which is good for us, as it means they probably won't still be around.'

'How can you tell?'

'Otherwise they'd have buried 'em properly.' Khayrik turned around to take a last look at the charnel house beneath the suck and rush of running water. 'It looks as if your green knight put up a good fight, at any rate,' he said.

Lara nodded, and found that there was something in her throat that she could not dislodge, something which was fear, and disgust, and respect. Ahead, she could see a small group of houses, with an inn and a small roadside basilica. Without needing to be told, she could guess what those dangling shapes hanging like grotesque fruit from the surrounding trees might be, and she tried to avert her eyes. Yet as the path took them closer, and through the trees, she found that she must just take one look, to check that her fears were justified. She opened her eyes, and snapped them shut again, but now the image of a child hanging naked by its feet was seared on her brain.

'Are we through?' she asked after a time.

Ormaas, who rode through stoically, as though the sight of such sufferings might do him good, replied that they were not, and so Lara hung her head down and let the mule thread its own route through the trees. 'Just a few strides more,' said Ormaas. 'Now, don't look back.'

Lara reopened her eyes. The image of the hanging child remained with her.

From Levafoln to Mornet was a long day's ride, and in the winter months it would have to be finished in the hours of darkness. It was this part they dreaded most. At the head of the company Consatiné-vaine-Mornet heard his old instructor's voice in his head, telling him about the Agaskan. 'Guard particularly against night attacks. It's not that they're night creatures, any more than me or you. No, left to themselves they'd spend the day much as we do, and spend their nights as we do too, sleeping and fornicating, which is far the most sensible arrangement. But we've harried them and made them change, driven them into the mountains where it's always dark, and now they come out at us after nightfall. They can see better in the dark than we can these days, that's a fact, and night attacks give them that bit of an advantage.' The old instructor's voice then had changed to one of contempt. 'Of course, there's not much chance of you ever meeting a real Agaska, not unless you go looking for trouble in the Thatter or in Orgral, like the Gyr Orland did a year or so back. All you'll ever meet – Menketh be thanked – are them degenerates up the Gilla Pass, and they're a different thing altogether, nothing next to the real thing. No, a real Agaska's quite a different proposition, two strides tall and broad across the shoulder.' Consatiné tried to picture the corpses in the river. Had they been bigger than the few Agaskan he had seen before? He couldn't decide. 'And they're not naked like the degenerates, either. They wear blackiron armour and long scarlet cloths wrapped about their wrists.' The corpses had been naked, but he felt he had seen red streamers below the water. 'Different creatures altogether, and a hundred times more dangerous.'

Meanwhile, at the back of the column, Streetpoet was faking nonchalance, pretending to tune his mandola whilst all the while his nerves strained into the failing light. The valley was wider now, cut by the rapid river to their right, but the trees along the banks were thicker, and occasional rocky outcrops suggested perfect ambushes. His eyes scanned the hillsides above him. Suddenly they stopped, staring at a darker mass on the darkening rocks. He reined the old horse back, waiting, and his heart beat more loudly than a drum: he heard it echo down the valley, and wondered his companions didn't hear it too.

There it was again, a slight movement in the shadows high above them. He spurred his horse on and spoke briefly to the nearest guard, who looked up just in time to see a hunched form scuttle along a ledge and vanish again into the shadows. Streetpoet took the guard's station escorting the mules whilst the soldier rode on to inform his sergeant.

Consatiné jumped slightly as Malver's approach disturbed thoughts which had been thick with Agaskan warriors, tumbling down the hills towards them. 'Yes?' asked the Vaine.

'Sir. Something following us, sir.'

'Oh.' Consatiné felt his stomach turn traitor on him, and fought the sensation. 'Agaskan?' His voice sounded far too careless he thought; it sounded ridiculous between the gathering darkness and the violence of the river.

'Couldn't say, sir. Haven't seen it myself, but Blenhe's a good man and he says it could have been.'

The darkness intensified; the nightmare continued. Consatiné tried to calculate how much further they had to travel. It couldn't be far, surely; that was the Mording's brook ahead of them, flowing down the hillside to join the Khalin. They would cross at the wooden bridge – wide enough to take a wagon so they wouldn't have to regroup – and then there would be just the wide belt of trees at the head of the Mornet Falls, the long descent by the Falls, then the lake at the Falls' foot to negotiate, and they would be home. Consatiné let his mind travel faster than his horse and pictured the great stone bridge across the Khalin, the lights of Mornet reaching up the foothills of the Northreach mountains, the pinnacles and towers of the Ranbrunsvag overlooking from its wooded hill the sprawling, busy, ugly city beneath. Consatiné looked up once again at the hills, and once again saw nothing. They reached the wooden bridge over the brook, crossed with a noise that was loud even above the noise of the river, and began to pad across the moist grassland on the far side. Straining his eyes against the darkness, Consatiné tried to make out their route through the trees that crowded the bank ahead of them. To his horror he saw a figure detach itself from the dark wood, and another. He paused his horse and felt the wave of anxiety that had threatened to engulf him all the long twilight burst over him. The others stopped behind him. To his surprise he felt calm. He turned his head, and made sure that the others had all seen them: they had. He drew his sword, and the others did the same. They spread out at the end of the bridge and

watched the dark figures move across the open space before
them. Suddenly Malver had rushed his horse forward, riding
past his lord and into the night.

'Malver!' cried Consatiné. 'Don't be a fool!' And then it was
he who felt the fool, for he too recognised the figures. They
were members of the Mornet guard, and men like themselves.
'Clonthel,' he shouted, addressing the nearest.

'Vaine,' cried the soldier. 'Thank Menketh you're safe. Some
travellers on their way north said they'd seen hordes of Agaskan
crossing the river, and your dad – the Gros of Ra, begging your
Vaineship's pardon – sent us out to find the lie of the land.'

For the first time, listening to the voice of this honest soldier
and feeling tears collect behind his eyes, Consatiné was glad
that it was dark.

Streetpoet was still plucking absent-mindedly at his mandola,
with it wedged against his hip as he rode. It was a large,
eight-stringed instrument with two curvaceous sound holes
and a bowl-shaped sound box, and it was horribly out of tune
after its soaking in the water supply of Levafoln. Each note
jarred hopelessly with the one which preceded it. 'Hang the
musician,' said one of the guards cheerfully. Consatiné saw
again the hanging bodies in the trees by the river, with their
intestines spilling lilac from slit stomachs and their eyes red
patches across which black flies marched.

It was quite dark now. The stars were bright and the
crescent moon a friend. Lara was aware of an increasing noise
from the river, drowning every other sound with its force.
Streetpoet gave up on his mandola and slung it over his
shoulder with an eloquent gesture of disgust that made those
who saw it laugh. Lara touched Ormaas's arm and pointed
ahead. In a bright shine of rapid movement the river seemed to
finish abruptly just before them, whilst the rest of their world
curved around the spot where the river had gone. Beyond was
noise and nothing: the world seemed to end where they stood.

They realised where they were, of course. They were at the
very edge of Northreach, and about to make the descent to the
lower level of Khalinreach. By their side was the flashing
maelstrom of the Mornet Falls, dropping vertically for six
hundred strides into a deep pool below. The path sloped

suddenly, sadistically downwards, almost throwing them, and Lara saw why mules would be no disadvantage when she saw the armoured Vaine ahead dismount and lead his horse. The noise was louder still now, impossibly loud, and by straining herself on her mule over the tangled thorns that surrounded the path down Lara was able to see, deep down in the abyss next to them, the phosphorescent display as the river plunged into the pool below. Lara felt her eardrums object to the weight of the Falls. A gap in the trees and rocks revealed the waters surging vertically past them, impossibly close, white against the darkness and frothing and bubbling so fast that nothing was more than a blur. She felt gusting spray wet her face and hands: the tiny water-droplets were a grey gauze in the night, passing in front of her like a mist, settling on her hair like dew on spiders' webs.

Down they went, and down further, until at last, when they felt they had never known flat ground in their lives, they were at the foot of the Falls. They found themselves riding around a great pool of dark water. Despite the noise, despite her knowledge of the great weight of water cascading down from the Northreach heights at every moment, the scene looked to Lara as though it were still, as though the Falls were a column of glass and the spray a tethered cloud at its foot. This impression was aided by the apparent stillness of the great pool they now skirted, and Lara heard her cousin question Consatiné about this.

'It may look still,' said the Vaine. 'But beneath the waters there are currents that would tear a man apart, and have. No man of Mornet would ever swim in these waters, but sometimes strangers, travellers from the south who are parched after crossing the deserts of the Rift, dive in joyously. We never even find their bodies.'

Chilled, Ormaas did not reply. The world, he reflected, seems full of things like this: innocent moments that are suddenly spoilt; beautiful places that kill. He wondered if Khayrik understood all this; Khayrik seemed to understand most things.

Consatiné no longer questioned the deceptive beauty of the pool. For him it was simply part of his home, part of Mornet, and he was recovering his composure with every step his horse

took. He lowered his voice and spoke privately down to
Ormaas, whose mule trotted contentedly alongside the
Vaine's grey war horse. 'That man, that musician. He's with
you?'

'I suppose so,' said Ormaas.

'He's not a servant though, I take it?'

'I don't think so. Not ours, at any rate.'

'You seem to have odd companions,' said Consatiné.
Ormaas bridled at this, but he could see that the Vaine was
not serious, and was grinning to himself in the darkness. 'A
cripple and a musician: like a circus.'

In deference to his companion's rank, Ormaas smiled too.
'Is he any good, this musician?' continued Consatiné.

'I honestly couldn't say.'

'Hey, you!' called Consatiné. 'Musician?'

'Sir?' replied Streetpoet, driving his horse on to join the
nobleman.

'Can you play "Hie the Boy Home"?'

'I can play anything you like, sir; you'll not recognise it till
I get this thing in tune.' He patted his mandola affectionately.

'Let's give it a try.' Streetpoet shrugged. Consatiné began
to sing, in a fine rich tenor which had been trained carefully
by some of the best and most expensive tutors in Cythroné.

> Hie the boy home.
> The same wind still plays through the trees
> As brought my young child to me.
> I should have known
> 'Twas better I let him run free
> As a loose leaf in the breeze.
>
> He's barely grown,
> He's still a child, and the trees
> Threaten, the north wind doth freeze;
> I hope that he'll rest in the lees;
> Menketh, sweet Menketh, sweet please,
> Hie the boy home, home to me.

By the time Consatiné's voice was declaiming the final
cadence, Streetpoet had decided upon some rudimentary but
appropriate accompaniment. He was disappointed, therefore,

when the Vaine stopped, with an apologetic, 'Of course, it should have been sung by a woman.'

Streetpoet continued to pluck out the tune. 'Is that it,' he asked. 'I was just getting the hang of it as well.' He added his own verse in his lighter voice:

> Hie this boy home,
> Away from the pain and disease,
> Away from the throat-ripping trees,
> Where bodies are hung, and the flies
> Circle about savaged eyes:
> Hie this boy home, sweet please.

There was a silence after he had finished. Only the sharp tapping of the horses' hooves and the background rush of the Falls could be heard as the travellers tried to forget Streetpoet's song.

'You have a dark mind, musician,' said Consatiné at last.

'It is a dark night,' replied Streetpoet. 'And a dark world.'

They reached the long stone bridge that crossed the Khalin and led them into Mornet. If the Falls are one of the wonders of the natural world, then the bridge must be one of the great man-made wonders. It stretches over a thousand strides, stepping in narrow arches across the shiny exposed rocks where the Khalin pours from the pool after the Falls. Khayrik looked ahead beyond the bridge. Mornet was a great pinnacled darkness flecked with lights from high windows. The hill on which it stood was separated from the mountains of Northreach that reared up behind it by a wide valley, but from where they were it was impossible to tell that: town merged into mountain and the windows were like caves, the towers like crags. They clattered on to the stone flags of the bridge. He listened to the river running beneath, and noted that its character had changed from the playful violence of the river that flowed through Northreach, as though the drop into the Khalinrift had taught it caution.

Thinking about Khalinrift made Khayrik look left. The darkness concealed the desert: all he could see was a long flat stretch of something that was white in the night, rolling away to an indistinct horizon, and broken by curiously formed rocks that threw short harsh shadows.

The drawbridge which isolated the bridge from the town was lowered, and as they approached they could see the silhouette of the portcullis blocking the lighted archway which was their destination. As they watched the portcullis was raised, noisily, heavily, slowly, and then, with a brief thunder of horseshoes on wood as they passed over the drawbridge, they had entered the city.

Lara and Ormaas looked around with wonder in their faces. Levafoln and Toothaas were small towns like Fenras: the situation of each was different, but the scale and layout much the same. Mornet was a revelation to them, a huge winding town of narrow anxious streets huddled about the wooded hill of the Ranbrunsvag, the castle of the House of Ra, which dominated the area. Although Mornet is considered to be part of Northreach – it is the administrational centre of the province – its isolated position beyond the mountains has given it a unique character which is neither of Northreach nor of the south. On the river front are great docks, where brightly painted barges are loaded and unloaded, and where a line of crookedly roofed warehouses force a break in the city walls; crowding the hillsides and occupying every available piece of land are tiny houses, often built quite literally on top of one another, and piling up towards the sheer cliffs at the foot of the Ranbrunsvag. From here the eye is drawn higher still, to a dense mass of pine trees, black that night as the companions looked, and then, proud of the trees, the dark towers of the castle itself. Consatiné and the guards led them through tortuous pathways and narrow squares, past fountains and basilicas, beneath carved decorative arches and huddled, over-hanging houses, and upwards towards the castle. They mar-velled at how the buildings seemed to fight for space, how their extensions vied and conflicted, how even the open spaces contained wooden lean-tos and canvas-roofed huts. It was, Lara realised, like a forest where everything grows towards the light, and it had an undergrowth of shanties from which the trunks of the houses fought for space. Then suddenly the buildings stopped, and they were clear and looking down on a mass of confused roofs while their path curved before them up a cliff. They continued upwards, circling right around the castle in a wide spiral that took them at last to another great gate.

Ahead of them was a stone keep, but they did not go towards it. Instead, Consatiné led them through the gate. They entered a bailey laid out as a garden, with symmetrical beds of shrubs and wide carriageways that led to a beautiful mansion with large, modern windows, built within the ancient stone walls.

Servants hurried out to take their mounts and lead them away. Until now the companions had simply been concentrating on their climb to the Ranbrunsvag. It had been no more than a continuation of their journey, but now they had arrived they were at something of a loss as to what to do.

Khayrik was helped to the ground before the fine building, and his string of mules led away to the stables at the rear. 'I'll go with them,' he told Lara and Ormaas, but a guard from those who had journeyed out and met them barred his way.

'The Gros will want to speak with you all,' he said. 'He's waiting in the library.'

Consatiné nodded to the companions, who shrugged but allowed themselves to be led into the house. Panelled wood doors admitted them into a domed hall. The walls were of stone, trimmed with grey marble; the floor was of marble of white and of black. Two flights of stairs curved gracefully away from one another, only to meet again at a landing two storeys higher. It was up one of these that they were led.

Halfway up there was a flat landing with a doorway leading off. The door was opened and they were led through. Ormaas took a last look back over the wrought-iron balustrade at the hall below, and then found himself in a wide corridor. A miscellaneous assortment of chairs suggested that they should wait, which they did, the Vaine of Mornet sitting with the rest of them. The soldier who had been leading them knocked delicately on a door that led from this corridor, and a gruff voice from within instructed him to enter. He did, closing the door behind him, and then returned a moment later to herd the others through the door.

They were in the library. The room was oppressive with dark leather books; soft and weighty hangings in pale green velvet all but obscured the windows; there was a large carved fireplace, ornate against one wall, which threw its brilliant light on to the spines of the books and made them orange. In the centre of the room, on a rug of dark green and gold, a desk crouched on intricately turned legs, like some stalking beast; on its top was a clutter of maps, letters and lists. Next to this desk was a globe representing the skull of Hrakar, subdivided like Va'alastar's, but four times the size and coloured in browns and blues. The lipless mouth grimaced in profile as they walked in and registered the room.

Next to the globe, with one hand resting on the mapped cranium, was a small grey-haired man in half-armour, with a heavy moustache and a tightly clipped, pointed beard. His hand covered that part of the skull which was Cythroné. As the companions entered he spun the globe in its wooden frame: the hollow eyes of Hrakar came to rest on Lara's face.

'Where is Gipethan?' asked the grey-haired man abruptly.

'I have not seen him father,' replied Consatiné. Ormaas had thought it was a geography question, something to do with that large and sinister globe. Consatiné continued. 'We were met by Clonthel here.' He indicated the commander of the guard who had met them by Mording's brook. The grey-haired man, who was apparently the Gros of Ra, nodded once at Clonthel.

'Did you see any evidence of the sort of Agaskan activity we've been hearing reports about?'

'No, your Grosarch,' replied the soldier, truthfully.

'I thought not. See one Agaska and they think they've seen an army, some folk. Well, what have you got to say for yourself, young man,' he said, turning on Consatiné. 'You were due back from Levafoln two days ago. Get lost?' There was something snide in the Ra-Lord's tone, but Consatiné's voice was nothing if not dutiful when he replied.

'We were delayed by Agaskan.'

'Agaskan? You too. My, my, it's becoming an epidemic.' The Ra-Lord laughed explosively, and then began to cough. Water reddened and moistened his eyes. Consatiné waited patiently.

'A large army of them passed Levafoln,' he said, when the coughs had turned back into chuckles. Lara could not see what was so funny, but said nothing. Consatiné continued to tell his tale.

'So why didn't Clonthel see these Agaskan?' asked the Ra-Lord.

'He wasn't in the right place, sir.'

'Hmm. You're exaggerating as usual. Any Agaskan rising I'd know about for certain.'

'Why?' Streetpoet's simple question was comic in its innocence.

'Why?' blustered the Gros of Ra. 'Why? Because I am the Ra-Lord. I am the Governor of Northreach. Things don't happen in Northreach without me knowing. I make things happen in Northreach.'

'Oh.'

A knock on the door saved them from further conversation. Consatiné smiled gratefully at Streetpoet; Streetpoet winked back. The newcomer was speaking as he entered the room. 'Ra-Lord, it's true. A huge Agaskan army moving south-east along the mountains between here and the Heront.'

The Ra-Lord looked first annoyed and then secure. 'Thank you, Gipethan,' he said smoothly. 'I have already been informed. My son has told me.' Khayrik laughed softly: the Ra-Lord shot him a venomous stare. 'Now we must make our preparations. When will they attack Mornet?'

'I'm not sure they will attack, sir.' Like his lord, the soldier was wearing half-armour. 'They appear to be marching around Mornet.'

'A ruse,' said the Gros. 'Where else is there to attack?' A reasonable question drawn from a false premise, thought Khayrik. The soldier simply shook his head. 'Exactly. Well, the first thing to do is raise the full militia. I need someone to lead the cavalry too, now that Hyoprad is too old.' The Vaine of Mornet coughed to attract his father's attention. The Gros eyed him speculatively, and then smiled wickedly. 'Oh no, not you my boy. You're going to accompany your mother to Cythroné. I don't want her here when the Agaskan lay siege.'

'I would rather stay here and fight, sir.'

'And I'm ordering you to get out of my sight,' roared the Ra-Lord unexpectedly. 'Now. And don't come back until you have arranged a boat. Understand?'

There was a long pause. 'Yes sir.'

Consatiné awoke, late, to a cold grey day. A persistent rain made even the lovely gardens of his father's mansion appear bleak and miserable. The bushes were wraiths marching nowhere; the few early flowers of the year mere baubles, impotent against the bitter day. A manservant held a towel and bowl out to the Vaine, and he washed and then was shaved. He felt better, but the day remained as empty as before.

He had forgotten about his guests, and was surprised when he was greeted at breakfast by six faces. They stood as he entered the breakfast room: the musician, the pretty girl and her cousin, the cripple, the penniless trader, and his mother. For a while his mother chattered on about what she intended to do when she got to Cythroné, and the others listened in respectful boredom, but then the Lady Ra left, and there was a pregnant silence accompanied by a certain amount of significant glances and nudging elbows. At length the girl stood. 'I hope you won't feel this is rude, and honestly we're only trying to help, but, well, we'd like you to know that we're going to Cythroné, and if you'd like to travel with us you'd be very welcome.'

Consatiné looked around the table. Only Blavni, the pedlar, seemed surprised at the girl's words, and he was staying in Mornet anyway. The others all waited expectantly for his answer. 'I see. This is a conspiracy. Well, yes, I'd be delighted. When do you want to leave?'

'As soon as possible.' It was the cripple who replied. 'We hope to find a boat.'

'We must go down to the docks this morning. There will be many people wanting to leave Mornet once news of the rising gets abroad.'

In comfortable silence they waited for Consatiné to finish his breakfast.

'It was Lara's idea,' said Ormaas, as he and Consatiné rode through the city and towards the docks. 'We all felt that you'd been treated unfairly, and, well, we wanted to help somehow.'

'It was very good of you.' Consatiné was genuinely touched. He met few people of his own age, and felt grateful to have friends again. The last friends he had known had been at college in Cythroné.

They rode on. Despite the friendly feelings inside the Vaine, he was sorry to be leaving Mornet. It was only three moons back that he had arrived, after two years in Cythroné, to find his father as irascible and his mother as carefree as ever.

They rode out through the main gate, but instead of crossing back across the bridge they went down a path towards the docks. Consatiné drew Ormaas's attention to this. 'Look. An attacking army doesn't even need to go through the main gate any more: it can go round it. This road, joining the gate to the docks, was here years ago, but since they pulled down the wall behind the docks it isn't really necessary. Pulling down that bit of wall was dangerous enough, but leaving an undefended flank vulnerable from here, which is where attack is most likely to come from, is suicidal.'

'Why isn't anything done?'

'Oh, it probably will be. When it's too late.'

They reached the riverfront. As Consatiné had said, behind the docks the walls had been knocked down, presumably to make trade easier. Ormaas could see that the journey through the main gate would be awkward, and wondered why Consatiné had taken him that way. As a form of protest, he decided; in fact it was from habit, as the walls had still been standing when last Consatiné had journeyed down to the river.

All along the riverfront was activity. Boats were being prepared for the journey south. Some were being pushed bodily from the dry docks where they had been beached over the winter into the river; some were being loaded, painted or trimmed; one or two were already leaving, and voices called out their goodbyes across widening stretches of water.

They reached the office of the High Rivermaster of Mornet. Ormaas said he would hold the horses while Consatiné would do the negotiating. The horses both belonged to the Vaine: Ormaas thought them beautiful, and stroked and fêted them all the time Consatiné was away.

Consatiné walked in. The office did not do justice to the High Rivermaster's title, being little more than a shed on the wharf. Light and cold draughts entered the room through gaps in the door. The whole thing was erected against the side of a large circular grain store.

'Yes?' The interior was dark. The High Rivermaster looked

up to see his visitor silhouetted in the doorway. 'Shut the door behind you,' he growled. A brazier burnt unenthusiastically in a corner of the room, giving off a faint redness. In this glow Consatiné could see a lined and intelligent face with a heavy nose and cracked lips.

'I was wondering if you could help me?'

'Might do. Who are you? What do you want?'

'I am Consatiné-vaine-Mornet, son to the Gros of Ra.'

'Are you now.' It was a statement, not a question. 'And how might I be able to help such an exalted personage as yourself, your Vaineship.' There was no mistaking the irony in the voice, but Consatiné chose to ignore it. The Rivermasters' cartel dominated trade on the Khalin, and they were fond of claiming their independence from any noble patronage or loyalty.

'Are there any boats going south?' asked Consatiné.

The heavy folds of flesh formed vertical instead of horizontal lines: it might have been a smile. 'Yes.'

'Good.' Consatiné had been worried by the boats he had seen leaving. 'We'd like to hire one on a bow-to-stern arrangement,' he continued, referring to the usual method by which the nobility hired boats—bow-to-stern, rather than hiring just a part as poorer people did.

'Would you really?'

'Of course.'

'Well, well, well. So the House of Ra is deserting before the first blow is struck. Very encouraging for the rest of us.'

'I would gladly stay,' said Consatiné, with some heat. 'My father has ordered me south to accompany my mother.'

'You'd gladly stay would you? That's good, because you're going to have to. I haven't any boats.'

'You just said you had.'

'I simply said they were going south. I didn't say whether there was any room on them. You can't have a boat, I'm afraid.' The flaps of broad flesh became even more pronounced as the High Rivermaster broadened his smile. Consatiné glared at him.

'I see. You will not, of course, receive any further trade from the House of Ra,' he said as he stood, picking up his gloves.

'Don't be daft. We don't need him, but he needs us. How are you going to get all them little luxuries you're so fond of in the castle if we don't supply them, eh? And if you're thinking of setting your troops on us, think again. If I wanted I could stop trade on this river dead, and then where would you be, you and your pompous little dad and your spoilt fat mum. I'll tell you where you'd be . . .'

But Consatiné had already gone. The unexpected light of the sun on the river almost blinded him, and as he blinked he felt tears squeeze through his lashes. The tears felt like weakness; he cursed the sun for making them, and the Rivermaster for making him want to hide them. Brusquely he returned to his horse and mounted it. Ormaas did not need to ask: the set of the Vaine's face said enough.

It was an unsavoury inn next to the open sewer they call the Bilkok Road. Consatiné stepped in. They seemed to be expecting him, for he was shown immediately to a dark booth at the end of a dingy room.

'The Vaine of Mornet? Good. I am Prothal, a merchant of the Rift. I believe I can be of some service to you, at a price of course.'

'You are taking a caravan across the Rift, I believe?'

'Soon, very soon.' The merchant was virtually bald. A few grey hairs sheltered around his ears; one or two braver ones clung ineffectually to a liver-spotted brown scalp. One eye was hidden behind a red patch, whilst the other looked at Consatiné alertly.

'How soon?' Consatiné was eager.

'When do you want to leave?'

'As soon as possible. Tomorrow? The next day?'

'It can be arranged.' The strong brown eye turned from Consatiné to the abacus on the table in front of him. Coloured beads clicked mysteriously from one end of the frame to the other. 'It will be expensive, but it can be arranged.'

'How much?'

'Sixty bitterns in gold. And in advance.'

Consatiné was relieved. That was less than he had expected. He said so.

'Of course, that is only for the inconvenience of leaving so soon. Unfinished business, you understand. I simply aim to reimburse myself for my losses. Then there is the usual rate for conducting people across the Rift. Another sixty bitterns.'

Consatiné looked aghast. Why do I always conduct these interviews in dark places, he thought inconsequentially, as the sum materialised in his head: six thousand talents!

'How many are there in your party? No, I can answer that. Yourself, your mother, two fur-traders from Fenras, currently staying with you, their two servants . . . And who else. How many soldiers will you have? How many servants?'

'My mother will have two handmaids. My father says he can spare us no soldiers.'

'No soldiers? I am afraid then I shall have to raise the price again, just a bit, to cover the cost of hiring my own guards.'

'You can't,' said Consatiné. 'I shan't pay.'

'Don't,' said Prothal One-Eye, carelessly pushing all the beads on his abacus back to where they began. 'If you can find someone else to take you across the Rift, be my guest. Or perhaps you were thinking of going on your own?'

Consatiné admitted defeat. 'How much more?' he asked.

'Ten bitterns,' replied the merchant. The beads spun across the frame again. 'And then we'll need guides, and food, and horses . . . '

Chapter 6

The Gros of Weir

The Gyr Orland, heir to the throne of Khalindaine, climbed to the head of the flight of steps which led from the exquisite gardens to the palace doors. Ahead of him, stopping every so often to smile encouragement, was a pretty serving girl. When he reached the wide terrace that ran the full length of his palace he stopped, leaning on the stone balustrade, and tried to get his breath back. Although he was only thirty years of age he was running steadily to fat, which was the only running he ever did. The girl remained tantalisingly out of reach. 'Just a kiss,' he panted. 'Nobody's hurt by a kiss.'

He had exchanged his health for fine food and wine, and only rarely did he regret the exchange; this was one of those occasions. 'That's as maybe,' she was saying, whilst he tried to shake off the sensation that he was trying to breathe under water. 'But you're never going to make an honest woman of me, I know that, are you?'

'I might, if you'd let me make a dishonest one of you first.'

'You are a one,' she laughed, nimbly avoiding his next lunge. 'What if the Lady Orland comes looking for you at this minute? What then?'

'A good question.' They both jumped at the new voice: the Gyr put his hands behind his back like a man hiding a weapon and began to whistle innocently; the girl blushed and giggled stealthily, until the Gyr suddenly relaxed.

'Oh, it's you brother. You made me jump.'

The Gros of Weir smiled his way from behind a pillar and on to the terrace. 'I intended to. Who is your pretty friend?'

The girl looked away from the Gros as he approached, and blushed. She blushed all the more when he rubbed his fingers down the line of her waist, as though approving the curves. The Gyr, who had been trying without success to get so close since he'd first employed the girl six days ago, looked at his brother furiously. 'Time you went,' said the Weir-Lord to her, and slapped her on the buttock as she started off.

'What do you want?' asked the Gyr Orland, resignedly.

'A quiet word. I take it we can talk privately here. You do your wooing here after all. Have you heard the rumours?'

'What rumours?'

'They say the empress is ill. The town is alive with talk. Some say that she is dying.'

The Gyr nodded. 'I have heard this. Surely you haven't come all the way here to Maldroigt to tell me that?'

'There's more. They say – they say she is talking about the bastard.'

'Is this true?'

'I don't know whether it is true that she's speaking of the bastard. I do know that everyone else is.'

The Gyr digested this. 'What are we going to do?'

'Kill the bastard?' hazarded the Gros of Weir.

'Easier said than done. I haven't heard a word from that man Hedch we sent to Northreach to find the bastard. He could have been eaten by wolves for all I know.'

'Not that man; he wasn't the type. Not enough flesh, for one thing,' he added, eyeing his elder brother's considerable paunch. 'Talking of which, you're putting on weight. A good idea that.'

'Why?'

'The people like their rulers to be fat. They look less dangerous that way. And if what I hear around the court is true, you'll be emperor within the year. If the bastard isn't, of course.'

'I should have told Hedch to kill anyone who fitted the description, instead of inviting the bastard down here.'

'Hedch wouldn't have done it. It was one thing to ask him to ask for the adopted son of any fur-trader; quite another to ask him to kill the lad in cold blood. He wasn't the type.'

'We should have sent somebody else then.'

'Nobody else could have done the job. He's quiet, but he's effective, is Hedch. Once he's agreed to something, he does it. I've used him once or twice before on delicate commissions.'

'You think he'll find the bastard then?'

'Certain to.'

'Good.' There was a silence between them, as they both thought about the bastard that was their half-brother, product of the passion between their father, Ravenspur, and his cousin, the present empress. The only proof of the bastard's existence was a note – long since destroyed – that they had found when dealing with their father's possessions after his death. It was from the empress. 'Our child is safe. He is with the Fur Trader in Northreach, and even the father does not know his true identity. Let it stay that way. Your darling, Elsban.'

'We must decide what to do,' said the Gros of Weir. 'Apart from anything else, if these rumours continue to fly you're going to lose credit in the city. How much do you owe?'

'I don't know.'

'Menketh! Is it as much as that?'

The Gros of Weir rode slowly back to Cythroné from his brother's estates at Maldroigt. The palace disappeared behind the trees. He was mumbling to himself incredulously: 'Doesn't know how much he owes. My own brother and he doesn't know how much he owes. He's a fool, my brother, an absolute fool. Menketh knows what sort of a mess he'll make of the government, when he can't even manage his own finances.'

And thus were the seeds of treachery sown.

'Economics,' he said, later that same day, whilst his new man-servant poured him a bath. 'That's the motivating force these days; that's what keeps the empire going. It isn't heroism or honour that holds us together nowadays, you know; it's trade, and money, and mutual dependence.' The manservant agreed dutifully; the Weir-Lord recognised he wasn't convinced. 'Do you want proof? Look out of the window. Look at Cythroné: it's doubled in size in the last twenty years, and the only reason for that is the power of money. Money makes people do things. Money makes things happen. You, where are you from?'

'I'm a Plainsman of Myr, your Grosarch.'

'Exactly. And what brought you to Cythroné. I'll tell you what. Money, nothing else.'

But Cluny, the manservant, testing the water with his elbow, knew that for him at least the attractions of Cythroné had been the old-fashioned ones: adventure and honour and love.

That night Cluny and his master dined out. The manservants stood in a ring behind the table as their masters ate, and poured wine or carved meat for them as required. The Weir-Lord ate and drank sparingly, and Cluny's duties were not arduous. He therefore had the chance to listen to the conversation that animated the table.

The Weir-Lord was, hardly surprisingly, dismissing the rumours about the bastard. 'Come now, you hardly believe that old tale do you? If there is a bastard, why is there no proof? Where is he? Why doesn't he come to Cythroné now and proclaim himself whilst Elsban can still identify him?'

'Perhaps he still doesn't know who he is?' suggested a dark-bearded merchant.

'In that case he's certainly no threat,' said the Weir-Lord smoothly.

'My dear Gros of Weir,' said their host, the Vaine of Alkal-Ka-Yran. 'You can hardly expect us to take any notice of your protests. You have an interest in the bastard, I believe.'

'Hear, hear,' echoed around the table.

The Weir-Lord, however, was as urbane as before. 'My dear Alkal-Ka-Yran,' he said, eyes wide with innocence. 'Why on earth should it matter to me which of my brothers takes the throne?'

Laughter trilled and rumbled about the table. 'Well said,' congratulated the bearded merchant. 'Well said.'

The Vaine of Alkal-Ka-Yran was not to be so easily satisfied. 'You are not expecting us, I hope, to believe that you are indifferent about the identity of our next emperor.'

'Not at all. Like all of us here, I recognise that the empire is rooted in trade; like all of us here, I would hope for an emperor who recognised that too.'

'Do you really believe that this anonymous bastard – if he exists – would understand the workings of the Khalindaine economy?'

'Do you really believe my brother understands it? I don't.'

As they travelled back by coach the Weir-Lord questioned

Cluny about the evening. 'More interesting than working for dreary old Halfyndruth, eh? Here you are where the real power lies. Halfyndruth's just an old courtier: he may dine with the empress but my friends and I could buy him out fifty times. Couldn't you tell the difference: the air at Alkal-Ka-Yran's is vibrant with power, whereas the air at the court is as stale as last month's cheese. And didn't you find the conversation interesting?'

'Yes sir,' said Cluny.

'You sound dubious. Perhaps you'd rather go back to that old fool Halfyndruth – if he'd have you back after that affair with the royal horse.'

'No sir, it wasn't that. It was just, well, you didn't sound very loyal to your brother, that was all.'

'And you believe we should be loyal to our brothers, is that it Cluny?' The Gros of Weir arched his eyebrows in mock inquiry, and then his handsome face broke into a grin. 'Well?'

'Well – yes, sir.'

'And I'm sure you are right,' said the Weir-Lord. 'But there are loyalties which must come above even family loyalties. Loyalties to the state, for instance. And I'm afraid my brother really would make a lousy emperor.'

'Oh,' said Cluny. Suddenly he understood.

The days passed. Cluny and his master visited many people of influence and wealth, and each time Cluny noted the delicately barbed insult, sometimes so subtle that it barely disturbed the refined Cythron air, and sometimes so blatant that it provoked guffaws, that the Gros made about his brother's financial prowess. He remembered their visit to the Gros of Treslan's luxurious towered town house, and the lovely Lady Treslan who smiled so knowingly at the Weir-Lord; he remembered dinner at the merchant Jyanwos's house, where even the servants had been fed off gold plates; he remembered the formal dinner of the Company of Spice Traders, where the speeches had all been in honour of the Weir-Lord's foresight, unusual in one so young, in investing heavily in commerce rather than frittering his fortune away on pleasures. Most of all though, Cluny remembered a cold spring afternoon on the banks of the Carpaccio, watching its light grey waters be absorbed by the duller brown of the River Khalin. A large boat from an exotic land moored near them; they watched the scurry of sailors telling on the sail sheets, the daring topmen clambering about the rigging, and the confident proud captain instructing them from the deck. The galleon put out a tender to the quay, and a group of merchants climbed into the small boat to be carried out to the ship.

The Gros of Weir turned to face Cluny. 'I should like such a ship,' he said.

'I thought you'd got one, sir?'

'Not to own, to command.' The Weir-Lord closed his eyes and sailed away in his imagination. 'Imagine: distant shores, where white beaches are backed by tall trees, and where gold can be found on the beach. Imagine: sailing through the mysterious Full Sea, where sea serpents rear from the weed. Imagine: storms in the night, the ship tumbling and tossing like a cork on the waves, the frantic yells of the seamen as they cling to the rigging, the wet spray of the waves clutching at the boat as if they want to grab it for their own.' The Weir-Lord stopped, as if to savour his thoughts. 'Imagine.'

'If you were emperor you wouldn't be able to go to sea,' pointed out Cluny. He always felt guilty about his master's ambition, which the Weir-Lord knew and enjoyed.

'Why not? A sea-faring emperor. That would be something. A navigator, piloting his kingdom through the rocks of state, or words to that effect. However, any slim chance of me inheriting' – he always spoke carefully, as though the crown were the last thought in his mind, when they were in public – 'must be thinner still now. My brother, Menketh bless and preserve him, is in the process of getting himself a divorce. Apparently there was some slight irregularity about the marriage – at least, the Order of the Green Dawn say so, and they should know, as my exalted brother is their Grand Master.' The Gros suddenly started walking rapidly along the riverbank towards the new Bourse, where the stocks and shares of the empire's traders were exchanged. 'Come on, let's see what the market's doing.

'What was I talking about? Oh yes, the divorce. Anyway, he'll doubtless get it, even though his wife's brother is Grand Master of the Order of the Twin Stars. My dear sister-in-law, Marle, couldn't say boo to a goose; she's hardly likely to put up a fight over this. Which is unfortunate, because one thing you could guarantee about Marle was that she wasn't going to be producing litters all over the place. It must be her that can't have children – my brother has produced hundreds. But it's all over now: new wife, new heirs, and no more chance of the crown for the Gros of Weir. A pity.'

They climbed up the elegant marble stairs of the Bourse. 'Personally, I suspect it would be a disaster if ever my brother did become emperor,' he continued. Cluny noticed that his voice was suddenly louder. 'Politically he would be walked over by bad advisers; economically, he would always go for the cheapest and easiest way out, and let the consequences go hang. I can see him now, debasing the coinage and raising taxation, to raise more money, which would only go to cover the fact that he can't manage his own affairs.'

The Weir-Lord's remark caught the ear of a passing merchant, as it was meant to. A florid gentleman in half-breeches, wearing a rich glossy fur jerkin and with a gold chain about his neck, came up to them. Cluny recognised him as Adel-vaine-Belkh, one of the richest and most responsible merchants on the Bourse. 'I beg your pardon,' said the Vaine. 'I couldn't help but overhear you, Weir-Lord, as you walked by. I hope I didn't hear you speak of debasing the coinage?'

'Nothing will happen immediately,' said the Gros, as though he were speaking of a confirmed fact. 'I was simply speculating on the likely effects of my brother's succession. A marvellous man in many ways, my brother, but no financier. He can't even manage his own affairs. I hope he doesn't owe you anything?'

'A trifle. No more than sixty thousand talents.'

'Exactly. You see how it is. He borrows a little here, a little there. Sixty thousand from you, a hundred thousand from me, and a rubek from his gardener. And now he is suing for a divorce – well, we all know how expensive justice has become. He'll be ruined in a year unless – Menketh forfend – Our Lady dies in the meantime.'

'His finances are so precarious?'

'They are appalling. But still, I shouldn't be talking here like this: it isn't fair on my poor brother. Is there security on the loan you made him?'

'No, but surely the Gyr Orland ... '

'Everything he owns is mortgaged to the hilt, and then mortgaged again.'

'I am horrified.'

'So will many others be when he collapses. For myself, I intend to extricate myself as soon as possible; there are some things thicker than blood, you know.'

'Exactly, exactly,' said the Vaine, who would gladly have sold his entire family for a loss if only he could get rid of them. 'Well, I must be going. So nice to have met you like this. Give my best regards to the Gyr when you see him.'

'I'll be seeing him tomorrow.'

'Tomorrow.' Like a card player arranging his cards. Adel-vaine-Belkh arranged this piece of information and worked out its value. He smiled internally; externally he remained the same. 'Thank you, my lord. I will no doubt see you again in the near future.'

'No doubt. Goodbye.'

'Goodbye.

The Vaine of Belkh left them: the Weir-Lord hurried Cluny away into a quiet part of the Bourse's great modern portico. He was smothering his laughter only with difficulty, and when they reached the privacy of the shadows it all poured out in silent chuckles that were almost sobs. 'Well Cluny? Well?' he said, with tears rolling out of his eyes. 'Do you see what I have done?'

'You've lent the Gyr Orland some money?' tried Cluny, and his lord burst into new fits of laughter. The laughter was contagious; Cluny found himself giggling too.

'No, you imbecile. But if Adel thinks I'm recalling my loan tomorrow, you can bet your last rubek he'll recall his today.'

'But the Gyr'll be ruined, sir,' laughed Cluny.

'I'm afraid not. His situation isn't quite as bad as I made out. But he will be acutely embarrassed. And do you know what he does when he's acutely embarrassed?' Cluny shook his head. 'He comes to visit me.'

Like schoolboys over a dirty joke, they chuckled in their corner, and then, settling down but still smiling, they set about the day's trading in the Bourse.

There was a furious ringing at the door. A servant let the Gyr Orland in. 'Is your master at home?' asked the noble.

'I believe so, sir.'

'Good. Tell him his brother has come to visit him.'

'Sir.' The servant withdrew, and the Gyr paced up and down the hall until he returned. 'This way, sir.' He was led up a flight of stairs that curved around the modestly sumptuous walls of the hall.

At the top of the stairs they were met by a pleasant-faced young manservant. 'The Weir-Lord will see you now, your Gyrarch.'

'Good,' said the Gyr, and was admitted into a darkened study. He saw his brother raise himself from a low chair and bow once, formally. The Gros of Weir wore a long silk gown, foreign work obviously, which bore a design of green leaves entwining on gold. The gown bent and straightened with the bow.

'What a surprise,' said the Gros, avoiding Cluny's eyes. 'To what do I owe the pleasure of this visit?'

'Sit down and be quiet,' returned the Gyr Orland. 'You must have heard. It's your lot that have done this to me.'

'My lot? Done what? What do you mean?'

'I mean that today I've been visited by the Vaine of Belkh, who has calmly handed me notice on an unsecured loan of sixty thousand talents and given me until tomorrow to raise it.'

'I wonder why. It must be this talk of a divorce: everyone knows how frightfully expensive divorces are, and as Marle is sister to the Grand Master of the Order of the Twin Stars, I expect people think that it'll be a long case.'

'Nonsense. Marle couldn't fight me; she wouldn't.'

'I believe you, of course, and Cluny here does too I'm sure, but I doubt you would persuade Adel-vaine-Belkh so easily. You have to look at it from a merchant's point of view. He has two good reasons for not wanting you to get a divorce. First, it will cost you a lot of money, and still will even if she doesn't contest. And, secondly, it will put you out of favour with the populace, because they don't like divorced men, and that would mean the chance of some pretender getting support would be increased . . . '

'You think so?'

'I'm certain of it. Anyway, you try looking at it from the merchants' point of view: it all becomes perfectly understandable.'

'No divorce?'

'It isn't a good idea. Not unless you want the whole of your debts called in like Adel's.'

'She's such a pretty girl, but she won't sleep with a married man she says.'

'Have I met her? Oh yes, I remember. Yes, very pretty, but is she worth an empire?' The Gros of Weir dismissed the subject. 'Cluny, pour us a drink apiece. The fortified wine, if you please.'

Cluny poured from a crystal decanter into a pair of crystal goblets. A drop of the rich red splashed on to his hand and he licked it off. 'What about the bastard? Any news?'

'Nothing. There's been no news from Northreach since before the winter.'

'Perhaps the thaw is late. Oh well, we'll just have to do something to raise your popularity here, and sort the bastard out when the time comes. How about a military campaign against the Agaskan?'

'I'd rather not.'

'You won't have to do anything, except wait for the empress to die.' Cluny almost gasped at this heresy. The Gyr Orland seemed, however, impressed; he nodded thoughtfully. 'A big campaign will give you an army, which will also be insurance should any pretender to the throne appear. All in all, the more I think about it, the harder it will be for you without an army. No, this is the perfect plan.'

'What will I do for money? Can you lend me some?'

'I have none, but I'll raise some, I'm sure. My credit is still good.'

And with that the Gyr had to be satisfied. The Gros reclined further into a chair, drew a white lace handkerchief from his sleeve, and draped it over his face.

'Well, I'll be leaving you then,' said the Gyr, without either enthusiasm or confidence to support him; he withdrew awkwardly.

The Weir-Lord waited until the sound of his brother's boots on the stair carpet was replaced by the sound of those boots on the floor of the hall, and then raised a corner of the handkerchief to grin out at Cluny. 'Were you impressed?' he asked.

'Sir?'

'Were you impressed? No, I see you were not. A shame, for you have witnessed tonight a performance that would delight connoisseurs. Did you appreciate the way I secured my succession by talking him out of the divorce; did you regard the skill with which I plunged him further into debt; did you recognise the true master-stroke of arranging he should write another page in the annals of military incompetence?'

Cluny was not sure that he had noticed any of these things, but he took his master's word for it that something had been achieved; by the time he had drunk, at the Weir-Lord's invitation, his second glass of the fortified wine, Cluny would have believed it if his master had said he could fly.

The public theatre at Frognoi, on the outskirts of Cythroné, is the largest such building in the land. It is squat, circular and, as befits a theatre, is not what it seems. Its grandiose fluted columns are repainted annually; its marble floors are granite slabs faced with painted slate; its silken flags are canvas dyed in shot colours. None the less, even those who mock the theatre for its vanity and its cosmetics have to admit that it always looks good for the Poets' Spoils, the competition to judge which of the season's plays is the best.

Like all such competitions in Cythroné – and anywhere else, for that matter – the Poets' Spoils are not so much about plays as they are about patronage, prestige and privilege. To be accepted as an entry a play has to have the sponsorship of the organisers and the approval of the authorities. This is costly. After having been accepted as sufficiently competent and sufficiently orthodox, then it has to be put on. This is even more expensive. And even then, after the carpenter and the actors and the man who operates the stage devices have all been paid, and the scenery erected, and the coloured flares prepared, if the play is going to win the judges must be bribed. Even the judges agree that the cost of this is exorbitant.

That year, the Gros of Weir had secretly but effectively put a considerable quantity of money behind a new interpretation of the old story of Kythen and Deteth. The story the play told was a familiar one: Akhran the Golden, at the height of his power, is poisoned by his wife, Nathatan, and by Posyx, her lover; Kythen and Deteth, the sons of Akhran, swear to avenge themselves on Nathatan and Posyx; finally, locked in combat, Posyx and Deteth plunge to their deaths in the waters of the River Khalin, whilst Kythen inherits his father's vacant throne.

The Gros of Weir, in his munificence, not only gave Cluny time off to see the opening night of the play, but also paid for his manservant, and even arranged for a girl to accompany him to the theatre; although Cluny knew the story of Kythen and Deteth well, he was not going to complain about this arrangement. They sat in a private box, overlooking the stage from the right, and watched two tumbling acts, a man who made small birds do tricks, and a rather talented man who could play any tune the audience cared to name by tapping his cheeks with his fingers.

Then the stage was cleared, and the leader of the actors stepped forward into the circle of sunlight which defined the playing area. He donned his painted mask, and began the play.

> I, Akhran, victor of the chase
> That coursed the mighty Khalin to the sea,
> Have reached at last my vegetable age,
> My venerable age, my vulnerable age:
> But soft, here comes my wife, my Nathatan.

Nathatan came on stage, followed by their eldest son Deteth. It was at this point the audience realised that something new was happening, for this Deteth was not like any who had gone before. Convention portrays Deteth as handsome and vigorous; this production had him fat, the worse for drink, and unmistakably like the Gyr Orland. Cluny found this very amusing indeed, and kept nudging the girl next to him to tell her so.

Deteth had come on stage eating a mammoth sandwich, thus sparking off an exchange in which the conceit of food was much exploited. 'The food of my ambition is desire,' said Akhran. 'Nothing shall quench my thirst, nor ease the hunger in my belly save your love,' replied his wife. It was obvious that Deteth did not follow very well: first of all he offered his father a bite of his sandwich, and then when that was refused he fetched a tray of sweetmeats.

His father's response was brutal and to the point.

> In every generation there is one
> Whose mind is not full-formed; my eldest son
> Is an idiot – go, get thee gone.

Akhran dashed the tray to the ground and stormed away. Deteth turned to his mother for comfort. 'I thought he was hungry,' he said. His mother smiled behind the mask; her voice purred like a cat's.

> And so he is. Here, take this pretty flask,
> And drop one drop from it into his meal;
> Then he'll be free from hunger ever more.

This proved to be correct when, at the beginning of the next scene, Akhran entered, clutching at his throat and belly, staggered dramatically, and dropped down dead at the feet of his queen.

At once, Posyx entered, and embraced Nathatan passionately. Deteth walked in to return the flask to his mother and explain that he had done as she suggested: he was shocked when he saw his mother and Posyx kissing. 'You're a married woman,' he said. Nathan pointed to the corpse at her feet. 'Not any more I'm not,' she said.

There then followed the compulsory erotic scene between the two lovers; the scene ended with Nathatan and Posyx using Akhran's corpse as their love-bed, a rather macabre detail which one Cythron broadsheet described as 'inspired bad taste', prompting a local preacher of the rather strict Order of the Daln to say that 'When bad taste is inspired, then good taste has expired'. Such is the stuff of which history is made, thought Cluny, when he later read the reports; for the time being, however, his attention was riveted to the stage.

Kythen, played by a dashing young actor, was on stage and soliloquising about life and death in blank verse.

> Life is but the outfit we all wear
> About this bag of bones, for we are blood
> Wrapped with flesh and flaking fading skin;
> Our bones are as a scaffold; our rib-cages
> Are ladders to ascend up to the noose;
> Our hearts are beating drums, their slow tattoo

Announcing death upon that gallows tree
Which is our corporal form. Our only life
Thus leads us to our deaths and our despair.

There is but one thing certain that we know:
The tightening of the noose about the neck,
The stretching, kicking jerk, the body hanged
And hanging up there like a bag of bones.
That drops before us all, as at the start
Of our lives we dropped into this life
By the clumsy act of birth. The midwife
And the hooded hangman are well wed:
We all were engendered in their bed.

Deteth came on and tried to explain what had happened to
their father. Tried to explain, because his understanding of
the implications was far from perfect. Kythen's quick mind
soon grasped the salient points, however, and together they
rushed off stage.

There was an interval. Cluny bought hot chestnuts for
himself and his lady friend, and they washed these down with
watered wine. The play began again.

Kythen and Deteth are standing on stage, listening to the
approaching lovers. The brothers hide; the lovers enter. Polyx
is swearing his love for Nathatan and says he will marry her and
'take care' of her sons. At this Deteth emerges from his hiding
place. Is this where Deteth redeems himself?

Posyx backs away from his mistress's son. Deteth throws
himself at Posyx in an ecstasy of gratitude. 'Thank you for
saying you'll take care of me,' cries the prince, as Posyx takes
one further step backwards, misses his footing, and careers
through an open window taking Deteth with him.

There was an uneasy silence in the theatre, although the
ribald drunks at the front had enjoyed Deteth's demise, and
then the clapping began. When the play resumed all that was
left was the long spectacle of the coronation of Kythen, and the
epilogue in which Kythen tells of his plans for future greatness.

Again there was a pause before the clapping. Audiences are
conservative by nature, and this play had certainly upset their
expectations about the story of Kythen and Deteth; nonetheless, it was well received by those who did not mind mock being

made of ancient mysteries, and whilst it did not receive the Poets' Spoils, it did quite well in the provinces before disappearing from sight as such plays so frequently do.

The Gros of Nanx rode at the head of a column of thirty armoured knights, up the long driveway to the Gyr Orland's palace of Maldroigt. He wore a suit of burnished steel armour which seemed to gather what little light there was in that dull wet day and to fling it violently back, and a crest in the form of a red swan swimming in a stream of blue and white plumes. His visor was up, revealing a face of handsome intensity: a firm mouth above a cleft chin, a trim moustache, a straight nose, and dark eyes. He halted his men before the white façade of the palace and dismounted. Other men might have been impressed or overawed by the dazzling architecture of Maldroigt, with its high walls broken by innumerable windows and arches, and its great roof richly embellished with domes and spires, turrets and dormers, and tall and fantastic chimneys; the Gros of Nanx did not even notice this splendour. He climbed the marble steps that led to the main door, waited impatiently as a guard opened the door to admit him, and then paced the hall until the Gyr Orland appeared.

'Your Gyrarch,' said the Gros of Nanx. He had taken his helmet off. 'Permit me to join your army.'

'Why, certainly,' said the Gyr Orland. 'Nice of you to come along.'

'It was not nice,' corrected the handsome Gros. 'It was my duty.'

'Ah, yes. Duty. of course.'

'I am, I believe, the foremost military thinker of my age, as well as being one of the finest warriors in Khalindaine. I do not think it right that my talent should not be used by my empress or her appointed minions.'

'Oh,' said the Gyr Orland, who was neither appointed nor a minion. He explained this to the Gros of Nanx. 'Actually, you know, I'm not appointed particularly: I more wanted to make this a private venture, kill a few Agaskan, get home by Endyear. That sort of thing.'

'What? Have you no ambition?' The Gros strode more furiously than ever about the hall, his armoured heels tapping loudly on the stone floor. 'This is an opportunity for eternal glory, a chance to live in the annals of Cythroné as one of the heroes, the immortals. We need a royal commission, so that we can raise a real army, and a target. We must march on the Thatter.'

'I'd rather we didn't,' muttered the Gyr Orland, but it was too late, for the Gros of Nanx was embarking on a favourite theme – his own glory. With mounting anxiety the Gyr listened to the plans the Gros of Nanx envisaged: a two-pronged attack following the valleys of the east and west branches of the River Elmath would open the Thatter up to them; a cavalry army would be mobilised in Nerith to cut off the danger of counter-attack; eventually the Agaskan would be driven from the Thatter to the Broken Plains or even to the sea. During this monologue the Gros of Nanx let slip two pieces of information which, amongst the mass of words the Nanx-Lord was unleashing, somehow got lost: the first was that he had been sent by the Gros of Weir, who had encouraged him to thus present himself; the second was that he would be billeting his knights in Maldroigt. Thus, it was with some surprise that the Gyr Orland discovered thirty knights in half-armour roistering in his cloisters and being sick on his stairs.

Two days later the Gyr was joined by his brother, who came, he said, for a fraternal visit rather than to fight, and who was therefore allocated a room, according to the Gros of Nanx's system, that was on the wrong side of the palace and already inhabited by a pipe-smoking colonel of the foot from Myr. The stench of the pipe filled the room.

There was much discussion about what should be done. They had amassed an army of some eighteen thousand men, including more than five thousand cavalry: now they needed somewhere to fight. There had been no news from Northreach, of course, which was hardly surprising at the time of year, and all their attention was focused on the Thatter. The Gros of Nanx was all for a major attack; the Gyr Orland felt he would rather not simply march into the Thatter again, and would like to spend some time familiarising himself with the situation. The Gros of Nanx demanded that they should announce themselves as a royal army of Khalindaine, and obtain a royal commission and the right to press troops; the Gyr Orland, whose only aim was popularity, had no desire to do this. Other nobles joined them, confusing the situation further. The Gros of Peltyn, who was a distant cousin to the Gros of Nanx as well as being a fine soldier, arrived on the same day as the Gros of Weir; the Gros of Weir was outraged to learn that the Peltyn-Lord had been given a state-room. The Vaine of Gramal was a day later: he brought not only his experience in the field and a force of eleven hundred armed infantrymen, but also his two vast sons, whose silent strength in the rich corridors and panelled halls of Maldroigt made everyone else feel uncomfortable and inadequate.

Meanwhile, in Northreach, the Agaskan march continued, and not a word leaked out to Cythroné.

The empress lay behind shuttered windows and on her great hard bed. Above her was a wooden canopy. She could not move her head, but by swivelling her eyes she could see the carved pillars which supported the canopy. The pillars were turned to resemble the tall pillars of Cythron antiquity, before Akhran the Golden had swept from the north to impose a new order, and were wrapped with writhing serpents. Festoons of gathered lace and velvet drapes hung from the pillars, bound by thick cords of tasselled gilt. The doctor took one damp flannel from her forehead and replaced it with another, fresher one. She smelt lemon and camphor. She felt him draw back the sheets to reveal her withered body, and the dull numb tug as he removed two bloated leeches from her stomach. There was a ringing sound as he dropped the leeches into a metal bowl, and then he made wide-fingered passes before her eyes with soft pale hands. The hands fingered the air above her face, and she experienced momentary panic. The hands went away, however, and she controlled her fear.

The hands came back, containing a small silver-bound phial. Above the hands was a bald shiny face with heavy eyebrows. It smiled in what it took to be encouragement. The empress, knowing what was coming, tried first of all to indicate to the doctor that she did not want the bottle opening and then, when that failed, she tried not to breathe as it was held beneath her nose. That failed too: she heard the doctor's voice turn from soothing solicitude to a hollow boom, until it was round-edged and awkward like a voice from a well, and then she was asleep. As always after the sleeping draught, she dreamt of leeches.

The Gros of Weir paced the room he had been given in his brother's palace, and cursed the Gros of Nanx. Still, he reasoned, it's my own fault: I invited Nanx here in the first place because I thought he'd make things awkward for my brother; I hadn't appreciated that he'd make things awkward for everyone, that's all.

The Weir-Lord paced back and forth, so far as was possible in the cramped confines of the room. Behind him, Cluny tried both literally and metaphorically to follow his master, as the Gros and his ideas twisted and doubled about the room. 'I must decide on my objective,' he told his manservant. 'That's been the trouble; I haven't known exactly what I've wanted; I've simply tried to make trouble for my brother. Time to reassess.

'First, I want the crown. I want the crown not for myself, you understand, but for the sake of Khalindaine's economy, which simply could not survive my brother's incompetence.

'Therefore, secondly, I want my brother out of the way. That much is fairly clear. But then the question comes: how do I get him out of my way? So far all I've tried to do is discredit him – you didn't know I wrote that play, did you? Thank goodness it didn't win the Poets' Spoils; it would have been so embarrassing. But that doesn't get him out of the way, it simply makes him less popular and less likely to succeed against the bastard. The bastard will be point number three, when I get there. Now, listen carefully Cluny, and tell me what you think. I have by subtle manipulation got my brother to the point where he is leading an army against the Thatter. This is a completely pointless gesture as, so far as anyone can tell, the Agaskan haven't killed so much as a sheep since last time my brother sent an army up there. None the less, it is the sort of gesture that romantic fools such as my brother or the Gros of Nanx believe will make them legends, even though a cynical pragmatist such as myself sees that the likelihood of glory from such an exploit is remote. The question is, do I want to discredit my brother, which would make it easier for me to take the throne but also make it easier for the bastard, should he survive, or would I rather my brother had a successful and, with luck, short career which would keep the bastard out?'

Cluny thought about this. 'I think you should try to keep the bastard out,' he said at last. 'But really, of course, you shouldn't plot to take the throne at all.' They often had this conversation, master's machinations versus manservant's morality.

'Not even for the good of the empire?' asked the Weir-Lord.

'No, sir. Because the empire is best served by the heir to Akhran.'

'But I'd be the heir to Akhran if my brother was out of the way.'

'Yes, sir. But that means removing your brother.'

'Exactly. And what have I been talking about for the past good-Menketh-knows-how-long?'

'But you haven't said how you are going to remove him,' said Cluny. It sounded as if they were talking about a stain, he thought.

'That's irrelevant,' stated the Weir-Lord, but he knew, of course, that it wasn't. In a sense, that was where his whole plot fell down. He could scheme and devise, sending his brother's fortunes up or down on a whim, but he couldn't actually kill his own brother, or even imagine how it could be done. Impatiently, knowing that the manservant had won, the Weir-Lord sent him away, back to the cellared servants' quarters where even manservants were forced to sleep now the palace was full with billeted soldiers.

Cluny opened the door to leave, but his way was blocked by the bluff weight of the Myrian colonel. 'Thank you,' said the colonel, winking inexplicably at the manservant. The omnipresent pipe jutted inanely from layers of dark brown beard and twisted wreaths of rancid smoke about the colonel's ears. It joggled up and down as the man talked, distractingly. The smell coiled its way rapidly to the Gros of Weir's fastidious nostrils; coughing ostentatiously, the latter went to the window and opened it, only to find that the colonel took this as a cue for conversation. Wisely, Cluny slipped away, before the colonel could draw him in on his chat.

'Look over there. You can see my regiment from here. They arrived this morning; naturally I got here first because I came by horse, but they made it too. Good chaps they are. No, not them; those over there in the yellow tabards with the green designs, by the pond.'

'Really?' said the Gros. 'How nice.'

'That's right.' Sarcasm was entirely wasted. 'Can you see that chap in front of the tent, not the one in the felt hat, that's Derbraph Molleswahe; the one next to him with the beard. That's Mendiprex, that is. He's my sergeant-at-arms, now, but he used to be my steward at home. Have I told you about him?'

'Frequently.'

'Good. Then you'll know the situation. So Mendiprex, he's my steward, did I mention that, and a better man as never counted bales of wheat, worked for me for fifteen years, and his wife too, Menketh bless her, and his son too, called Pelgan, and Mendiprex was going into town one day and – hold on, I don't think that Mendiprex's son is called Pelgan, because Pelgan's the name of the son of the miller of Belpenth, which is a really nice place by the way and well worth a visit if you haven't been there already which I know you haven't because you keep telling me you haven't, but if you had you'd have really liked Belpenth, and you'd have met the miller too, which would have been a real coincidence because his boy's ever so like my steward's boy. Have I told you about my steward?'

The Weir-Lord looked at the drop from his window. A man would die if he fell from here, he decided: it's either you or me, my friend; one of us will be out of that window if you don't shut up.

Chapter 7

Khalinrift

When the seas receded they left Khalinrift, a great flat plate of impermeable rock deserted by the waves and scattered with abandoned rocks whose smooth and grotesque shapes witnessed the action first of the sea and then of the wind. Great sand dunes form there: the millennia have eroded away the plate of rock in piling sands and yawning, unexpected craters. The dunes are combed by the wind, until geometric patterns like an antique script ripple across them, and then the wind veers and the dunes rearrange themselves.

On three sides of the Rift there are mountains. North-east lies the snowcapped peaks of Northreach, from whence the mighty Khalin flows into a great seismic flaw which has severed the floor of the Rift; west is blocked by the Taliolan massif; south-east are the ranges of Astesch and High Tor. Only to the south-west, where the Khalin leaves the Rift for the fertile Plains of Myr, are there no mountains.

For a third of the year the Rift is inaccessible, snow-covered, lethal. Violent blizzards scourge it from the mountains to the north; the cold can freeze a man's hand to his sword. For the rest of the year the conditions are very different. The clouds collect on the bordering mountains, the desert sand refracts and reflects the heat, the summer sun scorches the Rift and makes it unbearable. The only water is the Khalin, in its deep inaccessible gorge. The temperature rises, the air loses its moisture, the sand is tossed by the wind: breathing itself becomes a pain. It was across this landscape that Prothal was to lead the companions: they watched its changing contours, so like an ochre sea, from the towers of the Ranbrunsvag, and were afraid. Six tedious days had passed since Consatiné had made his arrangement with the one-eyed merchant. Lara had read more books in those days than she had read in her lifetime before; Streetpoet had got drunk but kept the soldiers entertained; Khayrik had almost felt whole again as he slept in the barracks and ate with the men; Ormaas had explored the castle.

The Ranbrunsvag is the largest castle in Northreach, and one of the largest in Khalindaine. Built atop a volcanic plug, as so many of Northreach's castles are, it consists of two baileys, one of which now serves as a courtyard for the old castle, with its keep and its stables and barracks, the other of which is now the garden of the new mansion. The mansion is built against the outer wall of the bailey, although the original curtain wall has been hollowed out and windows put in. This gives the mansion a southern aspect. It was decorated in the modern way, with wooden panels and plaster mouldings, in contrast to the plain stone hung with tapestries that had been fashionable for the century before: none the less, the room that Ormaas had was hung with tapestries, indicating the low status that room had in the castle. In Northreach, where there were no skilled plaster-workers to decorate in the modern style, such craftsmen had to be imported at great expense from the south; the old keep of the Ranbrunsvag was, at the same time, filled with attractive tapestries which would do for the minor rooms.

Ormaas liked the tapestries. He liked the crudely rendered figures on their disproportionately small horses who rode around his room hacking the heads from stylised Agaskan. He liked the way that each head was either facing forwards or was in profile, and the way that each eye, whichever direction the head pointed towards, was an elongated egg of white blemished by a round black iris. These eyes, all of which stared back at the viewer, made it look to Ormaas as though the galloping men were performing a well-rehearsed dance rather than fighting a battle, for none of them needed to look at what he did.

Sometimes, Ormaas walked out into the gardens. In recent years the defences of the Ranbrunsvag had been given second place to the considerations of luxury and elegance, and the pine woods between the inner and outer curtain walls had been turned into attractive woodland gardens. Small gates, militarily indefensible, let people from the mansion to the woods. It was through these that Ormaas particularly liked to go; it was cool in the woods, as though the pines took what little heat there was in the early-year air and exchanged it for their own dark green coolness. The scratched smell of the pines was cool too, and dark green, and friendly.

Through the trees it was possible to catch glimpses of the ochre Rift. It was curious how the clouds clung to Mornet, and yet how, but a few thousand strides away in the Rift, the sun lent a painful brightness to the sand, and scorched and parched the land. There is something sinister about the Rift, thought Ormaas. Usually he was glad to see the sun, for in Northreach the sun means warmth and good crops, yet overlooking the barren Rift he knew that there was a different, wilder sun out there, a sun that was an enemy.

He was standing amongst the trees when Lara found him and told him that they would be departing the following day. As he left the pines, he kissed his hand and placed the kiss reverently on to the trunk of the last tree. He looked back, but the trees blocked his view and all he could see was the thorny phalanx of the pines and the patched grey sky above. He walked beneath the gate and into the formal garden. The Rift would always be there, channelling the Khalin to the sea.

The southern gates of Mornet were opened, and a string of horses paced out. Many of the horses carried panniers, and were strung together behind a cripple on an adapted saddle. The caravan followed the river south-west, until the crack in the earth, the geological fault which carried the Khalin, cut them off from the waters which tumbled below, and they were isolated on the great Khalinrift plateau, with a pair of mournful buzzards as their only company.

Following the river was no longer possible. The earthquake which had split Khalinrift had thrown up great frenzies of rock which line the canyon in a confused medley of piled stone and drifting sand. Prothal led the caravan due west now, away from the river and into the desolation of the desert. Two scouts went before them, trying to map a route through the changing pattern of dunes. The dunes here were low compared to those they would encounter further in the Rift, yet the scouts had soon gone from sight.

The scouts were both Rhav tribesmen. The homelands of the Rhav are in the foothills of Taliola, and are the only permanent settlements in the Rift; their knowledge of the terrain is unrivalled. Many tribesmen, however, supplement their existence by banditry, and around the Rift the ferocious raids carried out by Rhav on caravans are notorious. Consatiné, knowing full well the Rhav reputation, watched the scouts vanish over the dunes with trepidation, and then spurred his horse forward to join Prothal.

'Weren't those men Rhav tribesmen?'

'They were indeed, my lord. How clever of you to notice; how observant you are, my lord.' Whether Prothal's remarks were intended to flatter or to mock was often difficult to assess: certainly the ochre garments and the brightly coloured turbans of the Rhav made them unique amongst the peoples of Khalindaine.

'Can they be trusted?'

'Here, my lord, they can be trusted. We have many thousands of strides before us until we reach Rhav country, and whilst I confess I would not like to depend upon them too near their homelands, here so near Mornet they are perfectly safe. Their loyalty to their tribes will be great – which is why I have two men from different tribes – but it will not be called upon here.' Prothal One-Eye waved an expansive arm at the horizons. 'After all,' he said, viewing the emptiness. 'Who is there to betray us to?'

Consatiné gave a word of thanks, reared his horse, and rejoined his mother. She was travelling in a litter slung between two docile black mares. The first mare was ridden by one of Prothal's men; the second simply followed on wooden yokes.

'Mother?'

She drew back the lace curtains of her litter, designed to keep out the desert air, and the desert grit. 'Consatiné?' The drawn curtain revealed a plush interior that was mostly cream cushions; despite this, however, the litter was not at all comfortable, and joggled alarmingly at every step the horses took. 'What did Prothal One-Eye say?'

Consatiné told her. 'It seems that they are safe enough.' He eyed the litter cautiously. 'How safe are you?' The litter had been an idea of the Ra-Lord; he had designed it himself when he heard his wife would have to cross the Rift overland. Like its designer, the litter was sophisticated, expensive, awkward and well-padded.

'I'm all right,' she replied. 'I may ride tomorrow though.'

'I'll arrange something,' said Consatiné, solicitously, bending down on his horse to be nearer the level of her litter.

'Thank you, my dear.' The Lady Ra looked at her son as he straightened in the saddle and rode off. He was a good boy, she decided: it was a shame his father had never taken to him, but that was the problem with adopting; the Ra-Lord had been agreeable enough to the suggestion – he knew he would never have natural children of his own – but had then found it impossible to love the child. He found it impossible to love anyone, thought his wife, privately; she smiled to herself in the lurching litter.

The Lady Ra had reached that age where anything new worried her and anything routine bored her. She had been a lady-in-waiting to the young empress when she had married her husband, and it was considered quite a match for the impoverished daughter of a minor court official that she had caught herself a Gros, albeit a Gros with a reputation for being difficult and for being fierce. Then had followed Consatiné, rather too soon after the marriage, but then there hadn't been much choice, and after that she had endured fifteen long years of exile in Mornet. She hated Mornet. She hated its twisting thwarted streets with their twisting thwarted buildings; she hated the constant rain and the desolate view over the Rift; she had even come to hate the sound of the falls. But now she was moving away from Mornet, moving back to Cythroné where she had been born, she was worried about what life away from the Ranbrunsvag would be like.

Behind the handsome horses of the Ra stables was a line of indifferent mounts. Khayrik had traded the mules for horses, who would cope far better with the desert terrain. It was not an exchange he had wanted to make, not least because being strapped to the saddle of a horse is a very different proposition from being strapped to the back of a sober and short mule; nonetheless, he recognised the need for haste when crossing the Rift, and even managed to make a reasonable bargain.

Streetpoet did rather worse. His nag, broken winded and ailing, had been sold for slightly more than it was worth and considerably less than it had cost, to a cheerful man at the knackers' yard; his present horse was borrowed from Ormaas. Eight horses, strung together in a line behind Khayrik, carried the load previously taken by twelve mules; flanking these were the attendants Prothal had engaged for the journey.

Streetpoet had twice worked his way across the Rift, as these men were doing now. He knew the sort of men it attracted, men like him who needed to keep on the move because they could not cope with staying still, and others whose reasons for moving were even more pressing and less savoury. Murderers, robbers, extortionists and runaway husbands were the staple of the caravan teams; looking around him, Streetpoet wondered which of that list they had travelling with them on this journey. He remarked as much to Ormaas, who rode between the minstrel and Lara and tried to make this look accidental.

'Where do they all come from?' asked Ormaas, looking around.

'All over the place. They're people like me and Khayrik: cripples, vagrants, musicians. The scum of the earth. See if you can guess where they're from, and I'll tell you if you're right.'

'He's from Northreach,' said Lara, indicating a tall man who wore a dark fur but no shirt. He had a thick beard and a blackiron skull-cap.

'Good,' said Streetpoet. 'What about him?'

'Lindos,' said Ormaas, guessing wildly to keep himself in the game and the conversation.

'Hardly,' said Streetpoet. 'Your turn Lara.'

'Myr?' It was the only place apart from Cythroné that she could think of outside Northreach.

'No.' Streetpoet laughed. 'You can tell he's not from the north by the colour of his skin: even the Rhav tribesmen who live all their lives in the Rift here aren't as dark as that. So that cuts out both your guesses.'

'Where is he from then?'

'That dark blue head-scarf he wears to protect his neck says that he's from somewhere in Nerith.'

'What about the man with the green cape over there?'

'He's hard to say. Somewhere around the Thatter, I should guess, but I'm only going by the colour of his skin and the way he's split his beard into two plaits. There are lots of other people in the west who do that.'

'I thought only Agaskan lived in the Thatter?' The moment she had said it, Lara regretted having spoken of the Agaskan. But Streetpoet did not notice.

'In the middle, yes, but there are lots of places where people live, on the outskirts.'

'Isn't it dangerous?' asked Ormaas.

'I've never tried it.'

Conversation came to a halt: perhaps they were all thinking about the Agaskan.

'Why do people move about so much?' asked Lara. 'Why doesn't everyone just stay where they were born?'

'You haven't,' said Streetpoet.

'I had a reason to go, though.'

'These people have reasons. I have a reason. People travel because if they didn't they wouldn't get anywhere.'

Lara was not impressed by this axiom. 'All right. Why did you move away from wherever you were born.'

'I was bored.'

'Why don't you go back?'

'It'd still be boring. Besides, they're probably still not there,' he said, ungrammatically, revealing the Northreach roots of his ubiquitous accent.

'Shut up,' said Ormaas, suddenly. They looked at him in surprise.

'What's the matter?' asked Lara. She couldn't make up her mind whether to snap at him or to be considerate: instead she sounded uninterested.

'It doesn't matter,' he said, and then added: 'How do we know we've got a home any more, Lara. It might've been overrun by Agaskan.'

'Let's sing a song,' said Streetpoet, softly. He took his mandola from his back and strummed it gently. 'I hate playing on horseback.' The song began:

> I've got my pack – upon my back.
> I've got my road – and my load.
> I've got a horse – a horse of course.
> I've got my reins – and my brains.
>   I've got these things and a little tin drum,
>   Ho hum, ho hum ho hum ho hum.

The others caught on as he sang the next verse, and by the third they were supplying the first half of the lines while Streetpoet found the rhyme. 'I've got my saddle,' sang Lara; 'It's hard and I waddle,' came the reply. 'I've got my tunic,' said Ormaas, and there was a pause before Streetpoet replied 'Ready for the new nick.' 'I've got my loincloth,' tried Lara, certain that this would fool him, but without hesitation he had added 'Which does for a groin cloth.' They rode on, singing together until dusk.

They travelled sixty thousand strides that day, making excellent time through a fortunate series of lateral valleys between the dunes, and eventually stopping for the night at the foot of a tall narrow rock that stretched into the evening. Under the direction of Prothal and his two lieutenants the outriders swiftly erected six patched tents and started cooking. Lady Ra and her handmaids had one tent, and Lara was invited to join them; Streetpoet, Ormaas, Khayrik and Consatiné had another, with one of the outriders sleeping in with them; the others went to Prothal and his companions. The drab smell of lamb's meat was punctuated by the sharper aromas of spices and herbs, and dinner, when it came, was plentiful and tasty although rather monotonous. Despite the stunning heat of the day the nights in Khalinrift were cold, and Khayrik advised the cousins to wrap themselves carefully in their furs. Consatiné was talking with Streetpoet as the others settled down, persuading him to play a few songs they could sing. 'I love singing,' said Consatiné. 'But my father couldn't stand minstrels.'

'Neither could mine,' said Streetpoet with a grimace, and then he looked sharply at Consatiné. 'You said he couldn't stand minstrels. Why couldn't; why not can't?'

'I don't know. Yes, I do. It's because I'm not going back to him. You've seen how he treats me. He doesn't even like me, much less love me. How old are you?'

Streetpoet was startled by this sudden change of subject. 'Seventeen years old, eighteen years old? Nobody has ever bothered to count.'

'Exactly,' said Consatiné. 'We could be brothers. You see, I'm adopted. I don't know who my real parents are, only that my father and mother aren't the ones. Well, my father isn't anyway. I'm not sure about my mother: she knows more than he does about my past but she talks about it less.'

'Skeletons in the House of Ra?' asked Streetpoet. He reached into his jerkin and pulled out a bottle of clear liquid. 'For medicinal purposes only,' he said as he removed the cork. He took a mouthful, grimaced, swallowed, and then let out his breath with his mouth open, as though he were trying to cool his mouth down.

The harsh smell on his breath caught the Vaine. 'I should think it is for medicinal purposes only.'

'Do you want some?'

'What is it?'

'Orlach.'

'And what's that?'

'Barley wine twice distilled.'

'For Menketh's sake! What does it taste like?'

'You'll have to try some; it isn't easy to describe.'

The Vaine put the bottle to his lips gingerly, swallowed and then gagged, fanning his open mouth with his hand. Streetpoet encouraged him to try some more. Taking a smaller amount this time, the Vaine did as he was bid. This time the burning sensation in his chest and throat seemed more pleasant than painful. He took another swig.

The resting travellers encamped around the fading fire were surprised when, in the dark of the Khalinrift night, the songs began again.

The first day had been enjoyable, the second day acceptable. The third, however, was downright miserable. As the heat and the desert dust settled on the travellers it carried with it an ennui and a numbness which buried all animation. The second day had been much like the first, save quieter, but the third day was silent.

Prothal directed by gestures, usually simply pointing out the direction they should take with a repeated stab of the air. His only confidants were the two Rhav tribesmen, whose coming and going were the only breaks in a routine of weary journeying. The Lady Ra had given up on her litter, and the net curtains had been adapted as veils, whilst the wooden frame was abandoned on a dune, where the ants explored it.

The third day became night, and then it was the fourth day and they were still travelling between dunes and rocks at the silent bidding of the one-eyed merchant. There was no sense of progress: the purple line of the Northreach range on the horizon had long since gone, leaving no distinctive landmarks by which they could measure their journey. On the seventh day a horse died; on the eleventh day a snake nearly caused Khayrik to fall, and made his horse bolt, by suddenly rearing in the animal's path. The horse was shocked and lifted itself desperately on to its hind legs, throwing Khayrik off the saddle so that he was suspended only by the leather thongs, one of which had caught around his neck. For a frightened moment while the horse pummelled at the snake Khayrik was being throttled and dangled at once, unable either to stay where he was or move, and then the horse had killed the snake and was exultant, straining at the lead rope which tied it to the other horses and then snapping it. Once more Khayrik was in danger as the horse ran away with him, whilst at the same time the pack horses, reacting to the lead animal's euphoria, tried to stampede in the other direction. Prothal, moving with surprising speed, whipped his horse up and headed off the strung horses, calming them in the simplest way, which was to let them run themselves out. At the same time, Khayrik's horse, rather than running in a straight line, had circled around the caravan and now stood – panting, and wriggling its back from time to time to shake off the badly slung deadweight that was Khayrik – on the skyline behind them, where one of the outriders was able to recapture it and bring it back. Khayrik was bruised but claimed he was not badly hurt; he even claimed to have enjoyed the experience, which his companions thought was unlikely since he had been, not unreasonably, crying out through most of the performance. They lost half a day's travel through the incident, but did not mind: even losing time meant variety.

Nevir, one of the Rhav scouts, encouraged his horse up the smooth sweep of a dune, traversed the lip, and then dropped almost sheer from the edge to a heap of soft sand which collected at the foot. His horse floundered for a moment in the yielding sand, regained its footing, and pressed on. Nevir felt his sore back where Prothal had beaten him: sometime in the last day they had missed the waterhole of Ggaya-Iya, and Prothal had been furious. 'We can't go back for water; we'll have to go on,' he said, keeping his voice low so that the fur-traders or the nobles wouldn't hear his worries, and then thrashing Nevir until blood had come through the punctured skin. Every time the scout moved the rough robes he wore rubbed against his wheals, but he was a Rhav and a Rhav does not complain. Instead he spurred his horse toward the next dune and took stock of the situation.

They were seventeen days out from Mornet now, and progress had become painfully slow. The dunes that had rolled like waves and so helped them in the first days of the journey had gone, and now the waves were against them, head on as they battled like sailing ships against the slowest of winds. Nevir looked out from the crest of the dune. Although these waves of sand looked still, he knew that their positions changed moment by moment, and that their lives might depend on not only his skill in navigating but also in anticipating the movements of the dunes. He had never seen the sea, yet had much in common with sailors.

A strip of red on the northern horizon surprised and heartened him. Even as he looked the mountains seemed to come nearer through some trick of the heat. He could make out the shapes of the Taliolan mountains now, and their rough red-brown forms of shadow and darkness, highlight and plane. The temptation to abandon the caravan was strong: even allowing for the distorted distance caused by the heat, those mountains could not be more than two days ride away, and then he would be home. He thought about home, about tents in circles and skewered meat cooked over an open fire. He dismounted and led his horse along the ridge, looking for a way down. He knew he would not be going home that day, however charming the prospect; he had a job to do. A withered, improbable bush in the trough between him and the lip of the next dune was the only feature of interest around him, and he smiled at it fondly. 'You're as daft as me, little bush,' he told it, as he walked on, searching for a route down.

His awareness of the buzzards came slowly as he concentrated on finding a route through the dunes. First one, then a second, and now a whole flock, wheeling in the sky overhead.

For an uncomfortable time he thought they were flocking over him, and offered prayers to Nett-Rhav, the god of the desert. But then he realised that the intended victim was somewhere to his east: warily, but knowing he must find the cause of the birds' activity, he remounted and set his horse in the direction of the circling birds.

The victim was not yet dead guessed Nevir. The birds soared and swooped, but did not settle. His progress towards the axis of their circling was slow, hampered partly by the terrain and partly by the need for stealth. Whatever lay ahead of him, in the inhospitable landscape of Khalinrift, it was sure to offer danger.

He was now beneath the birds, although still unable to see what it was they mocked. He drew a spike from his belt and thrust it firmly into the sand, tethering his horse in the valley between two dunes. Then he scurried forwards, climbing the dune ahead on his hands and knees to spread his weight on the soft sand and to keep his profile low. An inquisitive buzzard swooped low over him, the shadow of his great black wings passing over him terrifyingly, but Nevir had steeled himself; his only response was to pause in his climb, draw his curved Rhav dagger, and place the knife in his mouth.

Just before the lip of the dune Nevir stopped, knowing that he would be vulnerable against the skyline. He chose a point where the combing edge was already broken, quarried by a fall from below, and cautiously raised his head. Then caution was abandoned: he raised himself up and half-fell, half-ran down the edge below him, rolling and struggling in his desperate haste to join the scene he saw below.

A group of Rhavs was attempting to scale the dune on the far side from him. Nevir counted fourteen including five small children. All but three of the Rhavfolk were crawling: these three, two women and a man, were shielding the others from the impatient buzzards which swept low over them. Exhaustion and despair marked every movement. Only the encouragement of one of the standing women kept the party moving, and even as Nevir approached the man fell to his knees and then slipped slowly and painfully forward to lie spread-eagled on the sand.

The determined woman prodded the prone figure with her

foot, but there was no movement. As she bent to attend the man she saw Nevir running along the sands. Wearily she drew herself upright, her sword ready to defend herself and her party against this fresh attack.

'Woman!' cried Nevir, almost running on the spot in his attempt to sprawl his way up the slope. She looked at him without recognition as he pushed against the loose footing, slid down, climbed again, and then slowly lowered the sword.

'Rhav?' she asked.

'Nevir, son of Agix of the Cham,' he panted in introduction. 'What has happened? What are you doing so far from home?'

'We have no home. Have you not heard? We are of the Girn. We have no home.'

Nevir was confused. The Girn were established by the banks of the River Ytral, where the Grey Scree ended. He knew the place well. 'What has happened?' he demanded again.

The woman was joined by her companion. The others remained where they lay, heads down in the sand so that they could not see the talons and beak poised to rend them apart. Now that the woman had stopped her urgent injunctions that they should keep on they realised how spent they were; some, in the dry heat of the desert and beneath the grasping buzzards, even slept. Nevir could see now that many of them were wounded, and all badly blistered. The leader introduced herself. 'I am Welak, daughter of Weydrol. This is my sister, Paltra. And this' – she indicated the bodies on the ground around her, stained black with grime and dried blood and the sun's harsh heat – 'is the Girn.'

'But what has happened?' Nevir did not know if he was awed or impatient.

'Agaskan. Three days past. Thousands of them, marching from the hills. We were just in their way: they didn't even need to stop their march to destroy us; they just marched straight over us. We might have killed thirty or more of them, but it made no difference. They just kept on coming. In the end we fled. We had no choice. You have never seen such an army. Thousands? Millions perhaps.'

'But why?'

'They were heading due south. I think they may be going to the Thatter.'

'Across the Khalinrift? The Agaskan have never been across the Rift; they would surely perish.'

'Nothing can stop an army like that. Nothing.'

Nevir looked across the stillness of the desert. 'Where are they now?'

'West of here.' The woman stopped talking abruptly and turned away, again bending over the fallen man. Nevir watched her, feeling pity and panic in his throat.

'But where are you going?' he asked insistently.

'Leave her,' said the girl called Paltra. 'It is her husband she tends. I will try to answer your questions if I can.'

Nevir turned around and kicked a small pile of sand so that it scattered in the warm air. 'What of the other places? Was there any news of the Cham?'

'I do not know. But perhaps they will be all right.' To his surprise the girl took his hand, comforting him. 'The Agaskan were not interested in killing. They were not interested in anything, I think, except their march.' Her voice was gentle, though roughened by lack of water. How can this girl be comforting me, thought Nevir, when she has suffered so much. 'So long as the Cham was not in their way, I think that your people will be safe.'

The girl's goodness saddened him more than her sister's tale had done. 'Where are you heading?'

'To death.' It was a simple statement, with nothing self-conscious or dramatic about it. It was the truth, but Nevir could not accept it.

'Come with me,' he said impulsively. 'I have a horse. We could escape. We could live.'

The hand that held his squeezed and then released its grip. 'I shall stay with my people,' she told him.

Nevir stood, abandoned, on the edge of the group. A buzzard had settled on one of the children; the child did not stir. Anger filled Nevir. He ran forward, curved blade flashing viciously. But the bird flapped safely away and the knife slashed only air. Feeling grotesque, feeling impotent, Nevir returned to the girl's side. 'Is there nothing I can do? Water? Perhaps I could send for help? Please.'

But the girl only shook her head, stepped forward, and placed her hand on her sister's shoulders. 'Is he well?'

'He will die soon.' The woman who was called Welak stood, looking about her. A child was crying, an old man sobbing. The buzzards were settling on the ground now, only a few strides away from them. 'It is over. We will stay here.' She looked at Nevir. 'Leave us, but remember us. We are the Girn. We did what we could.' And then she knelt down again, placing her arms around her fallen husband and cradling him in her arms. She started wailing in a low soft voice. It was the Death Song of the Rhav, and hearing it, Nevir knew that there was nothing to be done. He looked again at Paltra, but the girl's eyes focused on nothing, and her lips mouthed the words of the Death Song.

'I will remember you,' he said.

He turned away from them, the keening sounding in his ears like the noise of busy flies. He climbed the valley side and reached the lip of the dune separating the Girn from his horse: the horse was still, and content, and flicked its tail instinctively against the flies. Nevir stood at the lip of the dune and looked back. The birds were settling now.

'I will remember you,' he called, and the buzzards were startled into the air for a moment. Nevir scrabbled down the slope and mounted his horse. Tears were in his eyes as he spurred the horse away.

The dust got everywhere. Clouds of it rose from the horses' hooves ahead, to fall in an irrepressible haze that surrounded them and penetrated them. It entered their noses and eyes, despite the material that they had now wrapped about their heads, and collected in the folds of their clothes. Lara lifted her hand to her face and found a lock of her hair which had escaped from the confines of her headgear. When she touched it, it powdered as if she were dead.

A dull warm wind had made matters worse, curling the dust from the dunes in bitter twisting plumes. Prothal was aware that the trough they followed at present led them due south, and was of no use to them, but he could not face the prospect of the rise and fall of dunes that he knew would stretch into the horizon between them and their destination. He chose instead to go south, to risk the river and its tremendous canyon, and to see if he could find a way around the barrier of dunes. He

forced his eyes open into the dust, and found that there was
nothing to see. Where, he wondered, were his scouts?

Whilst Nevir viewed the victims, Calad, the other of Prothal's
Rhav scouts, was viewing the victors. Concealed at the lip of a
dune, his brightly coloured turban covered by a dull khaki
wrap and his horse tethered carefully in the deep shade of a
weathered outcrop of cream-brown rock, Calad watched, and
was appalled by what he saw.

The vast Agaskan army was less than a thousand strides
away, and appeared often nearer in the fluctuating desert air. It
came through the Rift like a slow black flood, like oil on the
troubled tides of the dunes; diverting around obstructions,
swelling between the raised peaks of the dunes, dividing and
joining and moving ever south, it was more liquid than living.
The Rhav had seen the head of the column approach, and had
hidden himself: now he waited as it passed. It was four
hundred strides away now, and approaching. Calad lay prone
against the sheltered edge of the dune, and prayed to every god
he knew that he might not be discovered. The column moved
into the hollow directly before him. At its head was a line of
drummers, their long thin drums strapped to their waists; the
rhythm they played was harsh and unvaried, and the drummers were thirty abreast.

Behind the drummers came the standards, held aloft by
officers riding Vedi, foul beasts which had the proportions of a
horse and the appearance of something flayed. The standards
themselves were wide-armed tridents, each prong tipped with a
human skull, and each skull trailing long streamers of bright
silk from where the ears once were. Even the omnipresent dust
raised by the marching feet could not settle on those dancing
streamers: alone in all the view before Calad, the streamers
seemed unpolluted by the ochre of the desert as they flapped
and waved through the larded air. Their cheerfulness seemed,
to the concealed Rhav who studied their progress, only to
emphasise the grim terror all else in sight held for him.

After the standards came the élite guard – shields of purple
and black, plumed helms of blackiron and violet-dyed feathers
– with, in their midst, the canopied litters of the Oligarchs,
raised up on muscular shoulders. Following the élite guard

came more troops, and more, and more, until the hollow before him was filled with the sound of marching feet and the swirl of billowing dust.

Time passed and so did the Agaskan: neither showed any sign of stopping. Calad became aware, through the shifting patterns of dust that filled the air, that there were variations among the Agaskan. He saw whole companies of Agaskan mounted on Vedi, and could make out the exposed veins and muscles of these massive creatures and the grossly plumed lances of their riders, the Vedi-detch. He watched supply wagons, four wheeled and clumsy over the rough terrain, each pulled by a string of labouring figures, and continually being overtaken by more rapidly moving and mobile troops. Twice through the dust he saw figures stumble and fall, yet such was the strength of the force which drew this army on towards the Thatter that even the fallen continued to drag themselves on, until they were trampled and broken by the ranks behind.

Unstoppable, inevitable, the column continued past him, wrapped in its own fat cloud. Patient carrion birds circled over the cloud, waiting for the fallen. Calad, lying on his stomach and with his head drawn into the sand of the dune until only his eyes were exposed, watched them as if transfixed.

A sudden noise behind him broke his reverie, made him turn and duck his head instinctively beneath the edge of the dune. The sight which met his eyes filled him with a dread even more immediate than had the Agaskan: coiled on the sandy slope of the dune, its sharp head snapping a livid blue tongue, was a small tense snake, poised for the kill. Its venomous eyes were fixed on Calad's calf.

The Rhav moved slowly, despite the rushing blood in his ears and the desperate thumping of his heart. Gradually, delicately, steadily, he moved his hand towards the knife sheathed at his belt. The fingers moved gently, the arm straightened carefully. But suddenly the snake's head drew back, the mouth opened in anticipation, and the neck jerked forward towards the Rhav's leg.

The moment froze for Calad. His fingers reached the hilt, pulled, slashed upwards, met resistance, and carried the stroke through. The knife flashed once in the desert air before it descended on the writhing snake with the gaping throat; the second stroke, more carefully aimed, smashed the pointed skull and fixed the head to a coil which wriggled beneath.

Breathing hurriedly, shallowly, Calad lay still behind the rim of the dune, feeling the comforting drain of adrenalin from his veins, the slow return to normality in his heartbeat. He was still lying there when the first of the Vedi-detch, attracted by his flashing blade, crossed the crest of the dune beside him, and had barely moved at all before the pennoned lance had driven through his ribs, pinning him to the sand.

The Vedi-detch debated for a short while in their oddly pitched language, decided there was no time to perform the ritual desecration of the corpse, and rode off to join their company. Calad lay next to the body of the snake, and flies settled on their eyes.

Although the desert day brought searing heat, the spectacular sunset soon drained the warmth from the land, and reminded the travellers that it was still early in the year. They rode on, exhausted, thankful only that another day was drawing to an end. The dust had died down with the setting sun and the failing breeze when, barely acknowledging the return of one of the Rhav scouts, they pulled their cloaks from their saddle-bags and prayed Prothal would soon call a halt.

The Rhav rode up to Prothal, and the merchant's sharp single eye saw at once that something was wrong. His first fear was that Nevir's agitation might mean the Rhav was planning something, for his ride today must have taken him fairly close to the Rhav homelands, and he was therefore in no mood to be polite.

'What's the matter with you?' he asked, drawing the scout to one side of the caravan. 'If you've been planning anything silly with anyone you've been meeting out there I advise you to think again. There's not a bandit in the Rift that can match Prothal One-Eye at his own game, and you should know it.'

'It's nothing like that, honestly. It is worse, much worse.'

'Lower your voice, damn you,' said Prothal, for indeed Nevir's voice was almost shouting in its anxiety that Prothal should listen and understand. 'You'll frighten our guests.' Prothal dropped the threat from his voice and smoothly, silkily, continued. The tone did not match the language. 'We have the Lady Ra travelling with us. I do not want that lady disturbed by any plot or fantasy dreamt up by a lousy stinking unwashed Rhav who can't even find water when he's asked to. Do you want another beating?' Prothal smiled indulgently at the Rhav.

'Quickly Prothal. Before the sun sets. Come with me to the dune-crest.'

'What is the matter with you?' Prothal struck impatiently at the imploring arm which Nevir stretched towards him. 'And keep your voice down,' he added, as the Lady Ra herself rode past, with her maidservants. As she passed she called out that she hoped they would stop soon.

'Very soon, very soon,' soothed the merchant. 'Just as soon as we find somewhere suitable.' He turned to the hapless Rhav. 'My best customer ever. If you louse this up for me then I shall kill you very slowly and feed your remains to the worms. Easy pickings, the House of Ra is, and I'll not have my easy pickings threatened by you.'

Nevir shook his head. 'Prothal, we will all be dead.'

The merchant suddenly leant over from his horse to Nevir's and caught hold of the Rhav's ear. 'Is this some plan you and Calad have dreamt up? Try it out on the buzzards,' he said contemptuously. 'Where is Calad anyway, skulking?'

'Has he not returned?'

'No.'

'Then he is dead.'

'You really are daft, aren't you. Why should he be dead? Have you caught the sun?'

'There are Agaskan everywhere.'

'I suppose that's one of them now.' Prothal pointed at Khayrik riding past with his string of horses, but so swift and violent was the Rhav's reaction that the merchant was disturbed himself. 'Hey, steady on. Perhaps you had better tell me what you have seen.'

Briefly, Nevir explained. 'Come with me.'

The others had passed now; no one would see them go if they rode off, scouted around, rode back. Prothal was worried now; he did not believe the tale of the Agaskan – Agaskan in the Rift was ridiculous – but on the other hand something had obviously caused the Rhav to be so agitated. And there was the mystery of Calad's disappearance as well. 'Where are we going?'

They rode laboriously up the slope of a dune, their horses' hooves making little purchase on the loose sand, until eventually they reached the crest. There they stopped, and the Rhav looked about rapidly. He pointed to a blur on the horizon to the north-west.

'What is it?'

'It is the Agaskan army.'

Prothal looked at it: it was just a dust cloud, but if whatever was making it was as far away as it looked, then it must be something big. 'It might be. We ought to avoid it, whatever it is.'

'What shall we do?'

'Do? How in Araketh's name should I know?' Prothal was alarmed now: his usual calculating violence was replaced by flashes of temper. Bandits he could fight, but this was something new, something which he had never experienced before. 'Follow me,' he instructed, and the two of them returned to the caravan.

Prothal rode to the head of the caravan while Nevir was dispatched to summon Prothal's lieutenants. When they had assembled in a tight mounted group ahead of the rest Prothal asked the Rhav to relate again what had happened. They absorbed the information carefully.

'You're certain it's Agaskan?' asked Cleob, a sturdy man of Northreach with a full black beard.

'We aren't certain of anything,' replied Prothal. 'On the other hand, even if it's not, whatever it is I don't like it. There is a large dust cloud following us, gentlemen. Let us not examine too carefully what might be causing it, or all that we'll do is bring along nightmares; let us simply make sure we avoid it.'

'We could go back, let them pass,' said Cleob. 'We could hide easy in the desert.'

'We certainly could hide. We could also die of thirst: you may have forgotten it but our friend here' – Prothal struck Nevir a series of painful blows on the back which jarred the beaten nerves and made the bruised flesh livid again – 'missed the watering place.'

'All right, what do you suggest?'

'We could try to get ahead of them. They're to the north. We could try to get to the west of them before they pass.'

'Could we do it?' said Gelthro, a Plainsman of Myr with fair skin burnt scarlet and fair hair bleached white. 'I think not. Not with the caravan.'

'Bugger the caravan,' said Cleob.

'No,' said Prothal. 'Or at least, not yet.'

'What else can we do but leave the thing here?' asked the Northreacher. 'What is it to us?'

'A lot of money. Imagine what the Gros of Ra would give to his wife's saviours.'

'So what do we do?' insisted Cleob.

'What's the river like here?'

'Wet,' said Gelthro. 'We cannot get to it though, you know that.'

'And the banks. What are they like?'

'I don't know. Broken I suppose, as they generally are around the middle part of the Rift.'

'Exactly. Gelthro, you and Nevir here can go and examine the canyon sides. We are going to need somewhere to hide.'

'It's getting dark,' complained Gelthro.

'What do you expect me to do about that? Move.' The Rhav and the Plainsman rode off into the gathering dark; Prothal and Cleob waited for the rest of the caravan to catch them up. 'Ladies and gentlemen,' prefaced Prothal, as the horses stomped in the rapidly cooling night air. 'I'd like to be able to say that we could stop, but I can't say that. There are technical reasons why we cannot, which I hope you'll not mind if I don't explain; meanwhile, we'll be travelling just a little bit further. Can I ask you not to light any torches tonight, or to make any unnecessary noise.'

'Technical reasons?' muttered Khayrik. 'Bandits, more like.' The bruises to his chest were ugly discolorations, and kept him awake in the night. Unbeknown to his companions, one of them had started to fester unpleasantly just beneath the top layer of skin, and Khayrik was worried about it. 'Better to go in a fight than in a ditch,' he decided, and sat bolt upright in his adapted saddle to wait for the bandit attack.

'Technical reasons,' echoed the Lady Ra. 'Blow them: I'd rather sleep.'

The night was as black as it would become before Nevir and Gelthro returned, and their arrival out of the dark startled Prothal, who swore at them in a low voice. The news they brought was both welcome and unwelcome. The trough between the dunes led them directly to the river, where the ground was so broken by the collapse of the canyon walls over the centuries that it should not be difficult to hide; on the other hand, such country would make travelling difficult.

'We don't have much choice, unless the Agaskan have gone home for their supper,' said Prothal One-Eye. 'Nevir, follow me; Gelthro, take the caravan into those rocks. Get them there safely, please.'

The delay whilst they had waited for Nevir and Gelthro to return had done tempers no good. The companions were tired and puzzled, and reluctant to move when Gelthro asked.

'Araketh,' swore the Plainsman. 'We can't stay here all day arguing. Follow me if you like, or stay if you like. I'm going.'

He struck his horse about the neck with the loose end of the reins, and galloped away, following the valley between the dunes. In thirty strides he had gone from their sight: the half moon cast a pale and wintry light on the desert, but it was shadowy among the dunes. Without looking at the others, Khayrik whipped his own horse on, tugging the string of pack animals behind him. They started forward awkwardly, in a shuffling group across the moonlit sand, and then they too vanished into shadow. Many of Prothal's outriders followed Khayrik; a small group hung back, unwilling to move whilst Prothal and Nevir were still climbing a slab of rock that jutted out of the desert near where the caravan had rested. They had heard Prothal's instructions to Gelthro and Nevir, and were curious to learn what it was that had made their leader behave so uncharacteristically; they could see him now, climbing up the slab behind his scout, and then standing with him in the dark. They muttered amongst themselves. 'He's seen something that has frightened him'; 'Bandits?'; 'Must be, and a lot of them'; 'Rhav?'; 'Rhav's still with him'. And then the decision was taken. 'I'm off. I don't want no trouble.'

Horses were encouraged and spurred, pulled around so that they faced west up the dune, and then ridden up the soft yielding sand. 'They're deserting us,' whispered Streetpoet. 'Come on. Let's catch up with Khayrik.' He rode forward, with Lara and Ormaas following. Consatiné and the Lady Ra followed them, and with the Lady Ra's handmaids they rode off into the dark.

'Do you see anything?' asked Prothal, pulling himself up on to the top of the slab next to Nevir.

'Over there.' Nevir was pointing towards a glow in the sky to the north. For a time Prothal was unable to identify it, and then realisation struck.

'It's their dust-cloud, illuminated by lots of torches. They're marching through the night.'

'Prothal, look, down there.' Prothal turned quickly, expecting to see Agaskan, but it was only the outriders leaving.

'Let them go. I hadn't paid them.' The merchant made a move to climb down the rock again, to where his horse was tethered below.

'Wait,' said Nevir. The time for his usual deference to the merchant's temper had passed: they were equals in the face of the oncoming army. 'Can't you hear it?'

'What?' said Prothal, and then he was silent, listening. Here, above the routine noises of the caravan, the rattling of bridles and the chattering of handmaids, the groaning of saddles and moaning of men, the desert sounded different, moribund and dangerous. Deep below the gentle swish of the wind on the sands they heard a new noise, the dull muffled beat of the Agaskan advance. 'I hear it,' he said. 'Let's get away from here.'

They soon caught up with the Lady Ra and her company, who formed the unlikely rearguard to the caravan, and urged them on. Consatiné rode alongside Prothal, hoping to find out what was going on. 'Where have you been?' he asked. He had not forgotten that he had paid for this journey, and paid heavily. 'What have you been doing?'

Prothal decided he did not have the energy to argue. 'The desert is full of Agaskan,' he said. 'We're getting out of their way.'

'Agaskan.' Consatiné had a giddy vision of bodies hung from grim trees, and nearly lost his seat on his horse.

'Are you all right?' asked Prothal. He did not want the young Vaine to die: he wanted him to be a grateful survivor.

'Yes.' It occurred to Consatiné that there were no trees in the desert, and for a ridiculous moment he found himself laughing, until Prothal grabbed the reins of his horse and pulled both animals up.

'Pull yourself together,' said Prothal One-Eye, roughly.

Consatiné apologised, and together they rode on, Prothal herding the long broken line of the caravan as best he could.

From time to time the merchant stopped his horse to listen. There could be no doubt. The sound of the advancing army was louder: the beat of drums could now be distinguished from the shuffle of feet. Consatiné could hear it too now; he thought they sounded tired.

They reached the different landscape that skirted the Khalin hundreds of strides below. Here erosion from beneath had hollowed out vast caverns which had in their turn collapsed, causing rough terraces in the original stone plate. The terraces were strewn with gargantuan rocks, thrown up by the movement of rock beneath, and cracked and broken like old crockery. Their paths descended some thirty strides down a wide, long slope and then was no more, and they were amongst the rocks. Gelthro paused, and waited for the others to catch up.

Prothal and Consatiné were last to arrive. The place chosen by Gelthro was open and exposed, and Nevir kept jerking his eyes at the top of the slope overlooking them for the first sign of the Agaskan. The merchant spoke to them in a low voice, so that they had to strain their ears to hear.

'You will be wondering why we have not stopped tonight. I will tell you. We have not stopped tonight because behind us, ladies and gentlemen, is an army of Agaskan. They are likely to catch us at any time. Therefore we will hide in these rocks, and pray to Menketh and any other god we know.'

They all heard it now: the sound of the advancing army thrust the desert silence aside. 'What are we going to do?' asked Khayrik. *He does not look frightened,* marvelled Consatiné. *I dare not speak even.*

'We must split up. I do not think that the Agaskan are looking for us. From what my scout tells me they are simply marching across the desert, destroying all that is in their way, but not stopping for anything. Unfortunately, we are amongst the things that are in their way, but perhaps if we split up and hide we might survive.' He amended that. 'Some of us might survive.'

'Can't we make a run for it?'

'Across this.' He waved to the gruesome random rocks of this part of the Rift. 'We would not make a thousand strides before daybreak.'

'Across the desert then. We were making good time just now.' Ormaas was asking the questions; he doesn't sound scared either, thought Consatiné. Am I the only one?

'We were travelling down the dunes, where the going is easy. To travel either forwards or backwards – to travel, in short, in any direction other than by the one we came – would be impossible.'

'Must we hide? Can't we carry on running?'

'The river is behind you. How else would you account for these rocks?'

'Quickly, please,' said Nevir. Consatiné was comforted by the fear in the Rhav scout's voice, and thrilled by its urgency. 'They will be upon us soon.'

'Lady Ra, your son, your ladies, shall join my party; the rest of you must fend for yourselves. I shall leave Nevir with you, and wish you luck. If we survive, perhaps we shall meet in Akbar.'

Prothal rode off, and the Lady Ra and her handmaids followed. The Lady Ra was almost asleep in the saddle, and the reality of their situation had not yet reached into her to chill her. Streetpoet looked at her. She was not dressed to be chased by Agaskan. Consatiné held his horse still for a moment, and then turned away from the companions without speaking, to follow his mother into the rocks. The others were not to know it, but it was pride and the fear of fear that made him silent.

The cousins turned instinctively towards Khayrik. 'What shall we do?'

'Let's get into the cover first, and then decide.' Nevir had already ridden out of view of the desert behind them, and they found him a short way into a labyrinth of tumbled rock. In the desert there had been a predominance of sand, with the occasional rock breaking the monotony; here the landscape was mostly rock, puddled in hollows with pools of sand, like a shore when the tide is leaving. Khayrik had once seen the sea, north of Comtas on the Aphde shore. He remembered piled rocks that were arranged in lunatic heaps, and tunnels that bored secretly through rearing cliff faces. On that dark night, pursued by the Agaskan, Khayrik remembered different nights, of kissing and smiling and watching the starfish the tide had left, spent on that shore with a friendly local girl.

'Khayrik!' Ormaas's whisper broke in on his thoughts. Khayrik broke off from his memories, annoyed at his own nostalgia. Memory was not usually something that plagued him, and he wondered if he was remembering things because he was about to die. He shrugged off the speculation as he had shrugged off the memory, steeled himself for the night, and made a decision.

'We'll go left, then right, and then left, and then right, until we're well into these rocks, and then we'll look for somewhere to hide the horses. We'll need the horses later, if we're ever to get out of here, but it's too dangerous us all staying with them. Come on.'

They followed him. They were in a dark hollow between towering rocks. Narrow defiles led in all directions, darker than the night rocks that formed them. They had not gone far before they had to turn back, having reached a drop. Khayrik's horse would not approach the edge ahead, and the cripple could not dismount, so it was Lara who crept forward to investigate. She leant over a darkness that was broken by a thin trail of white at the bottom, like a snail's track. With a sudden sickness, she realised where she was. 'The river,' she said hoarsely.

They could hear it now, a murmur against the Agaskan beat. Rapidly they moved away from the edge. They did not want to be driven into the river so far below by the Agaskan army when it came.

It was Streetpoet who found the place. A crack in the rock just above head height, which could be entered by standing on the back of his horse, led him into a hollowed out rock like the inside of a wisdom tooth. 'We can hide here,' he said.

Khayrik shook his head. 'What about the horses?'

Streetpoet looked glum, but the Rhav was growing more and

more agitated. 'They are so near now,' he said. 'Come on. Be quick.'

'Khayrik, I'll look after the horses,' said Ormaas. 'You all hide.'

'All right,' said Khayrik. 'But don't just do this to be noble. If the horses are lost then we'll all die anyway.'

'Quickly,' said the Rhav. Streetpoet threw down a rope. He always carried rope, and it had saved him on several occasions. None had been more pressing than this, however. Nevir climbed it, followed by Lara; Khayrik was still strapped to his horse.

'Come on,' he said to Ormaas. 'Let's find somewhere to hide this lot.'

Prothal had broken his larger party up, until he was alone with the Lady Ra and her son. They were as well concealed as they could manage behind a heavy stone arch, formed when a boulder had wedged between two solid rock faces. They had dismounted and led their horses up a ledge that took them on to the level of the boulder, and there they waited.

Consatiné squatted down, patting his horse's nose to quieten it down. He had brought two horses on the journey, but his spare had gone with Khayrik in the confusion of their parting. He was sorry: it had been a good horse.

He listened. The curious noises of the Agaskan were much nearer now. He could make out a sort of song, a hollow wailing that seemed to wrap about the rocks. He thought of his father's maps. Where were these Agaskan from? Where were they going? The second question was easy to answer. There was only one place they could be going to that was south of the Rift, and that was the Thatter. And where they were from was irrelevant, for the very fact that an Agaskan army had done the unheard of and had crossed the desert suggested some deep compulsion, and Consatiné thought of the words of the Leva-foln shaman. The Ingsvaal would explain it. Nothing else could lure the Agaskan across the inhospitable sands of Khalin-rift. He wondered how they felt. Did they feel anything, or were their minds so full of the Ingsvaal that all other sensations disappeared?

He heard his mother's restrained gasp, and saw Prothal had

one hand over her mouth. He was about to act when he saw what they were staring at. Below them, the tip of his lance reaching the level of their faces, was a Vedi-detch on his fear-inspiring mount.

Ormaas looked about himself in horror. He was alone. Somewhere amidst the rocks he had lost Khayrik and the horses. He listened for sounds that would lead him back to the cripple, but in the confusion of possible routes and the mayhem of Agaskan sounds it was hopeless. He tried to retrace his steps, but realised he could not tell which end of the passage that he had entered he was now in. He guessed the right, and pulled his horse round to take him that way. The darkness was now his greatest enemy. He even found a comfort in the noise of the Agaskan. Then suddenly his horse had stumbled, and he was sliding down a scree-ridden slope, to drop from the end and to hang, suspended, Menketh only knew where.

Lara pushed herself deep into the shadows, even though no Agaskan had yet so much as looked into the hollow of stone that concealed them. The noise of the Agaskan swelled around them and overwhelmed them. They saw the light of many thousands of torches, and the occasional shadow, distorted by torchlight, that grew high against a rock face for a moment before disappearing.

They heard voices, piping and growling and barking commands, and listened to echoing groaning and breathing. She heard the thump of heavy weights against the stones, and the clash of metal on rock. And sometimes they heard screams, long drawn wails that fell off into the darkness ominously, and brought their own exquisite terror. The night went on and on. Lara felt Streetpoet's fingers in hers. Sometimes they were tense and sometimes they were not. She could not tell what he was thinking.

He decided he was at the edge of the gorge. He reached out an arm and touched rock, and gingerly tried again. There it was once more. He could see nothing.

A neigh behind him made him turn in terror, his hand reaching for the hilt of his sword. The neigh repeated, and he recognised it for the sound of his horse in agony. He whispered comforting words and crept forwards towards it, tearing his clothes on a sharp rock. He reached it and touched it, speaking its name softly like an incantation: Juhrai, Juhrai, Juhrai. The animal lay still and he ran his hand along the nearest leg, checking for damage. Almost immediately he felt the stickiness of blood where a broken bone had pushed through the skin. As he touched that place the horse rolled violently away from him, kicking as it did so and just missing his head. And then, suddenly, Ormaas was aware that he was alone in the darkness, that the horse had somehow left him: its breathing had gone, its presence had gone. He crawled after it, and then remembered the gorge, so he dropped a pebble just ahead of him and heard it tap reassuringly on stone. He crawled a step further and dropped another stone, which again tapped on to rock. But the third stone did not hit anything. It dropped into eternity. Nothing happened at all.

He must have stayed there on the brink for a long time, until the cold gripped him and made him feel the damp blood from a tear on his knee. He crawled back from the edge then and returned to the security of the scree, where the long day caught up with him and, despite everything, he dozed.

The Agaskan had not stopped, even at this dreadful obstacle. They reached the mighty Khalin gorge and carried on, plunging deep into inevitable death. Their ranks had been disorganised by the rocks they had marched through, but the impulse of the Thatter was as strong as ever. Forward, always forward, pressing against the backs of comrades who did not travel so fast, following the unearthly beat of the Wells. Pushing their way to the south, they did not realise that the Khalin stood in their way until, in a vicious gut-guttering moment, they balanced on the brink and the weight of those behind drove them on. Some screamed; others were still marching as they fell.

Figures crashed past Ormaas in his resting place, and the scree rattled and roared as it fell. The yelling seemed to continue endlessly in his ears. Often Ormaas felt that he must be dislodged, but accident had chosen the place where he sheltered well. Gradually, eventually, the night ended, but not the massacre. As light reached Ormaas he curled still tighter, found himself on a slope just beneath a low ledge, and watched the figures plummet past. They came with dreadful frequency, tumbled through the air before him, scrabbled at the scree, and then slid away.

Sometimes figures seemed to see him as they stretched, desperately, for the last handhold, and Ormaas felt pity and horror as the green distorted faces distorted further, the narrow eyes widened, and the creatures passed beyond sight. Twice hands reached out to hold him, and Ormaas drew back instinctively, to let the creatures fall into the pit.

And once a different instinct prevailed, and Ormaas reached out and held a flailing wrist as it passed him, and hung for moments on to a screaming body with a wide red mouth that opened and shut in desperation. Revulsion filled Ormaas. These were the Agaskan, the not-human. The green-white flesh was blackened by the sun, but still cold to touch. It was like holding the dead. Ormaas's hand opened, and the screaming body fell slowly away from him. Its face was stupid as it stared at him, but its mouth still worked with yells.

At last the deaths stopped. Eventually light brought reason and realisation. Strong characters blocked each of the many exits from the tumbled rocks into the gaping gorge, and they held back their fellows in spite of the crushing pressure from behind. The word was spread; order was restored. The odd scream still told of those who continued in their long drive south, but the sounds of an army on the move were replaced by the different sounds of an army at rest. Fires were lit, and the Agaskan ate for the first time since they had left their mountain homes. They looked about them, and wondered what to do.

In the numbness that followed the night, Ormaas could not think. It was as though the constant passing of Agaskan down the scree slope in front of him had scraped away his own identity, leaving him naked. The sun was hot on him now; in anguish he slept, and his dreams brought no release.

Chapter 8

The Fevered Sun

The world was stark sun and deep shadow, ochre and charcoal and blue. Sweat rolled into Lara's eyes and she blinked to clear them. She crawled between tall rocks along a trail of sand. Cautiously she peered out.

A small group of Agaskan rested beneath the great stones, talking listlessly in soft inhuman voices. The urgency of the Ingsvaal had left their movements now, and though from time to time an Agaska would bustle in, with a message perhaps or a suggestion, most of those she saw failed to react, or dismissed the messenger with a helpless shake of head. With sudden intuition, Lara realised the Agaskan were as lost and purposeless as she.

A sudden clamour drove her back into the shelter of the shadows. Instinctively she closed her eyes and waited, conscious of her breath and heartbeat, but the noise, although it grew nearer, did not seem to threaten her. She opened her eyes and cautiously crept forward to where she could see again.

Two figures were held by the Agaskan, two human figures. She recognised a pretty handmaid of the Lady Ra's party, and the Northreach lieutenant called Cleob. They were naked, and the Agaskan, whose asexual reproductive methods make them curious about such matters, were examining the differences carefully. The girl was wild with fear, and Lara could see her body flinch insanely at the Agaskan's touch; the man was apparently unconscious, for even when an Agaska took a sharp knife to his flesh, Cleob did not stir.

Lara returned as quickly as she could to Streetpoet, trying to forget the image of the knife in Cleob's loins, hacking and sawing away. Nevir greeted her. He could see from her face that she had been disturbed by something. 'Yes?'

'The Agaskan have captured some humans.' She felt faint. Streetpoet joined Nevir. They helped her back to shelter.

'Khayrik? Ormaas?' asked Streetpoet.

'No.' Lara spoke as though she were talking to herself. 'Others. One of Prothal's men, and one of the Lady Ra's serving women. They are killing them, just out there.' She indicated the way she had come. She wanted to cry, but the desert heat had dried her up and the sweat of fear desiccated her, leaving gentle sobs like hiccups that wracked her gentle youth.

For Ormaas, realisation was slower. He awoke from untidy dreams that were strewn with uncomfortable ideas, and found himself on a ledge above a scree slope. To his left was a drop to the river, and to his right a great boulder which blocked the way. Still not fully awake, he crawled along the ledge to the drop and looked down.

A vertical drop of two hundred strides swayed before him, and at the foot of the drop, like crushed ants, an Agaskan army lay dead. The corpses half-crossed the river, causing it to bubble and swell around them. Ormaas crept delicately back to the place where he had spent the night.

He had forgotten about the survivors. His mind was full of the dead. A shout echoed around him bewilderingly and he looked up, but nothing could be seen above the ledge save a broken wall of rock, through which he and his horse must have tumbled. He heard the shout repeated. It was an inhuman noise, too deep and croaking for a human voice.

On a small jutting platform, proud from the cliff face and about thirty strides to his right, Ormaas saw a small company of Agaskan, crowding and straining to look down. They were shouting to a single Agaska on the ledge below them, some twenty strides further down the crevice. It had apparently fallen, and was now picking itself up. It balanced on long stringy legs, resting on its haunches, and then called back a stream of gibberish to its companions, who replied in kind. One or two Agaskan dangled useless arms towards the trapped one, but it rejected that suggestion with an upward flourish of both arms. It looked down at the vertical cliff below, but not even an Agaska could descend that. Finally it looked at the ledge on which it stood. The ledge was wide there, but narrowed almost immediately to left and right. The Agaska chose the left, and moved beneath Ormaas and out of sight.

Ormaas remained still, transfixed like a rabbit. The days of desert travel had bleached and stained his green cloak to a dull pale khaki and he pulled it around him as though he were cold.

He saw another Agaska leap from the crowded platform to the ledge and set off in pursuit of its fellow. The sun climbed higher, striking Ormaas and making his fervid dreams more feverish than before. Snatches of dream danced just beyond the grip of memory, and when he shook his head they were gone, leaving only the faint afterglow of something foul.

Khayrik had been very, very lucky. The cave had been wider than its mouth had suggested, and the Agaskan had been too busy to explore it. He sat on his horse in a darkness made all the more intense by the light that now streamed past the cave's entrance. He was all right for two days, he decided, but he'd have to kill the horses and eat one if he was to survive beyond that. He had every intention of surviving, but he wished that the tight pain in his chest would go away.

A cheer drew Ormaas back to consciousness. Wearily, he watched as the Agaskan on the rock platform leaped and cheered, and wondered unconcernedly about what had excited them. While he watched one of them improvised a drum and began beating out the rhythm of the Ingsvaal. The echoing boom-boom-boom circled around him, and he could not tell if it was one drum or many that played the mesmeric rhythm.

Ormaas craned his neck cautiously, looking down to see what had caused the excitement. He saw the piled corpses below, beginning to smell in the desert heat, and saw that the corpses were already thick with birds of prey and carrion eaters. And then he saw, amidst the corpses, a single living figure, jumping and waving two hundred strides below. The drumming from the platform ceased abruptly as the drummer, throwing down his impromptu drum of cuirass and rock, leapt on to the ledge beneath and began to follow the first two down the cliff.

Others followed, or picked up the rhythm of the Ingsvaal for themselves. Urgency entered their movements. The dull vibrations of the Wells of Glavkcha filled their minds. Their journey had begun again.

Streetpoet crept up to the position where Lara had watched the Agaskan. Where she had been sick was just an inoffensive dry stain beneath the hot sun. He looked cautiously out at the hollow, and it was empty, except for two corpses pegged out in the shadows. He did not look at them, but lowered himself out of his concealment.

Quickly he ran to the edge of the hollow, where a small break in the wall led to the drop to the Khalin, and looked down. He saw thousands of Agaskan fording the river, and it was some moments before he realised that they were dead. 'They didn't stop,' he thought, and realised the explanation of the horrible screams that had pierced the night.

There was movement in the deep crack that bore the river, as well as the stench of the dead. The slow winged attention of hundreds of carrion birds dawdled the air between him and the river, whilst in a solid line of bodies that passed below him and out of sight, the Ingsvaal continued.

Many of the Agaskan had reached the bottom of the ravine now, and were crowding on the bank. Most of their officers, standards and drummers had been killed in the night, for the first to die were those at the head of the column. Vertical stakes which had been the shafts of the Oligarchs' litters punctuated a motionless writhe of limbs. Flies clouded everywhere. To cross the river they used the bodies of their dead, pushing them into the water and using them to dam it. When the pressure on the dam proved too much, great numbers of bodies were swept away downstream, often taking the living with them. The survivors assembled on the far bank. They did not pause, but searched for a way out of the ravine. The Ingsvaal was called: nothing would stop them now.

Perhaps it had been that there had sounded too many other noises in the night, but somehow the Agaskan had not heard their tethered horses. Now Consatiné, the Lady Ra and Prothal One-Eye were perched over a deserted alley between two rough-hewn slabs that the ancient earthquake had squeezed out of the earth, and they were wondering what to do next.

Consatiné's nerves seemed better now it was day, and he felt stronger and better able to cope. He even felt resentment against the merchant, who still gave the orders.

'My lord, how do you feel after our long night?'

'Better than earlier.'

'Good, good. You will have noticed, I do not doubt, the Agaskan seem to have gone. I will see if I can find a way out of here in safety. We are not well stocked with water. I will not be long.'

Prothal let himself down the rough purposeless track that had taken them to their place of safety, and then turned and ran. His bald head looked like part of the scenery to Consatiné.

He was gone a long time, and the boom of the drums had faded, although it could still be heard. Consatiné and his mother told one another stories about the two years they had spent apart. Consatiné told her about the day he had ridden in a butter churn, and she had laughed quietly; she told him about her father accidentally shooting one of the gardeners in mistake for an intruder, and how the man had been pierced through the foot with an arrow. A sudden sound beneath made Consatiné look down, expecting to see Prothal. Instead, he found himself looking at a small band of Agaskan who were resting in the alley.

They were mostly wounded, or exhausted, but the light of the Ingsvaal which had dragged them thus far was bright in their eyes, and in stately single file, tongues flicking in anticipation, they climbed the path towards Consatiné and his mother.

Consatiné stood up and drew his sword from its sheath. It grated as he pulled it clear: he had not drawn it for days, and the omnipresent desert grit had collected in the scabbard. And then he stood, ready as he would ever be, with his sword held in his right hand, his back to the wall of rock, and the voice of his instructor in his ear.

'Don't give up any advantage. If you've got height, use it, but watch out for the low sweep around your ankles.' The advice came just in time, and he parried an ugly stroke aimed at his legs with a blocking movement of the sword. The two swords remained locked together, pushing against one another, until Consatiné, in an unorthodox manoeuvre which would have had his instructor speechless, stood on his opponent's blade and, raising his own above his head, cleaved the other's neck. He watched, fascinated, as the Agaska toppled into the space beside them, and only just remembered to draw out his sword before the weight of the Agaska would have pulled it from his grasp.

A second followed the first, undeterred by the fate of its predecessor. There was a clash as it parried Consatiné's first stroke, but it posed no real threat, and was dispatched into the drop by a similar stroke. It had only had one leg, and will alone had driven it into battle with Consatiné.

The third was a different proposition, not because it was stronger, because it wasn't, but because it was aided by a comrade with a pike, who stood below and threatened Consatiné with the weapon. Trying to avoid the pike, which was not difficult on its own, was impairing his opposition to the Agaksa, who had slowly made ground until it had almost reached the level of the young man. Consatiné struck out with his sword against the pike. Wooden splinters flew from it, for the dry desert air had done the wood no good, but relentlessly if awkwardly it pressed on, now seeming to have a life of its own as it preceded the climbing Agaska along Consatiné's ledge.

Consatiné struck at it again, deflecting a probing jab that was aimed at his chest and finding that the Agaska on his ledge had struck a small painful wound in his sword arm's knuckles. He parried and escaped with no more than a graze.

The weapons ahead of him, the six stride long pike and the curved bladed sword with its long cutting edge, danced in feints and stabs before him. He twisted to avoid one and was almost caught by the other, and he could do nothing to counter-attack. 'You've got a good wrist,' said the voice of the instructor. 'Use it.' Consatiné tucked the tip of his sword beneath the blade of his opponent, whilst keeping his body arched away from the pike. He curled more of his sword around the Agaskan weapon. The two blades were held together for a long moment, and then Consatiné had flicked with his wrist and the Agaska was weaponless. With pleasure Consatiné stepped forward, as he had done so often in practice, to deliver the coup de grâce, and his sword blade nearly buckled as it hit the Agaska's armour. Needing no second opportunity the Agaska flung itself at Consatiné who nearly overbalanced when confronted with this unexpected attack from a defeated opponent. At the academy they would have laid down their swords by now, he thought, but he had no more time for thinking because the Agaska was inside his guard now and behind his sword, leaving the sword as a length of redundant metal protruding from the back of their locked bodies. The instructor's voice dried up. Consatiné was fighting for his life.

Without warning, it was over. The Agaskan slackened in his arms and its eyes went blank. It seemed to take a pace backward off the ledge, and then to hang, suspended grotesquely like some puppet doll, with both its feet clear of the ledge, before it fell quickly to the ground. There was the sound of splintering wood as it fell, and Consatiné saw that the pike was embedded in the Agaska's back. Consatiné had forgotten the pike in his moment of victory, and the pike-wielder had taken advantage of that, only to be as much fooled as Consatiné by the unexpected counter-attack from the Agaska. The blow that was meant for Consatiné had instead taken the Agaska in the back, and Consatiné was safe again, if only for a moment.

He turned to face the next of his opponents, but nothing happened. Whether dispirited by the failure of their companions, or worried by the wasted time, the other Agaskan had left him, and were hurrying away along the cleft. Consatiné turned, and saw his mother. She put her arms around him and wept.

Khayrik poked his head out of the cave mouth and the fresh sun blinded him. He was still mounted on the horse: there was no way he could devise to dismount, save cutting the threaded leather thongs that supported him, and falling to the ground. There was no one in sight. He let the horse lead through the entrance, and out to the day beyond. He squinted into the sun to see if he could learn what time of day it was, and reckoned it to be midway through the afternoon.

'Ormaas?' he called, experimentally. There was no reply. 'Ormaas?'

He rode around in a small circle. He hadn't been able to dismount, but at least he had been able to cut his horse loose from the pack animal which followed. Both horse and rider

were stiff and sore, and both were uncertain whether the other
was a friend or an enemy. They settled for an uneasy truce, and
enjoyed the sunshine after the darkness.

'Khayrik?'

'Ormaas? Are you there?' Ormaas wasn't. Instead it was
Streetpoet who greeted him from behind the strewn boulders.
The musician appeared a bit at a time, pulling himself over
some circular stones which blocked an otherwise obvious route
between Khayrik's cave and the hollow tooth that had been
their shelter. First two hands, then a head and the neck of a
mandola, followed by elbows and chest, stomach, hips and
knees, until finally the entire minstrel was face down on the top
of a rock.

'You haven't seen Ormaas, have you?'

'He was with you.'

'We got separated, in the night.' Khayrik had not been too
worried until now. He had reasoned that, had Ormaas been
taken, he would have heard it, for the boy could not be very far
away. But if that was the case, where was Ormaas now? He
tried to urge his horse towards the edge, but the horse had more
sense than that, and simply refused to go. 'What is happening
in the gorge?' asked Khayrik, for the noise of the Agaskan was
constant.

'They've found a way down.' The cripple nodded impatiently, for he had already worked this out. 'Many of them
were killed in the night: I don't think they knew the gorge was
there, and they just kept on going. But now they've sorted out a
route down, and nearly all of them are in the hole. They're
using the bodies of those that were killed to ford the river.'

'What is the route down like?'

'Hopeless for us. The Agaskan can do it by jumping, but
their Vedi can't and keep falling off. There is a great corral of
tethered Vedi at the top of the cliff now, abandoned by their
riders, but I don't fancy going near them; they look so foul.'

'I don't blame you. Is everyone all right?'

'Lara and the Rhav – his name's Nevir, by the way – are safe
enough, but the greenskins must've captured Prothal and his
lot because there are a couple left dead not far from here.'

'I'm glad Lara's all right,' said Khayrik, not wishing to think
about the others. 'And the Rhav too: we'll need him if we're to

get out of here. I wish I could only find Ormaas. Ormaas?' he called. 'Ormaas?'

'Yes.' It was the faintest of replies. Khayrik tried to make his horse move forward to investigate it, for it seemed to have come from the ravine, but the horse would have none of this, and so Khayrik was left cursing whilst Streetpoet went to look for Ormaas.

It was difficult to work out where he was. The voice ceased, as though Ormaas had gone again, and had either of them been alone, Streetpoet and Khayrik would have doubted what they had heard. At last, however, Streetpoet found him. An ochre leg halfway down a scree slope by a large boulder was all that there was to see. Using his length of rope once more, Streetpoet climbed down.

Ormaas was a mess. His face was blackened and his lips swollen. He had not even taken advantage of the little shelter offered by the rocks. Streetpoet tried easing Ormaas back to consciousness, and then tried shaking him. Eventually Ormaas muttered 'Yes' once more, and then he was awake.

Despite his appearance he seemed fairly wide awake now, and even smiled when he saw Streetpoet. 'Is Lara all right?' he asked.

'Fine. Can you climb?'

'I think so.'

'Good. You go first.' Streetpoet helped Ormaas on to the foot of the rope, and gave him a push upwards. Ormaas grabbed the rope and pulled himself up, slowly but steadily, towards Khayrik. It was not a difficult climb: the slope was less than forty-five degrees and were it not for the scree could almost have been walked. Nevertheless, Ormaas had to stop twice before he reached the top.

'Hello,' said the cripple.

'Hello.'

They collected together their horses and possessions. They had, Nevir estimated, no more than three days water and four days riding: it was going to be difficult. They turned loose all but two of the pack horses and selected the very best of the furs. The freed horses did not go far, however, but stayed within sight of the companions as they rode away from the Khalin.

Nevir was cheerful now: they had survived the Agaskan; he was certain they would survive the desert. The others were quiet, and saved the moisture in their mouths by barely speaking. Lara's throat hurt her abominably; Khayrik was sore all over, from nearly a day and a half in the saddle; Ormaas was badly sunburnt, and his face was raw. Streetpoet was least affected by the conditions, but rode steadily. That first day he had hold of the lead rope that controlled the pack horses, and held it loosely in his hands. There was little danger of the horses running away, for there was nowhere for them to run.

Prothal was surprised to see the corpses in the rocky floor beneath their hiding place, but said nothing. He led the Lady Ra down to the level of the floor and then mounted up; Consatiné followed behind.

Prothal's calculations were not precise, and he wished he had kept the Rhav with him. Nonetheless, he believed he could survive, on the amount of water they had, for five days more. After that it would be a matter of luck. He decided to follow the river to keep the tumbled distraught slabs of stone to his left all the time as they travelled. It would not be the quickest way, as the river zigged and zagged across the country, but it would be the safest. Prothal had been travelling across the desert for many years; he knew, better than most, what happens to a man who gets lost.

The great red orb seemed to balance on the horizon, drawing up its strength before launching itself into the sky. They had not wanted to rest that night, but had been forced to, as the condition of their horses would have made any other course of action foolish. Ormaas held the rope which tethered the pack horses to the others. He seemed much better, more alert and more at ease. This was because he now accepted death. The Agaska he had dropped had returned again and again in his dreams. It spoke to him in his own voice, looked at him with his own eyes, until at last, like a revelation, it came to him that it had not been an Agaska he had dropped but himself, his own life. That was why the Agaska had felt so much like death. He remembered pressing his hand against the cool trunk of a tree, and the sweet smell of pine in the air. He looked at Lara, and smiled, but his cracked lips did not respond and his expression remained fixed and tired.

Lara was not in a condition to respond. Her parched throat felt swollen, as though she could not swallow even when offered water. Her legs were sore from the long ride, and her back tired. Yet it was only morning. The sun behind them had barely turned from red to yellow. She found that she had cut herself on the forehead sometime in the rocks, and did not even know when. The blood had matted her hair around her face, and she had no way to get it out.

Streetpoet followed. His mandola had cracked, weakened by the sun and then caught against a rock. Its tone was distant and empty, as though it came from the far end of a long corridor. He felt restless, and wanted to play or to sing, but to play made him sad and to sing was out of the question. They could barely talk.

Nevir rode ahead. His horse, a Rhav pony, seemed least affected by the conditions, and was still quite sprightly. The dunes were with them for a change, and they were making good progress. He felt he deserved a change of luck. Sometimes the buzzards that flew overhead reminded him of Paltra, and he felt sad; sometimes he thought of Prothal One-Eye, and of how the merchant's bones would bleach in the desert, and felt almost happy. Prothal had deserved what happened, and though Nevir was sorry about the plump friendly Lady Ra, he could not feel sorry that Prothal was dead.

Khayrik rode last. He did this deliberately, so that he would not be expected to make decisions and so that the others would not see the expressions of pain on his face. The wound on his chest was getting worse; the dark green ooze was puckering the skin now into ugly sores, and the slightest movement of the left side of his body was agony. Stoically he rode on, but the wound was worrying him for the future as well as for the present, and for the first time in his life he wondered if he really was going to die. It seemed ironic that he, who had survived so much, should die from a riding accident.

Nevir called a halt. He dismounted and pulled a large leather bucket out of his pannier, emptying various other items out with it: knives, spikes for tethering horses, flints. He took the first water skin out of the pannier as well, and poured a drop of water into the bucket. He offered it to Ormaas's new horse.

Suddenly, like a cavalry attack, the horses the companions had turned loose were upon them. Ormaas felt the horse he rode pull forward and tried to control it, as a dozen horses, wild with hunger, descended. Then his palms were seared by an agony so intense that he could do nothing to control his horse more, but could only stay on it, as it stampeded insanely with the half-wild horses, bucking and tossing up a dune and then plunging down the steep far side. For too long they rode, Ormaas clutching the reins to his chest as he could not hold them in his hands, and then the horses settled down, steadying to a trot that became a walk. One of the horses collapsed, slowly, and rolled head first into the sand, its long neck stretched out before it.

Ormaas looked first at his hands and then at the world around him. The raised pads of the fingers were rubbed down to black and crimson weals by the action of the rope; the palms were crossed by a blistered broken track of red and blue that wept as he watched; the inside edge of each thumb was burnt away to show white bone through the tattered flesh. He carefully folded each hand under the opposite armpit, as though they were something precious, and looked around.

Khayrik was next to him, but the cripple looked ill. His face was white and his eyes dark-ringed. A lot of horses were also around them, looking wrong. It took Ormaas some time to realise why they looked wrong: they were gasping, but were not sweating. The sun was lifting their sweat as it formed.

He looked for the others, but they were not to be seen. A line of hoof marks trailed away into the distance, rolling over the regular pattern of dunes, and still steaming a gentle shimmer of dust. It was impossible to tell how far they had travelled. The sun was directly overhead. There was only one thing to do, which was to go back to his companions.

The sun was too hot, and withered the world. He watched it make patterns of the scene. A warm breeze came from nowhere and kicked the tops of the dunes maliciously. He started back.

Lara and Streetpoet rode together in the direction they had been given by the Rhav. He had told them to aim for two large rocks, keeping them in line; when they had passed those large rocks they were to ride on, still keeping them in line behind them. They did not speak, nor often look at one another. For the second time they had lost Ormaas and Khayrik; it was difficult to believe that they could find them again.

It had happened so quickly. None of them had really been paying much attention as Nevir watered the horses. Yet suddenly, alerted by Menketh-knew what sense, the other horses, uncontrolled, had been riding them down, had knocked the water-bucket from Nevir's hand, and had galloped away, taking Ormaas and Khayrik with them. Their horses had bucked and pulled; there had been no time to think of the other.

The horses had gone north, said Nevir. He would follow, he told them, but would return soon. The wind was getting up and the tracks would be faint. Soon they would be gone, and then only luck could find them.

They rode on. The dunes were flatter here, a sure sign that they were leaving the despairing centre of Khalinrift, according to Nevir. The worst was behind them, he had told them; so, they thought but did not say, were their friends.

Everyone deserves to be lucky sometimes, thought Prothal, so why not me. We've been riding along here so long, surely we must reach Akbar soon. Three days I have followed the river west; the weather has been hot but not impossible; the landscape has been all right. We have journeyed well. So where is Akbar? Where are the spires and domes, and the high walls built against the sands? Where is Akbar?

Or, to put it another way, where are we?

Nevir followed the trail until the wind erased it, and then turned back to rejoin Lara and Streetpoet. At least the horses seemed to have been travelling in the right direction, north and then west. Perhaps the Northreachers will be lucky, he thought, and reach the River Nier as it flows down from Taliola. But he was not optimistic, and even less so when he saw the mummified corpses of the outriders who had fled from Prothal's company. The buzzards had stripped faces and hands to the bone, but where thick leather or chain mail preserved the bodies they were undamaged. So much death worried him: he heard the Death Song of the Rhav in his mind, and then rode as quickly as he could away from the corpses. They had obviously rested once too often, thought Nevir, who knew the ways of the desert, and the drowsiness that comes with the sun had overcome them. We must not rest, he told himself. Not during the day.

Lara and Streetpoet had veered from the course he had set them, and he rejoined them later than he had wanted, so they camped almost immediately. Lara found a scorpion which she killed with a rock, and Nevir was happy. The scorpion was a sign that water was near, he explained; that you were able to kill it means we are having good luck.

Streetpoet played his mandola. The soft new desert tone suited his mood, which was bleak. He felt he had caught the sun rather, lightheaded and strange.

Everyone deserves to be lucky: Prothal recited it to himself continually as he travelled, like a recitative. It was a way of making external all the worries within him, and of handing responsibility for their predicament, and their salvation, to some external gods.

He was a long time hearing the different noise of the river now before he could identify the difference. It was louder, and closer. He looked behind them. There was no doubt but that the horizon before them extended further than that behind them: they were moving slowly down the long slope which marks the end of Khalinrift. He was glad. Tomorrow would surely bring Akbar.

Lara awoke with a jerk. It was still dark. She wondered what had disturbed her and then saw the shapeless silhouette of Nevir in his loose-fitting desert clothes moving about carefully. He whispered to her that it was morning as he collected and packed their possessions, and that they should move on at once.

Waking Streetpoet was difficult. The spring sun was not as ferocious as the sun that burnt in the mid-year, which the Cythrons call Endyear, but it was hot enough to burn. All of them, even Nevir, were suffering from loss of water and from burnt, cracked skin, and perhaps Streetpoet's self-diagnosis was right; certainly he was not well.

They drank the last of their water. 'We are not far from Akbar,' said Nevir. 'We shall survive today, and this evening we shall be there.' They rode on. Lara found herself locked in her own thoughts. Her mind, freed from the immediate problem of survival by the Rhav's information, was released to wander over her other worries. Fenras: had it survived the Agaskan? Mabeta: where was she now? Ormaas: what had happened to him? For a while it seemed to her, indeed, that everyone else in the world was dead, and that only these three crossing an eternal desert had survived of the human race. Her horse stumbled wearily. The Rhav's back was the only thing she saw as they travelled on.

For Streetpoet the journey was quite different. He was wedged in the saddle, desperately uncomfortable, with a sore rubbed patch raw at the base of his spine. Like one who is entering a dream he felt the thoughts run sensibly through his mind, and then he found that the sense had become nonsense; jerking himself back to consciousness, he found that the whole edifice of thoughts both sane and insane had collapsed, and he was left only with the rubble. He felt so tired. Too tired. Again he forced himself awake. But I'm tired. So tired. With a shock he re-emerged, only to nod again. Tired; too tired; I'm far too tired.

He was on a cliff, with the sea behind him. He had never seen the sea, but knew at once what it was. All that water seemed fantastic, and he laughed at it. The laugh echoed slowly around the cliff, and turned into the slow boom-boom-boom of the Ingsvaal. For a moment he was frightened, but the echoes died away.

He was hanging on to the cliffs. He turned around, and a man was coming out of the waves. A naked figure, huge and scarred, stepped towards him. The figure must have been vast, for Streetpoet on his cliff was like a fly on a wall to him. And then the minstrel gasped. He saw the figure's face, and it was not the ornate crown it wore that made him cry out, but the face beneath the crown. It was his own.

Streetpoet felt the chill of foreboding in his spine and ribs turn to certain dread, which sapped his bone marrow and left him weak. The figure approached. Its brown skin was ripped and putrid, and hung from the angular bones that jutted just beneath the flesh. The unmistakable face was haggard and drawn, the skin tight and drumming across the cheeks and high cheekbones. The figure came nearer. A long scar on its chest began slowly, horribly, to open. The tissue which had joined the flaps of skin tore silently and regularly as the creature stepped closer. In the open wound Streetpoet could now see the internal organs, washed with strange juices and pulsing and twisting inside. Streetpoet turned his head away. He clung to the face of the cliff. Through his closed lids his eyes registered intensified darkness, and he knew he was in the creature's shadow. A smell of putrefaction entered his nostrils. The stench was death. He opened his eyes, and for a moment nothing registered in the darkness. Then he realised where he was. He was in the gaping wound.

Architectural vaults faded into shadow above him. He stood on a gently glistening, pulsating floor, finely honeycombed with dark veins on its maroon surface. He stepped forward, and as he did so vermilion light flashed about the cavity. He ducked to avoid a globular stalagtite suspended before him. The light flashed again. It was coming from somewhere behind him. Its message was a threat. He stumbled on. The maroon surface gave way as he crossed it to soft and glaucous grey, which sagged beneath his feet. The stench was unbearable, and the light flashes brighter.

There was no motive to his actions beyond fear. Fear drove him forward. Fear led him to find some hiding-place. Ahead of him was a tunnel. The floors and walls were damp, hard, and regularly ribbed. The vermilion light penetrated less effectively here, and he was grateful for the darkness.

He lay still for a moment. The cave seemed to echo the sounds of his breathing, of his heart, of the blood pounding in his ears, until the noises seemed to come not from within him but from around him.

He crawled further into the tunnel. He was now entirely out of the light. Unseen things scuttled away from him. The roof came lower, until the ribs rubbed slovenly against his head and neck. He lowered his head and at once his face encountered something thick and damp in the passage before him.

Revolted, he tried to pull away, but found he was fast. He raised his hands to his face's aid, and they stuck too. Raving frantically, he tore at whatever it was that imprisoned him, and as he did so he became aware that each struggling move he made was finding a response in the vibrations of the sticky substance. The realisation that it was a web he was caught in made his dread so much the greater. He pushed through desperately, and found his head had broken free, clear of the clinging web. He tried to pull his arms through too. The darkness which had comforted him impeded him now. He was lost in his own corpse, and trapped in a foul tight web; unhurriedly the great spider traced the anxious vibrations.

Despair, fear, dread: he felt the emotions inside him settle fantastically. In the dark he could now hear, at a distance, the brittle sound of hairy legs rubbing down the passage, the crisp clicking of vast jaws preparing for their feast. Two clusters of white eyes, small and faint, surveyed him now from the darkness: in their light Streetpoet could just see the spiny legs pulling the great heavy body towards him. The eyes glowed with greed. Fascinated, he watched the pincer-like jaws open and close. Their sideways movement seemed infinitely more unpleasant than anything he had ever seen before, and a thin juice dribbled from its jaw.

A plate above the mouth curled back like a lip into the parody of a smile, and at that Streetpoet's slumbering emotions were dragged back into play. Fear rose, panic struck out, dread chilled the cave around him and filled his body with ice. He felt the frost in his veins expand them like the ice in a winter rainwater barrel that pushes aside the staves and strains against the iron bands. His being swelled up with icy dread. He pressed against the walls of the passage, stretching them. They gave around his distended figure, and burst him out into another cavity of the body. Growing still, he shouldered aside the organs. The heart dangled obscenely from dull pastel veins, grey and pink; the lungs collapsed as he pushed between them. He saw daylight as the old scar gave again, and the reassuring wall of the cliff with the sea at its foot. The wall tilted nauseously, and a tired horse was climbing it as though it were flat and he looking at it from below. The sky above was blue and clear and the horse continued its curious ascent and the wall tilted again, became the floor of a desert, and the sky that had been above was now ahead of him. Hands were lifting him, a water skin was pushed at his mouth. He remembered the cadaver from which he had escaped and felt his own heart and lungs contract at the thought. He looked at his flesh, and it was burnt and lifeless: it was the flesh of the corpse. So that's what happened, he thought. I grew and grew. I grew into the body that imprisoned me, and my arms were encased in its arms, its legs in my legs. My head peered from its shrunken mouth. And then we were united. Bones fused, flesh joined. The ornate crown was subsumed within my skull. We became one.

The hands helped him up. He stood on legs that were only partly his, and only partly responded when he gave them instructions. He tried to walk, but stumbled and was only just caught. Some more water was put into his mouth, where it seemed to be absorbed without him having to swallow.

'I'm all right,' he told them. The words meant nothing to any of them. They helped him remount. The sun was an agony of unavoidable heat and light. Travelling slowly, they resumed their journey.

Lara rode by Streetpoet's side. Her pretty face was blotched with sun and flaked with rough skin and dry dust. Blisters formed in the shadows at the side of her nose. 'Sing us a song,' she said. Her voice croaked.

'I don't know any songs,' he replied. He was still wondering whose body he wore over his own. He could tell by sight that it wasn't his own, for his flesh had been firm and whole and this was raw and dying; he could tell too by touch, for the skin had no sensation and no feeling penetrated from the surface to the whole Streetpoet encased within.

'Yes you do,' she insisted. 'You're Streetpoet. You're a minstrel. Nevir,' she called in her hoarse croak, 'Nevir. Tell him he has to sing a song.'

Without turning the Rhav obeyed Lara's instruction. 'You must sing a song.' Then, with more interest in his voice, he added a request. 'Sing the Song of Tlot. Sing of the funeral of Tlot and of the river and the ice.'

Streetpoet thought about it. The request seemed reasonable, and the words came unbidden to his mind. In a voice that

was richer than that of either of his companions, for he had just
been given the last of their water, he chanted the song.

> Brave the warriors who loosed silver tears
> As the maidens sang of Tlot's virtues;
> Noble the great kings who watched the craft
> That bore Tlot's body towards the Rift.
> The shore was white with snow, and Khalin ran
> Swifter than a hart to the world's rim,
> And the burning ship of death was carried
> On the flood to Rathkerid,
> The land of death, where with a feast
> The King of Death will greet his guest.
> A frost is on the land, and we have lost
> Tlot, whose loss hath made our kingdom less.

'A frost is on the land,' repeated Streetpoet. 'A frost.'

They mounted an unusually high dune. The dunes had been
getting lower and less dramatic: gentle, docile waves instead of
the fixed wild lashings of the storms in the centre of Khalinrift.
They reached the top of the dune and looked about. The desert
stretched on ahead of them, but the horizon was green.

'The Plains of Myr,' said Nevir. Their journey was done.

Prothal reached Akbar at dusk. The town stands where the
River Nier flowed into the Khalin, and where the desert slopes
down to reach the Plains of Myr. The great gorge which
contains the Khalin widens before then, and the river takes on a
stately, processional air, curling through the flat and fertile
Plains with graceful meandering curves.

Akbar itself is a curious town. Its high walls are more a
protection against encroaching sand than against any mortal
enemy, and its towers are the homes of rich merchants rather
than of warrior lords. It is a bustling, prosperous town, the
most important on the Khalin's route between Cythroné and
Mornet, and trade dominates. Long low barges line its
wharves, great mechanical cranes, harnessing the power of the
river, swing out over a canal system of concentric rings that
irrigates the town as well as providing its transport system,
wagons and pack horses wend their way through busy streets.
It was the town Prothal One-Eye loved beyond all others: he

had a quiet upstairs room in a profitable brothel, friends in the judiciary, and money in the bank. His daughter lived there, and his daughter's mother, and in the sentimental moments that seemed to come over him at increasingly frequent intervals, he longed to settle down in a house overlooking a canal, and risk his money without risking his life in deals on the Bourse.

Consatiné rode next to his mother. He loathed Akbar. Filthy canals linked filthy overcrowded islands. Washing hung across narrow, bustling streets. Everywhere there is noise, smells, dirt. Old men line the streets and chew tobacco, spitting lurid streams of juice into ornate brass spittoons. Conjurers perform ineffectual tricks on every street corner, or troupes of Kapatar dance and swallow fire. To Prothal Akbar may have been life and opportunity; to Consatiné it was dirt and confusion.

They rode in along a wide track that led them through an unmanned gate. The silence and stillness was ominous.

'What has happened?' asked Consatiné through chapped lips. 'Where are the guards?'

'Be quiet,' ordered Prothal One-Eye, harshly. 'Stay here, outside the gate. I'm going in.'

Prothal rode on. His horse sensed its master's tension and stumbled forward reluctantly. Prothal mouthed words of encouragement to it, but dared to make no sound.

He rode along a street of cobbles, flanked by boarded shop fronts and shuttered windows. The horse's hooves echoed in the narrow confines. It was the only noise he could hear.

He reached another archway over the road, leading into the wide town square. One gate was shut; the other hung open, swinging slightly in the faint breeze. A soft-edged smell, not unpleasant, drifted in this wind.

Suddenly a door opened and a figure ran out: Prothal swung his horse to face an Agaskan attack and his hand reached for his sword. Then he dropped the sword back into its scabbard. Facing him was no Agaska. It was a child, naked from the waist down, his legs unnaturally pale and thin, and glistening with a dampness that was like snail trails.

'Cholera!' exclaimed Prothal.

The child reached up a pathetic, hopeless arm but Prothal had turned away. He watched the strange rider ride off, then

returned to the business of dying. All Akbar was dying.
Thousands of rotting bodies in the Khalin had begun the
epidemic; already, the Agaskan had inflicted a defeat as
devastating as any they could achieve in battle, and the water
still flowed on south.

Soon the cholera would reach Cythroné.

Khayrik and Ormaas blundered on through the desert. They
had travelled in a large circle in search of their companions, and
found nothing. They were lost, but now they no longer cared.
The drowsiness of the desert which had killed Prothal's
deserting men was settling on them, and only the shambling
steps of their horses kept them moving.

The sun was an intensity of heat overhead, burning the
moisture from their flesh. Existence had become a monotony of
yielding sand. The desiccating wind plucked twists of dust
from the heaving dunes. They did not speak, conserving with a
miser's care their wandering thoughts and the last of their
spittle.

At noon that day, when the vehement sun was at its height,
and halos of light burnished the sky, Khayrik's mount suddenly stumbled and fell. The horse slid gently down the side of
a dune: Khayrik was strapped to the saddle by his web of
leather thongs and unable to get free. Horse and rider lay
equally still, equally exhausted, and then the horse twisted and
raised its head, and was dead.

'Khayrik!' Ormaas clambered painfully from his own horse
and crossed to where the cripple lay. 'Khayrik!' His voice was
no more than a whisper. He bent over the motionless body.
'Khayrik!'

Ormaas tried to tear at the straps with his wrists and teeth,
biting and rubbing and keeping his useless hands well clear.
Sand had clotted the wounds. Unable to make any impression,
and with dry desert tears stinging his eyes, Ormaas tried to
undo the leather thongs with his fingers. They were too tender,
and could not manage the straps. The pressure on his hands
made them burn again: he found himself holding his hands in
front of him, staring at them as if they caused him surprise, and
unable to do a thing to help the cripple.

At last the pain subsided a little. Breathing deeply to master the agony, Ormaas carefully drew his knife from his belt. His wounds were a matted waste of sand and blood which cracked as he moved them to reveal a moist pale discharge beneath, and Ormaas felt the knife sticking to his palm. The blade had not been sharpened since Mornet; awkwardly Ormaas sawed through the restraining straps.

Carefully he pulled the cripple clear, slotting his wrists beneath the cripple's arms: at least, having no legs, Khayrik had not been trapped beneath the horse. He bent his head to Khayrik's chest. There was still a beat, but it was faint through the clothes, so he opened the cripple's tunic. Beneath, the skin was black and broken. Ormaas shook his head, and carefully closed the tunic again. Every action hurt his hands, but compassion made him hardly care.

Water, he thought. Khayrik had been carrying two skins of water, one on either flank of his horse. Ormaas turned back to the horse. The one on the upper flank was empty, finished the day before; the one on the lower flank was unobtainable if it was not crushed. Ormaas, in a desert that stretched to the horizons all around him, felt he had to check whether the water bottle was crushed. Water obsessed his thoughts. With feet and wrists he hollowed out a space beneath the dead horse. The pain and desert heat were unendurable, and yet had to be endured. He stretched out his foot experimentally beneath the animal's weight, and wriggled his boot off, knowing as he did so that he would never be able to put it back on again. And then the naked foot touched water, that evaporated as soon as it met the desert air, and he knew that the skin had split beneath the horse.

He stood, looking down on Khayrik, who was a neat figure on the sand with his arms stretched out and no legs, and then he bent down, pulling the cripple's weight with his wrists about one of Khayrik's arms until Kharyik was balanced across his back. He stumbled to his feet, with the body sprawled across his shoulders, and unceremoniously dumped him on the saddle, apologising as he did so. He was about to remount on the horse behind Khayrik when, prompted by a light-headed optimism, he returned to the cripple's horse and pulled free the large purse Khayrik had carried. It contained the money for their journey, and nearly eighty talents remained. Clutching it

to his body to avoid rubbing his hands, Ormaas struggled back
to the horse once more. It stood patiently waiting for him. He
poured the money from Khayrik's purse into his own saddle
bag. Money spilled on to the sand, ten or fifteen talents in gold,
but Ormaas ignored them. He remounted, pushing the cripple
forwards until he was safely in the saddle, and the horse moved
forward of its own volition. The gold in the sand blinked
mischievous light behind him. They crested another dune.

A mirage on the horizon mocked them with verdant trees.
Ormaas had been warned of mirages, and stifled the quick
surge of hope that the green ahead prompted. Without hope,
without choice, he rode towards it.

The mirage continued to tempt him. It hardened into leaves
that speckled in the slight movement of air. He could see trunks
and the scrubby undergrowth. He felt despair, and shut his
eyes to keep out the false promise.

The horse accelerated down a slope. Ormaas, fearful for his
balance and his friend, was forced to open his eyes again. He
saw a bright thread of running water ahead of him, lined with
swaying reeds. The horse ran through shading trees. It did not
stop but continued into the stream; Ormaas, his balance
entirely gone, tumbled heavily into the shocking playful
waters. He sat in the shallows and laughed for joy.

That evening Ormaas found a road, and by the road an inn.
The country around him changed. Water became plentiful,
and ran in noisy ditches by the side of the road. They passed
through a small wood. Their dusty, sunburnt features seemed
curious and frightening amongst the domesticated farms and
streams.

The innkeeper came out at the sound of approaching hooves.
He carried a pitchfork, which he thrust at Ormaas menacingly.

'I'll have none of you plague-dogs here.'

Ormaas looked at him. His mouth was still hoarse despite the
water he had drunk, and the voice that replied was a whisper.
'We carry no disease.'

'What's happened to him then?' said the innkeeper, pointing
at Khayrik.

'His horse fell,' said Ormaas, simplifying. 'He's unconscious. He might die.'

'I dare say he will. What do you want?'

'Help for him, and food and shelter.'

'There's a good many died around these parts recently. Where you from?'

'Fenras. In Northreach,' he added, for it was obvious that the name of the town had meant nothing.

'Northreach, eh? Then you'll have come through Akbar. Get out of here. We want none of your cholera here. Get you off.' He thrust the pitchfork close under Ormaas's nose.

'We have not been to Akbar. We're trying to get there now, but haven't succeeded. We got lost in the Rift.'

'What happened to your hands?'

Ormaas held them up for inspection. 'Rope burns,' he said.

'They're a mess. You'd best get them seen to.'

'You'll let us stay?' Ormaas was eager; the innkeeper contemplated them carefully from the length of the pitchfork.

'You can pay?'

'Yes.'

'And you're certain your friend's not got the plague?'

'Yes.'

'All right. You've an honest face, save that it looks half burnt away. I'll believe your story. You'll be coming in then?'

'Thank you.'

The innkeeper led them into a low ceilinged room, cool out of the sun. The innkeeper dressed Khayrik's wounds as best he could with coils of bandage soaked in warm water, and Ormaas, with a tankard of frothing Myrian ale on the table before him, fell asleep.

Chapter 9

Maldroigt

A dark rider on a dark horse galloped through the night. His journey had taken him from Brokmild, where an Agaskan army had first been seen, down the Heront valley to Fenras, where he had stolen a boat. A desperate five days down the rapids of the Heront, during which he had almost drowned when his boat had been splintered in the torrents, took him to the southern edge of the Northreach mountains, where the Heront curves back north to join the Khalin before the two rivers as one cross Khalinrift.

For two wasted days he had been in Mornet, trying to get an audience with the Gros of Ra, whilst his story of Agaskan uprising was treated with contempt, and then he had stowed away on a boat journeying south, his money having been lost with his previous boat.

He was four days out of Mornet and well into the Rift before he was discovered: he tried to explain what his purpose was, and was smashed over the head with an oar for his pains. Two days later, however, a faster moving boat overtook their barge, with news that an Agaskan rising was suspected; the messenger changed boats and carried on south.

He reached Akbar safely on the day that the companions left Mornet, and would have arrived in Cythroné within two or three days of leaving Akbar, except that he was robbed and beaten and left for dead. It was ironic: he had stolen a horse from an Akbar merchant, and the horse had been carrying money; he had spent the money on new clothes so that he would be more easily able to gain admittance to the court when he reached Cythroné, and the new clothes had tempted a gang of thieves. Days of delirium in the woods north of Morn had ended when a passing preacher, braver than others who had been confronted by the ravings of a naked madman in a wood notorious for robbers, had spoken with the man and believed his story. The preacher re-equipped him and sent him on his way and at last, on the same day that Ormaas and Khayrik reached their Myrian inn, Hedch the messenger, the man sent by the Gyr Orland to look for the bastard son of the empress, was returning to his master. Hardly pausing, Hedch went through the gates of the Gyr Orland's palace and through the massing soldiery towards the lighted building at the end of the drive. The windows were brilliant in the darkness.

The meeting was going on and on. The Gyr Orland and his brother stood over a large map and used wooden pointers to slide shallow disc tokens, representing armies, across the representation of Khalindaine. Every so often the Gros of Nanx would impatiently move one of these tokens across the map with the point of his sword.

The Gyr Orland was seriously worried. Each calm, temperate suggestion he had made had been greeted with howls of protest from the bellicose Gros of Nanx, who was all for mounting a major campaign, and 'running the green-skins into the sea at Comtas', as he put it. What was more, he felt that the meeting was having increasing sympathy with the Gros of Nanx, as the Gyr Orland and his brother found increasingly tortuous reasons for not committing themselves to anything.

The Gyr was dressed in his father's famous suit of armour. It was black, enamelled to a high gloss, and trimmed with pure gold. The matching black helmet was on a delicate walnut table near where he stood; the yellow plume shimmered and breathed in a draught from the open window, and the pointed throat protector beneath the visor's snout gouged a scratch in the tabletop. By the helmet were a pair of metal gauntlets, palms upwards with the fingers clutching air. They were like two dead scarabs lying on their backs, and the evening sun made sharp patterns on the articulated armour plates.

The nobles arranged around the table were the leading aristocrats of the many the Gyr Orland had attracted to his venture. To begin with the whole thing had seemed ridiculously easy: all he had done was to announce that he was leading a campaign against the Agaskan and half the chivalry of Khalindaine, bored after the long peace since the Gyr's last abortive campaign, had forgiven him the Débâcle of Othmasht and offered their support. His popularity had rocketed, and at just the right time too, for the news from the royal palace at Verdre was bad, and the empress was not expected to live to Endyear. There were forty days left until Endyear, and the Gyr Orland saw them pass by with something almost like wonder. But now the troubles were beginning. Everyone else seemed to have more forceful ideas than he did, and seemed keener to get them done. All the Gyr wanted was a public reputation and an army at his disposal when he took the throne after Elsban's death; what those around him seemed to want was a rapid victory so that the reign of Elsban would be crowned with glory. It was proving awkward, and the Gyr was growing daily more dependent upon his brother the Gros of Weir.

Now even the Gros of Weir's nimble mind and tongue were tiring, as objections were raised to every scheme he could think of. The Gros of Peltyn, in a suit of blackiron armour ornamented with gilded scrolls and trimmed with scarlet velvet, was nodding his sombre grey beard against his barrel chest while his younger cousin, the Gros of Nanx, elaborated a possible attack through Kuhiar-Hamun and Folhri. He is the danger, thought the Gros of Weir: he is the clever one.

Nanx himself wore an enamelled parade armour, geometric designs of red and blue competing on a pearl-grey ground. Tufts of fawn silk were arranged in the exposed parts at the crook of the arms and around the loins. Energetic gesticulations caused his armour to clatter noisily as he spoke, but he did not care. 'Any size of army could take the pass at Folhri. All I'd have to do is stand there and they'd run away.'

Peltyn smiled intelligently at his cousin's discourse, whilst the Vaine of Gramal and his sons tried to hide their confusion as plan after plan was suggested and discarded by nodding each time the Peltyn-Lord did, much to the annoyance of the Gros of Weir. The House of Gramal did not wear parade armour, did not believe in it. Although their armour was to the same design as that of their companions, it lacked that polished, finely tooled finish; there were no impractical details on their armour which might deflect a sword thrust or weaken a defence. Their bald blackiron suits were trimmed with steel. Six legs were defended by six long thigh-pieces, jointed like the segments on a lobster's back; three narrow waists filled out to formidable chests; six metal shoulders led to six finned elbows via strips of metal plate; at the wrists six incongruous lace cuffs led to six heavy red hands. The Gros of Weir found himself looking at those hands frequently as the debate went on: both of his would disappear into the grip of one of those.

The Gros of Nanx concluded his speech. 'Bravo,' said the Peltyn-Lord softly, and the Nanx-Lord looked at his cousin in pleasure. 'A very eloquent exposition. Come now Orland, Weir, what have you to say in reply to that?'

'Very cogently argued,' said the Weir-Lord.

'So you will accept it?' pursued the Gros of Peltyn.

'There are points we must consider carefully, certainly,' said the Weir-Lord, in a tone that implied that was the same thing, but the Gros of Peltyn still was not satisfied.

'But will you accept it?'

'I don't feel it really answers our immediate needs,' said the Weir-Lord. 'There are technical problems . . . '

No one has ever been convinced by talk of technical problems. The Gros of Peltyn snorted his laughter. 'The only technical problem I can see – forgive me if I am wrong – is that this plan would involve us in some sort of commitment, which as far as I can see is exactly what you two are trying your hardest to avoid. Indeed, and again I ask you to forgive me if I am wrong, the only purpose of this campaign, if campaign it is ever to be, is to raise the popular credit of the Gyr Orland with the minimum possible inconvenience to that gentleman.'

The word 'credit' stung the Gyr Orland, whose finances were still desperate, even more than the Gros of Peltyn knew. 'Er, no . . . that is . . . '

The Gros of Peltyn allowed the firm thin line of his mouth to compress into something which was almost a sneer. 'Yes, your Gyrarch?' he asked, innocently.

'It is a matter of, of . . . '

'Contingencies,' put in the Gros of Weir suavely, but while the House of Gramal might have accepted that, the Peltyn-Lord was not going to.

'Really?' He puckered up his mouth into a frown of polite incredulity after the half-concealed sneer of the moment before. 'And what sort of contingency did you have in mind?'

'Secrets,' amended the Weir-Lord. Contingencies had not

been as useful as he had hoped, so he tried something else. 'Certain political considerations make a . . . certain amount of secrecy necessary.'

'We're only going to fight a few Agaskan,' said the Gros of Nanx, unable to remain silent any longer. 'What sort of secrets does that involve, by Araketh?'

'I'm afraid, cousin, that the Weir-Lord is unlikely to explain that,' said the Gros of Peltyn. 'Secrets are only secrets when they are kept secret. Is that not so, Weir-Lord?'

'Indeed,' said the Weir-Lord, wondering why the Gros of Peltyn appeared to be helping him.

'However, I hope that these secrets do not involve us in anything approaching treachery. The empress is ill; I hope this army is not in any way related to that fact. I hope, in short, that its expressed aim is still its real aim, and that it is to fight the Agaskan and not each other that we have gathered here.'

'Oh, yes,' said the Gyr Orland fervently.

'Good. Then perhaps,' he continued, with a cutting edge on his voice now. 'Perhaps you would explain what possible contingencies or secrets could be involved in fighting the Agaskan.'

Silence. The Gros of Weir picked up one of his brother's metal gauntlets from the table. 'You'll damage the inlay,' he murmured. The Gyr Orland did not reply. The Gros of Peltyn studied the brothers for a while.

'I take it then, that the Gros of Nanx and I are not vital to your plans. I hope not, for I think we shall be leaving. Is that not so? I think we have been insulted enough, don't you cousin?'

'Certainly.' The Nanx-Lord looked hesitant and then, like the man of action he was, strode for the door, only to have it opened in his face before he had reached it.

'Sir,' said a servant in the livery of Orland. 'There is a man to see you. He says that it is of vital importance and of direct relevance to your meeting, and asks to be shown straight in. What shall I do?'

'I don't know,' said the Gyr Orland, irritably. He looked at his brother, but before the Weir-Lord could make a decision, Hedch had entered the room, followed by another servant. 'I'm terribly sorry, your Gyrarch. He pushed past me. I told him you didn't want to be disturbed.'

'Your Gyrarch. Listen to me please, and believe me. I have vital news from Northreach, and was going to Cythroné to tell the empress but heard that she was ill and that you were raising an army here to oppose them.'

'Not exactly,' said the Gyr Orland, who had recognised Hedch as the man he had sent to Northreach to find the bastard and who now assumed Hedch's information would concern the bastard.

'You do not know of the Ingsvaal?'

'The what?' said the Gyr Orland. The Gros of Peltyn coughed politely into his hand.

'An Ingsvaal, my lord, is a particularly large Agaskan rising, or holy war. How do you know that there is an Ingsvaal?'

'The stones, sir. I saw the armies, we all did, but they could just have been involved in a rising. It was the stones that told us it was an Ingsvaal.'

'Hoarstones?' smiled the Peltyn-Lord. It was fashionable to smile at the Old Religion.

'Of course, sir,' said Hedch, primly. 'After many days of extreme activity, the hoarstone at Brokmild told the shaman that the Agaskan were called by their Wells to an Ingsvaal, and that the Avatar of Akhran the Golden is the only thing between Khalindaine and total destruction. I have seen them, your Gyrarch: I have travelled through the wild foothills of the Heront valley and I have seen thousands – millions – of Agaskan, all intent on war.'

The Gros of Weir had followed Hedch's story, his emotions switching rapidly. At the messenger's first words he had been terrified, for he felt that Hedch would blurt out the story of the bastard; mounting amusement followed as he listened to the story of the Ingsvaal, watched the faces of his fellow lords, and realised how this news was exactly what was required to give their enterprise credibility; now he felt fear again, of a different sort, as he realised the implications of Hedch's words. 'Why has there been no news of sieges, of attacks?'

'I am the first to have travelled from Northreach since the thaw and the beginning of the Ingsvaal,' replied Hedch. 'But the Agaskan are not attacking yet; they are simply mustering, bringing together all of their forces in the Thatter.'

'We must follow my plan,' said the Nanx-Lord, on a reflex at the word Thatter.

But the Gros of Weir was having no one interrupting his moment of glory. He called one of the hovering servants over, whispered a few words, and then dismissed the man. In a loud voice, a public voice, he addressed the nobles. 'This, gentlemen, is the moment I have been waiting for. You understand now the need for secrecy; I wanted no panic before the news was confirmed.'

'You expected this, your Grosarch?' asked Hedch.

'Most certainly,' lied the Weir-Lord. 'There were indications, perhaps only to be recognised by we of the blood royal, which made it clear that there was a likelihood of such an event.'

'Have we the proof? Can this man be trusted?' asked the other nobles, including the Gyr Orland, but then the dispatched servant returned with a tray and seven glass goblets, each loaded with good red wine.

'To the success of our expedition,' said the Gros of Weir. Hedch reached across and took one of the glasses, leaving the Vaine of Gramal without a drink. The Vaine looked around in some surprise and then curtly took the goblet of one of his sons. 'To the success of our expedition,' chorused the nobles, loyally.

'And the survival of the empire,' added Hedch.

Messages were sent out across the empire. Information was gathered about Agaskan movement. The Ingsvaal was confirmed.

When the empress was informed she made a special effort. She was washed with purifying waters and treated with potions which would make her strong, albeit only for a very short while. They took her into Cythroné in a shuttered carriage, and gave her more of the potion when they arrived there.

Cythroné was full of people. Twelve days had gone by since Hedch had arrived with his news, twelve days of feverish activity to give Khalindaine a defence against its mighty foe. The word had spread quickly about the Ingsvaal, and many new thousands had converged on Cythroné, to offer their services or to flee. All of them seemed to have packed into Fragma Square and the surrounding streets, and the Cythron militia had been hard-pressd simply to keep the empress's route open. As it was, the ceremony began late, and thus strained the empress's failing health further.

It was a brief ceremony, of necessity, for the empress could not have managed a longer one. She was obviously sick now: she looked frail and the once comfortable cheeks had hollowed and sunk; she could not stand on her own, but was supported by two of the palace guard.

A third member of the guard held the great war-banner, and the empress laid her hands round the shaft in a parody of holding it whilst the guard handed it to the Gyr Orland. The war-banner was magnificent. The field was ivory silk, bordered with a complex design of twisting floral embroidery, which linked decorated lozenges of alternate red and blue. Within the lozenges were medallions containing the arms of her generals in this campaign. At the top, larger than the rest, a rearing gold stallion of Khalindaine on a ground of black memorialised the Gyr Orland's father Ravenspur and spoke also for the son; beside this, moving around the flag, were the arms of the old Gros of Brouma, red and white horizontal stripes, bordered with gold and black, and then the white swan on a shot blue ground which represented the Gros of Peltyn. The Gros of Nanx was next, his arms of a scarlet swan on a complicated ground of gold and deep blue leaves indicating both his family connection with the House of Peltyn and the modern taste for the exquisite. The stern arms of Gramal – a black anvil on a red square – were after these, and then the flowered monogram of the Vaine of Tygyri, the yellow eagle displayed of the Vaine of Hryr, the silver griffin of the Vaine of Dolm. Completing the border, returning the design to the arms of the Gyr Orland, were those of his brother the Gros of Weir: similar to his brother's, the Weir-Lord's arms show a rearing silver stallion on a ground of dark blue patterned with silver.

Encircled by this elaborate border was another embroidered design, which led the eye through a web of interlocking flowers and mythical beasts towards the device at the centre of the banner. A circle of scarlet, shot through with designs in purple and gold, was the focal point of the flag, and the circle bore a great rearing stallion, beautifully rendered in golden thread. Its mane was the air behind its arrogant head; its tail was a fountain of curving gold; its hooves were poised to dash the earth apart.

The Gyr Orland took the banner. The empress's hands seemed reluctant to part with it and she looked at them with surprise, whilst one of the guard who supported her unfastened her grip. The Gyr felt the unaccustomed weight test his strength, for the banner was large, and then, resting the end of the staff on the ground, found the point of balance by pulling the flag upwards. When it was vertical he lifted it off the ground and tried waving it, but its weight was too much and he lowered it to the ground again; none the less he had achieved what was needed, for the vast number of people, soldiers and civilians alike, had caught a glimpse of the banner, and their cheering rippled concentrically down the crowded streets that radiated away. The Gyr Orland handed the banner to his standard bearer, who carefully inserted it into the cup by his stirrup and then, with the horse taking the weight, the Gyr mounted his own horse and the two of them rode away, followed by a line of mounted knights. The banner unfurled, and swayed with the movement of the horse.

The Gros of Weir was relegated to the sixth rank. He acknowledged theatrically the constant cheers of the crowd, whilst his mind assessed the circumstances of the last few days. Since Hedch's arrival there had been no time to think, much less act: there was something determined and righteous about Hedch which made him difficult to ignore, and he had come down to them from Northreach like their consciences, telling them how to behave to the gods they were rediscovering and why sleeping with another man's wife was a sin. He won't survive long when I'm emperor, decided the Weir-Lord.

But the thought of Hedch brought with it the thought of the bastard, and the thought of the bastard brought both despair and hope. Despair, because they were no further towards tracing him than they ever had been, and hope, because that was the way to win back the ear of his brother, and thus regain some influence in court. Since the news of the Ingsvaal the brothers had hardly spoken: the Gyr Orland only had time for military men, it seemed, and strategy had become the only topic of conversation for a gentleman. The nobles had even taken up jousting in the courtyard of Maldroigt: the Weir-Lord hoped that the Gros of Nanx might break his handsome impetuous neck, but of course he never did, and was now the unofficial champion of the army.

The sound of the cheering worried the horses, and made riding and thinking simultaneously something of a hazardous occupation. The Weir-Lord's horse suddenly bucked, violently, and nearly threw its rider off. For a stomach-lurching moment the Weir-Lord was in the air, and then he was back in the saddle again with a thump. He resolved to concentrate on his riding from now on, and did just that.

The whole of Cythroné and half an empire of refugees must have concentrated here, it seemed to the Weir-Lord, but he was wrong. In the slums of the Quarter, where the shanties reach down to the Khalin, whole families were dying of the plague.

The following day the Gros of Weir returned to Maldroigt. He had demanded, and had been promised, a room of his own, and so it was with a good deal more cheer that he returned to his brother's palace.

He had been born in Maldroigt, when the palace had belonged to Ravenspur, and knew its familiar grounds well. The palace itself was less familiar: much of his brother's debt was incurred to pay for alterations, and the building was barely recognisable now.

The grounds are altered too now, thought the Weir-Lord. Untidy clumps of tents cluttered up the vistas as the soldiers bivouacked on the lawns and hung their washing from the trees. The Weir-Lord rode through an avenue of noble elms, but many of them had been felled for firewood. Groups of soldiers, with buckets or bundles of tinder, made their way along the drive, smoking and laughing. The Gros of Weir was appalled by their easy familiarity with his family home, and by the destruction they had caused. Am I responsible, he wondered, with something approaching alarm.

Ahead now was the palace itself, looking then as it does now. Its symmetry was designed to awe the onlooker, and even when spoilt by straggling figures and lopped, damaged trees, it did so. Its northern aspect faces the avenue along which the Weir-Lord rode. Two bulging towers mark the corners of the original keep, while two long arcaded wings, trebling the length of the building, reveal where fashion has replaced military expedience. Above the recently marbled façade, the dormer windows and chimneys of the palace's fabulous roof jostled and fought for space. Each pinnacle bore the flag of one of the hundreds of noble guests accommodated there.

It was a vast, splendid gateau. The Gros of Weir found it as difficult to believe that the building before him was built of marble and wood rather than icing as to believe that he was going to war. Then he reached it and dismounted, and caught his shin on the bottom step of the flight that led to the door, and was painfully convinced of the reality of things.

I must look for Hedch, he decided, but first he looked for Cluny. I wonder if he knows anything to take the swelling off a bruised skin, thought the Gros of Weir.

Hedch was not the easiest man in the army to speak to, both in the sense that he was always busy and in the sense that, once cornered, his idea of conversation was everyone else's idea of monologue. His experiences on his journey south had changed him: he no longer saw himself as a tired old mercenary with a liking for the old ways, but as a prophet and a preacher. Unsympathetic souls suggested that being hit over the head with an oar or being left naked in the woods north of Morn was more responsible for his conversion to active religion than any other factor; whatever the cause, reliable, cynical, self-contained Hedch had been replaced by a new Hedch who burnt as with a new fire.

Eventually, however, Cluny traced the prophet, who was addressing a troop of cavalry on the values of decency and honesty. Earlier that day, at Hedch's instigation, a man had been hanged for stealing the adjutant's seal and forging the requisition for twelve hundred loaves. He would have got away with it if he hadn't tried storing twelve hundred loaves in his tent; the tent had attracted every rodent in the grounds of Maldroigt, and the man had been forced to give himself up. His commanding officer had wanted to make light of the incident, let the man off with a flogging, and keep the bread – it was pointed out that the army quartermasters could not have procured so much bread with anything like so much efficiency. Hedch, however, saw this attitude as typical of the lenient and immoral attitudes that characterised the modern world, and demanded that the man be hanged.

'My master, the Gros of Weir, would like a word with you,' said Cluny, drawing Hedch to one side when the latter had finished his oration.

'Your master is not a man of god,' replied Hedch, 'but I shall not be tempted. I shall see him.'

Cluny led Hedch to the Weir-Lord, who now had a turret room, small and draughty, but at least private.

'Come in,' said the Weir-Lord in his most friendly tone. 'I'm sorry to keep you from your valuable business of stirring up the troops, but I'm afraid there are one or two things I must ask you.' The Weir-Lord hoped that his speech would do: he did not have much experience of dealing with those filled with the light of Menketh, nor of messengers whose message turned out to be that the end of the world was approaching.

Hedch seemed satisfied, and at his ease. 'Of course, Weir-Lord.'

'Well, first of all I want to know whether you found the man we asked you to look for?' The Weir-Lord found himself speaking more slowly and distinctly than usual, as though he were addressing an idiot. 'Did you?'

'I did.'

'Oh. Where?'

'In a town called Fenras, in the Northreach mountains. I watched him initiated into the worship of Menketh. The youth of the town all take off their clothes and beat each other with red-hot pokers.'

'Everyone to their own,' muttered the Weir-Lord.

'Unfortunately I did not see that part. After that they have to stay awake all night.'

'I wouldn't have thought there'd be much choice after being beaten with a red-hot poker,' said the Weir-Lord. Hedch's face hardened.

'It is my belief that we need to introduce a similar ritual in Cythroné. For too long the Cythrons have relied on the monarch making all the sacrifice necessary during the Rite of Endyear. Our nation has grown flabby and without courage. A new time of suffering is upon us, and a new man will be required.'

'Whereabouts is this man now?'

'The new man is within us all. He need only be released by the faith of the true believer and . . . '

'I'm sorry. You misunderstood me. I meant where is the man you were sent to find?'

'I do not know.'

'Could you guess?'

'He was intending to travel to Cythroné with his father's furs. That was before the moon had come and gone twice. He should either be in Cythroné or dead by now.'

'Dead, at a guess. He hasn't been here that I know of. Although, come to think of it, he could be in the next room for all I know, there are so many people about at the moment. Anyway, he was the only one, was he? What was his name?'

'He was called Ormaas of Fenras. He was the only one.'

'Ormaas of Fenras. Thank you. Thank you very much.'

'Thank Menketh, without whom there would be no mankind. It is he who hath made all things come to pass.'

'Perhaps you'd better thank Menketh for me,' said the Weir-Lord. 'You seem to be on better terms with him than me.'

'Menketh is open to all who approach him with an open heart,' said Hedch, leaving the room. The Weir-Lord breathed a sigh of relief. 'Thank Menketh that's over,' he said, and then smiled stupidly at his own words.

The Weir-Lord walked along the corridors of the palace of Maldroigt. Light from the late spring sun lingered on the carpets and tapestries of the gallery, and suspended dust moved gently in its beams. The carpet was stained with mud from martial feet, but the gallery itself was quiet, and the Weir-Lord had chosen it as a good place to write a letter. He sat under the portrait of his father, Ravenspur, at a delicate inlaid desk, and wrote a short note to his brother:

Dear brother,
    I must see you at once about a matter of relative importance.
Your loving brother,
Weir.

He handed the note to Cluny. 'Deliver this in person,' he said.

Cluny retraced his master's steps along the corridors, descended a flight of stairs, and discovered the Gyr Orland's door by the noise. A great seething mob of petitioners and lobbyists were trying to make their voices heard, whilst two guards stood stoically trying to ignore the tumult. Until this moment Cluny had always supposed that the two guards who stand outside the rooms of senior officers were more for show than for protection, but now, seeing that mob of tradesmen all anxious for their accounts to be settled, mothers hoping for preferment for their sons, and salesmen offering everything from cheap pikes to patent wound-healing potions, Cluny realised that the guards were vital.

He was about to despair of seeing the Gyr Orland when the gentleman himself appeared through a sliding panel in the wall behind them.

'Gyr Orland, your Gyrarch,' said Cluny. He felt he had to say something, as the portly figure of the heir to the crown of Khalindaine let himself out like a thief through a secret passage.

'Quiet, please,' said the Gyr. 'Oh, it's you. My brother's manservant, is that right?'

'It is, your Gyrarch.'

'Don't tell anyone, eh? Our secret.' The poor man is obviously desperate, thought Cluny. The Gyr was wearing the uniform of a common infantryman, and now pulled a scarf over his lower face like one who suffers from toothache.

'I have a note from my master,' said Cluny, and handed it over.'

'Thank you,' said the Gyr. For a few paces the Gyr sauntered away casually from Cluny's company and then, turning a corner and getting out of sight of the waiting petitioners, he ran. Cluny had not realised that being important was so unpleasant.

For two days the Gros of Weir waited for his brother's response to the note. He was rather pleased with the phraseology – 'relative importance' indeed. But nothing happened. The morning of the third day saw the Weir-Lord uncharacteristically awake, and watching the first light of dawn from his

bed. Naturally a heavy sleeper, a man for whom the dawn was
as remote as Ehapot, he found the idea of first light rather
interesting. For one thing, he hadn't expected to hear so much
noise. Birds sang complicated baroque themes outside his
window. In the court, armed men clapped their hands against
the cold and swapped the night's news and speculation. Beyond
his door servants were cleaning the corridor, their brushes
scratching against his door. Crepuscular light hardened into
crisp projections of his window on the wall above his bed; he
decided to get up.

He dressed quickly, for the room was cold. Cluny slept, like
most of the servants in the crowded castle, below the stairs,
which meant that the Weir-Lord had no one to call to for hot
water or assistance or breakfast. This is the price of ambition,
thought the Weir-Lord. The thought partly consoled him,
partly chastised him, as he stood one leg on the rush-strewn
floor and drew his hose over the other.

Having dressed, he crossed to the window. The lightness in
the sky had not yet reached the ground, and burning through
the darkness were innumerable camp fires. The Weir-Lord
turned away, wondering about his brother and the message
that Cluny had taken. He wondered too about the passage that
his brother had used to escape undetected from his room: the
Weir-Lord had played in those passages as a child; surely he
could still find his way through them. It was very early.
Perhaps it was a good time to find out?

The corridors were deserted by the time he had dressed, and
very dark. The Weir-Lord groped his way along the wall until
he came to a shuttered window. He pulled a long bolt and
folded the shutter back: light, grey and cool, puddled the
corridor. He continued on his way.

His brother's room, as befitted the owner of the palace and
the army's commander, was the main room in the building, a
large bedroom with its own suite of dressing rooms and
drawing rooms attached. The Weir-Lord made his way to it,
stopping just around the corner from the guards, and then
rapidly slipping round the corner with his back to the panelled
wall. He tapped each panel as he passed until he reached one
that was hollow. The guards still had not noticed him. He felt
for the moulding at the bottom of the panel. His fingers

encountered a piece that was loose. As he lifted it the door slid open; still holding it he stepped inside, and then let go to find it closed on him. Inside, it was utterly dark.

Cluny poured the old veteran who sat by him another tankard of ale and then mulled it with a poker from the fire. The liquid hissed and spat for a brief moment and then settled down. 'I suppose not,' he was saying, in answer to the other's question. 'At least, not in the way that you would understand it. He's not interested in legends or heroes or anything like that, it's true, but he's daft about boats.'

'Boats?' said the veteran. They had been drinking all night; his reflexes were slowing.

'Boats,' confirmed Cluny. 'He wants to be a sea captain. I've often heard him say that. He wants to explore the world. He's got this theory that there must be land to the south.'

'He's daft,' said the other. 'He'll fall right off the edge of Hrakar's skull. Serve him right too.'

'I suppose so, but you should hear him talk about it. He could persuade you to go, I'm damned sure of it.'

'He's persuaded you then?'

'Yes.'

'You're as daft as he is.'

Meanwhile the object of the veteran's incredulity was no more than two strides away. The servant and the veteran sat in a vaulted room beneath the main stairs; the master, entirely confused by now and wishing he had brought a torch, groped his way along a descending passage that passed right by them.

He had started well enough, feeling his way along the outer wall of his brother's room, but obviously some obstruction had been placed across the way into that room, for although the Weir-Lord had found it easily enough it had not given. In fact the Gyr Orland had at last persuaded the pretty serving girl to spend the night with him: she accepted his offer partly to get away from the thousands of soldiers who now littered Maldroigt. She could satisfy the demands of one overworked Gyr; two thousand bored soldiers were quite another matter.

Meanwhile the Weir-Lord, having given up on the door that led directly into the Gyr Orland's room, remembered another door from a corridor on the far side from where he now stood.

As he recalled it, you had to go down a flight of stairs, and then up another somewhat later. He had found a flight of stairs: he'd been going down ever since.

He continued on his way leaving the celler where Cluny and the veteran were talking far behind. His hands encountered thick damp moss on the walls as he felt his way along. The passage seemed to descend for ever, but was apparently now dead straight at last. Suddenly his toes were in water, and he stopped. Presumably this passage continues down, he thought pessimistically, straight into the water. I was lucky I wasn't drowned.

A faint light ahead of him, however, persuaded him that the tunnel reached its lowest point here, where the water was, and that it climbed again to daylight and freedom ahead. He had long since given up on finding his brother; all he wanted was a way out. He splashed through the water, feeling it creep up his hose depressingly, and fill his soft boots with damp unpleasantness.

The light ahead became a sombre shaft. With a start he realised where he must be: he had left the palace, passed beneath the old moat – now mostly dried up, thank Menketh – and was in the grounds. He walked towards the light: the thought of making a return journey beneath the moat was not at all appealing.

The light was an air-shaft, a circular pillar of stone sunk into the ground like a well. Up one side of it were rusty iron rungs, set into the wall; the tunnel continued before him, into darkness.

He chose the air-shaft. It was only fifteen strides or so to the top, after all, and should present no problem. The rungs were damp with dew, and slippery. Twice his feet slipped off the iron; his legs swung momentarily before his already battered shins found the rung again. None the less, tired and annoyed but safe at last, he reached the head of the shaft.

The top of the shaft was proud of the earth by a good half stride. He looked around him. He was surrounded by troops, of course: as nonchalantly as he could, but feeling like the stage Araketh who emerges through the floor in children's plays at Endyear, he appeared.

A familiar smell reached him. He climbed out, stood gratefully on the firm ground, and turned around. 'Ah! Gladge you could make it,' said the pipe-smoking colonel from Myr. 'Have a gladge of wine.'

Dusk fell over the royal palace of Verdre. The empress lay in the dark behind heavy deal shutters. Attendants brought soap and water.

Carefully they washed her, flannelling her face delicately. The doctors wrapped her jaw with bandages, and massaged the flaccid flesh of her cheeks. As though mimicking their actions, an apothecary mixed grey powders and kneaded them to a paste. They smoothed the paste over her face to the edge of the bandage and waited until it was firm. A black-gowned cleric from the Order of the Twin Stars chanted archaic songs from the foot of the ornate bed.

They removed the hardened plaster from her face. The apothecary melted a beaker of creamy wax over a small flame and poured it into the plaster mould, and the doctors washed their hands.

When the wax had set they broke the mould, and a message was sent out to Vlatri tan Bul who waited with his paints and his assistants in the ante-room beyond. Vlatri entered, and with swift dexterous strokes of his brush coloured the features of the mask, until it matched exactly its original. He handed the mask to the cleric, and a maidservant put out the candles. The cleric took the mask in his hands and held it out over the recumbent form in the bed, before laying it carefully on a chair beside his empress.

They filed out of the room slowly, to carry the news of the empress's death to the new emperor. The death mask lay beside the empress like a sloughed skin. The mask's painted features had more life and colour now than the vacant face on the bed, and an extinguished candlewick smoked spirals of grey into the room.

Chapter 10

The Plains of Myr

Ormaas stood by the open window, bending to look through it.
It was nearly noon he judged, by the position of the sun, and he
had only just climbed from his bed. He smiled: he had slept a
long time.

Fields of ripening corn and grass rolled complacently
towards the horizon, studded with square brown barns and
seamed by dry-stone walls. Copses of trees, entering their
summer foliage, were darker green in green meadows. He
listened to the birdsong, and trilled a short accompaniment
until the tension on his still chapped lips proved too much.

Ormaas crossed back to the bed. Khayrik still slept, band-
aged heavily, but his breathing had lost its awkward anger and
his sleep was now more like rest than an escape from pain.
Ormaas carefully pulled the blankets from the cripple to listen
to the heart beneath the thin black bandages: it beat comfortably, with a slow regular coupled rhythm. Tenderly he
replaced the blanket, pulling it carefully between his wrists.
'What a pair of cripples we are,' he told the sleeper.

Ormaas dressed with difficulty, mismanaging the swollen
bandages that were wrapped around his wounded palms and
having to repeat patiently each motion until he got it right, and
then he went down the stairs for a very late breakfast.

The Lady Ra had made the suggestion, and it had proved to be
a good one. The cholera epidemic in Akbar had confused and
disgusted them: they felt cheated and angry with the gods.
Nonetheless, the Lady Ra had kept her wits about her; whilst
Prothal and Consatiné cursed their fate and argued about their
next move, she remembered her cousin the Vaine of Akbar.

Prothal had laughed weakly at her suggestion. 'What is the
point of staying with him? We'd only catch the disease.'

'No, you don't understand. My cousin is only Vaine of Akbar
in name, rather as Consatiné here is Vaine of Mornet but

doesn't actually do anything. Luetah-vaine-Akbar sold his castle in the town years ago, to pay off some debt or another, and now he lives in a smaller castle on the Khalinwatch. He would put us up, I'm sure, and particularly if we offered to pay. I have never known a man so short of money.'

'Can you find this castle?' asked Consatiné.

'I believe so. I stayed there often when I was younger,' she said, referring to the time when her finances, too, were far from healthy. 'I haven't been there since I married, and the old Vaine's died since then, but I'm sure Luetah will remember me.'

She was right, of course. The Vaine of Akbar was delighted to see his elevated cousin, the Lady Ra. His castle was small and ill-kept, standing on the edge of a bow-shaped lake which had once, until the meandering river had deserted it, been part of the Khalin. Now the Khalin's nearest point was several thousand strides south; nevertheless, the castle was still considered part of the Khalinwatch, the string of fortresses which, in the years before Akhran the Golden had united Khalindaine, had guarded the southern borders of Myr from envious eyes. Many of the castles were in disrepair, or had been destroyed; only in the far south, where the river passed close to the mountains of Astesch and the Thatter, and where there was still a threat of Agaskan raids, were they maintained in fighting condition. Certainly no one would have described Luetah-vaine-Akbar's castle in such a way: walls had been knocked down, or had fallen; turrets were abandoned to ivy and alpine plants; arrow slits had been boarded up against the draught.

Unwashed and desperate looking, they had found it difficult to persuade the ill-disciplined guards that the woman before them was indeed the Lady Ra; fortunately Luetah himself, clutching a chicken bone and trailed by a pack of dogs, had waddled into the courtyard and had recognised them. 'Welcome to Hoej,' he told them. 'What can I have done to receive such an honoured guest as her Ladyship the Lady Ra and her handsome son the Vaine of Mornet. Come in, come in. Make believe you're at home.'

Despite this greeting, it was Prothal One-Eye who most felt at home in the tatty bastions of Hoej. Before nightfall he had won twelve talents from the captain of Luetah's disreputable guard, and was now playing cards with the steward.

A shout from the courtyard disturbed their game.

'Who can that be?' asked the steward. 'Krunf?' – he referred to the captain – 'Have your lads been drinking again?'

'Probably,' replied Krunf without concern.

The shout was repeated.

'Doesn't sound like one of your troops, I'll admit,' said the steward.

'Who is it then?' asked the captain, getting up and looking out of the shuttered window. 'Hey, you. What do you want?'

'I am looking for the Vaine of Akbar.'

'And who might you be?' The man rode a chestnut horse. Its flanks gleamed richly even in the half-light.

'I'm Cluny, messenger from the Gros of Weir. I wish to speak to the Vaine.'

'Hang on, I'll be down.'

The captain disappeared from the window, and Cluny heard steps approach the door, the bolt drawn back, and then was admitted to a dark corridor. 'Who are you?' asked Cluny.

'Krunf, captain of the guard.'

'What guard?' asked Cluny, amused.

'They're out,' said the captain. 'I'd have gone with them only I fancied a game of cards. We've got some strangers staying. Wish I hadn't bothered now – I'm twelve talents down.'

'Strangers? A young chap name of Ormaas of Fenras? A fur trader?'

'No. Only young chap we've got's the Vaine of Mornet. Can't be the same bloke.'

'An impersonator?'

'He's brought his mother if he is. Anyway, the Vaine knows them. Apparently they're his cousins or something. Is that what you aim to see the Vaine about?'

'Yes. I'm sure he will help, as a favour to the Gros of Weir.'

'I'm sure he will.' They were both thinking of the same thing: the vast amount of money the Vaine of Akbar owed, and the even vaster amounts the Gros of Weir possessed. 'I'll take you in.'

They entered a long dining hall, illuminated only by the light of the fire. A dozen dogs fought for scraps tossed them by their master, whilst he sat and listened to his cousin recount her adventures. 'I'm glad about that,' said the Vaine expansively, after having been told of the Agaskan army that had plunged into the Khalin. 'There's been too much silly talk about the Agaskan recently. People have even been talking about an Ingsvaal. The Gyr Orland has even assembled an army, I've heard, at Maldroigt, ready to fight them. There won't be anyone to fight, the way you tell it.'

'This was not the only Agaskan army. When we were in Northreach we saw many hundreds of thousands more.'

'That's Northreach,' said the fat Vaine, complacently, whilst the thinner one stared in amazement. There was a knock on the door and the captain of the guard and a well-dressed servant stepped in. He stood there before two Vaines and the wife of a Gros, and was smarter than any of them. He ignored Consatiné and his mother and spoke to the Vaine of Akbar.

'A messenger from the Gros of Weir,' said the captain.

'Oh.' The Vaine reached out and caught his captain by the sleeve, pulling him closer so that he could whisper in his ear. 'It's not about money, is it?'

His breath was garlic and wine. 'No,' said Krunf, straightening hastily. 'He's looking for someone.'

'A traveller from Northreach,' explained the messenger. Hoej really was the most peculiar place, he thought. No guards, no servants as far as I can see, unless those two at the table with the Vaine are servants, and they look more like tramps. 'A fur trader from some place called Fenras. Name of Ormaas.' He had asked the question a dozen times since his master had, without consulting his brother, decided it was time to hunt out the bastard, and each time the person he had asked had looked as Luetah-vaine-Akbar looked and said 'Never heard of him.' Cluny was not prepared, therefore, for the voice behind him.

'Ormaas of Fenras? Travelling with his cousin Lara and a cripple called Khayrik. We travelled down from Mornet with them, but lost them in the Rift.'

'And who are you?'

'Consatiné-vaine-Mornet. This is my mother, the Lady Ra.' The young man's tones belied his filthy appearance; Cluny was inclined to believe him.

'You know this man?' Cluny was surprised, but did not forget to add 'Sir' after a short pause.

'I knew him. I do not imagine that he is still alive.' Briefly he recounted what had happened to them in the Rift. 'I have not seen them since the night the Agaskan attacked,' he concluded.

'Why are you looking for this man?' asked the Vaine of Akbar.

'He was bringing some furs for the Gyr Orland, and my master thought he would do all he could to ease the Gyr's position. They say the empress is very ill, and the Gyr is entirely occupied, night and day, with preparations for war.'

'Oh yes, for war. There isn't going to be a war, according to what I hear from my cousins here,' said the Vaine of Akbar, but before he had finished the Vaine of Mornet had spoken.

'Where?'

'Maldroigt, my lord. The Gyr Orland has put his palace at the disposal of the empire. He has never been more popular.'

'I must join him at once.'

'Consatiné!' said his mother. 'You've only just come out of the Rift. You need rest.'

'How can I rest when the empire needs me.'

'It's getting on all right without you now, isn't it.'

'Apparently not,' muttered the Vaine of Akbar.

'Can you lend me a horse?' asked Consatiné.

'I can sell you one,' said his cousin.

'Good. Do you ride tonight?' The latter was addressed to Cluny.

'Yes, sir.'

'Then I shall come with you.' Consatiné stood, painfully. He had hardly been out of the saddle since that night of the Agaskan, and had been as weak as his mother until that moment. Now he seemed filled with new vigour as he walked, uncomfortably but confidently, to the door.

'I shall choose a horse,' he said.

'I'll come with you,' said Luetah-vaine-Akbar, and they descended the stairs from the hall to the court, followed by Cluny. Luetah had half a mind to try to sell Consatiné his own horse back, but one look at the crippled, dusty specimen which confronted him persuaded him that that was not pos-

sible. Instead, he settled for selling him a handsome-looking
stallion that was older than it looked, and whose wind had truly
gone.

Nevir led them to a pool of standing water; a few hundred
strides from where the last desert sands petered out amidst
coarse, thin bladed grass. There he left them, to return to his
people. He had a story to tell, of the Girn and of their revenge.

  They rode together through an increasingly verdant land,
and Streetpoet taught her the names of flowers she had never
seen before. They reached Akbar one dismal afternoon, and
had only to see the heavy pall of smoke as the town's wooden
slums were cleared, and to hear the tolling of a toneless wooden
bell as the death-carts did their rounds, to know what had
befallen it. They turned their horses away from Akbar, and
found themselves on the busy road that led to Morn and thence
to Cythroné. Streetpoet's horse died beneath him on that road,
and the refugees who fled from the Akbar plague and the
rumours of the Agaskan pushed it to one side of the road, for
these were the earliest refugees. Later would come those more
desperate, and they would have eaten the horse.

  It had not been a conscious decision, to travel towards
Cythroné; rather, they had gone the way of the many. None
the less, once made, it was easy to rationalise. Alone in the
world, all their friends apparently dead, where else could they
go but Cythroné? Where else could anyone go?

Cythroné was in confusion. Like legendary curses the blows
had fallen upon the city: the rumour of the Ingsvaal; the death
of the empress; now, most immediately and terribly, the
cholera epidemic.

  Far upstream, where the corpses rotted and great flaccid
gouts of maggot-ridden flesh still fell away from trusty bones,
the disease had first found a home. The corrupt water had
washed through Akbar and southwards. No town had any
defence. Now Cythroné was taken. The Khalin fed fifty
thousand Cythron homes. Only those rich enough to move
away escaped. Within five days of the ceremony in Fragma
Square the Quarter had been devastated and the living were
outnumbered by the dead; by the time of the death of the

empress the whole south bank was gripped by the wasting fever.

Fear was tangible in the averted faces of friends who no longer greeted each other on the street, in the suspicious eyes of children watching their younger sisters die, in the creamy pallor that was the first sure sign before the dehydration and the agony of wasting. There were empty houses and boarded rooms, and bitter epitaphs scratched on doors. Carts plied the streets to take away the dead, their ragged drivers calling their trade with relish. 'The Body-Burner has come. The Body-Burner has come.'

Unwashed children stood at the doorways of narrow houses, their tears smearing their dirty cheeks as they watched the Body-Burners heave away a parent and pile the corpse into the back of the cart, where it would lie, familiar and yet unfamiliar, until the rough tarpaulin was pulled over them and the cart was led off.

The Bourse was abandoned. Ships stood idle, unable to find crews, or became the tombs of those who stayed on board. Several were looted and then fired, and blackened hulks were frequent along the wharves. In the House of the Condemned, overlooking the fatal river, the Gaolmaster died, worrying over quotas and systems to the end, while the prisoners, who were due to die anyway, seemed immune.

In the confusion, the coming of the emperor Dalerath made little impression. Almost his first move as emperor had been to withdraw from his capital, and the court and army were moved inland to Rhalman, a small market town in the Plains of Myr. The empress had accompanied them, for they had decided to perform the cremation there. The religious orders had squabbled, of course: some felt that the emperor needed to be crowned at once, in Cythroné, whilst others felt that he should be crowned in Rhalman. Still others felt he should not be crowned at all, until the epidemic was over. Dalerath, caught between conflicting views, allowed himself to be persuaded one way and then another and wished that he was still Gyr Orland. Power was such a worry, he found.

The court reassembled in Rhalman, surrounded by the army. They overflowed the market town terribly, laying waste the neighbouring fields, and their numbers were swollen each day by refugees fleeing the Ingsvaal or the cholera. The situation was growing impossible.

Ormaas smiled shyly at the servant girl. He had seen her every morning, crossing the yard with her basket of twigs while he washed under the pump. He fumbled with the ties at the neck of his shirt, his hands still clumsy with torn nerves and bandages, and then reddened as she smiled back.

'Here,' she said. 'I'll do that.'

She put down her basket and stepped up to him. With easy fingers she sorted out the strings and made a bow. He saw that she had a tooth missing from her upper jaw, and that it only showed when she smiled.

She finished the bow, pulling it tight with a flourish. 'There now. Any time you want yourself dressing or undressing, you just ask for Melsi,' she said with a wink. Ormaas looked down to avoid her eyes, and stared into her cleavage instead.

'Thank you,' he said, she picked up her basket and continued on her way. He paused for a moment as her bottom wiggled its way through the door, and then followed her, looking for breakfast.

There was plenty to eat. The plague in Akbar was deterring many farmers from trading with the town, for even the offer of high prices would not tempt the steady Myrians into risking their lives, and so while the town starved the villagers had a surplus. Ormaas washed down the bacon with a tankard of ale and then stood up, wondering what to do next. He had exhausted conversation with the landlord and his greedy, pregnant wife days ago, and would have moved on had Khayrik been better and had he anywhere to go.

Melsi was in the kitchen. 'How is your friend?' she asked.

'Much better,' he replied. 'He was almost conscious this morning. The fever has gone entirely, and the swelling is reduced.'

'Ugh,' she said. Ormaas's small-talk had not been improved by his time in the Rift. 'What are going to do today?'

'I don't know. I might go for a walk.'

'Have you been to Chintup Topping?'

'Where's that?'

'Where's Chintup Topping? Why, it's the only hill for miles.

You can see right into Khalinrift from there, and almost as far as Akbar too. You must have seen it. It's huge.'

'I'm from Northreach,' said Ormaas, with a touch of pride. 'There are no hills on the Plains of Myr, none at all.'

'Then I'll show you a hill. Come on, I'll take you. I'll give you a view you won't forget in a hurry. You come to Chintup Topping with me.'

A small troop of mounted soldiers rode up to the inn. Although they all wore the blazon of the same master, their armour was different in every case. Some wore closed helms, others morions, whilst one had an archaic wide-brimmed helm with a domed crown. Legs and arms were armoured indiscriminately; quilted leather vied with burnished steel or blackiron. In several cases it looked as if a single suit of armour had been divided between many. Simply from their appearance it was possible to see what they were: the retinue of a poor man, who perhaps tried a little banditry on the side.

They tethered their horses and walked in.

'Where's Blunct?' asked Krunf, as he walked in. He was resplendent in yellow hose, a long black pleated pelisse, a polished breast-plate and a plumed morion, with a dagger thrust nonchalantly into his belt and a heavy black moustache grinning over his lip. 'I hear you've got a stranger, a lad called Ormaas, staying here?'

Blunct's wife, the landlady, looked up from sweeping the floor. 'Blunct's feeding the chickens, and yes, there is a young chap o' that name staying here. What's it to you?'

'Never you mind.'

'Ah,' she replied. 'But I do mind. I mind a lot, when the likes of you and your cronies come barging into my inn and asking questions. Come on, what do you want with this Ormaas?'

She was a formidable woman. The captain of the guard looked at her and then decided to take her into his confidence. 'Come here,' he said, and then bent over her so that his men wouldn't hear. 'This Ormaas might be worth a good bit of money to me. We got a messenger from the Gros of Weir, night before last, looking for this fellow. Shot us some cock and bull story about "being concerned as the lad is bringing furs for the Gyr Orland", or words to that effect. Likely tale. You don't send out messengers if you're simply "concerned" about some-body, you only send them out if you want that body. So, I reckon there's going to be a reward.'

'This chap hasn't any furs.'

'Oh.' Krunf was surprised, but rallied. 'He is from North-reach is he? Came across the Rift?'

'Yes, he did both of those right enough.'

'Must be the same chap then. Where is he?'

'What about my reward?'

'Your reward? What do you want a reward for?'

'For not telling Ormaas first. What's to stop me doing that, him going off, and you not seeing a rubek?'

'All right. Ten per cent.'

She laughed in his face. 'Ten per cent of what? Of your wild guesses? Forget it. Hard cash or nothing. Fifteen talents.'

'Never.'

'If that's how you want it. Ormaas!' she bellowed.

'All right,' he replied urgently. 'you can have your money. Just shut up.'

'Fifteen talents?'

'Yes.'

'Right then. He's gone out with Melsi. She took him to Chintup Topping. Fifteen talents please.'

'You crafty old cow.' Krunf laughed reluctantly. 'He'd better be no trouble. I'm sick of the sight of him already, and I've never even met him.'

'It was you wanted him a moment back,' she said reasonably. 'But I don't expect he will be any trouble. Not after having been up Chintup Topping with our Melsi. Half an hour with her, he wouldn't be able to lift a sword, never mind swing it.'

They laughed together. 'Good wench, Melsi. Seriously though, do you think he will fight. I mean, he might be a friend of the Gros of Weir, might really want to be taken to him.'

'I doubt it, but you won't have any trouble. His hands are cut to ribbons. He couldn't fight off a kitten.'

'Bad as that? Melsi'll kill him then. She's a lively lass, that one.'

'You should know,' said the woman, pointedly.

'Me and every other man from here to Morn.' It was his turn to be biting. 'Only attraction this place's got if you ask me.'

'Ah,' she replied, showing no concern. 'But we didn't ask you, did we? Anyhow, as you're here, and as you're waiting, how'd you like a drink of something?'

'On the house?'

'On your nelly.'

The door from the kitchen opened. Ormaas entered, a bemused half-smile on his face. He was embarrassed by the sight of the men in armour who crowded the room, and turned hurriedly to go. A voice held him. 'You Ormaas?'

'Yes,' he replied. He felt tired, and the tiredness was a heavy blanket behind his eyes.

'You from Fenras? In the Northreach?'

'Yes.' A sudden enthusiasm filled him. Streetpoet and Lara must have survived: no one else would be looking for him. The thought of Lara, however, brought with it a new embarrassment, and a sensation of guilt.

'What'd you say if I told you the Gros of Weir was looking for you?'

'The Gros of Where?'

'No, Weir. You can't say you've never heard of him. Gyr Orland's brother. You must've heard of the Gyr Orland?'

'Yes.' Ormaas's heart sank. Of course Lara and Streetpoet hadn't survived; it was only a miracle which had saved him and Khayrik. He thought about the furs, scattered about the Rift. 'You'll have to tell him I've lost the furs though.'

'He wants to see you, so I hear.'

'He can't. I'm going back to Northreach as soon as . . .'

'Grab him lads!' said Krunf, and his men did, pinning his arms painfully behind his back and sending flashes of agony as they rubbed his palms.

'Sorry about this, love,' said the landlady. 'Nothing personal. By the way, you owe two talents sixty rubeks for the room. I'll get it off your mate when he wakes up.'

'What mate?' asked Krunf, suddenly alert.

'Just a cripple. You don't want him; you never mentioned him.'

'Got some money has he?' said the captain. 'I'll go and get him down.'

'No you don't. My pickings. Understand?'

'You've had your pickings.' They argued bitterly, abusively.

Ormaas had already decided that this couldn't be happening, that it was some hallucination induced by the sun or by that exquisite secret Melsi had shared with him, and so was not surprised to see the captain eventually beaten out of the door by the landlady's broom, nor even to find himself dragged out after, picked up, and seated hurriedly on a horse. He was not even surprised to find, when the horse moved on, that the view he got was of what was behind him, nor to learn that in their hurry they had seated him the wrong way.

'Well,' said the new emperor. 'What's the situation?'

'It isn't very good. We've got an army of a hundred thousand men out there, and they're getting hungry and impatient. Some of the Hedchites are saying you had their leader killed . . . '

'He died of the plague.'

'I know, sire, but the troops don't. They are saying that he was poisoned because he spoke about the bastard in North-reach, the one you sent him to find.' Halfyndruth, pacing up and down as he spoke, suddenly stopped and looked the emperor in the eye. 'Why did you do that? Why send him?'

'He wasn't a religious lunatic when we sent him. He was just a mercenary, and a more reliable one than most. My brother chose him; blame him, not me.'

'Your brother is outside, sire, if you want to see him.'

'I think I'd better. The story of the bastard hasn't really got everywhere, has it?'

'I'm afraid it has, your high majesty. The Hedchites are suggesting that you are not even the true heir, because you are only a second cousin to the empress, Menketh preserve her soul, whereas the bastard is both second cousin and, more importantly, son.'

'Illegitimate though. Anyway, there's no proof that there is a bastard.'

'Nonetheless, sire, the troops are restless. Some more food might go some way towards quietening them down.'

'More food!' The emperor was incredulous. 'Where can I get more food from? You said it yourself. There are a hundred thousand troops out there to feed, and how many hundred thousand refugees? It's like being under siege. I can't even send messages out without danger, because the moment we open the gate to this disgusting little castle' – he indicated the small provincial keep which was his headquarters now, since they had fled to Rhalman from Cythroné – 'half a million people try to squeeze their way in.'

The door to the hall opened with a creak. 'Your high majesty,' said a familiar voice. The Gros of Weir stood at the door. Like everyone else in Rhalman he looked hungry. 'I have news for you.'

'Where have you been. I haven't seen you since the empress died.'

'I have been busy. But I have been busy on your behalf. Halfyndruth, if you would please leave us, I have information which is solely for the ears of his high majesty.'

The emperor Dalerath nodded, and Halfyndruth withdrew, shutting the door behind him. Immediately the voices of the brothers grew louder. 'A fine choice for a messenger, that Hedch,' said the emperor.

'Why on earth didn't you reply to the message I sent you?' demanded the Gros of Weir.

'A religious lunatic, for Menketh's sake. Thank Menketh he died in the plague, that's all I can say. You've heard what he's been saying: that we sent him to Northreach to look for the bastard; that he found the bastard; that the bastard is on his way to Rhalman now. What message?'

'The one I sent you via Cluny. "Relative importance" – the bastard. Remember?'

'Relative importance? I thought that meant I could put it off. You've no idea how busy I've been. Have you seen how many people there are here in Rhalman now. It's frightening.'

'I have seen. More than that, I had to ride through them. But listen. There is only one real way to sort this out, you know, short of handing the whole mess over to the bastard . . .'

'He's welcome to it.'

'As I was saying, short of handing the whole mess over to the bastard, there is only one way of solving your dilemma, and that is to prove you're the true heir, to beat the Agaskan, and to cure the plague.'

'Is that all?' The emperor Dalerath's laugh was sardonic.

'I haven't finished yet. These are the things you must do. Now we must work out how you can do them. First, of course, you must prove yourself emperor: I suggest that you don't hold the coronation here after all, but hold it on a barge on the Khalin and then go immediately to the Keep Akhranta and perform the Endyear.'

'You mean, be crowned on the day of the Rite of Endyear?'

'Why not? We can announce a double celebration, an end to the old year, and the start of the new reign. That should be enough to bring a few people on to the streets; all you have to do is perform the Endyear and you'll have proved that you really are the avatar of Akhran.'

'Brother.' The emperor spoke in a low voice, although there was no danger that they would be overheard. 'What if I don't carry the avatar? What if the bastard has it?'

The Gros of Weir smiled. 'That's all right,' he said. 'I have the bastard.'

'Where?'

'Shhh. Don't shout. He's not far from here, I gather, in the castle of the Vaine of Akbar. It'll cost us some money, but I'm sure we could have him silently lost.'

'I want to see it. I don't want to stick a knife in my guts on top of the Keep Akhranta and then find someone has blundered. I want to know he's dead.'

'Do you really believe that he has the avatar?'

'I don't know. What does an avatar feel like. I don't feel any different. Take the bastard down to Cythroné. Let's have him killed in the House of the Condemned. Can you arrange that?'

'I should be able to. There's a messenger from the Vaine of Akbar downstairs: I'll tell him we want the man, this Ormaas of Fenras, taking down to Cythroné and handing over to the House of the Condemned. The new Gaolmaster is a man called Belphats who would hang his mother for a golden bittern: I don't anticipate any problems there.'

'Good. Arrange it.' The emperor had spoken; the interview was at an end. The Weir-Lord bowed once, in a manner he hoped was ironic, and left.

A heart-hitting shock of cold, and then a dampness. Khayrik's eyes opened for the first time in days: he was lying on a bed, soaking, whilst before him stood a lady in an apron with an empty bucket in her hands.

'See, I told you he wasn't dead,' she said to a figure beyond Khayrik's limited view. 'Is there anything up here worth having?'

'Not much apart from this bag of money.'

'Keep looking Blunct. You never know. If the Gros of Weir wanted his mate he might be worth something.'

The Gros of Weir? Khayrik did not deny the reality of the scene before him, as Ormaas would have done in his circumstances, but he did wonder what on Hrakar could have happened since the Rift.

'Sounds daft to me,' said the man's voice. Khayrik guessed that he was Blunct. 'Why should the Gros of Weir want that chap. Poor bloke was half dead when he arrived here – I thought he had the plague, if truth be known. What should the Gros of Weir want with him?'

'I don't know,' the woman snapped. 'Get on with looking and stop talking.' She walked out of Khayrik's sight. 'Melsi! Where is that girl? I'm going to see if I can see her.'

He heard the creak of wooden stair-boards and then the voice announced it was going to kill that girl if she didn't come soon. It was further away. There was a shuffle, a change in the light that fell on him, and Khayrik saw a man's face looking down at him. 'You all right?' asked the face.

'You Blunct?' whispered Khayrik, virtually inaudibly. It seemed vitally important to him that he should learn as much information as possible.

'That's right. Your friend mention me then?' The man seemed eager for this to have been the case, so Khayrik mouthed yes. 'Seemed a nice chap,' continued the man called Blunct.

'Where is he?'

'Hoej.' The name meant nothing to Khayrik.

'Where am I?'

'Eight thousand strides from Akbar, on the road to Cythroné.'

'Why did they take Ormaas?' There was a tired pause between each word, and the man wondered if Khayrik was going to die.

'I don't know, mate. Wondered if you could tell me.'

The sound of creaking stairs made the man shuffle off. 'Well,' said the woman's voice. 'Found anything?'

'Nothing at all, my precious.'

'Have you asked him anything?'

'I was waiting for you.'

Khayrik realised why instantly. She sat on the bed and pulled the cripple into a seated position, holding him tightly around the upper arms. It was agonising: his chest felt as if it would collapse. She gave him a shake. 'You got anything hidden?'

'No.' There was no sound, only the movement of the lips and the slight inclination of the head to indicate the negative. She gave him another shake, and he tasted something metallic in his mouth. Despite her grip he found he could raise his hands to his mouth, so he did. He coughed uncomfortably and saw blood on his hands.

'He's telling the truth,' said Blunct, who had been unable to look. 'Leave him be.'

She threw him down on the bed. Khayrik saw she was smiling. 'Oh well,' she said, 'we've got sixty talents out of him and his mate, and they didn't cost us a lot. Let's get him out of the place. Where'll we take him?'

'I'll drop him off down the road when I go to Humbri's.'

'Make sure you leave him somewhere he'll not get back from, that's all. I don't like to think of cripples around the place.'

'Yes, precious. I'll do that.'

Khayrik found himself man-handled down the stairs. Because he had no legs, people assumed he would be light, like a child. There was much cursing, therefore, when they discovered it took three of them to carry him down the stairs. Blunct and the girl called Melsi had dressed him; the woman had thrown a few other valueless possessions into a bag for him. He asked for his shield, but they knew nothing of that: it still lay in Khalinrift, next to the body of Khayrik's old horse.

They put the cripple on to the back of a cart, and started off on the road south. The road was busy, and Khayrik heard Blunct shouting at fellow travellers: some he greeted politely, others he ordered out of the way. They reached a wood. Khayrik saw the branches close in over the cart, and heard the different sound of the cartwheels over mud instead of trodden road. Then the jolting stopped.

Blunct must have jumped down and walked to the back of the cart, for when Khayrik next heard his voice it came from behind. Then the cart rocked as Blunct climbed up, grabbed Khayrik by the arms, and turned him round. There was another jolt as the man jumped back down, and then his arms were pulled again. Khayrik found himself dragged, arms first, off the back of the cart, and then he was swinging to the ground. For an agony of moments the cripple found himself vertical for the first time for days, and then the arms that gripped him relaxed and he was allowed to fall to the earth. It was cool and smelt of loam.

'I've left you some food,' said Blunct.

'Thanks,' replied Khayrik, but the man didn't hear. He had climbed back up behind his horse and stirred it into motion with the reins. Khayrik heard it creak and clip its way back to the road.

Consatiné was tired now, but determined. A quiet anger drove him on. He held tight to his sword as they clashed, and then with a sudden thrust he had his blade against the other's chest, and his point touching the other's throat.

The instructor ordered them apart. They separated, bowed, and started again. Again Consatiné won.

He had been six days in Rhalman now, and had watched the disillusion that had swept through the gathered multitude in those days. 'Why don't we do something'; 'why doesn't the emperor do something'; 'we're hungry'. The town was engulfed entirely by makeshift dwellings: tents and huts stretched away from the walls of the old market town and out across the plains. There was no room for more, yet still more came, following the court and the army, fleeing the plague or the Agaskan. Not, as the Gros of Weir liked to point out, that the Agaskan had actually materialised: on the contrary, apart from a few more unconfirmed reports from Northreach, and the discovery of a vast number of bodies in the Khalin, the Agaskan were keeping very quiet, and two theories were current that dismissed the threat of the Ingsvaal. The first was that the Agaskan had risen, but had somehow fallen into the

Khalin and that was that; the second was that the whole business of the Ingsvaal had been orchestrated by the religious fanatic Hedch, founder of the militantly fundamentalist Hed-chites, as a way of drawing attention to himself. Rumour now had it that the army was to be disbanded; Consatiné, training daily in the roped off area at one end of the courtyard, hoped desperately that this was not the case. Others might doubt the coming of the Ingsvaal; Consatiné had seen the Agaskan, and knew that neither explanation would hold true against the evidence of his eyes.

No one would listen to him, however. He had bought a horse and a badly made suit of armour, on his father's credit, and had been given a position in the noble guard which attended the emperor personally, as befitted his rank, and then he had been ignored. Thus, every day he trained compulsively until exhaustion took him over, and every evening he would ride out in his cheap armour to encourage the troops. He did not speak to people, for he felt awkward and tongue-tied about doing that, but he did do his best to look as if he, at least, was always prepared. It seemed to do little good, and recently rumours had suggested that Cythroné was no longer so gripped by the plague – 'there's no one left to kill', said the cynics – and that it was safe to return. He knew that if something didn't happen soon, there would be no army left when eventually the Agaskan did attack.

It was that evening that Lara and Streetpoet arrived at Rhalman. The road they travelled down was lined with people. Many of them were armoured in some way, but few of them seemed organised. Running between the armed men were dirty children and innumerable dogs; it was like some great picnic gone wrong, and in place of the food the people chewed rumours. Between the outlying pickets which hedged the great seething mass of people and the walls of the town Streetpoet and Lara heard seven conflicting accounts of what was going on. An eager old crone who sat atop an upturned wagon smoking a pipe had stopped them and told them that the emperor Dalerath was dead; this surprised them as they had never even heard of this Dalerath.

'Dalerath: the Gyr Orland as was.'

'You mean that Our Lady is dead?'

'Dead? Aye, and half Cythroné with her.'

'And the emperor too?'

'Aye, else why's he not been seen these many days?'

This was too much. They journeyed on.

A young man spoke to them next, haranguing them about their lives. 'Sin and wickedness have brought about the collapse of our powers. Soon the Agaskan will be upon us, for Menketh cannot be mocked nor the power of Hrakar set aside.'

'I'm sure,' said Lara, politely.

'The emperor is not the emperor. Hedch is dead, killed by the imposter for he and only he came to announce the bastard king.'

'Which emperor?'

'Dalerath the Ungodly. Soon Ormaas the Menketh-Blessed will join us though, and drive the Ungodly from his throne.'

They rode on. Ormaas? A curious coincidence, and the name Hedch rang a faint bell somewhere in Lara's memory. She worried over the name for some time, and then realised that the messenger who had started her and Ormaas on this fantastic journey had been called Hedch. Another curious coincidence.

After having been berated and shouted at, it came as a pleasant surprise to meet someone who spoke to them in a civil way, even if the man had no nose. 'Wermbek,' whispered Streetpoet, by way of introduction, as the man with no nose walked up to them.

'Streetpoet. How are you?'

'Living,' replied the minstrel.

'Still got the mandola then?'

'Out of tune.'

'And the women?'

'Wermbek, meet Lara. Lara is my friend, and the friend of my friends,' said Streetpoet firmly.

Wermbek smiled. 'How long you been in town, or should I say out of town, since you'll not get into town for love nor money.'

'We've just arrived. We're going to Cythroné. Why are so many people here. We heard rumours of a plague?'

'Dead right, I'm afraid, although they say it's getting better

now. I'm getting out soon, anyhow. There's no pickings here
for the likes of us.'

'To Cythroné?'

'Or maybe Myr. They say it's still all right there. It's this new
emperor as done it. Till him we were doing all right. Now it's
chaos. No one knows what goes off. There's a million people
wandering about the country, and if you ask me it's only
rumours as 'ave started most of 'em off in first place.'

They continued on their journey, after having arranged to
meet Wermbek again that evening. A young man with a
broadsheet was holding it out to passers-by, asking them if they
could read it to him. Streetpoet shook his head with a smile,
and was surprised when Lara took the paper from the youth
and began to read. 'The emperor Dalerath has announced that
he and the court shall return to Cythroné before the Endyear.
They intend there be two celebrations, the Coronation and the
Endyear, on the day of the Endyear. Never before has such
pomp been seen as shall be seen that day.' It went on, stating
which nobles would be there, and welcoming all who wished to
watch the spectacle from the banks of the Khalin. Lara stopped
reading suddenly. 'It says that the Vaine of Mornet is going to
be there.'

'Consatiné!' exclaimed Streetpoet. 'Did he survive?'

'He must have done.'

'Unless this is a list of who is invited.'

'The Gros of Ra doesn't seem to be on it.'

'Would you invite him?'

Bemused, the young man took his broadsheet back. These
tramps spoke as if they knew personally the nobles they
referred to, yet looked as if they came from the gutter. Still, it
was true that the girl could read. Very strange.

Their next piece of information came from a blind man, who
Streetpoet introduced as Vam A'Graivi, and was the most
surprising of all. After a long time talking of old times, the
blind man mentioned Khayrik.

'He's dead, I'm afraid,' said Streetpoet. 'He was a fine man,
and a brave one.'

'I'm sorry to hear that. Why, only two days ago I spoke to
him, and he seemed to be getting better. He was a good chap
I'll grant, though a bit hasty . . .'

'Two days ago.' Lara and Streetpoet together. 'Where?'

'Loutre. He told me he was abandoned in a wood by someone and then found by this widow. He was out in the garden keeping out the riff-raff for her when he saw me. Called me over, had a word. And now he's dead you say? Short and messy business, is life.'

Rapidly, tumbling words between them like jugglers, Lara and Streetpoet explained to the blind man what had happened. His face lit up with delight. 'Well, if that isn't just like life, eh? Downs and ups, downs and ups.' Chuckling, he wandered away from them.

'Ormaas would never have abandoned him,' said Lara.

'I know.'

'Do you think the blind man got it wrong? Perhaps he mistook someone else for Khayrik. It must be hard when you can't see.'

'Don't you believe it. Vam A'Graivi has spoken to you once, yet he'd know you if he met you again ten years from now. Faces change, voices don't, he's told me: he may seem simple but he's as sharp as they come. I think we'd better go and see Khayrik.'

They turned about, still leading their one, tired horse. A small, dark man, half-Kapatar from the looks of him, stopped them. 'You want to sell your horse?'

'No,' replied Lara, automatically. Streetpoet wasn't so sure. He wasn't used to a horse anyway, and found it an encumbrance.

'You want to buy one then?'

'No.'

'Ah. The young lady knows what she doesn't want, but does she know what she wants? She is like our emperor, who is also certain what he does not want, and announces that the army will not do this and will not do that, but who has not done a thing himself that is positive. Come madam, come miss, come whoever you are: do not be like our emperor. Take the decision. You are two people with but one horse. You want two horses, you want no horses. You sure as death don't want one horse.'

'We'll sell it. Look after it please.'

'I will give you four talents.'

'Done,' said Streetpoet, before Lara could complain that the price was too low. Whilst the dealer delved in his purse, he talked to them about the latest news.

'You have heard, perhaps, that the Gros of Nanx has become a Hedchite?'

'No,' they said, whilst their exchanged glances said 'Who's the Gros of Nanx.'

'Soon, perhaps, they shall find this bastard prince they proclaim all the time, this Ormaas the Menketh-Blessed, although I doubt it. A friend of mine, a Rift trader who knows this Ormaas, tells me that he is under lock and key and is being taken to Cythroné. There, I have no doubt that the emperor will make short work of him.'

'Ormaas, you say?' asked Streetpoet.

'That is what Prothal One-Eye said.'

'Prothal!' Again they spoke together. 'Did he say anything else about this Ormaas?'

'Nothing. What else is there to tell? He'll be killed before Endyear, you can guarantee that, and then either the Hedchites and their like will have to find somebody else, or the whole thing will drop. It depends on how soon the country gets back to normal after all this fuss.' The horse-dealer looked around at the people who surrounded him. There seemed no end to them. Again a curious holiday atmosphere suggested itself to Lara, but she dismissed it, picked the four talents out of the trader's palm, and walked off with Street-poet following.

'We'll have to find Khayrik now. What a shame we've sold the horse.'

'We'll be as quick on foot through these crowds.'

Riding through the field to the left of them, incongruous amongst the thronging masses in their shades of buff and beige, was a knight on a dappled grey. He wore an armour so shiny it suggested cheapness, and the trappings of his horse seemed somehow ill-fitting, as though made for a bigger and stronger animal, but none the less, the sheer buoyant enthusiasm of horse and rider as they capered about the field was compelling.

The dappled grey made Lara think of Consatiné, as they had first seen him in Levafoln. It seemed a lifetime away, yet it was

barely more than three lunar months ago. There was som-
thing else about the figure that suggested Consatiné: a certain
self-consciousness which belied the apparent confidence of this
show-off rider and made him human. At what point Lara
realised it was Consatiné, realised that the figure was far more
than simply reminiscent of the Vaine of Mornet but was he,
was difficult to say: one minute she was looking at a stranger,
the next at her friend.

'Consatiné! Consatiné!' she called.

Streetpoet took up the shout. 'Consatiné! Consatiné!'

Even so, it is unlikely he would have heard had he not passed
quite close, and then suddenly, rapidly, he had whirled his
horse to a halt and dismounted.

'Lara! Streetpoet! By Menketh! You survived!'

'Just,' agreed Streetpoet.

'Have you heard word of Ormaas or Khayrik?'

'Are they not with you?'

'We lost them in Khalinrift,' said Lara. 'We thought they
were dead, but now Khayrik's been seen in Loutre and there's
talk of someone called Ormaas being arrested, or something,
and taken to Cythroné.'

'I've heard the talk. Hedchite nonsense. The Hedchites are
strange people. I agree with them when they say that we must
be prepared for battle, and hate this talk of breaking up the
army, but all this talk of a bastard is ridiculous. Why, my
mother was the closest friend the empress had, until she
married my father and moved from the court, and I've never
heard her even mention the story except to laugh at it.'

'Somebody seems to think that the bastard is called Ormaas,'
said Streetpoet, more to get the information clear in his
own head than to communicate anything, but then Lara got
excited.

'Hedch! Hedch was the man the Gyr Orland sent to get the
furs from Murak, my uncle. Hedch was the man who started
this talk of someone called Ormaas.'

'Is it possible that Ormaas is the bastard?' asked Streetpoet.

'No, no.' Lara's mind was on quite a different track. 'If we
don't do something they'll kill him.'

'I'll speak to the emperor,' said Consatiné.

'I'll see if I can't start a new rumour, to the effect that they've got the wrong man,' said Streetpoet, who knew better than most the strength of the unwritten word.

'I'll go to Khayrik,' said Lara.

Khayrik sat in a rocking-chair. A low stool by its side explained how the cripple had climbed to its height. A warm fire glowed in the hearth, for though it was nearly Endyear the nights were still cool.

'Ysda,' he called, and the widow of Loutre answered.

'Coming, Khayrik.'

'There's no need to come. I was just thinking how much I owe you. You found me in that wood. You've nursed me. I must thank you.'

'No, you mustn't.' She brought in two bowls of broth on a tray, and steadied the rocking chair for Khayrik so he could drink. 'You're earning your keep.'

'It isn't me that keeps them out of the garden, it's the dogs, and you know it. Besides, there aren't nearly so many as there used to be. Soon I'll be redundant.'

'And who is it that keeps the dogs in the yard? Don't talk about being redundant, Khayrik. There'll always be something for you to do here.' She seemed on the verge of saying something important, but all that came out was: 'Drink your soup while it's hot.'

'Yes – mother,' he grinned.

A bell rang somewhere in the house, and the dogs began to whine, then bark. There were the usual sounds of doors being opened and messages relayed, and then a maid appeared at the door of Ysda's cosy sitting room.

'There's a woman to see you, ma'am. I don't like the look of her, looks like a bit of a tramp, but she's ever so insistent.'

She was indeed. The maid was brushed aside, and Lara entered. 'Khayrik!' she cried. 'What are we going to do about Ormaas?'

Ysda looked at the girl, heard the unfamiliar name, and felt like one woken from a dream. She saw the ungainly, beautiful figure of the cripple as he nimbly jumped from rocking chair to stool, and then to the floor. She heard him ask what was happening, and where Ormaas was, and why had it happened.

She watched him hurry to the door, on the new crutches he had made, and she said nothing. Only after he had gone, with a hurried goodbye and an even more hurried promise to return, did she say anything, and then it was a weak and tearful 'Come back.'

The dogs barked louder, and then settled down. He was gone.

Chapter 11

The Death of a Pretender

The wide river ran into the sea. A cormorant posed on a jetty beside the small quiet fishing boats. The bird stretched its wings behind it as if to yawn, and flapped into lazy flight. It climbed high over the estuary, until it could see from shore to reed-spiked shore, and then wheeled slowly down.

A large merchantman, a three-masted galleon, tacked past the jetty, heading up river. The report the ship's master had received from the shore had told him that Cythroné had thrown off the plague and that it was safe to go up-river again. The master was relieved: they had been waiting, anchored in the estuary with many other boats, for far too long. A boy on the masthead watched the circling cormorant and waited for it to dive. From where he hung from the purposeful ropes he could only see one shore; the other was lost over the horizon. The cormorant dived and reappeared, with a wriggle of silver in its beak.

The ship tacked back, starboard this time, away from the jetty and the north shore. It beat against wind and current a while and then gave up, anchoring mid-channel again and waiting for the evening tide. While it waited, a ketch flying the arms of Cythroné sailed out to them, chased by the wind and the morning sun; the captain of the ketch informed them that they would not be permitted into Cythroné the following day, whatever the state of the tides might be, because it was the day of the Rite of Endyear, and the river would be closed to all save the royal barge and its escort. The master of the merchantman acknowledged he understood, and then rid himself of his anger by beating the young boy. The river flowed on by.

The Namamorn was sticky with crowding people, who rubbed against one another beneath the sun as they walked. Lara found herself being pestered by a drunken man who had followed her, silently, since they had left Morn; now, as they approached the open mouth of the Anxious Gate and the city of Cythroné, he had plucked up nerve to speak. His first question had set the tone for their conversation: 'What are you doing here?' Lara had gasped with amazement. She was walking into Cythroné, as were half a million others who had fled the plague.

He smiled at her, and swayed. 'Have you been this way before?' he persisted.

She tried not to answer, but he kept on asking the same question, until in the end and in exasperation, she said 'No.'

It was a mistake to say that: he was a road-maker, and knew the Namamorn, as he put it, like the top of his own head, which made Lara smile. He told her in some detail about how to dig the initial trench, sprinkle a layer of aggregate not more than a quarter of a stride thick into the hole, and then top it all with well-chosen cobbles. 'Really?' said Lara, at intervals.

Streetpoet, suddenly aware of the drunk's attentions, walked faster to join Lara. He called out her name, and as she turned he caught her in his arms and kissed her passionately on the lips. By the time she had wriggled free, grateful but embarrassed, the drunken man had gone.

Khayrik travelled ahead of them. He drove the wagon that Consatiné had bought in Morn. Until Morn they had been taking rides in any vehicle that would have them – Khayrik could neither walk nor ride: his sore chest, although healing, would never stand the chafing of the straps needed to secure him to a horse – but now at least they were self-sufficient. Lara wore a wide brimmed hat, also bought in Morn by Consatiné, for the day was hot despite an early shower as they had left the tavern which had put them up for the night.

Alongside them, around them, and stretching as far as the eye could see before and behind them, were others making that same journey, similarly equipped with wagons and bundles and wide brimmed straw hats, for the refugees were returning to Cythroné. In the competition between death and life, life was winning again, and was flowing back into the beleagured city to make it vital once more.

The crowd had come to a virtual halt. Ahead of them Lara could see the towered barbican of the Anxious Gate, red stone climbing above red brick, but no reason for the hold up.

Meanwhile, behind, she could feel the increasing pressure of thousands of bodies trying to return to their boarded up homes.

The people who had fled had been the well-to-do, the prosperous river merchants, butchers and petty officials who had been able to afford the hire of a wagon. To cater for their return, all manner of street-traders had set up their stalls, hoping to catch the rubeks cast aside by this long procession by selling sweetmeats and all manner of other produce. Lara had to be quite rude to a man who offered her a sack of water at an inflated price.

The houses they passed were brick, white painted for a single storey and then climbing up in red that was pointed in grey. All the ground floor windows were shuttered, against the throng of homecomers. The houses had benches, and sometimes, where there was more money, terraces too, in front of them: most of these had been taken over by the street-traders. Between these comfortable, pleasant houses ran twisting alleys, leading to small dank courts. In one of these Lara saw rats worrying the carcase of a dog; in another grim-faced children played with a knuckle-bone in the dirt.

The shoving, sweating crowd carried her through the gates. Just before, she had a glimpse of one of the excise-free drinking-houses that are arranged all around the city walls, to take advantage of the different licence laws. A bottle of wine would be four rubeks in these drinking houses; ten in the city itself, and five of those would go in tax. Inside the drinking-house, although it was midday, was drunkenness unlike any she had seen before. The room seemed full of bodies, like a charnel house, save these bodies snored and yawned, and sometimes urinated where they lay.

She found herself pushed against something hidden on the ground. Her foot went through flimsy wooden bars and, with a frantic flapping of clipped wings, a hen fought its way through the crowd. So thick were the bodies that the hen was travelling almost at shoulder height, running from person to person in terror until, with a practised thrust of the thumbs behind its head, its neck was broken. An angry stall-holder bore down on Lara, but as he left his stall others started pulling dead chickens out of the baskets in front, and so he was forced to return. The chickens' necks flopped, nakedly, out of the top of the baskets, and the stall stank of fowl.

A fresher, citrus fragrance replaced that of the chickens. Lara sniffed the aromas with delight, and looked with wonder at the exotic fruits laid out on display: brilliantly coloured, like birds or butterflies, and regimented according to colour or shape. Some she recognised, others she did not.

She moved on with the flow of the crowd. The next stall was fronted with sacks of spices, coloured in a range that ran the gamut of yellows and browns, through oranges and reds to the faintest soft cream. She recognised some of the spices. That red was paprika, the light brown was ginger. Many of the others she could not identify, and like many others who passed the spice stall, Lara trailed her fingers in the powders and tasted them. Some tastes were warm and some tastes were sweet; one, a dark red, was overpoweringly hot. Serves me right, she thought, as the tang continued to scorch her tongue.

She looked round for her companions, and found she was alone. She felt herself gripped by a claustrophobic fear, as the weight of the city pressed against her. A passing banker on a mule offered her three talents and a wink; she realised she must move on.

She decided to hurry. She guessed she had lost her companions when dawdling by the market stalls. They must be ahead, she decided. The street led on, and then broadened abruptly into a great square hemmed in by tall and ornate buildings; in the centre of the square was the large statue of a knight on horseback. Forced by currents she could neither see nor control, Lara found herself swept against the tall plinth of the statue, and at eye level she saw the words 'Gyr Orland' set in the stone. Then the crowd had drawn her away again.

There were many exits to the square, and Lara could no longer distinguish where she had entered even, so knowing where to go was impossible. She let the crowd take her. She had never experienced so many people, she decided. Even the vast spread of refugees and soldiers around Rhalman had not compared with this.

Rather to her surprise she found herself by a great river. She saw huge stone bridges with wooden superstructures that spanned the river, and across the water the wharves and cranes

that marked the commercial areas of Cythroné. A set of steps
led down to a muddy foreshore and, to have a moment away
from the crowd, Lara descended them. She sat on the third
step up, and looked around.

She was next to an ugly building, low and featureless and
built of sinister grey slabs that were tightly jointed against the
river's rub. She raised her eyes up the smooth wall until the
smoothness ended and, with an all too human confusion,
there were dozens of corpses hanging and banging in the wind
in front of her eyes, and she knew that this was the House of
the Condemned. This was where Streetpoet had said that
they would take Ormaas, and was her companions' destination. But now her thoughts stopped wondering about
Khayrik, Streetpoet and Consatiné, and turned back to her
cousin. She wondered if she could get to see him. The Rite of
Endyear would be performed tomorrow, and the Hedchites
were saying that the emperor Dalerath would not, or could
not, perform the ceremony unless the bastard was killed
beforehand, as Dalerath did not contain the avatar of Akhran
which would knit together his severed flesh and animate
the damaged organs. Unless the bastard was killed beforehand . . .

She looked up at the dangling corpses. They were in
various stages of decomposition. Some were mere skeletons,
and would soon be hacked down and replaced; others were
barely dead, and hung like marionettes, turning lightly in the
breeze. The worst were those in between, where the carrion
birds had pecked away the flexible flesh in places, and she
avoided looking at those. There was no sign of her cousin.

She wondered how she could get in. She knew that she
must see Ormaas, although she had no idea what she would
say to him. She had a feeling that, somehow, being with him
again would sort out this mess: 'Look, look,' she would say,
'this isn't the bastard heir to the throne; this is my cousin
Ormaas from Fenras.' She climbed back up the steps and
worked her way around the House of the Condemned until
she reached a large gate. It was manned by a single soldier,
whose face was disfigured by a large wart over one eye. She
approached the gate and he smiled at her.

'You wanting something?'

'My cousin's in there,' she told him. 'Could I speak to him. Please?'

'I don't know about that. Nobody's meant to get in, not even for cousins. And anyway, how do I know he's your cousin. He might be your lover, and then I'd be letting you in for immoral purposes.'

'He's not my lover. Honestly he's my cousin.'

'Not your lover? Hope you've got a lover? Pretty girl like you needs someone to look after her.'

'Yes.'

'What do you mean: yes?'

'Yes,' she said, carefully. 'Yes, I'll sleep with you if you'll let me see my cousin.'

Streetpoet had not noticed that they had lost Lara until they reached Fragma Square. He worked his way through the crowds towards Khayrik's wagon, calling out her name as he went. A woman stood in his path and he tried to get around her, only to be confronted with a face full of angry goose. He tried the other way around her, with the same result. She had a pole over her shoulder, and tied to each end of the pole was a pair of live geese, suspended by the feet. The length of the pole kept the geese from biting the woman who carried them; it did nothing to defend passers-by. Streetpoet stepped back to avoid the birds and stumbled into a candle-seller who carried his cheap wares in a wooden tray around his neck. The tray spilt: Streetpoet hurried in a different direction.

Khayrik's wagon seemed to have disappeared, which was unlikely because the wagon would surely be thoroughly bogged down in this throng. Streetpoet made a wide circle of the square, looking for it, and found it twice until further investigation proved him wrong. He walked through a series of stalls where the acrid yellow smell told him he had found the fish market, and climbed on to the back of carts in the hope of seeing the cripple. That hope was running low, until a voice behind him called his name. He turned round and saw Consatiné on his grey horse, with Khayrik's wagon next to him.

'We've been watching you for ages,' said Consatiné. 'Where's Lara?' His voice contained an unexpected note of concern.

'I don't know,' replied Streetpoet, climbing back down from the cart with hurried words of 'All right, I'm going,' addressed to its rightful owner.

'You've lost her?' The concern had become anxiety.

'She's not with me,' said Streetpoet.

Consatiné turned to Khayrik at once. It's funny, he thought, how people come to trust Khayrik's judgement and sense, because they all mistrust him terribly when they first meet him. Perhaps it's because it's got so much sense.

'We'd best carry on to the House of the Condemned,' decided Khayrik, exhibiting some of that sense. 'We'd never find her in this crowd. When did you last see her?'

'Before we got to the square.'

'Then we'll just have to hope that she has the brains to go to the House of the Condemned on her own.'

They pushed and forced and squabbled their way through the square, and then down other streets where the throng was equally thick. Consatiné, who knew Cythroné better than his companions, led the way: he took them up alleyways barely wider than the axles of Khayrik's cart, and made them cross dirty streams where the water was flecked with filth or oiled with colours. They went over treacherous wooden bridges and beneath sullied stone arches. At last they arrived at the House of the Condemned.

Consatiné went ahead. The crowd was less dense here; there was little to attract them to the House of the Condemned. One guard stood, alone at the gate to the compound, watching the people go by. He looked up as Consatiné approached.

'Consatiné-vaine-Mornet, of the House of Ra,' he said, introducing himself. 'I would speak with Belphats.'

'You may enter, sir.' The guard was thinking about that pretty slip of a lass he had concealed in his quarters. He logged the entry of the Vaine of Mornet into his book by making a cross and went back to looking at the crowd and smiling about the girl.

Belphats sat in his darkened office. 'Ah, the Vaine of Mornet,' said Belphats, who wouldn't have known the Vaine of Mornet from the Vaine of Akbar, but who greeted all people with titles with the greatest of dignity. 'Welcome to the House of the Condemned. What can I do for you?'

Consatiné found something ghoulish about the smile that was directed at him, and hurriedly came to the point. 'You have a prisoner called Ormaas of Fenras?'

'Yes sir, a very famous prisoner he's becoming too, thanks to the Hedchites.'

'Are they still trying to say that Ormaas is emperor?'

'Isn't he, sir?' Belphats was being coy.

'Of course he isn't. He's a friend of mine from Northreach. He's no more emperor than I am, or you are.'

'I see.'

'So can't you let him out?'

'It isn't my job to release prisoners. But even if it was, I doubt that I would.'

'But he's not the bastard. It's absurd to even suggest it. You believe me, don't you?'

'Most certainly. But it occurs to me. He may not be the rightful emperor, he may not even want to be, but there are two thousand Hedchites who want to make him emperor. That's why he's got to die.'

'For nothing?'

'For the empire. What better reason has a man to lay down his life than for his empire's sake?' Belphats settled himself comfortably in his chair, wriggling his hips sensuously between the arms. His fat, flabby, lard-coloured face beamed at Consatiné. 'That's why we're killing him tomorrow.'

'Tomorrow?' Consatiné was ashen.

'It's the Rite of Endyear tomorrow. The emperor wants a good display. Your mate's lucky: he's only going to be hanged. Because of the danger that the Hedchites might want to do something daft if we tortured him, I suppose. But we've got three autos-da-fé and a good eight hanging, drawing and quarterings. Ormaas of Fenras will be going early, at dawn I think.' Belphats consulted a parchment on the desk, running his fingers down various columns to check on various facts. 'You wouldn't believe the complexities involved in running a place like this. I only took it over a short time ago: my old boss was topped by the plague.' His podgy fingers found what he was looking for. 'That's right. Ormaas of Fenras: dies at dawn tomorrow; straight hanging with no frills.'

Consatiné wanted to get out, into the fresh air. He fought the sensation. 'Who has authorised the execution?'

Belphats' smile turned ever more benignly repulsive. 'The Gros of Weir, countersigned by the emperor himself.'

'Thank you.' Consatiné turned to go. 'Can I visit him?'

'Oh no. Not in the House of the Condemned. Nobody gets to see them once they're in. It's a sort of kindness really: stops them remembering as much.'

'Good bye,' said Consatiné. He was sweating inside his armour, and he felt it an uncomfortable dampness that stuck his shirt to him, cool and warm, slippery and sticky at once. He walked out of the Gaolmaster's office and through the maze of offices that led him back to the compound. Lara saw him leaving through a window overlooking the compound and nearly called out to him. But then he was gone, and she was glad that she had kept quiet, because she desperately wanted to see Ormaas and did not want to spoil her chances.

The guard came off duty and clumped his way in hobnailed boots back to his room. Lara was sitting on the bed, huddled. He poured himself a mug of watered wine and then, as an afterthought, poured her one. She took it from him.

'Your cousin's going for the swing tomorrow. Did you know that?'

'Yes,' said Lara, she found herself lying compulsively, as if by deceiving this man she was not giving all of herself to him.

'Going at dawn, I hear said.'

'Yes,' she repeated.

'That nobleman was here wanted to see him too; if we're not lucky they'll double the guards on him and then you'll be in trouble. I can get you past one: I'll not try getting you past two.'

'No.'

'You want to go down and see him now? Or shall we play first.' He slipped his hand into her jerkin. She felt his fingers rub over her breast roughly. She found herself staring at the wart above his eye.

'I want to see him first,' she said.

He took her down long passages. Infrequent torches in brackets on the wall lit their progress. They stopped once or twice in the shadows to let people pass them by, for they did not want to be seen. Lara was grateful to the man that he did not try to touch her.

They came to a vast vaulted hall lined with wooden galleries. The arched ceiling was just a darkness above them, defined only where it met the slightly lighter grey of the walls. The guard led her up a spiral staircase of roughly hewn wood. The wood was littered with dirty straws and powdery with rot. As she followed him she realised that she did not know his name, and was on the point of asking, when she decided that she would rather not find out. It was like the pointless lies: it was a way of distancing herself from him.

The man pulled her into a dark cavity between two vast wooden pillars, and an armed guard shuffled past. 'Just the one of them: your luck's in.' He whispered to her in the blackness. 'He'll have heard our feet and be wondering who we are. You nip down to cell 47 – can you read? That's lucky – and you'll find your mate's in there.'

'Can't I have the key?'

'Not on your life you can't. You can speak to him through the hatch in the door. Go on, and be quick. I'll have a word with this chap and keep him away from you. When you hear me start singing, though, you come back here. Got it?'

'Yes,' she said miserably. She had not realised she would not be able to get in to see him, and she felt cheated.

'Right. When I start whistling.'

'Singing,' she corrected him.

'Don't matter. Either way, you get back here.'

He hurried off, and she heard the sound of the voices of two men recede along the gallery, and then their feet re-echoed as they climbed down the stairs. She ran down the row of cells. Each of them had a large wooden door in this part of the House of the Condemned, and set within the door was a small square hatch, low down and well away from the lock, which could be opened from outside by removing a pair of heavy bolts and pushing the wood up.

'Forty-one, forty-three. Where's forty-two? Forty-five. Oh, I see, odd numbers only. Forty-seven.' She bent down and pushed up the hatch, getting splinters in her hands as she did so. The hatch was heavy, but by replacing the bolts after she had lifted it she was able to prop it up. There was no noise from within.

'Ormaas,' she called, as loudly as she dare, and that was too loud in the strange acoustics of the House of the Condemned.

She heard a dragging shuffle, and the sound of metal scraping stone. For a time that was the only noise, and then a faint outline of a face appeared in the darkness behind the hatch. It was Ormaas. 'Lara?'

'Ormaas. Are you all right? Are you all right?'

'I haven't seen a light for a long time. I wondered if I'd gone blind.' His voice sounded happy, which was incongruous in the bleak certainty of the House of the Condemned. Lara suspected hysteria. 'I'm so glad that you've come. You've heard that I'm to hang tomorrow morning?'

'Don't talk about it. We might be able to do something to rescue you.'

'What? Capture the prison building? Force the emperor to change his mind about me? It's already been explained, dear Lara, that I'm going to have to die. The Gros of Weir told me why. It's because I'm a threat.'

'How can you be? You're just Ormaas, Murak's boy. The one who was found on the streets?'

'That's the problem actually. You see, the bastard son of Ravenspur and the old empress Elsban was taken to North-reach and adopted by a fur-trader. I'm the only person they could find in Northreach who fitted that, which is why we were asked to bring those furs.'

'You sound very calm about it.'

'Sometimes,' he said. 'What was I saying? Oh yes, they enticed us down here. But the man they sent to find me, this man Hedch that Murak talked about but that we never met . . .'

'If you never met, we could say that you were somebody else and he wouldn't be able to deny it.'

'He wouldn't anyway. He died in the plague. But you see, what he did do before he died was to start this religion, called the Hedchites. The Hedchites believe in all the things in the Old Religion, all to do with hoarstones and things like that, but above all they believe in me being the true emperor. The Gros of Weir believes that too, actually, but he won't admit it to anyone.'

'So you can't be saved.' She spoke almost harshly, angered by his dispassionate description of the circumstances which had condemned him. And then she felt sorry. 'Ormaas?'

'Yes?'

'I'll miss you.'

'I love you,' he replied.

'Ormaas. Do you remember when we set fire to Mabeta's kitchen?'

'And she chased us round and round until she discovered she'd have to put it out?'

'And we knocked over all that milk? Do you remember? Do you remember?'

'Yes, I remember. And when we dropped that flower pot from your window, do you remember that?'

'And it nearly hit Va'alastar. I love you.'

'Lara.'

And then, ominously, tunelessly, the sound of a popular song pulled them back to the present. 'I've got to go,' she said.

'Good bye.'

'Good bye then. Good bye, Ormaas. Good bye.'

She lay on her back in the darkened room. The guard had not even taken her clothes off, simply pushed them aside where necessary. She felt anxious hands explore her. Her mind was not on that; she was thinking of Ormaas. And thinking of Ormaas gave her strength against the guard's fumbling heavy body: the guard would never know it, but for her this was an act of love.

It was a disturbed night in Cythroné. The Hedchites had learnt that Ormaas was in the House of the Condemned some time during the day, and several hundred of them were picketing the building, and writing abuse against the emperor Dalerath, engraving their hatred into the smooth stone walls. Drunken people celebrated the coming of Endyear with markets and fairs throughout the town. The celebrations were double, for coronation and Endyear, and then given extra impetus by the end of the plague. Squabbles reacted on squabbles and erupted into acts of shapeless violence. Khayrik, Streetpoet and Consatiné sat in Consatiné's hired rooms and tried to decide what to do. Consatiné was impatient and angry, and his anger was made worse because the others did not share it.

'But it's so unfair. He never did anything. He's innocent. Even if he was the bastard there'd be no reason really to kill him, but why should he be? Belphats talked about him having to be killed whether he is or isn't: surely that's not fair?'

'No,' said Streetpoet. 'It isn't fair. Let me tell you a story. A year ago tomorrow I was in the House of the Condemned awaiting execution, and by a miracle I was saved. I was given a pardon, and do you know I was the only one in the House of the Condemned by the time the pardon reached us. Everyone else had been killed.

'But that's only part of my story. The other part is more difficult to tell, in a way. You see, I'd been very short of money for a while, and so I'd decided to try this trick I'd been taught. I won't explain it in detail, but with a little bit of help from this merchant's wife the trick earnt me nearly forty talents. But I got caught, and sentenced to death. The merchant's wife was so ashamed at having been caught out too that she threw herself off the Bridge of Towers. And do you know something, nobody was interested at all in that: nobody said, Streetpoet, we're going to kill you because you caused the death of a merchant's wife who was a nice lady and who you dallied with. If they had done so, I might have replied, "All right, I'm guilty. I'll go to my death like a happy man." But they didn't. All they ever talked about was the money.'

'Proving what?' asked Consatiné, dubiously.

'Proving that there is no justice. I was sentenced to death for an unimportant crime, and a matter of life and death was ignored. And afterwards I was freed on a whim. There is no justice. All there is is luck, and accident. Luck and accident are what are killing Ormaas.'

'I think that you're both wrong,' said Khayrik. He had not spoken for so long that the two younger men had almost forgotten he was with them. 'It isn't just luck and accident, for if it was then life would have no purpose. And before you tell me that life has no purpose, I caution you against that. All you'll succeed in doing if you try thinking like that is drive yourself off the Bridge of Towers too. But on the other hand, your life soon shows you that there's not much use looking for justice. Look at both of you. You're neither of you sure who your real parents were. You're the same age as each other, and as Ormaas. Shuffle a few babies some seventeen or eighteen years ago and you'd find that one of you would be in Ormaas's place now. Think yourselves lucky that you weren't adopted by a fur-trader.'

'It's funny,' said Consatiné. 'Fur-Trader was my father's nickname. He used to be always trying to sell things he'd shot, or so they say, and anyway, people who live in Northreach are all fur-traders as far as Cythroné is concerned.'

'You see,' said Khayrik. 'It doesn't seem like justice, but it doesn't seem quite like luck and accident either. Things just happen, but they happen according to patterns.'

'Well then,' said Streetpoet. 'This should confirm your ideas that it's all designed. You see, when I was first adopted by that hard-faced pair of crows I call my parents, my dad was a fur-trader too.'

They looked at one another in a silence that was filled by noises from the street. A great torchlit procession was going past, with an effigy of the emperor Dalerath on a litter on many shoulders. Directly beneath Consatiné's rooms, a youth threw a stone at the effigy. Streetpoet and Consatiné went to the window to watch the procession go by. As the stone neatly removed the effigy's head, the light from the torches climbed the walls of the street. It made holy haloes round each of their heads.

The guard smuggled Lara out through the gate and wished her luck. She thanked him gravely. It was an hour before dawn, but it was a warm night and she didn't need the blanket he had given her in a moment of unexpected tenderness.

She walked down the street that bordered the high smooth walls of the prison, and saw by the light of braziers in the street that there were many people about. Most of them were sleeping or nearly so, but a small group by the House of the Condemned chanted 'Or-maas, Or-maas,' regularly into the night. She tried to make the connection between the young man she loved and the object of their devotion, and could not. Ormaas was not a demi-god, surely.

She reached the steps that led down to the strip of muddy foreshore. It would give her a view of the proceedings; not the best view in Cythroné, perhaps, but a view nonetheless.

Streetpoet and Consatiné were about too at that early hour. Consatiné would soon have to ride up to the palace, but wanted to have a last look at the place where Ormaas would die. The dull inevitability of it still made him cold and angry. He rode up to the prison with Streetpoet riding behind on another borrowed horse. 'Good bye,' he told the smooth, chilling walls, and then he had wheeled his horse about and was riding as fast as he dared in his impractical fashionable court clothes and his long flowing cloak. Streetpoet watched him go, and then dismounted. He walked the horse around the walls until he reached the river, and decided to wait there, so he tethered the horse and made his claim on a stretch of embankment wall. He wanted a spot where he would be able to see both the events on the river and the death of his friend. Below him, on the narrow strand, Lara sat on her blanket.

There were men on the execution square above her, bringing down the gibbets and the scaffolds until only one remained. The emperor had specified that there should be only one scaffold, so that he would be able to tell at once that the right man had been killed. Soft light climbed from inland from the hostile mountains of the Thatter. It became a flat slice of orange at the foot of the sky, and then a scarlet eye. It expanded into a ball and balanced on the horizon. A drum roll broke into the monotony of 'Or-maas, Or-maas' and the noisy scuffling yells from the streets.

They led him out. He was blinded by the light. His cell had been so dark. He walked across a stone bridge that led to the single, awkward arm of the scaffold. His shadow stretched behind him, long and shapeless, leaning over the parapet in angular jerks.

Each step echoed. The stone flags seemed to vibrate under foot, exaggerating the sound of his boots. It was like walking on a drum. Around him were the guards, bored and tired, with dull eyes and beards, sardonic pouting mouths. The sound of his feet drowned all other noise, the boom of his feet told him that the world was hollow.

He crossed a vast plain of sound, It resounded against him whilst his eyes focused hopelessly on a tall dark shape silhouetted in the morning sun. Sound and vision competed. He was led up the steps and his head placed through the noose. A drum roll only emphasised how empty the world was. A cavity opened beneath his feet, and confirmed that the earth was hollow, and then his neck was broken, his legs still after their convulsive dance, and he was dead.

They left the body hanging so that the emperor would see it from his barge. Lara saw it, clothes ruffled by a slight breeze, and knew too that the world was hollow.

The Gros of Weir stood by his brother on the deck of the royal barge, whilst his brother let servants arrange the theatrical folds of his superb cloak. The Weir-Lord watched as the battle between Tlot and Ashgat was tucked behind the throne, and Tlot's journey to Reythiuge allowed to flow down the dais steps. The emperor Dalerath sat as motionless as he could and spoke without moving his neck at all.

'How is everything going?'

'There are no problems, your high majesty.'

'Good. This Ormaas of Fenras?'

'Taken care of. The Hedchites have rioted a little around the main gates here at Verdre, and some of them have spent the night outside the House of the Condemned, but the bastard will be dead by now, I can guarantee.'

'Thank Menketh. Are we ready?'

'I believe so.'

They cast off, the rowers pulled effortlessly with the current of the river. They passed the line of dockland that formed the southern banks, and the House of Condemned to the north. The emperor Dalerath looked at the body that still swung beneath the single arm of the scaffold, and he smiled.

They anchored the royal barge between the two great bridges, within sight of Ormaas's dangling corpse. The coronation began. The emperor had first wanted the coronation to take place on the barge because he had thought it would be safer against the plague, but now the danger of the plague had almost gone they continued with their plan, as more people could overlook the ceremony if it took place on the river than anywhere else. It had been his brother's suggestion, and it was a good one, symbolically confirming too that he was indeed emperor of the Khalin. Dalerath, made more confident by the body that hung in the breeze, relaxed and let the ceremony take its course.

A smaller barge, decorated in gold and cream, pulled out from the banks. In it were the Grand Masters of the many religious orders, thirty-seven in total, each in a decorated coat that was quartered with the designs of his order and the rearing stallion of Khalindaine. The senior grand master that Endyear was Parselk-vaine-Erdam of the Order of the Yellow Bear. His venerable old hands were clasped around a golden crown, and he stood in the front of the barge.

The two barges met, and at their meeting a band on the shore began to play. The music was familiar, the Glory Song of Akhran, by the long dead composer Fubra-tro-Arc, and the emperor Dalerath found himself humming it as Parselk approached him, with the gold crown still in his hands, and with a junior member of the order supporting it.

Parselk stepped up the steps of the dais, and the music came to a halt. There was no silken canopy over the throne this Endyear, for the people were to be given the opportunity of seeing their new monarch. There was a silent hush as the Crown of Crowns was held above Dalerath's face, and then lowered over the thinning hair until it rested, slightly awry, on the sweating forehead. The face broke into a grateful smile, and the cheering began.

It followed them to the Keep Akhranta, a cheering swearing enthusiasm that blocked out entirely the bitter chants of the Hedchites. The river rounded a gentle bend to reveal, ahead of the waterborne procession, the forbidding heights of the Keep Akhranta. It rose sheer and grey from the river, at the end of a low tidal causeway that seemed to push it out almost to the middle of the Khalin. Pale granite walls rose from harsh river-washed boulders, stark pale towers climbed clear in the morning. The royal barge approached the keep, whilst its escort anchored a little way off. The Gros of Weir felt the faint shudder as the prow of the barge nuzzled the side of the quay, and the rowers on the port side, as of one accord, raised their oars to let the boat dock. As the barge moored the men waiting on the bank ran into action: heavy ropes secured them at bow and stern; a small troop of soldiers, dressed in their plain white shirts without the fancy embroidered tabards, rapidly arranged a structure of planks between the barge and the shore; another troop unrolled a blue and gold carpet over the planks, effectively disguising the distinction between land and river-craft. A band was assembled on the quay, and it began to strike up some martial tune.

Whilst the horns and drums battled in the morning air, the courtiers disembarked. Finally, when they had all lined up on the quayside, the emperor rose from his ivory throne. He stepped down on to the blue and gold carpet, walked carefully between two files of bowed courtiers, and approached the steps that led up to the gateway to the keep.

He climbed the steps heavily, puffing slightly as he did so. The band continued to play. At the top was a great pointed arch set into the masonry of the walls, and standing at either side of the arch were veteran Akhranta pikemen, five in each company, and commanded by a tall captain in a pale blue cloak. The pikemen wore, like their sovereign, the traditional colour of black. Standing, slightly breathless, before his magnificent troops, Dalerath removed his crown with a barely-concealed expression of relief. A silk-clad pageboy ran forward from behind the legs of the pikemen, took the crown from the emperor, staggered under the weight, and withdrew rapidly, bowing as he went.

The emperor had been bathed in potions all night in preparation for this moment. He rubbed his hands together and made a spark fly, whilst he spoke the words that would begin the Endyear.

'The Akhranchild is among us,' he said in a firm low voice. The sparks were becoming more frequent.

'We hear you, Akhranchild,' replied the captain of the guard.

'I am Dalerath, emperor of Khalindaine, keeper of the Soul of Akhran, and I demand you admit me to my keep and my inheritance.' He spoke to the very walls of the keep, as though it were they would respond.

'We hear you, Akhranchild,' said the captain.

'Then let me pass.'

He stepped forward: the portcullis remained down. The terrace of grey stone before the great gate was bleak and exposed, and the expectant crowd pushing on the Khalin's banks could see the tracery of yellow power that seemed to lick around the small figure of their emperor. They watched from a distance as he stood at the top of the flight of arched steps and then they gasped as he stepped forward. He raised his arms at the portucllis, and the yellow energy that flamed around him concentrated at his finger ends. He moved towards the arch that led into the keep.

As he approached, he screwed up his face in concentration. Energy compressed within him, spluttering and spurting at his finger ends. He forced it from him, and orange spat from his hands. He reached the obstinate portcullis. The black wood resisted as his powers attempted to force through, and then charred, and burnt, and flamed quickly away from the emperor, and he had stepped through. The fire died down quickly and only ashes, rising into the keep as though sucked up by some great chimney, marked his passage.

He stood within the deserted keep. There seemed to be neither light nor sound within these thick walls. He eyes adjusted slowly to the darkness, and then, accustomed as he was going to be while the fire-spell still licked and caressed his fingers, he walked through the passageway ahead. The passage led him straight into the heart of the keep, and to a broad and twisting flight of stairs. Although it was warm outside, and the sun shone fitfully from behind grey cloud, it was ice cold in the keep. He spiralled up these stairs in utter darkness, spinning ever upwards until, dizzy and confused, he stumbled into the dusty shafts of light that were the Hall. He crossed the rush strewn floor. His confidence, which had been immense on the barge, nearly failed him as he walked across the hall. The stairs were ahead of him, bands of grey and black, light and shadow, climbing in a lingering curve ahead. Even the hall was much darker than the day outside: only the sharp swirling daggers of light that burst through its shuttered window like shards gave it illumination.

From the shattered floor of the hall, broken up by the shattered light of the windows, he climbed a wheezing flight of ornamental oak that led to the gallery beyond in a broad curve. Here he turned left through a narrow archway that led to another flight of stairs. They spiralled upwards in a mean spiral until they reached the very top of the keep. The cold air hurt his chest and mouth as he climbed, and he could taste his own poor health in his throat. He reached a trap-door, felt for the handle in the light that escaped in through its warped cracks, and pushed it upwards. Dazzling sunlight greeted him, and the sound of cheering crowds.

As he emerged, a tiny and remote figure at the summit of the keep, the people below fell to gradual silence. Elbows urged ribs: 'Can you see him?' Ribs gasped back that they could. The crowd settled to an expectant hush, dramatic and somehow shocking after all the noise, and fixed their eyes on their emperor.

He began to chant, too softly for any ears but his own and the gods he was propitiating. He cast his eyes over the floor of the platform, and found at once the wicked dull blade he was searching for. Trembling slightly, he bent and picked it up; with his other hand he plucked at the tie which secured his shirt. The shirt parted, exposing a chest that was stained with curling black hairs. He raised the knife above his head, hesitated, and then drove the knife into his heart, praying loudly now that he was the avatar. The knife entered him to the hilt, and the scene stood still. The heart pumped once, twice more, driving thick red blood down his chest inside his shirt, and then he fell forward as the crowd gasped.

The doves were released, to perform their ritual antics about the keep before flying off in a white cloud, and with the doves the Endyear was announced.

Later, much later that day, when Cythroné had abandoned herself to another night of processions and celebrations, the commander of the Akhran pikemen led a platoon of his men on a search of the keep. The first place they went was to the top of the tower where the emperor Dalerath had last been seen. It took two of them to lift the trap-door, and when they did they discovered their emperor had been lying across it. Now, shouldered off by the raising of the trap, he was sprawled against the parapet with his neck extended against the wall and his eyes tight shut as if in pain. He was quite dead.

The Gros of Weir waited at the foot of the keep. The news of his brother's death arrived at the same time as news that the Agaskan had moved out of the Thatter, with a larger army than had ever been seen before.

The Gros of Weir turned to the blood-stained messenger who had travelled from the Ingsvaal. 'What on Hrakar do I do now?' he asked. The messenger did not know. Neither did anyone else. 'Bother everything,' said the Weir-Lord. 'But if that Ormaas wasn't the bastard, who is?'

Chapter 12

Akhran the Golden

The Gros of Weir stood, rather uncertainly, behind the closed doors, whilst Cluny adjusted the fall of his cloak and straightened his hat. Then the door was opened and the Weir-Lord stepped out, on to the balcony, to be greeted by suspicious silence.

'Friends, citizens,' he said.

'Louder,' whispered the Vaine of Alkal-Ka-Yran.

'Friends and citizens,' tried the Weir-Lord again. 'I have come to you as the descendant of the House of Akhran, through the bloodline of emperors and warriors, to say what must be said.'

'You're not saying anything yet,' whispered the Vaine of Alkal-Ka-Yran.

'Khalindaine is beset by emergency. The empire is threatened. The emperor is dead.' For the first time the crowd reacted, with an uneasy shuffling of feet and clearing of throats. 'I therefore feel I must take on the responsibility of leading the empire, as befits my birth.' The noise of shuffling was joined by sounds of discontented words. 'Therefore I announce myself Regent of the Empire of Khalindaine, until such time as the rightful heir and avatar of Akhran presents himself.'

'What a long way of saying anything,' whispered the Vaine of Alkal-Ka-Yran, but this time the Weir-Lord did not hear him for the cheers. The new regent and his courtiers returned to the palace.

'Thank Menketh that's over,' said the regent, as Cluny handed him a full glass.

The Weir-Lord took the advice of the Gros of Peltyn. 'We must not let the Agaskan get a foothold on the flat lands this side of the Khalin. They are assembling on the far side near the foothills of the Thatter. We must make sure that their army cannot cross the river.' They moved the armies of Khalindaine down to the Khalinwatch, where a long line of solitary towers still patrolled the river and guarded every crossing. Meanwhile, opposite, across a mere eighty strides of torpid meandering river, the Agaskan mustered their own forces.

Khayrik looked out from the tower. A steady drizzle obscured his view of the far bank and reduced what could be seen to a hazy monochrome. Summer was turning to autumn, and with the fall came shorter days and colder nights. The army was dispirited by inactivity, and even the proximity of the Agaskan had become a familiar and uninspiring thing, just another irritant like the cold and the omnipresent damp. There were times when Khayrik felt himself to be the only truly enthusiastic member of the army, as the damp soaked through to the skin, and he smiled at the irony that made him a 'supernumerary' in the Vaine of Mornet's regiment whilst the fighting force was composed of people who did not care for army life. 'I might not be able to fight,' he told himself, and anyone else who would listen. 'But I can keep as good a watch as the next man.'

The drizzle eased off temporarily, allowing Khayrik an unhampered view along the banks of the river. The watchtower stood at the end of a narrow ford, a submerged causeway built in the time of the Old Kingdoms, before Akhran had united the empire. Behind the tower was a grassy meadow, rather waterlogged, and then a slope led to the higher land away from the river. Most of the army of Khalindaine was stationed twenty thousand strides east, at the bigger crossing by the town of Jorg, but even so the force assembled at the foot of Khayrik's tower seemed impressive. There were four regiments of foot, and a large troop of horse: the Vaine of Mornet's regiment, in their distinctive livery of red and white; the Vaine of Hyrdal's, dressed in light blue; the Kopp militia, in yellow and green; the Kala-Katahn regiment in blue and green; and the miscellany of colour and style that was the cavalry. In addition, the numbers were swollen by supernumeraries and camp followers, cooks, whores, beggars, tinkers, pedlars, musicians, rogues, stocksmen, drivers, wives, children, grooms, valets, factotums, drudges, ostlers, retainers, and all the other satellites and parasites which make up an army.

Looking east, Khayrik was surprised to see a column of

horsemen approaching. 'Hello,' he said. 'Who is this?' He screwed up his eyes to examine the flag at the head of the column. A scarlet swan swam across a decorated blue, making it the emblem of the Gros of Nanx. 'I wonder what he's doing here,' thought Khayrik.

He had arranged for a bell to be hung in the tower, beneath the wooden superstructure of the pointed, spiring roof, and he tolled the bell now. Men tumbled comically from their tents at the sound, pulling on their armour in readiness for an Agaskan attack and then looking first blank and later angry as the tolling ceasd. Khayrik had devised a number of signals which used the bell, and Consatiné had been glad to authorise them, but the army had not yet learnt to distinguish them.

'What's up, Khayrik?' shouted a sergeant from below, while his troops stared across the river in expectation of an attack.

'Reinforcements. Four rings for reinforcements. You remember.'

'Go to Araketh,' called the sergeant. 'Who's coming?'

'Nanx-Lord.'

As they called to one another Khayrik watched the nobles, including Consatiné, mount their horses and go to greet the Gros of Nanx. The Nanx-Lord outranked all the commanders on the Khalinwatch save the Gros of Weir himself, and rumour had it that even the regent did not dare argue with the stubborn, glamorous Gros of Nanx. It was not surprising that the nobles fell over themselves in their attempts to impress him.

A rattle and a scrape from below told him that someone was attempting to climb through the trap-door. Khayrik swung himself down from the battlements, feeling only the slightest twinge from his battered chest now, and eased open the wooden trap.

'Hello,' he called.

A good-looking young soldier with a soft, boyish face looked up. 'Hello,' replied the soldier. His voice had not broken. He climbed out of the trap and stood, holding two cups of steaming broth, on the flagstones next to the cripple. 'How are you?'

'Fine. How are you, Lara?'

The soldier with the pretty face sat down. 'Fine,' she replied. Like Khayrik and Streetpoet, Lara had volunteered to join the

Vaine of Mornet's regiment the moment she had heard that Consatiné had been empowered, under the Regulations Concerning the Governance and Implementation of the Royal Power to Impress, to raise a regiment of infantry. She had walked the streets of Cythroné for three days since the bitter tragic Endyear, until Streetpoet had found her and taken her to Consatiné's plush lodgings, and during that time her mind had been occupied only with the need for action. That Consatiné was raising a regiment seemed to her the perfect opportunity to escape from Cythroné and her memories; when she learnt that the Regulations Concerning the Governance and Implementation of the Royal Power to Impress expressly forbade women from joining the army she was first incredulous and then livid. 'Ridiculous,' she said. 'I'm an initiate. I've travelled from Northreach with you, shared your discomforts, your fights. Why can't I fight with you now.'

It was a good question. 'Because I would lose my commission,' replied Consatiné.

'Coward,' she accused, and he felt a bitter pain at the word.

'Lara, no, please,' he began, but she was not listening. She drew her sharp hunting knife from her belt and held it to her head. 'There,' she said, and she tugged the knife through a thick tress of hair. 'There. Now perhaps I can fight with you.'

Illuminated by the fire, surrounded by the comfortable trappings of Cythron prosperity, the angry girl who hacked through her hair made a strange, anachronistic figure. When she had finished she threw the locks on to the fire, where they burnt with a passionate intensity and vanished into the sad sharp smell of their burning. Consatiné had been unable to refuse her after that: they found her a uniform and a position on the staff which would give her limited privacy, and let her travel with them. Khayrik sipped his broth as he thought of this, and smiled.

'What are you thinking about?' asked Lara.

'You,' he said. 'And Consatiné.'

Unaccountably, Lara blushed. 'What about us?'

'How you joined the regiment.'

'Oh,' she said, sounding relieved. 'That. He's with the Gros of Nanx now, you know,' she continued, conversationally.

'He would be. I saw him go. Quick, sound the alarm.'

There was so little change in Khayrik's tone that for a moment the words did not register, and then looking beyond the cripple she saw what had inspired his demand. A line of black boats were pushing off from the far bank; a column of Vedi-detch was entering the river at the ford.

'Quick,' repeated Khayrik, more urgently now. 'The alarm.'

She pulled on the rope loud and hard, until it was clear that the troops below had understood, and then handed the bell-rope to Khayrik. 'I'm going down to fight. Menketh bless you.'

'And bless you,' he replied, and she was gone, and his attention concentrated entirely on the enemy that approached across the Khalin.

The fighting part of a Khalindaine regiment consists of five battalions of sixty-five men apiece, including officers. Four battalions are armed with the traditional pike, five strides long and tipped with blackiron, whilst the fifth is more lightly equipped with sword and buckler. In Khayrik's active days the pikemen had carried large shields, but the modern infantryman carries a longer pike which requires both hands.

Streetpoet gripped his pike as his platoon was arranged in front of the ford. The sound of the bell had been replaced now by loud alarms on the trumpets. A platoon, of which there are four in each battalion, consists of fifteen men, including three non-commissioned officers. Streetpoet was not one of these. He was just a pikeman, second rank, and popular with his fellows because he played a good tune.

Khayrik watched in disbelief. The Gros of Nanx was assembling the Khalindaine cavalry as though he intended to charge into the river. It was true that the Vedi-detch, mounted on their pulsing mounts, were fording the river, but surely, thought Khayrik, even the Nanx-Lord won't be daft enough to try to engage them in the water; apart from anything else Consatiné's regiment had just assembled at the near end of the ford, and the only way that the Nanx-Lord'll be able to get to the river will be through them.

But that was exactly what the Nanx-Lord had in mind. Unable to contain himself any longer, he brought together the various cavalry regiments and, as rapidly as he could, changed their formations from column of advance to line of attack, ready to charge.

The commotion behind him, as the cavalry were lined up and approximately arranged in blocks of swirling caparisons and flowing plumes, distracted Consatiné. He was having troubles of his own, trying to get his own regiment in line. His men, in the red and white colours of the House of Ra, seemed unendurably slow today, and fearfully clumsy. They had performed this simple manoeuvre – assemble, pikes at the ready – a hundred times in practice, and it seemed to Consatiné that the worst practice had been a hundred times better than this.

Suddenly he was aware of a herald, dressed in the arms of Nanx, trying to attract his attention. The herald rode up behind Consatiné and shouted from horse to horse over the heads of several pikemen. 'The Gros of Nanx sends his compliments, and asks you what on Hrakar's skull you think you're doing.'

'Deploying my men as was agreed. The Vaine of Pylai's regiment guards the left flank, the Mornet militia the right flank, and the Vaine of Gylandril's men are kept in reserve.'

The herald saluted to show that he had understood, touching his sword to his nose, and then rode back at the gallop to his commander. Consatiné again bent his energies to lining his men, painfully aware that the approaching Agaskan were more than halfway across the sluggish powerful river.

The herald returned, again bearing the Gros of Nanx's compliments. 'The Nanx-Lord intends to rout the enemy in the river by charging them in person. As your commander he therefore orders you to move your men aside and permit him to charge.'

Consatiné stared at the herald, who simply saluted again and returned once more to his master, and then rode in front of his men. This will be marvellous for morale, he thought, as he ordered them to move aside from the head of the ford in good order, to re-form in front of the tower. As he had expected, the troops responded badly to this, and instead of moving aside in good order, they simply moved.

The moment that the way was clear the Gros of Nanx charged, swerving past those infantrymen who still stood in his way, and therefore breaking the order of his charge. He led his men straight into the water: Streetpoet watched with fascination as Gallants in armour of silver plunged clumsily into the unsuitable element of the river. He saw knights in scarlet and green plunging into the muddied water by the ford, and saw some of them swept away.

As soon as the Nanx-Lord had led his charge into the river, Consatiné ordered his men to return to their positions at the head of the ford; inspired by the bloodshed that was now taking place in the waves, and by the sight of their cavalry charging into action, the soldiers surprised him, and did.

Streetpoet held a pike in the second rank of Consatiné's regiment again. They formed up once more at the end of the ford. Already they had been disturbed in their defences by the Gros of Nanx and his glorious, fated cavalry; now the stragglers and survivors of the cavalry charge were retreating, pushing through the ranks of their own infantry to escape the deadly river. Streetpoet found himself pushed out of line by a riderless horse that fled from the carnage in the river. The Gros of Nanx and his men had done little but blunt the swords of their enemy: the pressure of the Agaskan advance did not falter. Another horse, splashing water all over them, emerged from the river and sped away from them, running uncontrollably along the bank. Streetpoet risked a glance around. Behind him the watch tower seemed secure enough, although the Vaine of Gylandril's Regiment, dressed in surcoats of green, looked dangerously disorganised in reserve. Left and right was the real danger, it seemed. The Agaskan infantry were arriving by boats in increasing numbers. The moment their boats reached the shore the oarsmen dropped their oars and picked up spears, and the unit organised itself into a firm phalanx that could not easily be dislodged. In contrast, the Khalindaine forces were not so well organised. The Gros of Nanx's charge had drawn many of their mounted officers with it, and the leader of the Mornet militia, a burgomaster called Elkathraps who had been a tutor to Consatiné in earlier and more ordered days, was battling now for his life as his men retreated in chaos about him.

Streetpoet's thoughts were interrupted. A Vedi broke out of the water in front of them, its broken, veiny flanks dripping with water like sweat, its distorted rider swinging a long notched sword that ran with watered blood. Behind it came another, and another. The cavalry had been defeated, and the Vedi-detch had broken through.

Streetpoet tensed, holding the four stride long pike in front of him over the shoulder of the rank ahead. The Vedi did not bother to form up against the insignificant opposition offered by Consatiné's single regiment at the end of the ford, but charged them as they arrived on the bank. Streetpoet saw them coming at him, their swords waving and swinging dangerously, their voices thrilling the air with dreadful cries. With a crash that almost threw him over, Streetpoet caught one of the Vedi on the end of his pike, and saw terror in the creature's eye as it tried to thrash clear of the barbed spike. The rider was not yet aware of the wound to his mount. He slashed a descending blade into the shoulders of the man in the rank before Streetpoet's own, and the man fell, crying out horribly. Then the wounded Vedi collapsed, throwing its Agaskan rider forward on to Streetpoet, who was forced to drop his pike and draw his sword to deal with the danger. The Agaska landed badly, falling on an arm that most certainly broke beneath the weight, and Streetpoet had no difficulty in dispatching the creature, running it through the exposed nape of the neck as it crumpled before him.

Dropping the pike proved a dangerous mistake. The Vedi came constantly at them, and without a pike Streetpoet had lost the infantryman's one chance against cavalry. He found himself almost caught between the veined and glistening sides of two great Vedi, and ducked between them as they bore down upon him. A notched blade slit his jerkin from neck to hip. Reflex took over: without thinking about what he was doing Streetpoet lay in a tightly curled ball to avoid the threshing legs that threatened to overwhelm him. He lay still for a moment until the vibrations around him ceased, and then picked himself up and sprinted, still bending double. The ranks of Consatiné's men were butchered or smashed through, and men retreated towards the stolid stone of the watch-tower. One of the Vedi-detch singled out Streetpoet as he fled from the carnage and rode at him, intending to ride him down. Street-poet stood upright quickly and jumped back to avoid a singing

lance as it impaled the ground in front of him. The minstrel
bent down and grappled with the quivering tip of the lance,
pulling the Vedi's rider clear from his mount. For a moment
the two fought along the length of the plumed lance, and then
Streetpoet had thrust the Agaska back and the latter was
sprawling over the body of a comrade: the Agaskan lance was
pulled back and then shot forward, ripping through the armour
of the Agaska's chest. Streetpoet stood for a bare moment
above his victim, feeling a hungry sorrow, and then ran on
towards the tower.

At the foot of the watch-tower Consatiné was rallying his
men, and the men of any other regiment around. Streetpoet
ran towards his friend and his commander, reached the tower,
and felt again the comfort of comradeship as Consatiné formed
them into ranks against the enemy.

'Streetpoet!' He half turned. Next to him, a sword in her
hand, was Lara. 'Haven't you got anything to fight with?'

Stupidly, he looked down. As she had said, he was without a
weapon: his sword and pike had long gone. He felt a pushing
next to him and then Lara had broken ranks, pulled a sword
from one of the dead, and was returning to her place when a
Vedi charged at her from the flank. The unexpected attack
would have reached her had not one of those who were lined up
alongside Streetpoet stepped forward. The soldier's head was
cleaved from his shoulders, but Lara was saved.

Wordlessly, Lara handed Streetpoet the sword that had cost
a man's life, and he felt its weight in his hands.

The flank attack on Lara suggested what Khayrik had
already predicted: that the tower would prove indefensible. On
both sides of the tower the Khalindaine forces had fallen back.
Indeed, the charge of the Gros of Nanx had denuded the
reinforcements of any leadership, and the defence seemed
entirely in the hands of the original regiments. Many of the
reinforcements still waited, in column, for instructions, while
before them the regiments battled for their lives. Khayrik was
horrified.

Between the Gros of Nanx's column, as yet unengaged, and
the solitary tower, was a causeway of fighting men, constantly
pressed back by the advancing Agaskan. Consatiné, his horse
killed beneath him and cut in a score of places, fought bravely

and firmly, but was aware that his men, falling back on the tower, were being gradually isolated. He spoke to the infantryman at his side. 'Can you get a message through? Tell them that we need reinforcements.'

'At once, sir.'

The man pushed through his own ranks, nearly being killed by a large comrade with a bristling black beard who thought the messenger was trying to desert, and only just escaping a charge of the Vedi-detch that swung into the right flank of the Khalindaine army. Then he was away, and running across open ground, until a different echo behind his feet told him he was being pursued. He stopped and turned, just in time to see the notched blade that sliced through his head. The messenger fell to the ground, and the Vedi trampled his body.

Consatiné drew back from the front row of the fighting, to learn what the situation was. The tower was, temporarily, the safest part of the battlefield for those from Khalindaine: the Vedi were still cutting down stragglers, whilst the Agaskan infantry was forming up, ominously but at a distance, before advancing against them. Consatiné was forced to admire the discipline of the Agaskan: their infantry manoeuvred on the battlefield as though it were a parade-ground.

He was aware of a smell of burning, and looking up saw that Khayrik had lit a fire in the tower. It looked dangerous but Consatiné had no time to worry about it: he was set upon again.

The Agaskan infantry had regrouped now, and were advancing to the beat of regular long thin drums. Like a tide the Agaskan swept around the foot of the tower, and eroded the defences as though they were sand about a rock. The smell of burning intensified, and Consatiné was not the only one who looked up to wonder what the cripple was doing, before being forced to concentrate on the present as the Agaskan advance, shield overlapping with neighbouring shield, short thrusting spears jutting dangerously ahead, moved onwards as inevitably as time. To the sound of a thousand cheering voices they marched forward, and the enthusiasm of the voices contrasted frighteningly with the measured advance of the feet. There was power as well as violence poised and coiled in that advancing line as it swirled around some obstacle, or stuttered over some fallen horse; it never broke, never wavered, until it faltered against the infantry around the tower, and broke like a wave over them.

Lara found herself fighting for her life. Black armoured figures pressed on her, and she was forced to struggle against her comrades before she could oppose the Agaskan, as the pressure of body against body increased. The nearest of the Agaskan approached her, and its thrusting spear was shafting towards her viciously. She twisted aside, and the head of the spear rattled harmlessly against the armour of the man to her left. She collided with Streetpoet as she moved, not without force, and he took a step forward, breaking the shield wall in front of him. Lara found herself behind the shield wall. She was darting and thrusting with her sword into the backs of the Agaskan, and then they had fallen back, leaving her and Streetpoet unmolested and standing back to back. The two of them sprinted safely the two strides that would unite them with their comrades, and joined the line just before the attack began again.

It seemed ridiculous to die in such chaos, thought Streetpoet. It should have been organised better than this. He hardly had room to swing his sword against the omnipresent enemy as they crushed them closer against the grim grey walls of the watch-tower.

He grabbed Lara by the hand. 'We've got to make our way round to the back of the tower,' he told her.

She nodded, but whether she had really heard he could not tell. Nonetheless, they found they had no choice. Their defences had broken at the front of the tower, and the Agaskan were forcing a wedge between the men to left and right. There were still some soldiers resisting in small numbers against the front wall, but they were soon overwhelmed, and could not even fall in the weight of numbers pressed against them, but were carried by the oncoming Agaskan like parody fighters, marionettes or trophies, to be thrown against the next opponents the Agaskan met.

Consatiné found himself being driven around the base of the circular tower as the middle was split by the Agaskan wedge. At least, being at the edge of the line, he had a limited freedom of movement; at least, standing where he did, he could be sure that every time his ducking weaving sword encountered flesh,

it would be Agaskan flesh. He found himself driven further
and further back, however, until he found himself more or
less facing away from the river. Here, where the Agaskan
advance had not struck so hard, numbers were more even,
and there was space to breathe from time to time. Nevertheless, Consatiné was aware, as he looked back towards the Gros
of Nanx's still waiting column of reinforcements, that even
the narrow peninsula which had kept them in contact had now
gone.

Khayrik could see that too. With an axe and a bottle of fire-
spell he was doing his best to set fire to the tower, but it was
producing only a few red flames that flickered around the edge
of the flagstones, before dying away when the fire-spell was
exhausted. Khayrik cursed at it and threw the bottle hard
against the parapet, where it burst into a hundred burning
shards, most of which went out. 'Second-rate-lousy-fire-spell,'
he shouted. With his axe he smashed into the wooden bench,
trying to build a fire over one of the drops of fire-spell that
was still alight, and then, as he did so, he saw the sight he had
hoped for: the distant dust of a rapidly travelling body of
men, coming their way. Quickly, he swung his body between
his crutches, efficiently snuffing out the flames that played on
the stones. There was no need for a beacon if the reinforcements were already on their way, and Khayrik had no death
wish. Carefully, he made sure that the last of the flames were
out.

From the column of men on the higher ground a shout
went up, as they too saw the approaching reinforcements, but
around the base of the tower the situation got no better.
Khayrik saw the narrow margin of men around the tower
grow narrower still, until it had whittled down to nothing at
some parts. He tried to see Lara and Consatiné fighting
below, but was unable to.

Something struck his tower with the force of an earthquake,
and it seemed to rock before settling. He looked towards the
river. The Agaskan had assembled siege-engines, virtually
redundant against the limited opposition the tower could
afford, and the catapults were firing heavy stones. Another
one aimed towards the tower, and even the steady nerve of
Khayrik failed him as the rock grew in the sky above him,

plummeting towards him dreadfully. There was another great
sound, but no vibration, and he discovered that the top of the
tower, the spiked roof, had been knocked clean off.

It fell with a dusty clatter amongst many embattled men.
Figures were crushed beneath masonry or trapped against the
walls by wooden beams. Agaskan and Khalindaine alike were
killed by the falling, shredding, tiles. Khayrik, face down on
the stones of the tower's roof, felt bits of loosened wood and
lead drop all around him, but he was lucky, for the parapet kept
the larger, heavier bits of debris from him, and all that struck
him were tiles, that travelled only a few strides down. Bruised
but not badly damaged, he stayed where he was until the
immediate danger seemed past, and then levered himself to a
vertical position on his crutches.

Fortunately for Khayrik, the Agaskan artillery, realising that
they were doing as much damage to their own side as to their
opponents, re-aimed their weapons, firing now against the still
leaderless column that had been intended as reinforcements.
Many of the individual commanders now took the decision they
should have taken well before, and advanced their men forward
into the battle; others continued to wait at one side.

The confusion was confirmed by the sudden appearance of
the Gros of Weir and a small retinue of knights and heralds,
over the brow of a small rise not two hundred strides from the
column. The Weir-Lord rode forward, looked at the situation,
and then returned to his force, still advancing behind him. To
his surprise, for he had no experience of the way that men
behave in battle, many of the waiting column, for want of
anyone better to follow, followed him, and he found himself
taking a ragged collection of soldiers back with him to the brow
of the hill.

The catapults still tossed up boulders. One landed between
Cluny and the Weir-Lords, and made the former's horse bolt
wildly. The animal charged into the fighting, attracting
support from a squadron of as yet unengaged cavalry, and for a
moment the tower seemed relieved, until the horses were
hacked down and the riders killed or forced to join the infantry
crowding at its base.

The Gros of Weir and his army drew up now on the rise,
overlooking the battlefield. The Gros was faced with an

awkward decision: should he rearrange his men into a more aggressive formation. The men being killed at the foot of the tower could only be saved by instant action; dare he leave them to be butchered before him. The whole battle was focusing on the tower now, and he wondered if that might not be to his advantage, because the Agaskan were distracted. Perhaps he could attack them now: it was raining, and his troops were getting wet; an advance in good order down the slope ahead of them might be what is wanted, he decided.

He gave the order and the army started moving. The cavalry travelled much faster than the infantry, and the Gros found himself steadily further ahead of his men. He wondered whether to turn around, which would perhaps confuse them again – he had learnt his lesson – or whether he should let his horse stand still if it would. He decided on the latter, and felt himself drawing the Agaskan fire as they turned their bows on this new threat from the higher ground.

Khayrik, on his tower, looked out at the battlefield aghast. That the Agaskan would win the day now seemed beyond doubt, and he had been professional soldier enough to appreciate the need that the Gros of Weir had to preserve some of his army in good order, to fight another day. But now the Weir-Lord had begun an advance down the hillside, and then had stopped. Khayrik did not know what to do, and nor did the Weir-Lord's troops by the look of them.

Consatiné was facing the Weir-Lord now, his back to the tower. He saw the advance and applauded it, and then saw the Weir-Lord hesitate. 'No, you fool,' he shouted. 'Not like that.' He raised his sword and in a single blow had taken two Agaskan heads from their shoulders. He drew back his arm and struck a third. As the pincer movement on the tower completed and the Agaskan forces surrounded it entirely the Agaskan between Consatiné and his target thickened. The Vaine's sword swung faster and truer through the throng, driving them back as he advanced. A rapid parry; a lightning thrust. Bodies fell around his feet, forcing him to step high to get over them. He saw an Agaskan standard before him, and without undue effort seemed to reach out and break it. Khayrik, from above, watched with amazement that became comprehension as the Vaine of Mornet scythed through the ranks of the Agaskan, but even he was shocked when the young Vaine raised his head for a moment and revealed his face: the soft, almost effeminate lines were gone, exposing harsher bone; the soft eyes with their heavy lashes thrust forwards, bulging and glowing with a golden glow; a golden glow diffused around him, forcing back even those opponents he had not encountered. Akhran the Golden had returned.

The face of the warlord contested with Consatiné's and won. The avatar's face and thoughts, the avatar's strength and skill. Consatiné's body peformed Akhran's will, and Akhran's will was destruction.

He forced a corridor through the Agaskan. 'Heart-Cleaver,' they cried as they died. 'Heart-Eater.' Now many of the men at the foot of the tower were aware of the commotion, and tried to follow their leader into the fray. Many were killed as they dived into the ranks of the enemy, but the inspiration of Akhran seemed to be reaching the entire army. 'Akhran,' cried an inhuman voice through Consatiné's mouth. 'Akhran!'

The men on the hill overlooking the battle, who still paused in their advance, were suddenly driven forward by those higher who had seen the golden figure hacking and cutting his way towards them. They charged down the hill, all order gone again, and screaming their belief in their new-found emperor. The advancing troops tore into the flank of a now confused enemy: from his watch-tower Khayrik saw the Agaskan army recoil from the new attack as Consatiné, in the centre of them, tore the heart from their left flank.

The golden figure fought his way out of the Agaskan ranks, and rejoined his own army, although that terrible face looked no more human than it looked Agaskan, with its bony high cheekbones and its long, cruel upper lip. Swiftly, Akhran surveyed the scene. His eyes were filled with a magnetic gold light that drew the stares of all those about him. He walked to the standard bearer and, without speaking or doing more than staring, ordered the man to relinquish his horse and the flag. There was no choice and the knight obeyed with alacrity. Mounted now, and with a banner to be recognised, Akhran returned to the fray.

His ebullient violence seemed to flow into those around him. Seared with wild madness, they charged the enemy again and again, battering their way through to the river banks for the first time since the battle had begun, and then forcing the Agaskan back towards the tower in a curious parody of the Agaskan manoeuvre. Lara and Streetpoet were still back to back in the shadow of the tower, and both of them bleeding from a dozen cuts. The pressure had relaxed on them for a moment whilst Consatiné's fury had drawn the enemy off, but now that same fury was focusing the Agaskan back on to the tower and forcing them to fight again. Wearily they raised their swords, and then the ethereal power that came from Akhran gripped them too and became something tangible, and with new strength they fought, battling back as the Agaskan crushed in on them. The Agaskan did not know which way to turn. Lara's sword pierced the back of one and the front of another with a single inspired jab; Streetpoet lost his weapon to the rushing crush of Agaskan, in the back of a dead Agaska who could not yet fall because of the pressure of his comrades.

The Gros of Weir still sat on his horse, as though immobilised, and then turned it about and let it trot up the hill away from the battle. Even Cluny had left him, and alone above the field of devastation, he watched as Khayrik watched and waited for the end.

It was not long now. The line of Agaskan between Akhran and the tower grew thinner, and thinner. At the foot of the tower bodies, human and Agaskan, were piled so deep that those who survived were forced to stand on them as they defended themselves. A red stain in the river showed where blood drained off the marshes. Pocket by pocket, incident by incident, resistance ceased. At last the final groups of Agaskan were isolated and the tower liberated. Of the hundreds of soldiers who had fought before it, barely a hundred still stood. Lara was on the ground, unconscious after a flat-bladed desperate blow; Streetpoet, bending to attend her, was ripped from temple to temple and a great jagged flap of skin flopped over and into his eyes, dripping blood on to Lara. Cluny nursed an arm, broken where he had been struck with the edge of a shield. Only Khayrik, of the companions, survived the field of battle in the same state as he had entered it, and he stood at the battered and ragged top of the tower and looked out.

His eyes followed Akhran the Golden, the Avenger, as the

avatar drove Consatiné's body ever onward. The field of battle was now indisputably Khalindaine's, and the Agaskan who still resisted were in isolated pockets, and would soon be over-whelmed. Even now the fury of the Avatar was not sated, but charged his horse into the river at the ford, drawing many of the cavalry of Khalindaine behind him. The horse he rode was as wild and furious as he now, and plunged across the ford throwing out gouts of furious water. Behind him rode the cavalry, sharing their leader's immortal lust for blood.

Khayrik returned to the business of freeing the trap-door. It had been blocked by the falling roof, and he had to drag the rubble away. He no longer wanted to watch Akhran and the chivalry of Khalindaine as they massacred the Agaskan. He pictured the Oligarchs fleeing on their litters, and then the Agaskan who carried the litters spilling their masters out. He saw the Oligarchs, using leg muscles that had been redundant almost since birth, waddling away from the scything swords of the men, and the men ignominiously striking them down from behind. He imagined Akhran the Golden, exulting in victory, severing the Agaskan heads to make a cairn, and then saw Consatiné, abandoned as soon he must be by the avatar, faced with the awful consequences of the actions performed by his arms.

He opened the trap-door at last and eased himself slowly and carefully down the spiral stairs. A step at a time, placing the crutches on the stair ahead and then swinging his body down to meet them. He smiled to himself behind his beard: it is over, he decided. It had all been about the identity of the bastard: that was why Ormaas had died and why they had suffered the terror of a journey by twilight or a journey through the desert of Khalinrift. Khayrik, who had always believed in the pattern behind events, who had always denied that it was luck alone that decides human affairs, was satisfied.

He got to the bottom of the stairs at last, armpits sore with the rubbing of the wooden crutches. After descending the darkened stair he was surprised when, unlocking and opening the strong wooden door, he found it was still daylight outside. The day had felt longer than that. He pulled himself outside, and down a further short flight of stairs that took him to ground level. Bodies were piled on the steps, grinning faces with necks bent back in agony: only they weren't grinning, nor were they in agony; they were just dead, whatever that means, and Khayrik avoided them as he would have avoided any obstruction. He limped his way around the base of the tower. The corpses were heaped high against the walls as well, but the cloud of busy flies annoyed only the living. Khayrik passed the Gros of Weir, down on one knee and offering his water-bottle to an injured man. 'Come on Cluny, drink some more. You've got to get better you know, otherwise you'll miss my voyage to the south. You'll want to come with me when I discover those rich new lands, won't you?'

'Don't blame me if we sail straight into one of Hrakar's eyes,' moaned the wounded man, and the Weir-Lord laughed, and so did Khayrik, for they knew that Cluny would survive.

He hobbled further, hampered by the dead. Already the people of the nearby village were sifting through the corpses, looking for anything of value. They would name the battle after the village of Klau, thought Khayrik, and yet all the villagers will have done all day is to rob the dead. He glared at a peasant woman picking through the pockets of an armoured noble, and she glared straight back. 'He's mine!' she called. 'Find one of your own. There's plenty for all.'

At last he found Streetpoet, cradling Lara's head in his arms. She had recovered consciousness, but her eyes were vague and unfocused.

'How are you both?' asked the cripple.

'We'll live,' said Streetpoet. 'Though I don't know what we're going to do. It all seems over now, doesn't it. Like the pattern is finished but we're somehow left alive, superfluous.'

'I thought you didn't believe in patterns,' accused Lara.

'Did I say that? I'm a poet; it can't be true. What else is a poet but a finder of patterns. But sometimes I can't see the pattern. Now I know why Ormaas died: he had to die to save Consatiné. And knowing that makes it all right.'

'Perhaps,' said Lara. 'I spoke to a man of Mornet yesterday, one of the militia. They say that Fenras was not harmed.' Khayrik smiled at her wisely. He saw the connection between Ormaas and Fenras, cousin and parent. She continued, 'I think it is time I went home.'

Streetpoet's smile was less benign, more wicked. 'What about Consatiné?' he asked.

'What about Consatiné?' she asked in surprise.

'Don't you want to be empress?'

'He's never asked me.'

'He will,' he laughed. 'He will.' He recoiled in surprise as she stood up quickly, and put a hand on her elbow to steady her. She seemed cross with him, and he did not know why. 'Where are you going?'

'To say goodbye to Consatiné,' she said, and left them.

Streetpoet turned appealingly to Khayrik, who just looked back, appraisingly. 'You know,' said the cripple at length. 'For a poet you're not very subtle.'

Streetpoet thought about this in silence, and then brightened. 'But then, I was never much of a poet.'

'They'll not wed this year,' decided Khayrik. 'She's too full of Ormaas. But next year perhaps.'

'He'll be emperor.'

'She'll be empress.'

They looked around the battlefield. The Gros of Weir still tended Cluny, the villagers still squabbled like vultures over the corpses. About them, twilight gathered in the shadows, and camp fires burnt through the dusk. 'Come on, old friend,' said Streetpoet, as he lifted himself painfully to his feet. 'There's a bottle hidden in my tent. Old Consatiné won't miss it now he's emperor.'

'You stole a bottle from Consatiné?' Khayrik was shocked.

The musician turned his eyes innocently towards the cripple. 'He wasn't using it,' he said.

Khayrik laughed. 'I suppose not,' he conceded. 'Which way?'

'Over there by the tents.'

'It's treason, you know, stealing from the emperor. They'll put you back into the House of the Condemned.'

Many of the tents had fallen down in the fighting. Someone had lit a fire in the middle and was roasting autumn chestnuts; another group danced to the sound of a pipe. Khayrik and Streetpoet walked out of the dead and towards the living.

'I hope you hid that bottle well,' said Khayrik.

THE SILENT TOWER
Barbara Hambly

Another thrilling fantasy from best-selling author
Barbara Hambly.

Antryg Windrose, dog wizard student of the Dark Mage,
has been imprisoned in the Silent Tower for seven long,
lonely years.

But have his powers been limited by the spell-bound
tower walls, or is the life-sapping Void and the appearance of appalling abominations throughout the countryside somehow connected to him?

And is he linked to the strange occurrences noticed by
young computer programmer Joanna Sheraton at the
San Serano Aerospace Complex? Joanna has the feeling
that someone is following her, but who, and why? At a
party thrown by her boyfriend Gary, she is soon to find
out: whirled through the Void into an unfamiliar world,
accompanied by a mad wizard and a beautiful sasenna
swordsman, she is about to discover depths within herself
she had never dreamed of, and horrors worse than any
nightmare ...

to be followed by

Book Two: THE SILICON MAGE

THE SILICON MAGE
Barbara Hambly

Concluding the nail-biting story that began with the SILENT TOWER ...

The corrupt Archmage Suraklin has taken over the body, brain and computer of Gary, Joanna's ex-boyfriend. Through magic he is already able to leech the life-force out of two worlds to fuel his lust for eternal power and life: now he will harness science as well.

His main adversary, Antryg Windrose, dog-wizard and Joanna's lover, is imprisoned again in the Silent Tower, his mind and body broken. Joanna is on her own. Somewhere, in this strange medieval world full of superstition and corruption, where worship of the Dead God, lord of entropy, has emerged once more, where human sacrifice is practised and abominations abound, Suraklin has hidden his computer. Armed with a backpack full of software, a worm disc and a .38, Joanna Sheraton is all that stands between the Dark Mage and the death of the universe.

THE DARWATH TRILOGY
Barbara Hambly

Book 1

The Time of the Dark

For several nights Gil had found herself dreaming of an impossible city where alien horrors swarmed from underground lairs of darkness. She had dreamed also of the wizard Ingold Inglorion. Then the same wizard crossed the Void to seek sanctuary for the last Prince of Dar and revealed himself to a young drifter, Rudy. But one of the monstrous, evil Dark followed in his wake and in attempting to help Ingold, Gil and Rudy were drawn back into the nightmare world of the Dark. There they had to remain – unless they could solve the mystery of the Dark. Then, before they could realise their fate, the Dark struck!

Book 2

The Walls of Air

In the shelter of the great Keep of Renwath eight thousand people shelter from the Dark. The only hope for the besieged is to seek help from the hidden city of Quo. Ingold and Rudy set out to cross two thousand miles of desert. Beyond it they have to penetrate the walls of illusion that separate Quo from the world.

Book 3

The Armies of Daylight

The survivors of the once-great Realm of Darwath shelter, squabble and struggle for power. Meanwhile the monstrous Dark threaten their great Keep. Is there a reason for the re-awakening of the Dark? The final volume of *The Darwath Trilogy* builds to a shattering and unexpected climax.

THE LADIES OF MANDRIGYN
Barbara Hambly

Determined to win back their men from the cruel fate assigned to them by the evil Wizard King Altiokis, the Ladies of Mandrigyn set out to hire the services of the mercenary leader Sun Wolf to destroy him. But not even a fortune in gold would tempt Sun Wolf to be fool enough to match his sword against the wizard's sorcery ...

Sun Wolf awoke, some hours later, on a ship bound for far-flung Mandrigyn, lethal anzid coursing through his veins. The ladies held the only antidote, and Sun Wolf found himself an unwilling participant in a very danger-ous game ...

DRAGONSBANE
Barbara Hambly

It was said to be impossible to slay a dragon. But Lord John Aversin had earned himself the name of Dragons-bane once in his life and had become the subject of ballad and legend. Fired by the romance of his tale, young Gareth travelled far and wide across the Winterlands from the King's court to persuade the hero to rid the Deep of Ylferdun of the great Black Dragon, Morkeleb, oldest and mightiest of the dragon race. But Morkeleb was not the greatest danger that awaited John Aversin and his witch-woman. Just as Morkeleb posed the hardest test of skill and courage for the Dragonsbane, so Jenny Waynest would find her powers pitted against an adversary as deadly as the Black Dragon, and infinitely more evil.

'This is literary alchemy of a high order, and it confirms Hambly's place as one of the best new fantasists.'

Locus

THE SUMMER TREE
Book One of The Fionavar Tapestry
Guy Gavriel Kay

The first book of a fantasy trilogy on a grand scale, in the epic tradition of THE LORD OF THE RINGS. Five young people find themselves flung into the magical land of Fionavar, First of All the Worlds, there to play their part in the vast battle against the forces of evil led by the fallen god Rakoth Maugrim and his dark hordes.

THE WANDERING FIRE
Book Two of The Fionavar Tapestry
Guy Gavriel Kay

Continuing the story that will echo through the fantasy genre for years to come, THE WANDERING FIRE takes the five young adventurers from THE SUMMER TREE back into the land of Fionavar, there to join forces with the legendary Warrior in the struggle to save the Weaver's worlds from the evil might of the Unraveller.

'Guy Gavriel Kay might well have created the major fantasy work of the 80s.' Charles de Lint

'One of the very best fantasies which have appeared since Tolkien.' Andre Norton

THE DARKEST ROAD
Book Three of The Fionavar Tapestry
Guy Gavriel Kay

Concluding this vast epic fantasy, THE DARKEST ROAD carries the young heroes from our own world to the final titanic battle for Fionavar against the evil of Rakoth Maugrim. On a ghost-ship the legendary Warrior, Arthur Pendragon and Pwyll Twiceborn, Lord of the Summer Tree, sail to confront the Unraveller; while Darien, Child of Light and Dark, must tread the darkest road of any child of earth or stars . . .

THE PASTEL CITY
M. John Harrison

In his melancholy sea-tower, moody reclusive tegeus-Cromis, hero of the Methven, puts away his nameless sword, thinking that he had finished with soldiering forever. Then, on the road from Viriconium, came the massive mercenary, Birkin Grif, roaring out a filthy brothel song, bringing news of the war between two queens. In the great Brown Waste lives Tomb the Dwarf, as nasty a midget as ever hacked the hands off a priest. They must join forces to fight for Queen Jane and Viriconium, for Canna Moidart and the Wolves of the North have awoken the *geteit chemosit*, alien automata from an ancient science, which will destroy everything in their path, and now they march upon the Pastel City ...

'If you like elegantly crafted, elegantly written sword-and-sorcery, this book is all you could ask for.'
Michael Bishop – *Fantasy & Science Fiction Review*

A STORM OF WINGS
M. John Harrison

Eighty years have passed since Lord tegeus-Cromis broke the yoke of Canna Moidart, since the horror of the *geteit chemosit*. The Reborn Men, awoken from their long sleep, have inherited the Evening Cultures. In the wastelands, to the north and west of Viriconium, a city is being built – but not by men.

In the time of the Locust a paralysing menace threatens to turn the inhabitants of the Pastel City into hideous, mindless insects ...

'the best writer of heroic fantasy working today ... Through the spoiled wastelands of our ancient planet travel a resurrected man, an assassin, a magician, a madwoman, a dwarf ... A superior read.' *Daily Express*

THE INITIATE
Book 1 of the Time Master Trilogy
Louise Cooper

The Seven Gods of Order has ruled unchallenged for an aeon, served by the adepts of the Circle in their bleak Northern stronghold. But for Tarod – the most enigmatic and formidable sorcerer in the Circle's ranks – a darker affinity had begun to call. Threatening his beliefs, even his sanity, it rose unbidden from beyond Time; an ancient and deadly adversary that could plunge the world into madness and chaos – and whose power rivalled that even of the Gods themselves. But though Tarod's mind and heart were pledged to order, his soul was another matter . . .

THE OUTCAST
Book 2 of the Time Master Trilogy
Louise Cooper

Denounced by his fellow Adepts as a demon, betrayed even by those he loved, Tarod had unleashed a power that twisted the fabric of time. It seemed that nothing could break through the barrier he had created until Cyllan and Drachea – victims of the Warp – stumbled unwittingly into his castle. The terrible choice Tarod has to make as a result has far-reaching consequences . . .

THE MASTER
Book 3 of the Time Master Trilogy
Louise Cooper

Tarod had won his freedom – and lost the soul stone, key to his sorcerous power. Cyllan, the woman he loved, had been taken from him in a supernatural storm. With a price on both their heads, Tarod had to find her before the Circle did. Only then could he hope to fulfil his self-imposed pledge to confront the gods themselves – for they alone could destroy the stone and the evil that dwelt in it. If touched by the evil in the stone, Tarod would be forced to face the truth of his own heritage, triggering a titanic conflict of occult forces, and setting him on the ultimate quest for vengeance . . .

MIRAGE
Louise Cooper

Raised by a sorceress from the depths of limbo he came
into the world without a past or a name.

They called him Kyre – Sun Hound – avatar of an
ancient hero; summoned as the last chance to save the
dying city of Haven from the ravages of the evil witch-
queen Calthar and the sea-dwellers.

But Kyre sensed that he was more than a cipher: he felt a
power within him, and a past existence which lurked in
his dreams and hazy memories. He had to solve the
mystery of his true identity before the hour of the final
confrontation.

In the sky, the Hag cast down its baleful light: the Great
Conjunction was close at hand. Soon the followers of
Calthar would rise from the sea and obliterate the city of
Haven and its people, forever.

Also available from Unwin Paperbacks

The Armies of Daylight (The Darwath Trilogy: 3) *Barbara Hambly*	£2.95 ☐
The Darkest Road (The Fionavar Tapestry: 3) *Guy Kay*	£2.95 ☐
The Deep *John Crowley*	£2.95 ☐
Dragonsbane *Barbara Hambly*	£2.95 ☐
Freedom Beach *James Patrick Kelly & John Kessel*	£2.95 ☐
The Initiate (The Time Master Trilogy: 1) *Louise Cooper*	£2.95 ☐
In Viriconium *M. John Harrison*	£2.25 ☐
The Ladies of Mandrigyn *Barbara Hambly*	£2.95 ☐
The Master (The Time Master Trilogy: 3) *Louise Cooper*	£2.95 ☐
Mirage *Louise Cooper*	£2.95 ☐
The Outcast (The Time Master Trilogy: 2) *Louise Cooper*	£2.95 ☐
The Pastel City *M. John Harrison*	£2.50 ☐
Prince of Stars *Ian Dennis*	£2.95 ☐
The Silent Tower *Barbara Hambly*	£2.95 ☐
The Silicon Mage *Barbara Hambly*	£2.95 ☐
A Storm of Wings *M. John Harrison*	£2.95 ☐
The Summer Tree (The Fionavar Tapestry: 1) *Guy Kay*	£2.95 ☐
The Time of the Dark (The Darwath Trilogy: 1) *Barbara Hambly*	£2.95 ☐
Viriconium Nights *M. John Harrison*	£2.95 ☐
Walls of Air (The Darwath Trilogy: 2) *Barbara Hambly*	£2.95 ☐
The Wandering Fire (The Fionavar Tapestry: 2) *Guy Kay*	£2.95 ☐
The Witches of Wenshar *Barbara Hambly*	£2.95 ☐

All these books are available at your local bookshop or newsagent, or can be ordered direct by post. Just tick the titles you want and fill in the form below.

Name ....

Address ....

....

....

Write to Unwin Cash Sales, PO Box 11, Falmouth, Cornwall TR10 9EN.

Please enclose remittance to the value of the cover price plus:

UK: 60p for the first book plus 25p for the second book, thereafter, 15p for each additional book ordered to a maximum charge of £1.90.

BFPO and EIRE: 60p for the first book plus 25p for the next 7 books and 15p for the next 7 books and thereafter 9p per book.

OVERSEAS INCLUDING EIRE: £1.25 for the first book plus 75p for the second book and 28p for each additional book.

Unwin Paperbacks reserve the right to show new retail prices on covers which may differ from those previously advertised in the text or elsewhere. Postage rates are also subject to revision.